DEATH ON BOARD

THE FLORA MAGUIRE MYSTERIES BOOK 1

ANITA DAVISON

Boldwood

First published in 2015. This edition published in Great Britain in 2023 by Boldwood Books Ltd.

Copyright © Anita Davison, 2015

Cover Design by Head Design

Cover Illustration: Shutterstock

A CIP catalogue record for this book is available from the British Library.

Paperback ISBN 978-1-83518-841-5

Large Print ISBN 978-1-83518-837-8

Hardback ISBN 978-1-83518-836-1

Ebook ISBN 978-1-83518-834-7

Kindle ISBN 978-1-83518-835-4

Audio CD ISBN 978-1-83518-842-2

MP3 CD ISBN 978-1-83518-839-2

Digital audio download ISBN 978-1-83518-833-0

Boldwood Books Ltd
23 Bowerdean Street
London SW6 3TN
www.boldwoodbooks.com

For Clive - Life is only temporary - Love is eternal

1

SATURDAY

Well-wishers stood four deep on Pier 39 in New York Harbour beneath a sea of colourful hats wide as sailboats, their owners waving handkerchiefs or sobbing into them. Horse-drawn carriages with crests on the doors lined up alongside hired hackneys to disgorge elegantly dressed couples and businessmen with their matronly wives, all of whom joined the clamour on the quayside taking farewell of friends and relatives. The clatter of hooves vied with shouts from newsboys and costermongers plying their wares to the waiting crowd, their voices combined in an inaudible concert.

Boisterous children darted between them, miniature flags held aloft on sticks; Union Jacks and Stars and Stripes in equal numbers. Harassed nurses made vain attempts to round them up, while their parents looked on with bored disinterest. Porters strained behind loaded trolleys calling out their warnings to make way, while imperious matrons issued braying instructions for the disposition of their luggage.

'It's huge!' Flora stood at the bottom of the gangplank, her foot tapping in time to the music from a brass band led by an enthusiastic conductor in a rendition of the 'Washington Post' march. She had seen ocean-going steamers before, even travelled on one, yet there was something awe-inspiring about the *Minneapolis*, with her gleaming black hull, bright red smoke stack and taut metal winch lines draped with multi-coloured bunting.

'This is her maiden voyage!' Eddy shouted as he waved the shipping line brochure that had been his constant companion this past week under Flora's nose. 'Listen to this,' he opened the booklet and read aloud. 'She's six hundred feet long, and 13,400 tonnes, which means she has the largest tonnage of any ship afloat, apart from the *SS Oceanic*.'

'Which was the ship we came over on three months ago,' Flora reminded him.

'I know, but Minneapolis is a brand new ship.' He looked up briefly from the brochure. 'This is her maiden voyage, and she's carrying only seventy-eight first class passengers and a hundred and fifty-five crew. That's almost two crew members for each passenger. Just think, Flora we'll be the first people to travel on her.' He tucked the booklet back into his pocket, his gaze following a man who walked past with a boy of about his own age. The man pointed items of interest out to the boy, who laughed and chatted at his side, both intent on each other.

'I'm sorry you have only me for company on the trip home.' Flora caressed Eddy's shoulder gently with one hand. 'Your parents would have stayed to see you off, but they had a train to catch.'

'I don't mind being with you, Flora. For a governess, you're a good egg.' Eddy swiped a hand across eyes that looked suspiciously wet, then trained a morose glare on the emotional farewells taking place on the quayside. 'Mama didn't even bother to get out of the carriage.'

Although tall for thirteen, with well-defined features that promised to mature into male handsomeness in years to come, Edward, Viscount Trent, was still very much a child.

'You're very important to your father.' Flora bit her lip at the disappointment in his voice. 'You're Lord Vaughn's heir, remember.'

She tried to imagine how she would feel if her parents had packed her off back to England while they toured the Eastern United States. The question was moot, for her mother had died when she was young and, as Lord Vaughn's head butler, her father didn't possess the resources to send her anywhere. Flora had resigned herself long ago to viewing the peripatetic lives of the English aristocracy from the shadows.

'I would sooner be just his son.' Eddy broke away from her and pounded up the gangplank.

Sighing, Flora prepared to follow, but was prevented by a young man in a shabby brown suit who stepped in front of her, a bulky camera raised to his face. 'Photograph, Miss?'

'Er no, thank you.' Flora stood on tiptoe to keep Eddy in sight, he had reached the saloon deck and was on his way to the outside companionway. 'Maybe later.'

Lowering the camera, the youth pressed a pasteboard card into her hand. 'Printed in our own darkroom, and available throughout the voyage,' his sales patter continued unabated. 'Perfect to send to your loved ones as postcards.'

'I'm sure.' Thanking him with a smile, Flora shoved the card into a pocket without looking at it, and joined a queue of passengers further up the gangplank.

An officer saluted her with a smile, and flattered, she stood a little straighter before proceeding to the packed deck where a group of sailors held out baskets of tightly coiled paper streamers in pastel colours. Flora grabbed a handful, pausing to allow an elderly matron to totter past with a tiny white dog on a leash. With a sharp eye open for Eddy, she eased through the press of bodies, where a barrage of feathers and silk flowers batted her face, their owners with world-weary expressions oblivious to her repeated and increasingly urgent "excuse me" requests.

She spotted Eddy again on the promenade deck, where he strolled the row of doors to the suites; she guessed he was trying to find theirs. Flora started up the companionway to join him, forced to a halt at the top when a noisy family shoved past her. She stepped back to let them pass, where her attention caught by an arrestingly pretty woman beneath the deck canopy. In a claret wool travelling coat with mutton leg sleeves and fox fur trim, she looked to be about Flora's own age. Her features were set hard, eyes narrowed and her fists clenched at her sides in barely restrained anger.

The object of her fury was older, with slightly receding hair, olive skin and thick eyebrows that met in the middle. He accepted her tirade in silence, while he repeatedly eased his collar away from his throat with a finger.

Her message delivered, the lady shot him a final hard glare, swivelled on her heel and stalked away.

The man inhaled deeply from a lit cheroot, shot the smoke in a straight upward stream, turned and leaned both forearms on the rail, hunched forward as if the encounter had drained him.

Flora took in his yellow-stained fingers and badly cut hair as she passed, intrigued as to what someone like him could have to say to the immaculate girl in her expensive clothes.

The clang of a bell interrupted her thoughts, and as the echo of its resonant peals died away, a booming male voice shouted, 'All ashore that's going ashore!'

A middle-aged lady who stood with a young couple to Flora's left burst into noisy tears and threw her chubby arms round the young man's neck. He disentangled her firmly and walked her to the companionway, while the girl remained behind, a hand raised in a weak wave, a wistful smile on her pretty face. At the gangplank, a steward took charge of the weeping older woman, while the young man returned to the girl's side, their combined expressions now of undisguised glee.

'Come on, Flora,' Eddy's shout commanded her attention. 'I've found our suite, now I want to go and watch for the pilot boat.'

A long, plaintive note of the ship's horn was greeted by a renewed burst of cheers and catcalls from the quayside, while the passengers on deck made a surge for the rail to wave their goodbyes. The brass band began a rousing chorus of 'The Star-Spangled Banner' followed by a cacophony of horns, hooters and whistles from the river that sent a shiver of excitement along Flora's spine.

'I can't see much with all these people,' Eddy said when she reached him.

'Let's see what we can do about that.' Flora grabbed his hand and dragged him through the press of bodies toward the ship's rail, responding to the scowls and outraged rumblings thrown their way with an apologetic smile.

'I'm dreadfully sorry, do forgive me,' she gushed. 'Please let us through. My little brother and I might never see our darling Grandpapa again.'

The disapproving looks faded, replaced by sympathy as both the aloof and the obliging shuffled aside to make room for them at the rail.

'Flora!' Eddy dragged out her name, his eyes widening. 'My Grandpapa lives in Knightsbridge and yours died years ago.'

'Hush!' Flora selected a paper streamer from the pile handed to her by a steward on the companionway. 'I had to think of something, or we would be stranded at the back, and you wouldn't get to see your pilot boat.' She tossed a strip of paper into the air. The streamer twirled in a graceful arc, then slowly unfurled and fell slowly into the sea of waving arms and blurred faces far below on the quayside.

'What are we doing this for?' Eddy asked, surly again. 'My parents left ten minutes after we arrived.' His penetrating dark eyes peered out from behind hanks of curly, nut-brown hair that resisted all attempts to tame it.

'Then pretend.' Flora raised herself on tiptoe and threw another streamer. 'Imagine there's someone running along the quayside as the ship pulls away, tears in their eyes and waving a damp handkerchief.' She clasped her hands against her breast and gave a mock sigh.

'You are funny, Flora.' His mouth twitched and he shook his head, then with a resigned shrug, snatched the rolled streamer from her open palm, pulled his arm back and tossed it into the air.

The boards beneath their feet vibrated and the twin-screw steam engines thrummed into pulsing, whirring life far below, while the long plaintive boom of the ship's horn came again.

They were leaving.

'There's the pilot boat!' Eddy's mood had evidently lifted as he scooted along the rail, his chin propped on his folded hands on the polished wood as the tiny vessel ran fast and straight towards the bow. In seconds it had disappeared beneath the hull as the vast ship eased away from the pier and swung into mid-river. A flotilla of small vessels jostled and bobbed on the froth-topped waves like minnows round a whale.

'Goodbye, New York!' Flora untangled the streamers that had snagged onto her straw hat as tiny scraps of paper fell around them like coloured snow and floated to the deck in a pastel layer around their feet, while the

receded into the distance like a cluster of toy houses heaped on a
een blanket.

'Goodbye, Meely,' Eddy whispered his childish nickname for his eldest
ister.

Experiencing a surge of sympathy, Flora slid an arm round his shoulders. 'Maybe Lady Amelia and her husband will come to England one day.
Once you've finished school, you could even visit them.'

'That won't be for ages.' Eddy snorted.

Aware that another platitude would simply worsen his mood, she
summoned a bright, if slightly contrived, smile. 'Well, I've had a wonderful
time on this trip. I'm so thrilled your parents invited me. I would never
have had the opportunity to see America otherwise.'

Invited was a somewhat generous term, for Lady Vaughn had included
Flora among the party as a temporary lady's maid for her bride-to-be
daughter. Her more usual role as Eddy's governess was what qualified her
as the most suitable candidate to escort Eddy home. 'Why do I have to go
back to rainy old England and school anyway?' Eddy mumbled into his
folded arms on top of the rail.

'School is a fact of everyone's life.' For boys anyway, she reminded
herself, for her own education had been conducted in the schoolroom at
Lord Vaughn's Gloucestershire home along with his three daughters. Not
that their syllabus included Latin or Philosophy, which would be expected
of Eddy at Marlborough, but Flora considered herself was well versed in
most subjects, which fitted her for her post as Eddy's governess.

One by one, the passengers peeled away from the rail to settle in their
accommodations or converge in the public rooms, leaving the young girl
and the schoolboy virtually alone on the deck. The Statue of Liberty
glowed in the evening light as it slid by on Bedloe Island, an arm raised in
perpetual salute, while lights blinked on in the receding city as dusk
approached.

'Papa said the French gave the statue to America, but he didn't say
why.'

'They gave it as a gift to commemorate the War of Independence.'

'You mean because we lost, and they wanted to rub our noses in it?' He
slanted a sideways look up at her which conveyed his scorn.

'I doubt that was quite their intention.' Flora smiled, tightening her arm round Eddy's shoulders in a one-armed hug; the only sort he allowed these days. 'Did you know the statue is about the same age as you are?'

He shook his head, frowning. 'Is it made of real gold? It's not very shiny.'

'It's copper, but I've been told it will turn green eventually, which is what happens to copper in the air.'

'Why?'

'Oxidisation, but for a more comprehensive explanation you'll have to ask your new chemistry master. 'Now Eddy, which suite is ours?' she asked, in an attempt to distract him.

'That one.' He cocked his chin at the closest of the white doors, where a hand-written label in a brass frame had been attached to a door that stood ajar; the words *Edward, Viscount Trent and Miss Flora Maguire*, in cursive script, set above a brass doorbell.

'Well then, what are we waiting for?' She tugged him forward. 'Let's go and explore.'

The cream and white panelled sitting room was no bigger than ten by eight but, with its ornate gilt fireplace at one end, exuded an air of opulence and style, combined with a tang of beeswax polish, fresh flowers and linseed oil.

A writing bureau with a hinged lid stood near the door, together with three wicker armchairs upholstered in dark red plush fabric. Two square windows framed by dimity curtains of white with a tiny red rosebud pattern overlooked the covered promenade deck. A door at either side led to two compact bedrooms, each with a tiny bathroom complete with white ceramic fittings, polished brass taps and gleaming mirrors.

Flora strolled to the mock fireplace, on which was a trio of cards, propped against the gilt mirror above. One was the passengers list, though she didn't recognise any of the names but for one Member of Parliament. Beside it sat the menu card for the day and a programme listing the week's activities.

She made a mental note of the treasure hunt and horse races, which might interest Eddy, before replacing the card.

Their luggage had already been delivered and a maid bustled between the open steamer trunks and the bedrooms, tutting good-naturedly when Eddy got in her way in his bid to try out the beds, open drawers and peer into cupboards.

Inhaling the smell of fresh paint and clean linen, Flora released a satisfied sigh at the thought this luxurious new suite would be her home for the next week or so, and she would be at no one's beck and call but Eddy's.

Removing her straw hat, she tossed it onto the bed where the maid had arranged her things, simultaneously running a hand across the soft white coverlet that matched the dimity curtains in the lounge. Her room also had the luxury of a large square window, not the tiny porthole in the cupboard euphemistically referred to as a cabin on the outward trip.

'Did you know there's a wireless telegraphy room on board, Flora?' Eddy braced both hands on either side of the door frame to her room, making no attempt to enter. 'The *Minne* class ships are among the first to have one.'

'I'll have to borrow that brochure of yours, Eddy, because I have no idea what a *Minne* class ship is.'

'That's easy.' His enthusiasm for anything connected to engineering had returned. 'The shipping line gave some of their new ships native names like *Minnehaha, Minnetonka, Minnewaska*. They all begin with *Minne*, see?'

'Of course, why didn't I think of that? And this one has a wireless telegraphy room?'

He nodded. 'Do you think the crew will let me see how it works?'

'I don't see why not. We could ask the purser.' Flora guided him back into the sitting room, and at the same time, she impulsively dropped a swift kiss onto his cheek in response to his renewed enthusiasm.

Eddy's lips puckered in a moue of distaste, he scrubbed at his face with a fist and threw himself into the nearest chair.

At the sound of a trumpet being blown with enthusiasm from outside, he leapt up again.

'That's the bugle call for dinner. Good show because I'm starving. At least we don't have to change because no one dresses on the first night.' He slicked down his hair with both hands, then gave her a swift top-to-toe look. 'Hurry up, Flora, or we'll be late.'

Sighing inwardly at her reflection in the mirror above the mantle, Flora reminded herself that on a first class-only ship, she couldn't disappear into a third class dining room like she had done on the outward voyage.

Her cinched-waist grey jacket above a matching straight skirt and high-necked white blouse conveyed the tailored image of a new century professional woman; nothing like the rest of the lady passengers in their couture silk moiré gowns and abundance of furs.

The creeping worry that had plagued her all day found a voice. 'I'm not very hungry, Eddy. You go along on your own.' She hoped her stomach wouldn't growl, making her a liar.

'Are you sure?' Eddy peered at the printed menu card on the mantle. 'They're serving roast lamb, and Charlotte Russe cake.'

'It's been such a busy day what with all the packing.' She feigned a yawn. 'I'll ask the stewardess to bring me something here.'

'If you're sure.' Eddy frowned, his hand already on the door handle. Not much kept him from a meal. 'I'll see you later, then.'

The door closed behind him at the same second the stewardess appeared from Eddy's bedroom. 'I've finished now, Miss. Is there anything else?'

'Might I have a tray sent in for supper?' Flora asked. 'Something light, perhaps?'

'Of course, Miss, I'll arrange it straight away.' She pronounced it 'awee', revealing her Celtic origins.

Once alone, Flora chastised herself for foolishness, her excuse to Eddy struck her as feeble now; combined with guilt at having left him to face a room full of strangers on his own. Not that the prospect would bother Viscount Trent. He took social occasions in his stride. In one sense she was proud of his confidence, even took credit for it, but its existence only served to emphasize the differences in their worlds.

In what seemed like no time at all, the stewardess returned with a hot, fluffy omelette, a selection of tiny, sweet biscuits, fruit and cheese, together with a pot of aromatic coffee on a tray; all of which Flora demolished in half the time it took to arrive.

Anticipating a solitary stroll on deck before Eddy returned, she let herself out of the suite into the internal corridor that ran the length of the ship. At the stern end, she pushed through a glazed door into a staircase hall grand enough for a London hotel.

A crewman saluted her as she emerged onto the saloon deck; the only indication the vessel was moving was the rhythmic whoosh of the ocean below. A soft glow of yellow light from the long windows in the dining room reflected on the water, while the muted strains of the orchestra serenaded the diners.

Flora headed for the aft saloon deck, where land was no more than a blur on the horizon beneath the purple and navy of a darkening sky. A gust of cold air lifted her hair at the temples and she shivered, glad of her shawl. She passed a stack of steamer chairs piled beneath the metal companionway, and the massive round winches on a deck empty but for a square, bulky shape under canvas, fastened down with thick ropes.

Flora recalled from Eddy's lecture that the *Minneapolis* was designed to carry livestock, but sailed in ballast this trip, used to keep the vessel upright and discarded when the ship reached port.

The strange object stood a few inches taller than herself, several feet wide and distinctly square, but with vague shapes protruding from the front; that it was ballast seemed unlikely.

With a swift backwards glance to ensure she was not observed, Flora eased into a gap between the swaddled shape and a stack of fenders piled beside the companionway.

The oiled canvas proved heavier than she imagined, but a brief struggle and a determined tug revealed a rubber wheel more than two inches thick, beneath a curve of black-painted metal. Smaller than a cartwheel, the wooden section was painted in cream with thick spokes picked out in brown; some sort of wheeled cart, but much sturdier.

'Magnificent, isn't it?' a male voice said at her shoulder.

Flora jumped backwards, her head colliding with the metal support, sending a sharp pain through the crown of her head. She raised one hand to her scalp and swung round to where a young man stood, his feet splayed and both hands tucked into the pockets of a dinner suit. His tie lay undone against the lapels of his jacket, the collar open on his throat and his fair hair in disarray from the evening breeze. Penetrating eyes of an indistinguishable colour in the low light behind a pair of rimless spectacles regarded her with unnerving intensity.

And he was laughing.

A reprimand rose to her lips, suppressed when he removed his hand from his pocket and held it out, whether to draw her from beneath the metal support, or to shake hers, she wasn't sure.

'I cannot tell,' Flora snapped, taking small revenge by ignoring his hand. 'Whatever it might be is still mostly covered by this canvas sheet.'

'Quite right. And I shouldn't laugh, not when you might be hurt? I apologise, but I've simply never seen someone look so guilty, and yet so angry at the same time.'

'I'm not hurt, not really.' Flora rubbed the crown of her head. 'However, next time, I would appreciate some sort of warning before you creep up on me like that.'

'Next time?' His lips twitched. 'Should I assume you make a habit of skulking round ships in search of treasure then? Because if so, you do know that makes you a pirate?'

'I beg your pardon?' Flora tucked in her chin, frowning. Either her throbbing head was making her dizzy, or he was deranged.

'I've never met a pirate,' he chattered on. 'But as I always say, life is an adventure.' He thrust out his hand again. 'Bunny Harrington, pleased to meet you.'

Gingerly, she accepted his hand, startled at how firm and warm his grip was in hers. Her pulse raced uncomfortably and, unnerved, she snatched back her hand.

'Actually, it's a nickname,' he said in response to her surprised start. 'My real name is positively unmentionable.' He guided her from beneath the overhang with one hand, his other at her waist. 'Do you have a particular interest in motor cars?'

'Is that what this is? One of those horseless carriages?' Her thoughts flowed again, though with less clarity than normal, hampered by her throbbing scalp.

'Indeed, yes. Would you like to see her?'

Before she could answer he had hauled the canvas aside, revealing what resembled a scaled-down hansom cab, but on four wheels as opposed to two, with a fifth wheel on a pole behind a sheet of glass where the driver should be. Instead of traces for a horse, there sat a rectangular metal box with rounded corners.

'It's, um – quite impressive.' Flora stared, fascinated. 'This is yours?'

'She is indeed. He ran a hand gently over the fender in a caress. 'A Panhard-Levassor Landaulet.'

'They make these in America?' Flora's nerves receded and curiosity took its place, though her head still throbbed a little. Following his example, she stroked the caramel paintwork, surprised to find it was smooth as glass beneath her fingers.

'This particular masterpiece is French.' He adjusted his glasses by a sidebar. 'I had her shipped over in the autumn to show to the Duryea Motor Wagon Company.'

'And it really goes all by itself?' Flora had seen pictures in the *London Illustrated News* of motor cars, but she had never seen one.

'Not exactly.' His bemused frown made him even more attractive. 'She's powered by a front-mounted engine with rear-wheel drive, a sliding-gear transmission—' His mouth closed with a snap. 'Well, never mind all that, I'm sure it's of no interest to you.' He pushed a hand through his hair, revealing a well-defined brow and arched eyebrows slightly darker than his hair. 'Besides, I still don't know your name.'

'Flora. Flora Maguire,' she said, disarmed by the intensity of his stare that made her think they had met before, but couldn't possibly be the case.

'Delighted to meet you, Miss Maguire.' He placed a hand flat against the metal box in a possessive gesture. 'I plan to start my own manufacturing company making similar vehicles once I return to England. Not the first to do so, you understand. The Daimler Company beat me to that particular accolade. At present, I'm seeking partners to provide the engineering expertise, while I—' He checked himself with a wave of his free hand. 'Do forgive me, but when I get started, there's no stopping me.'

'I'm fascinated, but this is all quite new to me, I'm afraid.' Flora bent to study the front-mounted lamps that looked like eyes peering back at her. 'It looks as if it has a personality.'

'Splendid!' His face lit up like a schoolboy's. 'I'm so glad you see it too. Most people think it's ridiculous that I should attribute a character to a pile of metal, wood and rubber. He leaned towards her, his breath warm on her cheek, 'Actually, I've named her Matilda.'

'That's not so outrageous.' Flora smiled, enjoying his closeness, despite the fact he was a stranger. 'After all, they call boats "she" and give them feminine names.'

'Exactly.'

'There you are, Flora.' Eddy's voice called to her from the far side of the deck. His rapid footsteps clattered across the boards. 'I've been searching for you everywhere. I thought you'd fallen overboard.'

'There's no need for melodrama, Eddy.' Flora's governess tone emerged by habit. 'I was taking a walk, when I happened to meet Mr Harrington.'

Eddy wasn't listening. 'Golly! It's a motor car.' He eased between them, his feet trampling the canvas to get to the vehicle.

'Panhard-Leva-um,' Flora broke off, failing miserably in her attempt to display her knowledge.

'Panhard-Levassor Landaulet,' Bunny corrected, following Eddy's progress round to the rear.

'Mr Harrington plans to open a factory in England making them,' Flora added, wondering when, if ever, she would be able to call him Bunny. Then remembered he hadn't asked her to.

'Well, perhaps not these,' Bunny said. 'I hope to make one from a design of my own.'

Eddy's head appeared above the rear canopy. 'Do you have your designs with you?'

'I do as a matter of fact. I would be happy to show them to you sometime.'

'Oh, yes please.' Eddy ran a hand along the bodywork as he circled the vehicle, firing rapid questions, to which Bunny offered enthusiastic responses.

Flora stepped back, an observer to these two who were so clearly from the same mould, who, though physically dissimilar, possessed the confident air of knowing their own place in the world.

She began to feel invisible; rarely remembered and easily replaced, which reminded her of a housemaid, called Molly, who had left Cleeve Abbey, the Vaughn's country estate in Gloucestershire two years before.

Her post had been held by several others since, but Lord Vaughn still called the girl who made up the fires 'Molly'. A habit Flora attributed more to absent mindedness rather than an arrogant disregard for his staff.

The night air had grown colder and goose bumps erupted on Flora's arms beneath her shawl. She cleared her throat. 'Eddy, I think we should leave Mr Harrington in peace. Perhaps, he will allow you to see the motor car another time?'

'Of–of course. Any time he wishes,' Bunny's perplexed stare made him look as if he was on the verge of saying something, but he changed his mind and let it go with a sigh.

'Goodnight, Mr Harrington. Come along, Eddy.' Flora strode away without looking back, though she was sure he still watched her.

'What did you think of Mr Harrington?' Eddy asked, catching up with her on the metal steps up to the promenade deck.

'He seems pleasant enough.' Flora tried not to think of that wayward hank of blond hair and the twinkling eyes behind his spectacles. Who would have thought a man in glasses could be so attractive?

'I think he's a really good chap.' Eddy's voice held disappointment at her lack of enthusiasm.

'Why? Because he owns a motor car?' She gave the sore spot on the back of her head a final, brief rub.

'Sort of, though I had a good long talk with him at dinner.' Eddy pushed open the door of their suite, and stood to one side to let her enter. 'He's seated at our table.'

2

'Isn't it time you got ready for bed, Eddy?' Flora placed the tray that contained their empty cocoa cups on the bureau by the door, ready for the stewardess to collect.

'I will but, I wanted to ask you something first.' Eddy hovered at her shoulder, shuffling his feet in a familiar precursor to either a confession or a request.

'Which was?' She hugged a book left on the bureau close to her chest, her head tilted in a listening pose.

'There was a chap at dinner the same age as me. His name is Ozymandias.'

'Really? Does his mother have a fondness for Shelley by any chance?'

'What?' A confused frown furrowed his brow.

'Don't say "what", Eddy. Say "pardon". Haven't you ever read, "I met a traveller from an antique land?"'

'I hate poetry. It's sissy.' He wrinkled his nose.

'Girls love poetry, especially if you can quote it from memory.'

'I don't like girls either.' Eddy's brows lowered as if she had committed blasphemy.

'In which case, perhaps I should save romantic verse for another few years.' Flora sighed. 'Go on, you were telling me about your friend Ozymandias.'

'He prefers to be called Ozzy.' Eddy threw himself into the nearest armchair, hooking his feet over one arm. 'It was that old lady's suggestion. Mrs Penry-Jones I think she's called.'

'What was?' Flora turned to him with a frown. 'Calling him Ozzy?'

'No, not that.' He threw both arms outwards in a gesture of frustration. 'She said Ozzy and me ought to take meals with the other young people on board and not in the main dining room.'

'She said that?' Flora gaped. 'How presumptuous of her!' An image of a woman with a thrusting bosom and chicken-lipped mouth puckered like a schoolteacher filled Flora's head. 'She wasn't rude to you, was she, this Penry-Jones person?'

'How can I tell?' Eddy shrugged, nonplussed. 'All adults address me in the same way, like I am a Labrador who has just fouled the carpet.'

'Eddy!' Though she doubted her display of shock was convincing, confirmed when he hunched his shoulders and grinned. His irrepressible sense of fun always made her laugh, which made discipline an uphill struggle at times.

'Flora, really, it's all right.' He wrapped both arms round his drawn-up knees. 'Mrs Gilmore, she's Ozzy's mother, thinks we would prefer it too. Anyway, I'd rather eat with the other boys, honestly. The old people in the dining room are so stuffy.' He splayed both hands in mid-air. 'They spent the entire time at dinner reading the passenger lists to see who is important enough to talk to. Then the Americans got into some angry debate as to whether or not McKinley will be re-elected as President. I'll have more fun with Ozzy, truly. He's a trump.'

'I'm sure not everyone is old and stuffy.' Flora recalled a pair of attractive blue eyes fringed with heavy lashes that sparkled behind a pair of glasses. 'But I understand what you mean, and why not? I'm glad you've found a friend of whom you think so highly.' She gently ruffled his hair, ignoring his frustrated sigh. 'Incidentally, did this Mrs Penry-Jones happen to have an opinion about where governesses should eat?'

'That's an odd question.' Eddy tucked in his chin and regarded her with his head on one side. 'Papa bought you a ticket, didn't he? Which means you've every right to sit with the other passengers. The dining room or the deck, what's the difference?'

'You're absolutely right. And I'm sorry, I didn't mean to whine or feel sorry for myself.' She smoothed his hair where it stuck up at the back. 'Now off you go to bed, it's after ten o'clock.'

As Eddy's bedroom door banged shut, Flora released a sigh. Now she would have to face all those stuffy people on her own.

* * *

Flora woke with a start, blinking into the darkness until the outlines of furniture emerged from the shadows. The thump that had woken her came again, as if something heavy had been thrown against the bulkhead. Pushing her hair away from her face, she rolled over and flicked on the bedside light. The hands on her travelling clock stood at twenty minutes past midnight. With a groan, she slapped her arms on the covers in protest at the sound of a male voice that came clearly through the bedroom wall.

'Things change...'

'...but I thought we agreed...' a high, female voice answered.

Fully awake now, Flora drew her knees up into a crouch and scooted to the head of the bed. She pressed her ear to the bulkhead, ignoring the surge of shame that ran through her. Anyone vociferous enough to wake her in the middle of the night must expect eavesdropping.

The man spoke again, his tone lower and more menacing, though Flora couldn't make out the words.

Then a door slammed, followed by silence. No rapid footsteps, or enraged sobbing, just the tick of the mantle clock that now read 12.26 am.

Muttering to herself about the selfishness of others, Flora turned over, and slapped the pillows into submission in an effort to settle back to sleep. The remaining hours of the night passed slowly, alternating with periods of wakeful restlessness, accompanied by the persistent low thrum of the engines far below.

* * *

Sunday

When Flora finally woke from a deep sleep engendered by a disturbed night, her head throbbed slightly, her room bathed in weak daylight. The clock announced it was still unsociably early, so with no pressing need to rise, she relaxed into the comfort of the soft mattress and crisp linen.

A vague recollection of shouts from the cabin next door came back to her, though she couldn't recall if she had dreamed it or not. What sat clearly in her mind was the charming young man with the uninhibited laugh she had met on deck, whose vivid blue eyes had a disarming way of regarding her as if he recognised her from another place and time, although she was quite sure they had not met before.

A warm flush spread through her when she recalled her abruptness towards him when Eddy arrived. With a resigned sigh, she threw off the bedclothes and padded to the bathroom. There wasn't much she could do about it now, and besides, she had saved him embarrassment. Handsome young men who owned motor cars did not associate with governesses.

After the luxury of a hot bath where the water geyser didn't splutter and bang like the one at home, Flora dressed leisurely, intent on taking an early walk on deck when there was no one about. Before leaving the suite, she eased open the door of Eddy's room, to find him lying spread-eagled among rumpled covers, snoring gently.

Confident the stewardess wouldn't arrive with morning tea for another half hour, she threw a shawl around her shoulders and let herself out onto the promenade deck: a line of doors to the suites and staterooms running beneath a protective canopy – the luxurious part of a very glamourous ship. Land lay far behind them, the sea sprinkled with white-flecked waves below a milky blue sky that augured the beginning of a calm day.

She decided the argument she had heard in the night wasn't a dream, and stopped to read the label on the door next to hers: *Miss E Lane*. Was the lady travelling alone? And if so, who was the man she had been arguing with? Another passenger, or a member of the crew?

A voice called from somewhere on the upper promenade deck above, followed by the sound of a door slamming. When no one appeared, she continued slowly along the deck, not yet accustomed to the gentle rise and fall of the ship.

Having completed a full circuit of the promenade deck, she arrived at an outside companionway of narrow metal steps that dropped steeply to the deck below. At the bottom lay what appeared to be a bundle of clothes, as if someone had laid out a dinner suit on the boards. Curious, she began her descent, but half way down the companionway, the bundle transformed into the figure of a man lying prone on the saloon deck.

A surge of alarm sent her clattering down the remaining steps, her boots ringing on the metal treads. Her enquiry of, 'Are you hurt?' died on her lips as she took in his unnatural stillness and the fact his eyes were open, sightless... and quite dead.

Bile rose in her throat and she covered her mouth with her hand, which quickly felt damp as a result of short, rapid breaths through her fingers.

She backed away several paces, then stopped, her gaze returning to the man's features which, though slack, were recognisable as the worried-looking man she had seen with the lady in the claret coat when they had boarded.

She stared round in panic in search of help, but the deck lay silent, except for the singing of the wind in the winch lines and a distant rumble of the engines as the ship glided over a calm ocean. Unlike the promenade deck, the staterooms on the lower saloon deck were reached from an internal corridor. She preferred not to bang on doors and risk frightening the still sleeping occupants, which was likely to cause panic. Surely someone would come by soon? Was the man here alone? Would anyone be looking for him? Where were the crew?

Her initial horror turned to curiosity as she debated what to do. She took in his black dinner suit, scuffed shoes and an odd purple bruise on his right cheek. Did he get that when he fell?

Her gaze slid to the three-inch long gash at the base of his skull, and she winced, but couldn't look away. The open edges gaped a deep liverish red partially covered by strands of matted black hair. Apart from a smear of red-brown on his shirt collar, there was no sign of fresh blood. Even the boards beneath him looked clean, if damp.

'Are you all right, Miss?' a male voice spoke from several feet away, making her jump. A man in naval officer's uniform stood before her, a much younger crewman at his shoulder.

She had heard no approaching footsteps, and his sudden appearance made her heart pound again and her mouth dry, so no words came.

'Has the gentleman had a fall?' Without waiting for her to respond, he eased past her and bent to the figure on the deck.

'I... I don't know,' Flora addressed his crouched back. 'I found him like this a few minutes ago. I think he's dead.'

'Blimey!' the younger sailor muttered, his eyes wide.

'Fetch Dr Fletcher immediately.' The officer gestured to the young crewman, who backed away with a brief, 'Aye, sir,' as he turned and pounded along the deck.

'Second Officer Martin, at your service, Miss, uh?' The officer rose to his full height and touched a hand to his cap, enquiry in his eyes.

'Maguire. Flora Maguire.'

He acknowledged her with a nod, then blinked, distracted, as if making a mental search of the sailor's manual but unable to find the part about dead bodies. Seconds passed in which he appeared to make up his mind, then he straightened and grasped her arm. 'Perhaps you should step away, Miss Maguire?'

'I'm fine, truly.' Flora rolled her shoulder out of his hold, unwilling to be shunted away as redundant. 'The captain might wish to ask me some questions.'

Her initial shock had dissipated, and curiosity took over. Who was the man, and had someone helped him fall down those steps?

'Oh yes, of course, Miss,' the officer stammered, staring round as if in search of guidance.

The sound of running feet presaged the return of the young crewman in the company of a man Flora assumed to be the doctor; confirmed when he bent and rested a finger on the man's neck and then lifted his wrist. His nut-brown hair was short, well cut, but untidy, as if he'd just got out of bed. Two more sailors had appeared from somewhere by this time, along with a steward, all of whom hovered expectantly a few feet away.

'Dr Fletcher.' He gave Flora a brisk nod by way of introduction and sat back on his haunches, his head turned towards her. 'Did you see the gentleman fall?'

'I didn't see it happen, no, but...' Flora lowered her voice, adding, 'Excuse me, but are you quite certain that he fell?'

The doctor's eyes narrowed. 'Why do you say that?' He frowned and swallowed, his Adam's apple bobbing like a fishing float.

'Well,' Flora began, turning over the details in her head. 'If he fell forwards, the way he's lying now, how did he get that wound on the back of his head?'

'He most probably hit the handrail on the way down, or perhaps the edge of one of the steps.' The doctor's gaze settled on her for the briefest pause before sliding away in dismissal. 'They're metal and quite sharp. Perfectly capable of inflicting such an injury.'

'Maybe. But if so, wouldn't he have tried to save himself?' Flora tried again. 'His arms are by his sides as if—'

'You've clearly had a shock, Miss Maguire.' Dr Fletcher rose to his feet and stepped in front of her, blocking her view. 'I suggest you return to your suite while we deal with this.'

Flora bridled. 'Why do you all keep trying to get rid of me? I'm not hysterical. A bit queasy maybe, but quite calm. And I did ask a perfectly reasonable question.' She summoned her most appealing smile, then braced herself for more censure as another set of heavy footsteps approached. However, the startled 'Good grief, what's happened?' came in a voice both familiar and reassuring, as the young man of the night before pushed through the knot of curious sailors and came to her side.

'Mr Harrington, thank goodness.' Flora grabbed hold of his arm, conscious of his warm, firm muscles beneath the fabric of his sleeve. 'I found this man on the deck.' She lowered her voice to a whisper. 'He's dead, and not only will the crew not answer my questions, they keep trying to make me leave.'

'The lady is a trifle distraught, Mr, er—' Officer Martin took Flora's arm with one hand and saluted Bunny with the other, a brow raised in enquiry.

'Harrington,' Bunny added, sliding an arm around Flora's waist, though she was in no danger of falling.

She left it there, his touch comforting and safe as the nausea she thought had gone returned.

'Were you present when it happened?' Bunny repeated Officer Martin's question.

'No, he was just lying here. I didn't know he was dead at first, I—' A metallic taste filled her mouth and she shrugged Officer Martin away and pressed a hand to her lips until she was able to speak again. When she did, her voice was calmer than she felt. 'The doctor said he fell down the steps, but I'm not so sure.'

'Coming upon a body like that could upset anyone, Mr Harrington, especially a young lady.' Officer Martin gently took her free arm again and tried to pull her away.

'I am *not* upset!' Flora tugged her arm away. *But if that was true, why was she shaking?*

'It appears to be a simple, but regrettable accident, Mr Harrington.' Officer Martin took a step back, his hands held palms upwards in surrender. 'Easily done when one isn't used to the motions of the ship. Added to which, the companionway is quite steep.'

'Are you saying fatal accidents occur often on board ships?' Bunny asked, tightening his hold on Flora's waist.

'Not at all, sir!' he raised his voice, evidently affronted. 'Falls do happen, especially in rough seas, but I cannot say we have many deaths. This gentleman must have been extremely unlucky.'

Flora frowned. Was his bland reassurance an attempt to shield the other passengers? Or to allay blame that the companionways weren't safe? A metal rail ran around three sides of the hole, but the steps were thin and metal, thus quite slippery. They had also been washed recently, judging by the sheen of water that clung to the treads.

'Do either of you know who he is?' Dr Fletcher asked without looking up. He had completed an examination of the body's hands and feet and now rummaged through the man's pockets.

Flora hesitated. 'N–no, I don't know him.' Her being witness to the dead man's conversation with the lady in the claret coat hardly counted as an acquaintance.

'His name is Parnell,' Bunny interjected. 'Frank, I think.'

'You knew him, Mr Harrington?' Officer Martin's expression hardened to suspicion.

'Not exactly.' Bunny's sigh showed he resented this implication. 'We met for the first time at dinner last evening. He was travelling in the company of a young lady. An actress, I believe.'

'I see. Well now, if you would excuse me, sir.' Dr Fletcher beckoned two members of the crew, both of whom proceeded to manoeuvre the dead man onto a sheet of tarpaulin that had appeared from somewhere as if by magic.

'Shouldn't the captain see the body before it's moved?' Flora whispered.

'I've no idea what the procedure is.' Flora felt, rather than saw, Bunny's shrug. 'I assume they know what they are doing.' He turned and addressed the doctor. 'Where are you taking him?'

'To my office for the time being,' Dr Fletcher threw over his shoulder, as he set off after the sailors.

'It appears the matter is entirely out of our hands now.' Bunny sighed, then turned back to Flora. 'Would you allow me to escort you back to your suite?'

'But—' she halted and exhaled, resigned. After all, she hadn't known the dead man, and whatever had happened to him was none of her concern. 'All right, if you insist. I mean – thank you.' She accepted his proffered arm, and started to climb the steps, pausing halfway up, her gaze roving the metal treads.

'Are you looking for something?' He halted beside her.

'There's no blood on these steps,' Flora said slowly. 'Or on the deck. In fact, there's not a drop anywhere.'

'Perhaps one of the sailors cleaned it up?' Bunny gave the steps a cursory search, a thumb and forefinger gripped to one arm of his spectacles. 'They wouldn't want to leave it there for the passengers to see.'

'No one came near with anything resembling a mop. I would have seen them,' Flora murmured as she resumed her climb. 'Besides, there was no blood to remove in the first place.'

Her confusion made the walk along the deck a silent one. Why did no one else wonder about the absence of blood from a wound deep enough to kill a man?

If indeed that's what killed him.

3

'Thank you for escorting me, Mr Harrington, I shall be perfectly all right now.' Fighting sudden dizziness, Flora inserted herself between Bunny and the door of her suite.

'I'm sure you will.' Bunny pushed the door open and indicated she should enter ahead of him. 'However, you look decidedly shaky, if I may say so. I wouldn't be a gentleman if I abandoned you now.'

'Maybe it wouldn't hurt for a while.' The door to Eddy's room was still closed and she raised a finger to her lips. 'He's still asleep, so if you could try not to wake him.'

He nodded and tiptoed past Eddy's door, lifting each foot in a pantomime that made her smile.

Discouraging him became too much of an effort, and appreciating his kindness, she sank into the thick cushion of the nearest wicker chair, her hands thrust into the folds of her skirt to still their shaking while he closed the door.

'It must have been a dreadful shock finding the body like that,' Bunny said gently.

'Actually, I was more curious than shocked at first. That is, until I saw that gash on his head, but no blood anywhere...' She motioned him into the chair opposite. 'I imagine it must have been worse for you as you knew him.'

'Not really.' He tugged up his trousers and sat, dwarfing the chair. 'After dinner, the others at the table repaired to the saloon for drinks. I only remember him because he instigated a game of poker.'

A light knock came at the door, and Flora half-rose, glad of a reason to break eye contact. The intensity of his stare made her uncomfortable, though she wasn't sure why.

'I expect that will be my morning tea.'

'I'll go.' Bunny halted her with an upraised hand, leaving her with little choice but to relax back into her seat.

She squeezed her eyes shut in an effort to banish the image of the man on deck. His prone body lying on the boards merged with that of a woman from her past. That she was Flora's mother was deeply ingrained, though the circumstances remained indistinct. Flora always saw her in a dream that ambushed her at odd times, leaving her with more questions than she could answer. That struck her as strange, because there was no blood in this instance, only what was matted into the man's dark hair, when her dream always featured blood; a good deal of it.

'The stewardess thought she had come to the wrong suite.' Bunny's cheerful voice brought her sharply back to the present. 'She evidently didn't expect to have the door answered by a man. Shall I pour?' He hovered above the loaded tray on the table between them.

She nodded, comforted by a familiar smell of tea that wafted into the room, reminding her of the Cleeve Abbey nursery in the afternoons. At first try he misjudged the arc of hot water and slopped some into a saucer. 'What were you saying about the blood?' he asked, dabbing at the wet tray clumsily with a napkin.

Flora attempted a smile. 'There was none. Not on the companionway, the deck or the handrail. What do you think about that? Did the man's death look like the result of an accident to you?'

'I didn't have time to form much of an opinion.' He adjusted his glasses, as if taking time to think. 'What with those sailors in such a hurry to take him away.' He handed her a full cup, a finger pointed to the sugar bowl.

'I thought it was odd, that's all.' She shook her head at the sugar, watching as he added a spoonful to his own cup which he stirred slowly. The thought struck her: he had nice hands. Slender though not feminine, with neat, well-kept fingernails.

'Flora?' The word made her jump, his face giving the impression he had said it more than once before she heard. 'The doctor didn't agree though, did he?'

'He didn't consider anything I had to say. But then I suppose the last thing the crew would want to put about on the first day at sea is a possible murder. That would certainly upset the passengers.'

'Murder?' His eyes glinted with surprise, magnified by his spectacles. 'Why would you think that?'

'I–I don't know.' Flora's confidence waned at his open scepticism. 'Maybe Dr Fletcher knows his business, and Mr Parnell did fall.' She met his gaze over the top of her teacup. 'Incidentally, what were you doing up so early?'

'I was on my way to check on Matilda.' His mouth tilted up slightly at one side. 'Why? Did you think I was on deck pushing card sharps down companionways?'

'No, of course not.' She tutted, mildly exasperated he should suggest such a thing. 'Unless you lost money to him, that is.'

'Should I be offended you think me capable of such a thing?' His pale brows lifted slightly.

'I don't, not at all.' Heat flooded her face. 'I apologise, my sense of humour can be somewhat dark at times. Comes from being around Eddy so much. I gather you're not a gambler?'

'Definitely not.' He relaxed again, apparently forgiving her. 'I work too hard to risk my money on games of chance.' The fact he was a man of high moral principle pleased her, for reasons she couldn't yet fathom.

'What was the late Mr Parnell like?' Flora asked.

Bunny thought for a moment. 'Early thirties, dark, heavy-featured with thick black hair.'

Flora had gathered that much for herself. 'I meant his personality. Aggressive, self-effacing, unassuming?'

'Well, from what I could make out, not the last two I suspect. He talked rather a lot at dinner, where he spoke with a Brooklyn accent. He claimed to know London, which didn't seem likely to me, though I have no reason to disbelieve him.'

'Hmm, what about this lady you told the officer he was with?' The hot tea began to relax her and she began to enjoy the exchange.

'Ah yes, the actress.' Bunny's eyes lit at the recollection. 'A petite, dark-haired girl who spoke with a Southern accent. Difficult to understand sometimes, but appealing on several levels. Despite her slow speech she was clearly more intelligent than him, if not in intellect, then common sense. I was surprised they were together.'

This description sounded nothing like the lady Flora had seen talking to Parnell.

'She appears to have made quite an impression on you.' Instantly she regretted the sharp edge to her voice. Why should it worry her if he found another woman attractive? To cover her conflicted thoughts, she poured more tea into her cup and held the pot up in a silent question. 'Was it a high-stakes poker game?'

He held his cup out for a refill. 'Depends what you mean by high. One chap lost $1,000 in the game.'

'A thousand?' The handle of the teapot slipped from Flora's fingers, though she managed to catch it before it hit the table.

'He didn't seem particularly upset by it.' Bunny shrugged. 'He is quite well-heeled, I imagine, by the look of his wife's clothes at least.'

'That could be ocean-liner talk.' In response to his sideways look, she continued, 'My employers warned me that when separated from our ordinary lives, one's history can often be embellished.'

'His wife's diamonds are definitely real.'

'Isn't it bad form to wear one's jewels at sea?' Flora recalled Lady Vaughn always locked up her jewellery on sea voyages, claiming that any well-travelled lady knew, that sea air spoiled the stones' lustre.

'Maybe so,' Bunny said, laughing. 'I don't claim to know much about it. Gerald Gilmore is a solid chap. I quite like him.'

'Gilmore,' Flora mused. 'That was the name Eddy mentioned.' His friend Ozzy must be their son. 'Had you met the Gilmores before this trip?'

'I don't know anyone on this voyage.' He turned his intense gaze on her and smiled. 'Except you, of course.'

Her stomach performed a lurching flip, and she dipped her nose to her teacup to hide the heat that flooded her face.

'I hope you don't mind my hanging about, treating you like an old friend?' He placed his cup and saucer on the table between them, and eased forwards, resting his forearms on his thighs. 'Actually, I wondered about why you left me so abruptly last night when I imagined we were getting along famously. Did I say something to offend you?'

'No, not at all.' She dropped her gaze to her lap. 'It's just that, well, Eddy—'

'Ah, yes, I see. Eddy.' He nodded slowly. 'I quite understand. You're his governess, aren't you?'

Flora nodded, while her heart fluttered like a distressed bird. 'How did you know?'

'He mentioned at dinner that he was travelling with his governess. I consider it my sheer good luck I ran into you later admiring Matilda.'

Her face warmed even more at the compliment, hopeful that at least now he wouldn't make an excuse and leave if he already knew who she was.

'The Minneapolis was the first ship with accommodation available when my employer booked passage.' She was about to add that she had a third class cabin on *The Oceanic* during the outward voyage, but feared it sounded too much like an apology.

'I don't see why that would send you rushing away like you did,' Bunny went on. 'I have very happy memories of my governess.' He produced a handkerchief from somewhere, removed his spectacles and proceeded to polish the lenses.

Flora focused on the tiny red mark the metal bridge had caused on his nose and had to resist the urge to stroke it away. It was only the thought of what Lady Vaughn would say about entertaining young men in her suite that prevented her.

'Tell me about the other passengers.' She offered him the plate of biscuits, hoping he wouldn't notice that her hand shook, but this time not with shock.

'If you hadn't avoided the dining room last night' – he took a garibaldi, pointing it at her – 'you would have met them yourself.'

'Well, I didn't.' She returned the plate to the tray, feeling more confident. 'Therefore, I rely on you to paint me a picture.'

'Let's see.' He took a bite of the biscuit and chewed. 'Gerald Gilmore is English, a businessman of some sort, though he didn't boast about it like some. Either he's extremely modest or he's involved in something not quite kosher. His wife is a social climber and spent the whole evening running through names on the passenger list to see with whom she should strike up acquaintances.'

'Eddy mentioned something like that.' Flora smiled. 'Do go on.'

'They have a son about Eddy's age. Ozzy's a nice lad, bright and knowledgeable, if young for his age and a little awkward. He got on well with your young charge at dinner.'

'Yes, Eddy mentioned him – Ozymandias.' A surge of guilt welled at her having abandoned Eddy to a room full of strangers the night before but was immediately suppressed at the memory of his enthusiasm over Bunny's motor car.

'Yes, well, I'm in no position to comment on unusual names.' Bunny fidgeted on his chair.

Flora reminded herself she must ask him about his own some time, when the occasion presented itself.

'The Cavendishes are our on-board honeymoon couple,' Bunny continued. 'What the newly-marrieds forget is that getting away from everyone they know for a while might seem like a good thing, but can backfire on them.'

'Why do you say that?' She recalled the young couple who had been so eager to wave off the grief-stricken woman when the ship left New York.

'Because take it from me, the people you know are not half as bad as those you don't know. They will be observed by the other passengers with fierce intensity.'

'What for?' Flora relaxed in her chair, enjoying his obvious enthusiasm of the subject.

'Schadenfreude, my dear Miss Maguire. The need to take pleasure in another's misfortune. The acquired knowledge that nothing good will last and has its origins in a misconception.'

'Oh dear, that sounds cynical. What sort of things are said about them?'

'That if the groom leaves his bride's side for a moment, his love is growing cold; if she gives her attention to another male passenger under fifty, she's a flirt who will never settle down. If the husband dozes in his steamer chair, he must be tiring of her. Should she dare to yawn in his company, married life is beginning to pall; if he dares raise his voice to her, he is a typical bullying husband, and if—'

'Enough!' Flora slapped his arm gently, turning an amused snort into a delicate laugh. 'You make your fellow passengers sound like a judge and jury.'

'It's the plain truth. I've seen it myself. If he doesn't call her "Sweetheart", he's a cold-blooded wretch, and if she wears more expensive clothes than he does, then he must have married her for her money.'

'What a depressing outlook, Mr Harrington. I dread to think how many new marriages have been thus tainted by shipboard gossip.'

'Dozens I should think.' He shook his head in mock dismay, and she joined him in a moment of companionable laughter. When they fell silent again, he asked, 'As to all these questions, are you an Arthur Conan Doyle fan, by any chance? I ask, because when I was a boy I enjoyed his detective stories when they were serialised in The Strand Magazine.'

'Isn't everyone?' She returned his flirtatious look with one of her own, becoming relaxed in his company. It was as if she had always known him, which seemed a strange thought to enter her head and one she would never have been able to explain. 'I read *Marked "Personal"* by Anna Katharine Green when I was in New York. Her father was a lawyer, so she gets the legal aspects spot on, and—' she broke off at the rattle of the doorknob which announced the arrival of Eddy, who fumbled with the cord of his blue and red plaid dressing gown as he entered the room.

'Why is everyone up so early?' he demanded in a voice heavy with sleep, pushing one hand into his disarrayed hair. 'There are people running along the deck past my window. Is the ship on fire?' He blinked as he realised Flora wasn't alone. 'Oh, hello, Mr Harrington. What are you doing here?'

'The situation isn't quite as dramatic as that, Eddy,' Flora said. 'Mr Harrington escorted me back to my room after an incident this morning. But it's nothing for you to worry about, there's no fire.' She exchanged a glance with Bunny, hoping he might take her cue to break the news gently. 'I'm afraid one of the gentlemen passengers has met with an accident. A Mr Parnell.'

'He's the one with the eyebrows that meet in the middle isn't he?' Eddy perched on the edge of the third armchair and peered at the tea tray, frowning.

'I'm afraid Mr Harrington used your cup,' Flora explained. 'You'll have to wait until breakfast.'

'I don't mind.' Eddy shrugged, plucked a biscuit from the tray and nibbled at it, one knee looped over the arm of his chair. 'What sort of accident?'

'He suffered a bad fall on the companionway steps,' she replied carefully. 'He was badly injured.'

'How badly? Will he die?' Eddy whispered round a mouthful of crumbs, his eyes wide, making Flora regret her having introduced him to Arthur Conan Doyle. Or would his penchant for blood and destruction have emerged in any case?

'Already dead,' Bunny replied, ignoring Flora's frantic hand signal pleading for discretion.

'Spiffing!' Eddy dropped his unfinished biscuit on the tray and headed for his room. 'Must get dressed and find Ozzy. He'll want to hear about this.'

'Mr Harrington, I really don't think you should—' Flora tried to intervene but no one appeared to be listening.

'You can tell him Flora found the body,' Bunny called after Eddy on his way out.

'Excellent!' Eddy's delighted yell came from behind his closed door.

'Why on earth did you tell him that?' Flora said, aghast.

'Don't look so disapproving.' Bunny smiled, unabashed. 'Shipboard gossip will soon fill in the gory details anyway.' He swept one of the two remaining biscuits from the plate. 'Besides, it will give Eddy some kudos amongst the other boys. These things matter, you know.'

'Hmm.' Flora narrowed her eyes at the strange proclivities of young boys, and older ones. 'Slightly morbid if you ask me. Besides, weren't you about to describe the honeymooners?'

'Hmm, I sense you are attempting to root out possible suspects for your alleged murderer.'

'Maybe, but Mr Parnell's death might very well be one. And isn't that what all sleuths do in the best crime novels?'

'As far as I know, but no one thinks he was murdered except you.'

'Indulge me then. What harm could it do?'

The crease between his brows told her he did so with reluctance but didn't wish to argue with her. 'Max Cavendish is in his early thirties, I would say; an affluent English businessman who puts me in mind of a bulldog puppy – no grace, but plenty of enthusiasm.'

'Very descriptive, which means I shall be hard put not to smile when we meet, and thus I will completely baffle him.' She conjured the young man with the woman she had thought might be honeymooners, but Bunny's description didn't resemble him at all. She dragged her gaze back to her cup. 'What's his bride like?'

'Cynthia? She's what one might call a society beauty, all brittle aloofness and perfect features. Quite a stunner. Slim with light reddish-gold hair and startling cerulean eyes. Extremely wealthy, if her wardrobe is anything to go by.' He waved his teaspoon in the air. 'Several chaps I went to school with had sisters just like her.'

'Really?' Flora said slowly. He had described the lady she had seen talking to the dead man on deck the previous day perfectly. But why was she arguing with a man who wasn't her husband? Had it had something to do with Mr Parnell's death?

'Did you really find the body, Flora?' Eddy reappeared in the doorway to his room, having apparently thrown on whatever clothes came to hand.

'Have you washed, Eddy?' Flora asked, suspicious.

'Was there much blood?' Eddy avoided her question, his head bent as he tied a loose shoelace.

'Not enough,' Flora said under her breath, then more loudly, 'never mind that now, Eddy. I rather think a yellow sweater with red socks is a little—'

'No time. The nursery breakfast is about to start.' Without glancing at either of them, he left, banging the door behind him.

The mention of breakfast made Flora's stomach lurch, though not from hunger. To be the focus of a roomful of strangers speculating on what part she had played in the death of a passenger did not appeal. She was bound to be the talk of the ship by luncheon.

Almost immediately, the doorbell rang, and sighing, Flora rose and flung it open, adopting her most patient tone. 'What have you forgotten?' The words froze on her tongue at the sight of the two uniformed men who filled the door frame. One of whom was Second Officer Martin.

'Miss Flora Maguire?' an older man asked, four rings of gold braid on his sleeves identifying him as the captain.

Her mouth dried but she gathered herself enough to nod.

'Captain Gates, how do you do.' Of medium height and a stocky build without being fat, his eyes glinted with amusement in a face that Flora expected to break into a laugh at any second. An aroma of old tobacco hung about him, echoed by the polished walnut pipe poking out of his breast pocket. 'Would you mind answering a few questions about this morning's ah, unfortunate mishap?'

'Of course not. Please come in.' She stepped aside to allow them to enter, her attention caught by the sight of a crewman in front of a cabin two doors down. A diminutive maid stood, feet planted apart, in front of him, a pile of white towels hugged to her chest.

'You had no cause to throw me out,' the maid said. 'I have to clean the cabin, or I'll lose my job.'

'I can't help that,' the crewman snapped, unmoved. 'Mr Parnell's state-room must not be touched. Captain's orders.'

'Then just you be sure to tell the housekeeper those things are missing, and it wasn't me who took 'em.' With a final sniff at the unbending sailor, she stomped off along the deck.

The crewman mouthed something at the girl's back before locking the door of the cabin, then pocketed the key before striding off in the other direction.

So Mr Parnell had occupied the cabin on the other side of Miss Lane's. Not that it mattered now. He wouldn't be using it.

Flora closed the door, aware the neat sitting room felt suddenly crowded with the addition of the officers, both of whom stood with their caps tucked neatly beneath their arms.

'Captain Gates, this is Mr Harrington, who was also at the scene of the accident earlier.'

'Mr Harrington,' the captain shook his hand firmly, then turned a smile on Flora. 'Thank you for assisting us, Miss Maguire.'

Flora nodded shyly and resumed her seat, slightly overwhelmed by the presence of the captain in her suite as she directed them to the remaining chairs.

'Should I leave you alone?' Bunny asked, the question in stark contrast to his possessive occupation of the room.

'Actually, Mr Harrington.' Officer Martin turned an amiable smile on him. 'It might be better if you remained, seeing as you were both at the scene, as it were.' He produced a notebook and pen from a pocket, at the same time looking to the captain for approval, which was given with a nod.

'As you wish.' Bunny now stood by Flora's chair, positioning himself at her shoulder; a gesture she found both protective and reassuring.

'What was the first thing you saw this morning, Miss Maguire?' Officer Martin's pen hovered above the page.

'You know what I saw.' Flora frowned, slightly confused. 'You were there too.'

'I'm sorry.' He exchanged a look with Captain Gates, who nodded. 'This needs to be kept formal as an official record.'

'I see.' Flora took a deep breath. 'Well then. I was out for a walk and about to descend the companionway to the saloon deck, when I spotted something at the bottom.'

'You didn't use the internal staircase lobby to get to the lower deck?' the captain interrupted.

'Well, no. I wanted some air, and it was a lovely morning.' Flora flinched. 'At least, it was before...'

'Quite.' Captain Gates instilled a world of speculation in the words. 'Do go on.'

'I–I thought it was a bundle of clothing at first, but a closer look told me it was a man. A dead one.' She aimed a nod at the younger office. 'Which is when you arrived.'

'That's true, sir.' Officer Martin nodded. 'When I got there, the young lady was bent over the body.'

'Of course it's true.' Flora tensed, then felt Bunny's hand come down on her shoulder in warning. 'I apologise, I don't mean to be sharp.' She bit her lip. 'I'm still rather shocked. It was the last thing I expected to see.' Not that she was in the least upset any more, but as an excuse, it would do.

'Did you see the man fall?' Captain Gates asked.

'No. In fact, the blood on his head had congealed, so it must have happened some time before I discovered him. Hours possibly.'

'We doubt that was the case.' Captain Gates twisted his cap repeatedly between his splayed knees. 'The decks are washed every morning at six. None of the crew reported a body in that location then.'

'What did Dr Fletcher say?' Flora glanced up at Bunny, who shrugged.

'He didn't appear to regard the fact as important.' Officer Martin cleared his throat.

Flora gave him a hard look. 'How could it not be important when a man died?'

'The doctor could only give the body a cursory examination,' Captain Gates said. 'The post-mortem will have to wait until we reach England.' His gaze shifted from her to Bunny. 'Were either of you acquainted with the deceased?'

The deceased. Flora shivered. A few hours ago he had been a living, breathing human being. Now his life was reduced to two stark words.

'I met him for the first time last night at dinner.' Bunny's hand squeezed Flora's shoulder, reminding her he had not removed it. 'Miss Maguire ate dinner here in her suite, so they never met.'

'I believe Mr Parnell won a good deal of money in a card game last evening?' Captain Gates said with a slight trace of accusation. 'What, might I ask, were the reactions among the players to his good fortune?'

'Gilmore took it in his stride,' Bunny replied. 'Although perhaps a chap called Crowe might have been more put out. He was one of our dining companions who joined the poker game. Parnell goaded him a little, and I suppose you could say Crowe appeared rattled, but there was no real hostility between them.'

Bunny hadn't yet mentioned this man Crowe to Flora, but then they had been interrupted quite early on in his description of their fellow passengers. There were likely to be others she knew nothing about as yet, which might prove interesting if her suspicions about Mr Parnell's so-called accident proved true.

'You didn't join this game, Mr Harrington?' the captain asked. Again that mild accusatory tone. Officer Martin continued scribbling in his notebook.

'I'm no gambler, Captain. Not for money at least.'

'Are either of you acquainted with' – Officer Martin paused, flicked back a page or two and squinted at what was written there – 'a Miss Eloise Lane?'

Flora shook her head. Raised voices heard through bulwarks didn't count.

'Again,' Bunny said, 'I met her for the first time last night. She and Mr Parnell were travelling together.'

Flora straightened, easing forward slightly. So Parnell was travelling with Miss Lane? Was he also the man who was in her stateroom last night? If so, she might know more about his death.

'Together?' the officer prompted Bunny. 'Do you happen to know the nature of their relationship?'

'That I cannot say. But I do know they had separate staterooms.' Bunny's slight hesitation told Flora he was uncomfortable, though she couldn't see his face to confirm this without twisting round in her seat.

'In your opinion, Mr Harrington,' Officer Martin asked, 'were Mr Parnell and Miss Lane amiable towards one another?'

'I got the impression their association was a business arrangement.' The vibration of Bunny's shrug went through Flora's shoulder. 'One where the lady's expectations outweighed Parnell's promises.'

'In what way?'

The interview had become a three-way discussion, with Flora relegated to that of spectator, which she found mildly annoying seeing as they occupied her suite. Though what Bunny had to say about his dining companions was infinitely more interesting than the snippets he had imparted to her. Perhaps he was right and she shouldn't have avoided the dining room, but instead relished the chance to observe these people for herself.

'Miss Lane intimated Parnell had got her a part in a London production of *School for Scandal* at the Theatre Royal once they reached London. He had claimed acquaintance with Cyril Maude, the producer.'

'How did Mr Parnell react to this claim?'

'Yes, how did he react?' Flora slanted a glance up at Bunny over one shoulder.

He gave a small start as if reminded she was there, then extended his look to Officer Martin. 'He appeared embarrassed, actually,' he said, as if the thought had just that moment occurred to him. 'He tried to dismiss it. Told her it wasn't a definite agreement and she still had to audition when they reached England.'

'And the lady? Was she disappointed? Angry?'

The captain sat with his forearms on his thighs, his head lowered but silently watching both her and Bunny. When she caught his eye his mobile face broke into an amiable smile, almost encouraging, as if to tell her that he, at least, had not forgotten her.

'More like petulant,' Bunny scoffed. 'She was adamant Parnell had guaranteed the part was hers and didn't like him denying it.'

'Did they argue?'

'Not that I saw. Miss Lane exchanged a few cross words with him and left abruptly, but Parnell carried on playing as if nothing had happened. I've no idea if it developed into a row afterwards.'

'Did anything out of the ordinary occur amongst other members of the company last night?' Captain Gates asked. 'An argument perhaps, or harsh words?'

'Well, I ah—' Bunny began, but when Captain Gates shot him a sudden, eager look, whatever he had been about to say went unsaid. 'Nothing, other than I've already mentioned.'

'You and Miss Maguire, sir?' Officer Martin pointed his pen at each of them in turn. 'The two of you had not met before yesterday?'

'That's correct,' Bunny replied, as if he resented an implication it might be otherwise.

A loaded look passed between the two crewmen, then Captain Gates cleared his throat and rose. 'I think that's all we need for the moment, sir. Miss.' He waited until his companion had pocketed his notebook, then cocked his chin as a signal for them to leave.

'What do you think happened to Mr Parnell?' Flora blurted at them, irritated at being virtually ignored in her own suite. And what did Captain Gates mean by 'at the moment'? They had told him everything they knew. Or at least she had.

Captain Gates turned back at the door, his expression bland. 'We have no reason to believe the gentleman's death was anything other than an unfortunate accident. I hope this incident doesn't spoil the rest of your voyage.' The captain went on, 'If there's anything you need – either of you – do feel free to call upon myself or one of my crew.'

Bunny saw them both out and Flora slumped back in her chair, disappointed but not surprised. After all, people died all the time from falls. Maybe the most obvious explanation was correct, and it had been an accident after all. Then an image of the body on the deck intruded and her disquiet surged again. They were wrong.

4

'It's quite evident they believe the man fell,' Bunny said, when he returned from seeing the crewmen out.

'They weren't prepared to discuss the alternative either, were they, for instance—' she broke off, wincing at the strident note of a bugle from outside announcing the first meal of the day. 'I'm never quite prepared for that sound.'

'It does take a little getting used to.' Bunny laughed. 'It's been a long morning already, yet it's only breakfast time. Shall we go in together?'

'Eddy has elected to eat without me, so I shall have to do without his company from now on,' Flora said, forgetting her resolve to avoid the dining room; not with Bunny offering to be her escort. 'I hope he hasn't been upset by this *incident*.' She had almost said killing, but to persist with her suspicions would make her look foolish. 'Despite his mischievous nature, he's a sensitive boy.'

'He didn't look too upset when he ran out of here earlier.' Bunny retrieved Flora's shawl.

'No, he didn't, did he?' She stood passive as he draped the soft wool over her shoulders. 'Will Captain Gates make an announcement during divine service about what happened?'

'Probably.' He reached past her and opened the door while shooting her a mischievous sideways look. 'I doubt he'll mention you, though. Women on board are considered bad luck. Sailors are superstitious that way.'

'You aren't making me feel any better about this at all, Mr Harrington.' She cast him an oblique look as she stepped out onto the deck.

'Sorry, just my perverse sense of humour. And I wish you'd call me Bunny.'

She smiled in response, not quite ready to enquire as to how he might have acquired such a name.

They reached an open suite door further along the deck, from which a young woman in a cream and white gown stepped into their path, her head turned to address someone behind her.

'Oh, do hurry up, Max,' she urged, both annoyed and seductive. 'I want my breakfast.'

'Good morning, Mrs Cavendish.' Bunny slowed, bringing Flora to a gentle halt beside him.

The woman turned to face them, her face lit to perfection by her bright smile. 'Good morning to you, Mr Harrington. How nice to see you again.'

His use of her name identified the female honeymooner who argued with Parnell on deck. So where did Miss Lane come in? Or did Parnell make a habit of upsetting women? Was Flora even sure it was Parnell Miss Lane was with, or had she made the wrong assumption? Which raised the question as to why Mrs Cavendish was also arguing with him? And was it significant her husband wasn't present at the time?

'Flora, did you hear me?' Bunny nudged her gently. 'I was just introducing you to Mrs Cavendish.'

'Oh, do forgive me, I was miles away.' Flora took the lady's limply extended hand.

'Call me Cynthia,' she gushed in a clipped Home Counties accent, as if conveying a rare privilege, while her gaze swept Flora's navy skirt and matching plain jacket.

Flora returned her smile, aware of how a sparrow must feel in the company of a kingfisher. Clumsy, brown and invisible.

'How did you sleep on your first night aboard, Mrs Cavendish?' Bunny asked.

'Perfectly fine, thank you.' Mrs Cavendish's wide, grey gaze slid over Flora before returning to Bunny. 'That is, until what sounded like the entire crew stampeded past our window at some ridiculously early hour.' She puckered her cupid bow lips and fluttered her sweeping eyelashes. 'I've a good mind to complain to the captain.'

'I'm afraid there was an accident earlier, which explains all the activity,' Bunny said. 'One of the passengers fell down a companionway.'

'Really? How inconvenient.' Cynthia fussed with her scarf. 'Anyone we know?'

'I'm not sure if you remember him. It was that Parnell chap from last night.'

'How awful!' Cynthia froze in the act of tugging on a white glove. 'Was... was he badly hurt?'

'He's dead,' Flora said, watching her closely.

The blood drained from Cynthia's face, her hand stilled in mid-air, her glove dangling from the end of her fingers. 'He can't be!'

'Hard to believe, isn't it?' Bunny said, seemingly oblivious of her discomfort. 'Seems he hit his head as he fell. Shocked all of us, especially Flora here, who was unfortunate enough to have found the body.'

'I'm sorry to have upset you,' Flora said, matching Bunny's bland expression. 'I didn't realise you were acquainted with him.'

'Whatever made you think I was? In fact, we met for the first time at dinner last night.' Cynthia's pigeon wing eyes rounded in an innocence that Flora found unconvincing.

Aware of Bunny's puzzled frown directed at her profile, Flora couldn't resist pushing a little further. 'Really? Only, I'm sure you and he were having some sort of disagreement when we boarded yesterday.'

'Was that the same man?' Cynthia's shaky laugh was unconvincing 'I have to admit I didn't look at him properly. He bumped me with his suit-case and bruised my ankle.' She looked down at an extended foot but there was nothing to see beneath her boot and skirt hem. 'I gave him quite a set down, I can tell you.' She cleared her throat and looked away. 'Any-way, I mustn't keep you.'

'We were just on our way to breakfast actually,' Bunny waylaid her at the last second. 'Won't you join us?'

Cynthia smoothed her gloves over each wrist in turn, as if giving herself time to think. 'I have to wait for Max. We'll be along in a moment.' She backed hurriedly through the suite door and closed it firmly behind her.

'As I'm sure you realised, Cynthia is one half of our honeymoon couple,' Bunny said as they reached the door to the interior lobby.

It was on the tip of Flora's tongue to ask him if he thought Cynthia was pretty, but changed her mind and she simply smiled at him instead. It would be like probing a sore tooth to check it still hurt.

'Did you really see her arguing with Parnell yesterday?' Bunny asked, frowning as they descended the staircase to the saloon lower deck where the dining room was located at the stern.

'That's what it looked like. I didn't see any suitcase either.'

'But she said she didn't know him.'

'She did, didn't she?'

* * *

The dining room door flapped open at Bunny's touch, releasing a low murmur of voices. Panelled in light oak with a domed, stained-glass ceiling that rose through two storeys, a blaze of jewel-tinted light flooded the scene below.

Long maple wood tables filled the room, arranged like a school dormitory; while wide windows gave onto the glistening ocean on one side, and tall gilt mirrors made the room appear twice its size.

Heads swivelled in their direction as Bunny guided Flora across the room to their table, a whispered remark aimed at a companion, who watched them pass.

Flora fought the urge to turn tail and run, but Bunny's grip on her arm prevented her. 'Keep walking. It won't be nearly as bad as you imagine.'

She didn't believe him.

'There you are, Harrington.' A broad-shouldered man unfurled from his chair as they reached the table. A wing of silver graced one temple in his black hair; a hereditary trait more than a sign of age, as Flora judged him to be no more than forty.

He clasped Flora's hand in both of his and held on. 'Is this the young lady who eschewed our company last night?' He raised her hand briefly to his lips. 'Gerald Gilmore. Lovely to meet you, my dear. This is my wife, Monica,' he indicated a lady in a dove-grey silk gown which did little for her sallow skin. Gerald Gilmore's solid build and inherent calm made a marked contrast to his wife's gushing mannerisms and flapping hands.

'How do you do, Miss Maguire.' Monica offered Flora her a limp hand as if conveying a blessing. 'I'm Ozzy's mother,' she added unnecessarily. 'This awful business about Mr Parnell is all over the ship. You must tell us all about it.' She waved Flora into a chair as if she had taken charge of the seating arrangements for the table, then ushered Gerald in beside her.

'Ah yes,' a middle-aged man with salt-and pepper hair said. 'The finder of our unfortunate dinner companion.' His words tinged with a slight Germanic accent.

'You didn't mention him either,' Flora said, *sotto voce*.

'I would have, had the captain not interrupted,' Bunny whispered back. 'Though I know nothing about him.'

'Carl Hersch.' The stranger introduced himself, taking Flora's hand in a firm, dry grip that was not unpleasant, though the contact lasted longer than politeness required. 'It's nice to meet you, Mr Hersch.' Flora retrieved her hand gently. 'I hope my reputation won't be held against me.'

'I'm sure it won't be.' His eyes softened with something like under-standing.

'Nothing to fret about. Storm in a teacup. Forgotten by tomorrow.' Gerald's clipped manner appeared to be his normal mode of speech.

'It could have been far worse,' Monica Gilmore said. 'I mean, he wasn't anyone of consequence was he? Nor did anyone on this table actually know him, not after only one night.'

'Miss Lane did.' Mr Hersch took his seat. 'They were travelling together.'

Flora watched each face in turn, but no one reacted to this comment.

'Have you met Miss Ames, our resident author, Miss Maguire?' Monica indicated a grey-haired lady beside her in her purple-frilled blouse coupled with a bright orange skirt.

'No, I haven't.' Flora examined another character Bunny had not mentioned, which surprised her as the lady was hard to forget. She had either dressed in the dark or simply desired to be noticed. Or maybe as a lady of a certain age she no longer cared about appearances or fashion. Flora hoped she had the courage to be so individual herself one day.

'Mary Ames, how nice to meet you.' Her firm handshake and voice were as loud as her clothes. Her place was taken immediately by a young man of around twenty-five with untidy dark hair and a waxen complexion which made him look as if he suffered from a chronic illness. His eyes were hooded, the lower lids sporting dark lines like bruises, though his cheery, 'Morning, everyone,' ascertained he was fitter than he looked.

'I'm Gus Crowe.' His lingering gaze slid over her in a way that made her want to shake it off. 'Nice to see another attractive face.' His limp, slightly clammy handshake repulsed her and she released his hand rapidly with a fixed smile.

'Sorry, I should have warned you about him,' Bunny whispered as Crowe threw himself carelessly into an empty chair, sending Mr Hersch's napkin onto the floor. A steward rushed forwards to replace it, while the German flicked an exasperated look at the miscreant.

'I take it everyone has heard about that Parnell chap?' Crowe addressed the table. 'Took a header down a flight of steps I was told. Quite dead, y'know.' He appeared oblivious of the combined looks of censure aimed his way.

'We're very aware of the situation, Mr Crowe.' Monica glared at him. 'They ought to put warning notices on those companionways. They're positively dangerous.'

'They do, Monica,' her husband said with a world-weary sigh. 'You need to wear your glasses more often.'

'Oh pish, Gerald, I barely need them.' Monica flushed as she spoke, the subject an evident issue between them.

'Is that all we know? That Mr Parnell sustained a fall?' Miss Ames asked.

'What's to know?' Crowe spread butter liberally on a slice of toast, took a large bite and chewed. 'He bashed his head and copped it.'

Flora bit her bottom lip, resisting the urge to offer her own opinion when it had not yet been asked for, though the sharp looks directed her way told her it was only a matter of time.

'Surely not everyone is ill this morning?' Miss Ames indicated that half the places at table were empty. 'I'm aware some people aren't accustomed to ocean travel and find themselves disturbed by the smallest swell.'

'That's odd.' Bunny glanced at the door. 'Cynthia said she and Max would be along for breakfast. Yet neither of them have turned up yet.'

'That's honeymooners for you.' Gerald winked as he sawed vigorously at a sausage. 'Most likely they had a tray sent to their suite.'

'Mrs Penry-Jones isn't here either, nor is Miss Lane.' Monica's brow creased in concern that formed ruffles on her forehead.

'I'm not surprised the actress isn't here,' Miss Ames said. 'She's probably too distressed after hearing what happened.'

'Doesn't explain the old lady, though.' Gerald appeared thoughtful. 'She struck me as an up-at-the-crack-of-dawn sort of person.'

'I should imagine Captain Gates and his first officer are still interviewing everyone, which might explain their absence. I saw him on the way here and he's asked me to make myself available later this morning.' Mr Hersch reached for the last bread roll from a basket, which Gus Crowe snatched from beneath his fingers, grinning like a schoolboy.

Hersch sighed and withdrew his hand, gesturing to a waiter to bring more.

'We've already been interviewed by the captain.' Bunny included Flora in his response. 'There will be a post-mortem when we reach London.'

'What sort of questions did he ask?' Miss Ames produced a moleskin-covered notebook and pen from her handbag.

'Only what we saw, which was very little,' Flora replied, then before she could stop herself, said, 'when I pointed out there should have been more blood on the deck, he didn't agree.'

Bunny's eyes narrowed and he gave a tiny shake of his head which Flora pretended not to see.

'How interesting.' Miss Ames unsheathed her pen. 'Do share your theory, Miss Maguire. I love a good mystery.'

'I don't have a theory, as such,' Flora said, regretting her impulse when Miss Ames began writing. 'I thought it odd, that's all.' She refrained from mentioning the gash on Parnell's head, or what the maid had said about the missing items from his stateroom, though the temptation to do so was almost irresistible.

Bunny gave an annoyed sigh, which sent a rush of defiance through her. 'Actually, I did wonder how Mr Parnell came to still be in his dinner suit at six forty in the morning.' She jumped as Bunny's shoe lightly connected with her shin.

'You mean he was there all night?' Monica asked, her eyes round.

Flora narrowed her eyes briefly at Bunny before turning back to her questioner. 'Not according to the captain.'

'How curious.' Miss Ames held each of their gazes in turn then carried on writing.

Gerald gave a half-amused snort. 'Something for your next book, Miss Ames? Fiction is more interesting than fact, after all.'

'I don't agree with you on that, Mr Gilmore.' Flora exchanged a defiant look with Bunny, who rolled his eyes but stayed silent.

* * *

At the end of the meal, Flora excused herself with vague promises of catching up with Bunny later. His disapproval of her thoughts regarding Mr Parnell's death had annoyed her, though on her walk back to her suite, she had to admit no solid evidence existed to disprove the accident theory.

Despite that, her head buzzed with unanswered questions. Had Miss Lane and Parnell been more than travelling companions, and the argument she had heard through the bulkhead turned into a lovers' quarrel, followed by a crack on the head? If so, how did Parnell end up at the bottom of a staircase hours later? And did Cynthia lie about knowing Parnell, or had she another reason for disassociating herself from him? A face from her past maybe she didn't want to acknowledge? Intrigued, she relished solving all the puzzles of human behaviour which had led to a man's death.

Thus preoccupied, Flora wasn't looking where she was going and collided with another lady passenger; the impact sent her sideways into a steamer chair.

'I'm so sorry!' Flora righted herself and made a leap for a clutch bag that had skittered across the deck. 'I wasn't looking where I was going.'

'That's quite all right,' the young woman replied in a soft, lilting drawl. Her cloud of black curls contrasted sharply with porcelain skin and a heavy layer of blood-red lipstick.

'I'm Flora, Flora Maguire. I don't think we've met.'

'How do you do, I'm Est—' her bag slipped from her fingers and hit the deck again. 'Oh, please excuse me I'm so clumsy this mornin'. I'm Eloise, Eloise Lane.' She dipped to retrieve the bag before extending her hand. Flora accepted it as if in a daze as she realised who the young woman was. The occupant of the suite next to hers. The actress travelling with Mr Parnell.

'You're the lady who found Frank's body, aren't you?' Eloise blurted.

'What?' Flora broke off from staring. 'How did you know?'

'Gossip moves faster'n a moth in a mitten, especially in small places like a ship.' She cast a teasing eye on Flora, then gestured for her to join her at the rail. Eloise leaned both forearms on the top and stared out to sea, her scarf whipping behind her in the wind like a small sail.

'You were missed at breakfast,' Flora said in the hope of instigating a conversation, though Eloise appeared in no hurry to leave.

'Was I indeed?' Her cornflower blue eyes beneath thick lashes widened, then sharpened. 'By whom, exactly?'

Flora thought quickly. 'The gentlemen, naturally.'

'Huh! I'll wager their wives didn't miss me one bit.' Eloise propped one elbow on top of the rail and dropped her chin into her hand; a gesture so perfect, Flora guessed she practised it in front of a mirror. 'I had no appetite after Frank—' she broke off and bit her lip.

'It must have been such a shock to hear he had died,' Flora said carefully.

'It was. Awful. I've just spent the most ghastly hour with the captain. He wanted to know everything. How long we had known each other? How did we meet? How close were we?' She ran the end of her scarf repeatedly through her fingers. 'Such impertinent questions, and all because the silly man fell down a set of stairs.'

'They're only doing their job. I doubt they think you had anything to do with it.' Flora's speculation as to any romantic involvement answered.

'O' course I didn't!' Her cheeks coloured, eyes flashing in an outrage that struck Flora as genuine. But then, Flora reminded herself, she was an actress. 'Now what am I goin' to do? I can't present myself to Mr Cyril Maude without Frank?' she demanded, apparently not expecting an answer. 'He promised to get me a part in a play.' She inclined her head, her thick lashes coming down slowly over her eyes. 'I'm an actress, ya know?'

'Is Mr Maude the producer?' Eloise nodded and Flora tried to think of something profound to keep the conversation going, finally settling on flattery. 'Perhaps you don't need his influence to get you the part. You could impress this Mr Maude with your acting ability alone.'

For a long second, Flora imagined she had overdone the flattery, but a few seconds passed in which Eloise seemed to consider this remark. Then she gave an acknowledging nod and puffed out her boyish chest.

'You're absolutely right. I don't need Frank. I'll go to that audition and prove to everyone what a wonderful Lady Teazle I'll make.' A beatific smile softened her expression as she consigned Mr Parnell to the past without a flicker of emotion.

'Of course you will.' Though as far as she could remember, Lady Teazle did not speak with a Southern drawl.

'Ah only wish I'd realised that before I—' Eloise broke off as gust of wind unravelled the knot in her scarf.

'Before you what?' Flora watched her as she caught the billowing end.

'It's nothin'.' Her eyes hardened. 'I didn't mean anything by it.'

'Even if you were most probably the last person to see him alive?' Flora wasn't going to let that go.

Her head whipped round, pinning Flora with a direct stare. 'What are you talking about?'

Flora hesitated. Challenging her directly was a gamble, but this verbal dance was getting her nowhere. 'I don't mean to imply anything, but I heard you arguing with someone last night. A man.' She broke eye contact and pretended to study a group of children playing hopscotch on the deck below. 'My suite is right next door to yours and I heard you quite clearly.'

'Oh, o' course. Ah remember now.' Eloise's feigned memory lapse indicated she had been caught out. 'Frank arrived at some ungodly hour last night wanting to talk. He smelled of whisky, so after a few sharp words ah sent him away. That's what you must'a heard.'

Flora was tempted to probe further, but Eloise had already turned away. 'I need to go and lie down. It's been a stressful morning and this wind is giving me a headache. Maybe we'll see each other later?'

'I expect so.' Flora watched her take small but confident steps back along the deck, unsure whether to believe her or not. Her story hung together, but loosely. Still undecided, she pushed away from the rail, turned to where a woman stood in the centre of the deck openly staring at her.

A few years older than herself, she wore a drab grey dress that clung to her ample curves wherever it touched, though with no actual shape or style. A flat, brown velvet hat covered her hair above features so bland, the woman's plainness might easily be mistaken for hostility. Flora couldn't recall having seen her before but wondered if her conversation with Eloise had been overheard.

Flora smiled in greeting, but the woman's pinched mouth and hard brown eyes refused to meet hers. Instead, she turned abruptly away and marched off down the deck. Dismissing her as the unfriendly sort and someone she wasn't likely to encounter again, Flora returned to her suite.

5

Flora descended to the companionway to the deck below, a wide-brimmed straw hat to keep off the sun, a woollen wrap to fend off the wind and a copy of *Northanger Abbey* to while away the morning. After a brief search, she located the steamer chair with her name attached in a row lined up facing the rail. When Lady Vaughn had volunteered to pay the eight shillings hire on two chairs for the duration of the voyage, Flora had deemed this unnecessary as Eddy was unlikely to use one. Her employer had insisted, suggesting Flora might find someone congenial to sit with in the afternoons. She doubted Bunny Harrington had featured in her lady-ship's calculations, but was now grateful for her foresight.

She settled down to read her Jane Austen, and having reached the part where Catherine had endured Mr Tilney's indignant tirade for trespassing in a private area of the house, Flora slapped the book face down in her lap with a sigh.

'I would have gone looking too,' she said aloud, her sympathies lodged firmly with the misunderstood heroine.

'It's a sign of madness you know, talking to yourself?' a male voice said.

Flora raised a hand to her eyes to where Bunny, the sun at his back, was little more than a shadowy outline staring down at her.

'Sort of. Won't you join me?'

'An attractive idea.' He eyed the row of labelled steamer chairs. 'Though I'd better not occupy someone else's seat, or I'll be in disgrace for the rest of the voyage.'

'Borrow Eddy's chair, I doubt he'll notice. He's at divine service with the Gilmores.'

'In that case, I will.' Bunny dragged the appropriate chair closer, tugged up his trousers and sat.

'I suppose everyone is still talking about this morning's drama?' Flora fidgeted as a man in a clerical collar turned to stare at her as he passed. His shoulders hunched beneath a long black coat and stovepipe hat reminded her of a disgruntled blackbird with his hunt and peck mannerism.

'Does that surprise you?' Bunny plucked a cushion from a pile beside his chair and tucked it behind his neck, his head tilted back and eyes closed against the morning sun. 'He's the last person you need worry about.' He nodded to the disgruntled blackbird. 'He's going to England to evade being implicated in a rather nasty fraud case. The dog collar is fake, by the way.'

'How on earth do you know that?' Flora gaped as she stared after the retreating man.

'I have a friend who works for the *New York Times* who wrote an article about him.'

'Then everyone aboard will know who he is, the poor man.' Her voice trailed off, distracted by a savoury aroma that drifted towards her on the wind, covering the salt water and carbolic smell of recently scrubbed deck boards.

'Poor man nothing. He's quite guilty, but by virtue of being the brother-in-law of a Governor, he's off to Europe to re-invent himself. My friend's editor cancelled the article in favour of some latest news about McKinley, so you are quite wrong in that everyone will know. Although gossip does have a life of its own aboard ship.'

'What's that wonderful smell?' Flora sniffed appreciatively, only half listening.

'Bouillon.' Bunny indicated to where a steward moved along the line of chairs, pausing at each one. 'It's served with these delicious soft floury rolls, which for some reason the Americans call biscuits. Would you like some?'

Without waiting for an answer, he beckoned the man over and requested two cups. Handing one to Flora, he tossed a coin onto the tray.

The steward examined the coin so closely, Flora half expected him to bite it. Then giving Bunny his effusive thanks, he pocketed it with a flourish before moving on to the next steamer chair.

'I see you're a generous tipper.' Flora wrapped both hands round the cup, allowing the steam to drift over her face.

'Stewardship work is demanding for those Southampton boys. Long hours for derisory pay, so they tend to rely on passengers' tips.'

'The housemaids at Cleeve Abbey work equally hard, but they never get more than a day-old cake or cut of left-over pork to take to their mothers on a Sunday.' She looked up from her cup and took in his expression. 'Oh dear, that sounds bitter, doesn't it?'

'Not really. I'm impressed you consider those less fortunate than yourself with some charity. So many people don't.'

'The same applies to yourself, apparently. Anyway, don't stewards have to hand their tips in to the steamship treasury?' Flora repeated what Lord Vaughn had used as an excuse for a measly gratuity on the outward voyage. 'It's not all added to their wages, either.'

'Really? I didn't know that.' He adjusted his spectacles with a disgruntled sniff. 'I'd like to think good tips keep them honest. The temptation to cheat must be irresistible amongst all this luxury.' He broke off to acknowledge a nod from Gus Crowe who stood twenty feet away in conversation with a prosperous-looking man in a fur coat.

'Talking of cheating,' Flora began, changing the subject, 'you told the captain Mr Crowe was angry when he lost at cards. Is it possible he suspected Parnell of double-dealing?'

'Ah, we're back to that, are we?' He kept one eye closed as he slanted a sideways look at her.

'I don't like mysteries.' Flora shrugged, mildly resentful at being dismissed, however politely.

Bunny shook his head. 'I doubt Parnell employed sleight of hand. He was just lucky. Biscuit?'

He held up one of the golden biscuits, twirling it like a conjurer.

Flora took it eagerly, surprised at how hungry she was, despite having eaten a good breakfast. Everyone who told her that sea air increased the appetite must have been right.

'What did the ladies do while the men played poker last night?' She bit into the still warm, floury biscuit, following it with a mouthful of hot, salty bouillon that slid warmly into her stomach.

'The old lady from Baltimore loudly disapproved of card games played for money.'

'The one who didn't make an appearance at breakfast?' Flora asked round a mouthful of crumbs.

'Mrs Penry-Jones. That's right. She claims to be one of the "four hundred".'

'Forgive my ignorance, but what's the "four hundred"?'

'Fascinating American idiosyncrasy.' Bunny chewed his biscuit and twisted to face her. 'Four hundred was the number of guests who could fit into Mrs William Backhouse Astor Junior's ballroom; thus, that was the number of New York society considered the elite.'

'Really.' Flora silently resolved to avoid Mrs Penry-Jones, not least because she'd been the one to dismiss Eddy to the children's meals, then remembered she was seated at the same dining table, making it unlikely.

'Perhaps she tripped Parnell with her cane and sent him to the bottom of the stairs because she objected to gambling.' Bunny grinned at her over the rim of his cup.

'I shan't rise to that, Mr Harrington.' She narrowed her eyes at him. 'And you? What did you do all evening?'

'Me?' He blinked, then thought for a moment. 'I chatted to Cynthia for a while, and then Mr Hersch joined us.'

'An interesting man, I thought. He's German, isn't he?'

'Originally.' Bunny swallowed a mouthful of bouillon, nodding. 'He's been a resident in New York this past twenty years, or so he said. Affable chap, but, well, buttoned-up is a good description.'

'Did he play cards last night?' Flora asked, not sure of the relevance of this game, but employed it as a starting point.

'For a while, but he folded early on. He was winning too, which struck me as odd. I asked him what he did for a living at one point, but he was vague. It wasn't until later I realised he hadn't answered my question.' He shrugged. 'I suppose he only agreed to play to be sociable. Not like Parnell.'

'What about Parnell?'

'Hah! He played as if his life depended on it.' He caught her eye and winced. 'Sorry, bit inappropriate in the circumstances. Ah, here's young Eddy.' He glanced to where Eddy and a boy of similar age but more athletic appearance approached them along the deck.

'What are you doing here, Eddy?' Flora cocked her ear to where the strains of 'Eternal Father Strong to Save' drifted from the deck above. 'Divine Service hasn't finished yet.'

'Um.' Eddy shuffled his feet, rubbing both hands down the side of his trousers. 'Me and Ozzy, we didn't go.' He indicated the boy with blunt-cut straight blond hair and mouse-brown eyes beside him. 'We played shuffle-board instead.'

'I see.' A reprimand died on her lips. She could hardly chastise Eddy when she had not attended the service herself. 'I'll forgive you this once, though you'll be expected to display more conspicuous devotion once you are at Marlborough.'

'Oh, I will, I promise.' Eddy's shoulders slumped in relief.

Bunny mouthed the words 'conspicuous devotion' behind the boy's back with a mock-horrified expression.

Flushing, Flora clamped her lips together to prevent herself laughing.

'Did you really find the body, Miss Maguire?' Ozzy could evidently not hold in the question a second longer.

'I did. However, I trust neither of you have discussed the gentleman's demise with the other boys. It's disrespectful.'

'How would *he* know if we talked about him or not?' Eddy demanded, with all the straightforwardness of youth. 'He's dead.'

Bunny chortled and Flora sighed.

'Captain Gates told my father that card sharps might be on board.' Ozzy peered at her myopically. 'Perhaps Mr Parnell was a professional gambler?'

'It was simply an accident,' Flora insisted, despite her own convictions on the subject.

'They'll bury him at sea, you know,' Ozzy announced with dispassionate authority. 'Wrap his body in a sail and sew it up like a parcel with the last stitch right through his nose.'

'Really?' Eddy's eyes widened as he tugged up a wayward sock. 'Straight through the bony bit, or just the soft end?'

'Eddy!' Flora half choked on her mouthful of biscuit.

Bunny's shoulders shook with ill-concealed mirth, and Flora threw him a 'don't just sit there' look. He withdrew a dollar note from his wallet and waved it in front of them. 'How would you boys like an ice cream?'

'Jolly decent of you, Mr Harrington.' Eddy palmed the note with the speed of an illusionist. 'See you at luncheon then.'

They were halfway along the deck before Flora spoke. 'You do know ice cream on this ship is complimentary?'

'Is it really? I had no idea.' Bunny's lips twitched as he dipped his nose into his cup, then immediately held it at arm's length, grimacing. 'Dash it, my bouillon has gone cold.'

* * *

Flora spent more time than usual selecting what to wear. Despite her worries about looking out of place with a wardrobe that would not match up to a ship full of wealthy travellers, she had found it reassuring that even society ladies regarded it bad form to wear their best clothes on board. The captain's dance on the penultimate evening would be the rare occasion silk and high fashion was expected and she intended to make an excuse in the unlikely event anyone asked her if she planned to attend.

She settled on a sage green blouse in soft cotton with pale grey trim over a grey skirt, confident she wouldn't instantly be recognised as being 'in service'. A gentle rap came at the door just as she fastened a gold and garnet brooch left to her by her mother.

Assuming it was the stewardess with clean linen, Flora's welcoming smile froze in place at the sight of Bunny in a dark blazer and buff slacks, one arm braced above his head against the door frame.

'I came to offer my services as your escort to luncheon.' His smile betraying he was not totally confident of his welcome.

'That's most kind of you.' Her voice came out surprisingly calm, considering how his slow, appraising gaze unsettled her. She pulled the suite door closed and fell into step beside him, throwing him the odd sideways look as they walked. His rimless glasses made him seem less studious than a horn-rimmed pair she had also seen him wear, and the question she had asked herself all morning resurfaced. 'How many pairs of glasses do you own, exactly?'

He slid them off his nose, peering at them as if he had never seen them before. 'Several. They're an indulgence of mine.' Replacing them, he reached past her and pushed open the door that led into the staircase lobby. 'Actually, I have a small confession to make,' he said as they descended the oak staircase side by side. 'I ran into young Eddy earlier, who suggested I call and take you to luncheon.'

'I see.' Her stomach did a tiny dip of disappointment, suspecting Eddy did so to assuage his guilt at preferring Ozzy's company to hers.

'Although I imagine every unattached man on board will be lining up to be your escort soon,' he went on. 'I simply thought to steal a march on them.'

'Well recovered, Mr Harrington,' she murmured to herself before turning to acknowledge Officer Martin, who stood to one side of the dining room doors as they passed. His benign smile reminding her of something she had meant to ask Bunny.

'When Officer Martin asked about anyone having cross words at last night's card game,' Flora began as she settled into her chair, 'you looked about to say something, but changed your mind.'

'Thought better of it.' Bunny grimaced. 'A chap shouldn't gossip if it's likely to stir things up for anyone.'

'Stir what up, and for whom exactly?' Flora asked.

'Max Cavendish. He said something to Parnell, I didn't hear what, but for a moment I thought Parnell was about to punch him.'

'Why didn't you mention that to the captain?'

'Don't know really. Why spoil the man's honeymoon by suggesting he held a grudge against a dead man?' His exaggerated shrug was reminiscent of Eddy when caught out in a misdemeanour.

Flora was about to suggest he had implied exactly that, when a voice sounded at her elbow.

'Miss Maguire.' Dr Fletcher loomed beside her, his ingratiating smile firmly in place. 'I'm glad to see you have recovered from our little upset this morning.'

'Not much recovering was necessary,' she replied, smiling sweetly. His patronising tone immediately set her on edge as she regarded him steadily, experiencing a small triumph when he looked away first. 'I had never met Mr Parnell.'

'Quite so. Though some of the other ladies on board don't possess your constitution. I've been handing out sedatives all morning.' He gave a curt nod and then strode in the direction of the captain's table, pausing to talk to passengers on the way.

'What are you thinking?' Bunny asked, his head tilted toward her.

'That he's a handsome, but somewhat superior man with good manners. I'm simply not convinced of his professional ability.'

'Because he dismissed your question about the blood on the deck?'

'Lack of blood.' She glanced across the crowded room to where Monica Gilmore approached with Gerald. She sailed ahead of her husband, ignoring all the bows aimed at her from the crew, while Gerald paused to exchange a word with everyone he met.

Monica reached their table and greeted both Bunny and Flora like old friends, with planted kisses on cheeks and pressed hands. Having noisily persuaded Gerald to rearrange the seats, her attention shifted past Flora's shoulder.

'Here's someone else whom you haven't yet met, Flora.' Bunny nudged her gently with his elbow. 'Mrs Penry-Jones and that odd companion of hers.' He indicated the angular lady who leaned heavily on a black cane as she limped towards them, an oversized black bag hooked over her other arm.

Three rows of pearls the size of hazelnuts encased Mrs Penry-Jones' wrinkled neck above a forest green taffeta gown in the style of some ten years previously.

'Assist me, won't you, Hester?' she demanded of the woman who followed close behind. 'Take my bag and place my cane where I can reach it.'

Flora recognised the companion who rushed to obey as the same woman who had cut her dead on deck. Her mousy brown hair was scraped back from her round face into a severe chignon which gave her eyes a cat-like tilt.

On Bunny's introduction, the old lady pressed the ends of Flora's fingertips, with a muttered, 'Adele Penry-Jones,' in a tone which intimated she should have heard of her. 'My companion, Hester Smith.' She directed a backwards wave at the woman beside her without looking at her.

'Flora Maguire,' she responded, though the lady's attention had already moved on.

'Maguire,' Mrs Penry-Jones addressed a space above Flora's head, turning the word over on her tongue, her lips curled slightly. 'Irish?'

'Somewhere in my ancestry, I believe,' Flora replied. 'Scottish grandfathers notwithstanding.'

'Every hansom driver and waitress we came across in New York was Irish.' Monica sniffed, making a show of arranging a silk shawl over her shoulders.

Flora groaned inwardly, anticipating the universal reaction when it was revealed she was a governess, the moment deferred when a heavy-set young man with floppy hair and slightly bulging eyes weaved between the tables towards them, his face brightening when Bunny introduced him to Flora.

'Max Cavendish.' He pumped her hand with enthusiasm, while his gaze constantly swept the room. 'I'm travelling with my wife, but she appears somewhat tardy.'

Flora blinked, having expected the exquisite Cynthia to be married to someone more physically impressive than this well-fed puppy of a man. Bunny's bulldog description returned and she found herself smiling, though she dared not look at him in case the laugh she fought so hard to supress would burst out of her.

'I run Beaufort's department store,' Max said, pausing when Flora hesitated. 'Ah, I can see you've not heard of it. We'll be opening a branch in Knightsbridge this year.'

'I'll be sure to pay a visit when I'm next there,' Flora replied, though she suspected her salary was unlikely to run to such extravagance.

At that moment, Mr Hersch joined them in company with Miss Ames, both seating themselves opposite Mr Crowe in what Flora surmised was a deliberate move. Crowe seemed not to notice, and took his seat with a scrape of wood and jangle of cutlery, making Flora wonder how such a wiry man could be so clumsy.

Amongst the ensuing clink of crockery and low hum of conversation, the doors opened again to admit Cynthia, who looked enviably beautiful in powder blue silk that skimmed her gentle curves. She moved with the measured glide of a woman seemingly oblivious of her surroundings but aware she commanded attention. She surveyed the room surreptitiously as she moved, her wide, pigeon wing eyes taking everything in. At the table she bent slowly and dropped a lingering kiss on her husband's head before taking her seat.

'Steady on, old girl, everyone's watching.' Max ducked his head, flushing a deep red.

'Give the busybodies something to talk about.' Cynthia smoothed his hair into place, her eyes narrowed in response to Mrs Penry-Jones' loud, critical tut.

Hester ignored the new arrivals and sat with her shoulders hunched while she nibbled at a bread roll, as if the dining room was the last place she wished to be.

Flora idly wondered if her red-rimmed eyes were her normal appearance, or maybe harsh treatment at her employer's hands might be a cause for tears.

'It was the Scotch with us,' Mrs Penry-Jones drawled, continuing a conversational thread already abandoned. 'I believe Queen Victoria insists all her servants are Scotch.'

'I think you'll find the inhabitants of that country are called Scots or Scottish, Mrs Penry-Jones,' Mr Hersch said slowly. 'Scotch is whisky.'

'Indeed?' The old lady sniffed and narrowed her eyes, a response the German accepted with aplomb.

'Has anyone ordered wine?' Mr Crowe asked as the waiters distributed bowls of ham and pea soup.

'Nothing stopping you doing so, old boy.' Max's good-natured grin concealed a criticism.

'Allow me.' Gerald waylaid a passing waiter and rattled off an order without consulting a list.

'How generous of you.' Max aimed his widening grin at Crowe, who slurped his soup without reacting, then demanded the salt.

Flora watched the various reactions to this man, which ranged from mild incredulity to open distaste, and lasted until the waiters returned to remove their plates.

'This morning must have been something of an ordeal for you, Mrs Penry-Jones,' Mr Hersch broke the ensuing silence, his tone casual, though his intense stare told Flora he was keenly interested in her answer.

'Ordeal?' The old lady's voice rose to a near screech. 'Why, pray should you think so?'

'I meant the death of Mr Parnell,' he persisted, watching from half-closed lids. 'Violent death is hardly a daily occurrence.'

'Members of the lower classes come to grief all the time. Mainly due to their choices in life.' She inhaled, narrowing her already thin nostrils. 'Why should this particular one have affected me?'

'And if that's not "Pooterism", I don't know what is.' Gerald snorted, picking bits of wood from his teeth.

'Sorry, what did you say?' Monica broke off her conversation with Miss Ames. 'What's a Pooter-um?'

'It means someone who takes themselves grotesquely seriously,' Gerald replied in response to a few surprised looks and Flora's admiring one, though this surprised her too. Gerald always looks bored when Monica and Miss Ames talked about literature, yet he evidently had tastes of his own and perhaps a genuine lack of vanity. She pondered this thought while aware Hester toyed with her food, pushing it round her plate as if there was something wrong with it. Or maybe the companion was not affected by sea air like everyone else and was not hungry?

'From the novel, *The Diary of a Nobody*,' Bunny added. 'I've read it.'

'As have I,' Flora said, determined not to seem unknowledgeable.

'I did so enjoy that story,' Miss Ames joined the conversation. 'I sympathise with the poor Charles Pooter.'

'I agree,' Flora added, relaxing into the company. 'A vain, pompous man but decent and honest. Sadly misunderstood I feel.'

'Either that or he was the author of his own misfortune,' Bunny eased back slightly to allow the waiter to slide a plate of lemon sole in lobster sauce in front of Flora. The savoury aroma brought her hunger back in full force. Her loaded fork hovered enticingly an inch below her lips when she became aware of Mrs Penry-Jones peering at her through a lorgnette.

'Didn't I read in the papers that Lord Vaughn's eldest girl married one of the Astor boys last month?' She dabbed her lips with a napkin. 'You must be one of the sisters.'

Flora stiffened, laid her fork down again, steadying herself for the moment she had dreaded since boarding. 'Actually, Viscount Trent is my charge. I'm escorting him home so he can start at Marlborough next term.'

'Charge? You mean you're his gov-er-ness?' She gave the word three syllables, her upper lip curled in disdain. 'How unconventional! When did it become acceptable for such persons to eat in first-class dining rooms?'

'When they have a ticket?' Flora replied, emboldened by Bunny's arm pressing against hers.

'Bravo, Miss Maguire,' Mr Hersch said from behind his napkin, laying it on his lap again to address the table. 'We've entered a new millennium. These are modern times, and we must all learn to adapt.'

'Not to my mind.' Mrs Penry-Jones's tone implied she ought to have been consulted on the matter. 'Being forced to share a table with those of lower class is most galling.'

'Come, Mrs Penry-Jones,' Mr Hersch adopted a patronising tone. 'I agree that in a hotel dining room a gentleman without prior acquaintance of a lady would never presume to speak to one who happened to be seated at the same table. However it would be churlish to ignore a fellow diner on board ship simply because the lack of an introduction.'

'I suppose that does make such associations acceptable.' Mrs Penry-Jones stared back at him down her pointed nose. 'As long as she confines her new acquaintance to the women on board and not flirt with the gentlemen. That would be most improper.'

Flora kept her gaze on her plate, not daring to look at Bunny in case the entire table could guess he had spent part of the morning alone in her suite with only a sleeping Eddy next door.

'I quite like it,' Gerald said. 'I've made some extremely good scrapers on board steamships. Besides, one never can be quite sure about people.' He glared pointedly at his wife, who kept her copy of her passenger list beside her plate, where she scribbled notes and outlined names at intervals. 'The most gentlemanly passenger may prove to be a confidence trickster. Even men in clerical garb might have an unsavoury reputation ashore.'

Bunny gave a shocked start beside her, and they exchanged a look. Did Gerald know about the disgruntled blackbird? Or was his purely a throwaway remark?

'Mr Gilmore, what, may I ask, is a "scraper"?' Miss Ames reached for her notebook that sat beside her plate.

'It's a term which refers to those one meets aboard ships. People one would be unlikely to associate with in the normal course of life.' Gerald ignored Mrs Penry-Jones's sour look. 'Here, everyone is exactly what they appear to be.'

'Or pretend to be,' Flora said under her breath, her thoughts still on the late Mr Parnell. Was he playing a part when someone took offence and ended his life?

'Has anyone seen Miss Lane today?' Monica asked, giving the room a sweeping glance. 'She must have been most upset about poor Mr Parnell's accident. They were friends, weren't they?'

Mrs Penry-Jones mumbled something incoherent, while beside her, Hester flushed a deep red. Flora didn't hear what was said, assuming Hester was being reprimanded.

Miss Ames leaned forward, her pen still poised. 'Miss Maguire doesn't think it was an accident at all. Do you, Miss Maguire?' Her steady gaze raked each face. 'As she found the body, she's in a position to tell us what really happened.'

Flora stiffened, aware all eyes had turned towards her.

'Really?' Max's ever-present smile congealed. The spoonful of custard that halted halfway to his mouth dropped back onto his plate with a splat. 'What do *you* think happened then, Miss Maguire?'

Flora caught Bunny's 'you-are-on-your-own' look and sighed. 'I didn't see what happened. I arrived afterwards. Nor do I have any proof, merely an impression that he might not have fallen.'

'To trust one's instincts is a creed of which I always approve.' Miss Ames underlined something in her notebook with a flourish. 'Perhaps he was murdered. Who knows what malign influences were at work?'

Hester stopped chewing. She inhaled a rapid, noisy breath. Her eyes widened and she began to cough.

'She's choking! Do something someone!' Monica flapped.

A wave of concerned murmurs circled the table, though before the coughs turned into a full-blown crisis, Mr Hersch delivered a single, hard and effective slap to her back between her shoulder blades. He handed her a glass of water which she grabbed at as if it were a lifeline, taking several rapid sips.

'Thank you. I'm quite all right now.' Hester handed the glass back, then patted her upper chest, blushing furiously.

Mrs Penry-Jones flicked a frustrated glance at Hester, then dismissed her with a slow exhale.

'What exactly are you suggesting?' Miss Ames asked, her pen held aloft.

'I didn't mean to suggest anything.' Flora's face heated uncomfortably, aware she was still being stared at by half the table. 'Maybe I shouldn't have spoken. If Dr Fletcher says it was an accident, I'm in no position to contradict him.'

'I heard a rumour Parnell was a professional gambler.' Monica's eyes gleamed with speculation. 'Perhaps he cheated at cards and someone decided to teach him a lesson?'

'One can't accuse the man of being a broadsman without proof, Monica,' Gerald snapped.

Hester's breathing was still shallow, and as she reached for her own water glass, she fumbled it at the last second, sending its contents across the table. 'I–I'm so sorry, Mrs Penry-Jones,' she stammered, oblivious to the fact it was Max who was forced to leap out of the way to avoid his trousers being soaked.

'Clumsy!' Mrs Penry-Jones's thin lips twisted into a sneer.

The companion dabbed at the spillage with her napkin, her feeble attempts annoying the old lady more. 'Oh, do stop that. Hester, you're making it worse. Summon a steward.'

Monica tutted in sympathy, while Cynthia stared at the ceiling, her eyes closed as if the entire scene were beyond her attention. Gus Crowe watched the small drama with the self-satisfied smirk of someone who rarely began an argument, but often provided the ammunition for others to do so.

Mr Hersch took command; summoned a waiter to replace the table-cloth and supervised the rearrangement of crockery with remarkable efficiency and the least disruption.

'I don't believe this speculation about Parnell helps matters,' Mr Hersch said when the waiter withdrew. He topped up his wine glass before ostentatiously offering the bottle to the rest of the table. 'Starting rumours will only make the situation worse.'

'I agree.' Cynthia toyed with the pendant at her throat, pulling the jewel along its gold chain. 'This voyage is going to be unutterably boring if that man's demise is the only topic of conversation.'

'One cannot stop people talking, my dear.' Miss Ames spoke with the relish of someone who was glad of the fact. 'We're all captive on this ship for another week.'

'If it's not inconvenient, Mrs Penry-Jones, may I return to the suite?' Hester rose unsteadily to her feet. 'The movement of the ship is making me queasy.'

Flora experienced sudden sympathy for the woman. The sea was perfectly calm and Hester didn't look ill, but perhaps having embarrassed herself had been the source of her upset?

'Oh, if you must.' The old lady sighed, and waved her away like a persistent fly.

'Take my bag back to my suite would you? Saves me worrying about it.'

'Yes, Mrs Penry-Jones.'

Passengers in the process of leaving hovered in the aisles while they waited for or assisted companions, forcing Hester to manhandle the cumbersome bag between them on her way out, each step hampered in some way.

'Poor Miss Smith, she's such a timid little thing,' Monica whispered. 'She made a dreadful fuss about tipping over a water glass.'

Flora nodded, her gaze on Hester's retreating back. It wasn't the falling glass that had upset her, but something that was said earlier. She wished she could recall what it was.

6

'It's a pity I chose to go straight back to my stateroom after dinner last night,' Miss Ames sighed, regretfully. 'I must have missed all the excitement.'

'There was none,' Gerald said. 'When Parnell left the bar he was in perfect health. We had no idea what had happened until this morning.'

'Oh well, anyway, I had this idea for a novel you see, and simply had to write it down.'

'Do share it with us,' Monica gushed. 'We could do with a distraction from this horrible business, couldn't we, Gerald?'

'Can't wait.' Gerald's lip curled. He cast a resigned look at Max, who rolled his eyes in sympathy.

Mrs Penry-Jones gave Flora a distracted wave as she and Bunny left the table, where Miss Ames was occupied in delivering her new story idea to an enraptured Monica and a clearly bored Gerald.

'What a beautiful day.' Bunny eased beside Flora where she had paused outside the lobby doors leading from the dining room.

Flora pulled her shawl tighter round her shoulders, nodding as a chill wind lifted the loose hair at her temples. The sea on the horizon was like glass beneath a powder blue sky, the air sharp and not quite warm enough to linger for long; the whoosh of the waves created as the vast ship cut through the ocean was accompanied by the steady thrum of the engines far below them.

'How about a game of poker?' Gus Crowe appeared at Bunny's shoulder, nudging him so hard he winced and rubbed a hand across his side.

'Good idea.' Max appeared, rubbing his hands together. 'Cynthia's busy writing letters this afternoon. Either that or she'll be poring through the passenger list in search of someone famous.'

'Thank you, no.' Bunny directed a weak smile at the two men. 'I'm sure Gilmore would join you.' He nodded to where Gerald had emerged onto the deck.

'Is that right, Gerald?' Max accosted him, a hand clamped on his shoulder. 'Are you game for a hand or two?'

'Long as Monica doesn't find out.' Gerald gave the door behind him a swift furtive glance. 'Let's repair to the smoking room before she finds something for me to do.'

'Ah well, see you later then, Harrington, Miss Maguire,' Crowe drawled and hurried to join them as the trio sloped away like schoolboys intent on mischief.

'Please don't feel you need to miss the game on my account, Bunny,' Flora said.

'I'm not a card player, and those three play for very high stakes.' He twisted toward her, lowering his voice. 'I see you're sticking to your theory that Parnell was murdered?'

'For all the good it will do me.' She fell into step beside him as he set off along the deck, pushing back strands of hair blown into her eyes by the wind. 'Besides, Mr Hersch was right about idle speculation. I should be more careful what I say until I have some proof.'

'You're probably wise. By the way,' he asked in a change of subject she suspected was deliberate, 'did I hear you mention Eddy was enrolled at Marlborough?'

She nodded. 'I hope he'll be all right, he's never been away from home on his own before.' When she had ventured similar misgivings to Lord Vaughn, he had dismissed her with talk of family tradition.

'I'm sure Eddy will cope beautifully. Speaking as an old Marlburian myself.'

'Really?' Flora halted in surprise, though there was no reason why she should have been.

'My father claimed it was because Charterhouse wouldn't take me. Which I suspect was a ploy aimed to keep me on my toes.'

'Did it work?'

'Indeed yes.' The lopsided smile she had begun to look for appeared, which raised goose bumps on her arms she couldn't attribute to the weather. 'Top marks all the way through to Oxford, and then a first.'

'Impressive. Shall I see you in the Commons, and will your speeches be quoted verbatim in *The Times*?'

'Definitely not.' He angled his head toward her, frowning. 'What's that look for? My motor car isn't simply an indulgence, you know. It's how I intend making my living.'

'I just thought—' Her gaze slid over his immaculate dark blue blazer, the diamond pin that held his tie in place, then down to the handmade shoes of soft leather. Bespoke Lobbs, if she wasn't mistaken.

'Appearances don't always tell the whole story,' he said, following her look. 'Granted, I benefitted from a privileged upbringing, but after my father died and the debts were paid, all that was left was a crumbling mansion and an annuity.'

'You have no other close family?'

'Only my mother. There's my father's younger brother and his family, but Mother and I manage well enough alone.' His change of tone reflected his devotion to his lone parent. 'She sold the crumbling pile, and we now share a charming eight-bedroom house on the Thames in Richmond, and the annuity of course. I've had to apply my expensive education into earning my living.'

Flora hid a smile, bemused that his idea of reduced circumstances was a house with eight bedrooms and a private income. She doubted Bunny Harrington had ever woken to a winter's dawn in an attic bedroom with a quarter inch of ice inside the glass.

'May I take you in to dinner this evening?' Bunny asked, suddenly.

She turned her face into the wind in order to hide the sudden warmth that flooded her face.

'I appreciate your kindness, but I don't expect you to escort me to every meal.' His face fell and she rushed on, 'I'll look forward to your company, though. After all, we occupy the same table.'

His unsmiling nod told her this was poor consolation, which expanded into an awkward silence, broken when he indicated a man in an overcoat who stood between two lifeboats, smoking a cigar.

'That chap over there asked to see my designs, so if you don't mind, I—'

'Of course not, please go ahead.'

Flora watched him go, surprised at the depth of her attachment to him, when twenty-four hours ago she had never heard the name Bunny Harrington. He didn't seem to mind she was a governess, but then why would he? Most likely he regarded her as a temporary amusement with whom to pass a few days aboard ship. Or was she denying herself the chance of friendship with a perfectly nice man who might be genuinely inclined to spend time with her?

A dilemma for her to ponder, almost as mysterious as who might have killed Mr Parnell.

* * *

Flora pushed open the double doors of the library and stepped inside. Tapestry upholstered sofas were set in horseshoe arrangements of three round low tables, the room divided by supporting white pillars. Like the dining room, a glass lantern ceiling flooded the space with light, while rows of polished walnut bookshelves lined the walls from floor to ceiling; every one entirely empty.

'Where are all the books?' she inquired of a passing steward.

'They were pledged as a gift by the City of Minneapolis in recognition of the ship bearing the same name,' a freckle-faced young man informed her with the air of a tour guide. 'Though, unfortunately they didn't reach New York before we sailed.'

'What a shame.' Flora reluctantly abandoned her intention to give Eddy some work in preparation for school.

'We do, however, have a few magazines to accompany afternoon tea perhaps?' The steward handed her a copy of *The Strand Magazine.* 'It's two months old, I'm afraid. I could find more if you wish.'

'This one is perfect, thank you.'

Flora had become engrossed in a story entitled 'The Brass Bottle', when she heard Mr Hersch's distinctive voice from a nearby table and realised she wasn't alone.

'You're certain as to the cause of that head wound?' he asked an unseen companion.

Flora straightened, confident the white painted pillar she sat behind shielded her from sight, though she could just make out Dr Fletcher's profile where he was seated on the sofa to her right.

'I cannot be sure,' the medic replied. 'However, the signs certainly indicate a fall.'

'Might the wound have been administered by something heavy?' Hersch persisted. 'An ashtray, perhaps?'

Flora's heartbeat quickened. Of course. The square brass ashtrays were a feature of every cabin and would be the perfect weapon. Eddy had knocked theirs off the table onto his foot that morning, his subsequent yell attesting to its considerable weight.

'That's rather specific,' the doctor said, an edge to his voice. 'What made you mention that?'

'A maid reported the one in Parnell's cabin was missing. Poor girl was worried she would be made to pay for it.'

'The housekeeping staff have their wages docked for breakages whether they actually break anything or not,' Dr Fletcher said. 'Harsh, maybe, but it's company policy.'

'When the crew were questioned,' the German continued, 'they insisted there was no body on the deck when it was scrubbed down at six that morning.'

'I don't understand the question. He could have fallen after the decks were washed, even slipped on a wet step.'

'In which case, why was there was no blood on the steps, or beneath the body?'

Flora only just stopped herself jumping to her feet to add that this was exactly what she had thought at the time, unable to help a certain satisfaction she hadn't been the only one to think it important.

'Must admit, I didn't pay much attention to that. I was too concerned about getting the body out of sight before any more passengers turned up. Bad enough that young woman was asking all those questions. What was her name again?'

'Maguire,' Hersch's slow pronunciation of her name sent a tingle down Flora's spine.

'Ah yes, I remember now. Although I fear it's destined to be one of life's mysteries.'

'What about the lividity on Parnell's face?'

'What about it?' The doctor's voice turned defensive.

'Can you explain how it appeared if the man had been dead only minutes?'

'I *am* qualified, you know,' Dr Fletcher snapped. 'I suppose you could say it was odd if he had only lain there a short while, but hardly conclusive.'

Flora hunched against the pillar, her excitement growing at the knowledge she wasn't the only one who believed Parnell may have been dead for hours, not minutes.

'Is it possible he was killed elsewhere?' Hersch asked. 'And his body left on the steps to make it appear as if he had fallen?'

'Steady on.' The doctor dropped his voice to a fierce whisper Flora struggled to hear. 'You could damage my reputation with such talk.'

'What is more significant, is that it would mean there's a murderer on board.' Hersch appeared to be losing patience with the good doctor.

'Quiet, man! You don't want to go spreading rumours like that.' Flora imagined him giving the room a swift, nervous glance to see if they had been heard. Then his voice came again in a fierce whisper. 'What do you expect me to do about it?'

'Nothing, for the moment,' Hersch said, unfailingly calm. 'However, I suggest you ensure your record-keeping is flawless, Dr Fletcher, or this could come back to haunt you.'

'I hope you're wrong, Mr Hersch.' The creak of leather signalled the doctor was about to leave. 'Anyway, I must be off, I've a patient due with a boil that needs lancing. One of the few ailments I can charge for as it didn't occur on board.'

His footsteps tapped across the polished floor, followed by his cheery greeting to someone on his way out. The room fell silent, the clink of china and the slap of the door the only sounds as stewards and passengers came and went.

'He didn't appear particularly interested in my theory, did he, Miss Maguire?' Hersch's low, clear voice reached her.

Flora froze. Then, aware it would be pointless to pretend she hadn't heard, she peeked around the pillar to where the German stirred his tea, the silver spoon dwarfed by his manicured hands.

'Did you know I was here all the time?' Her voice came out as a whisper.

'I doubt you wear perfume, my dear, but your soap is distinctive. Jasmine, I think.'

Sighing, Flora rose and eased round the pillar whilst bidding a mental farewell to the last remnants of her reputation. As if tripping over dead bodies wasn't enough, she had now been caught blatantly eavesdropping.

Hersch gave a low chuckle and indicated the seat the surgeon had vacated. 'Would you care to join me?'

'Thank you.' Flora sat. 'And I shan't pretend I didn't hear anything. Was it my imagination, or did Dr Fletcher seem nervous?'

'You noticed that, did you?' Hersch lifted the teapot in invitation. 'You don't suffer fools gladly, do you, Miss Maguire?'

'He's not a fool, but I think he's lazy.' Flora declined his offer of tea, but his compliment gave her confidence. 'Do I understand you examined Mr Parnell's body after it was taken to the doctor's office?' When he raised one brow in enquiry, she added, 'I ask, because you weren't there when he was taken away, so when else would you have seen him?'

'How very astute of you.' He took a slow sip from his cup while he kept his gaze on hers.

Flora stiffened, suspecting she was being teased. 'It's not idle curiosity, Mr Hersch. I have responsibility for a young boy whose safety is my chief concern.'

'I apologise, Miss Maguire. I don't mean to be flippant.' He leaned back in his chair as if settling in for a long talk. 'Tell me, what were your impressions when you first came upon the body?'

'Well.' Flora cast her mind back to her initial horror at discovering the pile of clothes was, in fact, a dead man. 'He lay face down with a gash on the back of his head that had already congealed. I couldn't see blood anywhere else. Not on the steps or the handrail.' Hersch looked about to ask a question, but she rushed on. 'I have no medical training, but on a large country estate, injuries occur quite often from farm equipment and horses. I can tell an old wound from a fresh one.'

'What did you conclude from these observations?' He steepled his fingers below his chin.

'That if Mr Parnell fell down those steps, he did not do so in the half hour before I got there.' Then something he had said earlier returned. 'This lividity you mentioned? Is it anything to do with the large purple mark on Mr Parnell's cheek?'

Hersch's mouth twitched, but the slight smile did not reach his eyes. 'Indeed yes. It's what happens when the heart stops pumping. The blood in the veins pools at the lowest points, causing that purplish-blue colour. It doesn't appear for at least half an hour after death. Similar marks appeared on his body as well. Such a head injury would have rendered him either dead or unconscious, so I doubt he could have moved on his own.'

'Then he was already dead when he went down those steps,' Flora said, almost her herself. When he didn't correct her, she added, 'There was a small amount of dried blood on his shirt collar.'

'Dried, you say?' Hersch's brows drew together, his glance drifting to the ceiling. 'The body had already been stripped when I saw him, but that also puts the time of death into dispute.'

'There's something else.' Flora waited until she was sure she had his full attention. 'He was still wearing his dinner suit at six in the morning.'

'Something else I wasn't aware of. You make a good point.' He stroked a thumb and forefinger down either side of his moustache, his eyes filled with either admiration or amusement. He had one of those faces which were not easily read, which made her suspect he was a much-misunderstood man.

'I'll reserve judgement until more information comes to light.' He leaned towards her, lowering his voice. 'But between you and me, Miss Maguire, I too am not happy about the circumstances of this man's death. It doesn't look right.'

A rush of excitement fizzed through her veins, but was irrelevant when neither of them had any proof. In which case, she would have to find some.

7

Flora dressed early for dinner that evening in a gown of primrose yellow with a fine lace overskirt and a lacy shawl over her exposed shoulders – inadequate for evening sea breezes on the Atlantic, but far too pretty not to wear.

Eddy emerged from his bedroom, his tongue protruding as he struggled with his tie. 'Some of the chaps want to listen to music after dinner. There's a piano in the smoking room and one of the crew has offered to play for us. You don't mind if I join them, do you, Flora? I promise to be back by nine thirty.'

'What sort of music?' Flora gently eased his hand away and completed the knot for him.

'It's not boring classical stuff like Mozart or dreary Bach. It's Tin Pan Alley mostly.' He stood passive while she completed his efforts, tweaked his collar and smoothed his hair.

'I doubt your parents would object. What was that tune your father liked, the one about the bank?'

'"The Man Who Broke the Bank at Monte Carlo?"' Eddy hummed in perfect tune. 'Hey, Mr Gilmore has a gramophone. One of those new ones that plays discs, not cylinders.'

'Maybe he'll let you listen to it sometime.' She dismissed him with a gentle push. 'Nine thirty at the latest, and remember, it's Sunday, so decorum is called for. Oh,' she added in mock seriousness, 'no smoking, either.'

'Flora!' He snorted in mock disgust. 'In any case, they chuck us out well before the grown-ups come in.'

* * *

When Flora reached the dining room on the deck below, she spotted Bunny through the filigree gold etchings on the glass in the doors. He was seated at their table opposite Cynthia, who propped one elbow on the table, supporting her chin while she stared into his eyes as if he conveyed the meaning of life.

Flora's confidence dwindled, despite reminding herself that Cynthia was a married woman – on her honeymoon, no less. Still, she was exquisite – exactly the type of woman a man like Bunny was destined to be with; not a shy girl raised below stairs who hovered in a doorway trying to summon the courage to go inside.

A group of diners approached the doors from another direction, all talking at the top of their voices; a trait of the upper classes.

Flora stepped behind a pillar as they passed, just as a blast of hot breath enveloped the back of her neck.

'Don't turn around, Miss Maguire,' a voice little more than a croak whispered, freezing her in place. Indistinguishable as male or female, yet the menace behind it combined with the use of her name sent her heart thumping at an uncomfortable rate.

'Leave well alone,' the voice went on. 'People disappear from ships all the time. Who would miss one nosy governess and a small, mischievous boy?'

Flora sucked in a breath, unable to believe she had heard correctly. Her mouth worked in protest, though no sound came. Too terrified to move, long seconds passed until she sensed the person had moved away and she was alone.

She ran to an alcove but found it empty, then back to the corridor that disappeared into the ship, the cool wind having driven the passengers to use the internal hallways. Her eyes darted into corners in search of a lone figure, but saw no one. On impulse she pushed through the double doors onto the saloon deck, the cool wind tugging her hair as she probed the deck with her eyes.

There was no one there.

Low laughter drifted toward her from the internal corridor and she ran back inside, in time for a group of approaching diners to sweep past her into the dining room, on an enticing wave of expensive perfume.

Smoothing her skirt with shaking fingers, she took a deep breath and joined the tail end of the line who entered the dining room. The pressing crowd made it difficult to judge who was missing, while couples and small groups stood between tables, talking in small coteries rather than being seated. She passed the Gilmores talking to a couple she didn't know and Miss Ames giving what looked to be an animated lecture to a young woman Flora had seen before at a nearby table. Mrs Penry-Jones arrived and glided past Flora on a cloud of parma violets without acknowledging her; a snub repeated by Hester who followed close behind.

Flora tried to assess who was missing, which thus far included Max and Eloise, though she found it difficult to believe anyone amongst the elegant diners with their benign smiles and expensive clothes would whisper threats. And yet she had not imagined it. Someone on this ship felt threatened by her.

Her slow progress through the welcome warmth, light and the plinking notes of a piano at the end of the room, combined with the clatter of plates and the savoury smell of cooked meat, calmed her nerves as she approached the table Bunny and Cynthia occupied with Mr Hersch.

Bunny rose from the table with a smile when he saw her, and Cynthia relinquished her seat without being asked.

'Are you quite well, Miss Maguire?' Mr Hersch enquired. 'You look somewhat shaky if you don't mind my saying so.'

'Y–yes. I'm fine, thank you.' Warmth flooded her face, her glance flicking to where Mr Crowe held out Miss Ames' chair, though not all the chairs were occupied. Not still nervous about being here, are you, Flora?' Bunny whispered as she stared about her, trying to discern who was missing.

'N–no, I'm quite all right, but outside just now, I—'

'Ah, here's our notorious actress,' Gerald announced as he and Monica drifted to their seats. 'Wondered when she was going to make an appearance.' He nudged Bunny with an elbow, distracting him. 'I don't care if my wife does disapprove,' Gerald murmured, 'I think our pocket Venus is quite lovely.'

'Gerald, really!' Monica glowered at him, then turned to welcome Miss Ames, the two falling immediately into animated conversation.

The crowd parted briefly to allow Eloise's approach in a slow and sensuous stride, despite her diminutive size. She dimpled at a middle-aged ogler at the next table and blew a kiss to another whose eyes popped when he saw her, while their respective female companions glowered like cross twins.

'Good evening, everyone.' Eloise's captivating smile and seductive drawl encompassed them all. 'Someone get me a drink, would you? I'd like a large gin and tonic to give me an appetite for dinner.'

At the word, 'gin', Miss Ames exchanged a scandalised look with Monica, who uttered the word 'actress' in a clear, disparaging tone.

Eloise must have heard her, but she gave no sign.

Monica's glare deepened when her husband leapt up to fulfil Eloise's request, although he extended the request for aperitifs to include everyone else.

'Sorry, Flora, you were about to say something,' Bunny said, once the waiter had left with Gerald's order.

Flora hesitated. The safe, warm atmosphere of the crowded room, the repeated clink of expensive glass among low laughter had made the incident in the lobby seem unreal. As if it had happened to someone else.

'It's nothing.' Flora shook her head and smiled. 'I'm fine, really.'

Eloise sipped her drink, flirting in equal measure with Gerald on one side and the lately arrived Max on the other, unaware of the hostility emanating from both their wives.

'Bank clerks, even secretaries travel to Europe unaccompanied these days,' Mrs Penry-Jones responded to a remark made about modern young women who crossed the Atlantic alone. 'I always say, if one cannot afford to employ a maid, one should not be permitted to purchase a ticket. Hester would never dream of travelling alone, would you, Hester?'

'No, Mrs Penry-Jones,' Hester acquiesced with little enthusiasm.

'I believe single, independent ladies should be permitted to enjoy foreign travel, even without husbands or male relatives to escort them.' Miss Ames tossed the trailing end of a canary yellow boa carelessly over her shoulder. 'It seems harsh to deny us the same advantage.'

'I agree,' Flora said, recalling Bunny's advice to stand up to the likes of the old lady. 'I don't have a maid or a male escort. I don't think Eddy counts.'

Gerald laughed and Bunny saluted her with his glass.

'Hmm...' Mrs Penry-Jones did not trouble herself to answer, but stared at Flora down her long, pointy nose. 'One also has to be wary of whom one associates with on board ship. A woman came out of Lady Radley's suite this morning and struck up a conversation with me. It was a full hour before I discovered I'd been prowling the decks with her maid. Everyone saw us talking too.'

'How distressing.' Cynthia's face was a picture of false outrage. 'What did you do?'

'What could I do?' Mrs Penry-Jones's mouth puckered in distaste. 'When she approached me again this afternoon, I cut her, naturally.'

Cynthia nodded sagely, while the corner of her mouth twitched as she concealed her amusement. Monica offered the old lady a moue of sympathy, while the men either buried their noses in their glasses, or pretended something fascinated them on the other side of the room.

'I've found maids and valets to be most useful in providing information about their masters, especially those who have suffered at their hands.' Mr Hersch's eyes twinkled with mischief as he gently stroked his moustache. 'It's shameful to listen to their stories, but who can resist?'

'If you want my opinion,' Monica said in tones which dared anyone to decline, 'the Baedeker guides place an asterisk on hotels that guarantee to be first-class, the steamship companies should do the same with the passenger lists.'

'I need another drink,' Gerald stared round in search of a waiter.

By the time her entrée arrived, Flora had convinced herself that the owner of the voice had played some sort of joke. Then as if from nowhere, the thought struck her that if it was indeed serious, a thirteen-year-old boy was an easy target.

She considered excusing herself to see that Eddy was all right, then she remembered, he would be at his musical evening with the other boys. He was safe there as anywhere for the time being. Besides, what excuse could she give for dragging him away? With this thought uppermost, she only caught the tail end of a question Miss Ames had directed at Eloise.

'...recovered from the death of your travelling companion?'

'We weren't exactly friends!' Eloise waved her fork in the air. 'Ours was purely a business arrangement.' Beside her, Gus Crowe shifted sideways in order to avoid a chunk of beef landing in his lap. 'Someone has since reminded me I'm talented enough not to need him.' She aimed a wink at Flora.

'That's somewhat callous.' Miss Ames puckered her thin lips. 'The poor man's been dead less than a day.'

'It was an accident,' Eloise said on a sigh. 'Tragic maybe, but still an accident. He had probably had too much to drink and missed his footing. It could happen to anyone.'

She held her empty glass out for a refill from a passing waiter, a careless elbow perilously close to a crystal rose bowl, which Gerald whisked away just in time to avoid disaster.

Monica suppressed a startled, though redundant cry, while Mrs Penry-Jones tutted loudly. Hester glared at Eloise in disapproval, her tiny eyes glinting, whereas the instigator of this possible disaster laughed and covered her mouth with one hand, then demanded her drink.

The table finally settled down and conversation resumed, with banter going back and forth, carefully avoiding all talk of bodies. Instead, there appeared to be a mutual agreement to confine talk to trivial subjects which could not offend anyone: usual for strangers forced together in close proximity for a protracted time, if a little stilted, while jokes were met with overenthusiastic and too loud laughter.

Flora sensed a simmering unease ran beneath the smiles and polite requests to pass the water jug; the subject of Mr Parnell's demise present, but never spoken of.

The entrée plates were removed and a waiter approached with a wide tray expertly balanced on one shoulder from which he distributed dishes of chocolate mousse among the diners at a nearby table.

Without warning, Eloise rose awkwardly from her chair, unbalanced and staggered backward, her arm flung out behind her in an effort to stay upright.

Flora brought a hand to her mouth, aware of what was about to happen but helpless to prevent it. Dismayed, she could only watch as Eloise's hand sent the tray of glass dishes flying from the man's hands.

Chairs were hurriedly scraped back. A man at the next table issued an expulsion of rage, his evening shirt sporting a large smear of whipped cream.

Eloise surveyed the damage dispassionately, offering a garbled but incoherent apology.

A steward led the cream-splattered man away, while a stiff-lipped waiter gathered pieces of broken glass whilst uttering repeated apologies.

'I feel quite woozy.' Eloise raised a hand dramatically to her forehead. 'Mr Harrington, Bunny. Would you be a darling and take me back to my suite?' She ignored a respectable offer to do exactly that from Gerald.

'Sit down, Gerald,' Monica snapped. Reluctantly, he resumed his seat.

'We're happy to oblige, aren't we, Flora?' Bunny rose, hauling Flora to her feet.

'What?' Flora gaped. 'Why me?'

'I insist.' Bunny wrapped an arm round Eloise's waist and addressed Flora in a whisper over her shoulder. 'I've no desire to be trapped in a stateroom alone with an inebriated woman.'

Eloise giggled and flung her arm round Bunny's neck.

'I never took you for a coward,' Flora said mischievously. Then the thought she was about to leave the safety of the crowded dining room brought back the earlier incident. 'I'll come, provided you promise to collect Eddy from the musical evening and bring him back to the suite for me.' She picked her way along behind them as Bunny guided an unsteady Eloise towards the doors.

This seemed to take Bunny by surprise, who blinked. 'I'll pour his cocoa for him if you like.'

'You don't have to be sarcastic. He isn't a baby. It's almost dark and... I simply want to make sure he's safe that's all.' She trailed after them, speculating on which of her audience had threatened her outside earlier, but only curious or bemused stares followed them out, not malicious ones.

* * *

By the time Flora had retrieved Eloise's key from her bag and unlocked her stateroom door, Eloise clung to Bunny like a rag doll, leaving him with no option but to hoist her into his arms and carry her inside. Lowering her limp figure onto the bed, he barely paused to see if she was likely to fall off again before backing away.

'Where are you going?' Flora demanded, bringing him to a halt at the door.

'My chivalrous deed is done.' He held both hands up in surrender. 'I'll order some coffee to be sent in, but I'll leave the rest to you.'

'You won't forget Eddy, will you?'

'Were you serious about that?'

She nodded, trying not to shiver as the croaky voice accompanied by a wave of hot breath on her neck returned to haunt her.

'Well, if you insist, of course I'll fetch him.' He gave an airy backwards wave of one hand and disappeared through the door without a backwards look.

'Black coffee is what you need, Miss Lane,' Flora addressed the prone figure on the bed. 'Or you'll be fit for nothing in the morning.' She plucked the coverlet from a nearby chair and spread it over Eloise's childlike form.

Eloise moaned but barely stirred, her cloud of messy black curls in stark contrast to the snow-white pillow. She looked just as pretty in sleep as she did awake, with dark eyelashes gently curved on her pale cheeks, her expertly applied red lipstick not even smudged. Even her bodice rose and fell gently with each silent breath. She didn't even drool.

The stateroom was similar to Flora's own, but with only the one bedroom and an identical tiny bathroom. Flora left the bedroom door open, the bed clearly visible from the sitting area. In both rooms, the detritus of Eloise's chaotic life lay strewn over every surface: open pots of cosmetics scattered on the dresser, a feather puff on a layer of flesh-coloured grains on the polished top. A string of agate beads looped over the corner of the mirror. The mess had spilled over into the sitting area too, with an oyster silk negligee discarded on an armchair. A pair of shoes had been discarded on the floor beside the bureau, its top messy with empty boxes and discarded crumpled scarves.

Despite Flora's close examination of the panelled wall that separated this room from her own bedroom next door, she could find no trace of whatever had struck it the previous night.

A light knock came at the door and Flora jumped, startled at almost being caught out poking through Eloise's room. She smoothed down her skirt to compose herself before answering it.

She huffed a relieved breath through pursed lips and went to let in the maid. The woman sketched a curtsey and lowered a tray onto the table in the sitting area and began arranging the cups.

'I'll manage that, thank you.' Flora ushered her out.

'Is that coffee I smell?' Flora swung round to where Eloise now sat, her arms wrapped round the hump formed by her raised knees, regarding her with eyes as clear as glass. 'Excellent! Good thinking, Miss Maguire.' She patted her curls into place with one hand. 'That should convince ev'ryone.'

'I–I thought—' Flora broke off in mute confusion.

'I know what you thought, which was entirely the impression I was tryin' to give.' She heaved the bed cover onto the floor, grimacing at her rumpled skirt before advancing on the coffee tray.

'You want everyone to believe you were intoxicated?' Flora demanded, her governess instincts rising to the surface. 'Whatever for? That's not going to do much for your reputation.'

'Pish, who cares about that, it's done for anyway.' Her attempt to smooth out the more obvious creases had no effect, and she gave up with a flap of her hand. 'And now I intend to take a look in Frank's stateroom.'

'Break in, do you mean?' Flora's hand shook slightly as she handed her a cup of the hot, fragrant brew from the tray. If Eloise was aware she had been nosing through her belongings she gave no sign.

'I quite understand if you want nothin' to do with it.' Eloise's smile dissolved and she gave a resigned sigh. 'In which case, feel free to go to bed with your cocoa like a good little governess.'

Flora bridled. 'If anyone finds out, you'll be the first one they'll suspect. You're the only one on board who knew him.'

'Perhaps.' Her eyes sparkled with mischief. 'However, I couldn't possibly have done such a thing. After all, I was so inebriated, that nice Mr Harrington and the governess had to put me to bed.'

'Please don't call me "the governess".' Flora took a mouthful of coffee to give herself time to think, but regretted it, the brew was too strong and quite bitter.

Eloise took a delicate sip from her cup, though her black-fringed eyes never left Flora. 'I have to admit, I expected you to go screaming for the captain. I also didn't bargain on you as my nursemaid, but you're here now, so do you want to help me or not?'

'You haven't yet told me why you want to search his stateroom. What do you expect to find?' Flora's heartbeat quickened, but she kept her face impassive.

'Money, my dear girl. And don't glare at me like that. It's my money. I gave it to Frank last night. He insisted he needed it to pay our expenses in London.'

So that was what they had argued about? The dead man's character slipped markedly in Flora's estimation if he had expected Miss Lane to pay the bills.

'How much did you give him?' Flora added more milk to her cup and ventured another mouthful.

'Three thousand dollars.'

Flora almost choked, a spray of coffee missing her dress by inches.

'Well why not? Frank won't need it now, will he?' Eloise's steady gaze challenged Flora to contradict her. 'I still have to pay my hotel bill in London. I want it back.'

'What if we get caught?' Flora's head filled with unwelcome images of her being escorted off the ship in London in chains by two burly police-men, watched by a distraught Eddy and a calm, but resigned, Bunny.

Eloise drained her cup and returned it to the tray. 'You don't have to help me, but it will be quicker with the two of us. Are you game, or not?' Without waiting for an answer, she made for the door.

Quietly seething, Flora followed. Which must have been what Eloise counted on: don't give your press-ganged accomplice time to reconsider.

On the short walk across the deserted deck to Parnell's stateroom, her father's stern, 'I'm disappointed in you' look floated into Flora's head but she pushed it away. She would never admit it, especially to Eloise, but the thought of finding something to prove she was right about Parnell's death to wave beneath Bunny's nose was tempting. It would also be the only chance she would have to go into Parnell's stateroom. She might even find something which could point to his killer.

'Warn me if anyone comes,' Eloise instructed, inserting what looked like a double hatpin bent at right angles into the lock.

'Have you done this before?' Flora whispered. At Eloise's slow sideways look, she added, 'Never mind, it's best I don't know.'

Flora scanned the deck on both sides, but the boards gleamed empty in the moonlight. The passengers had probably decamped to the saloon, but would start drifting back to their rooms any time now. She began to wish she hadn't come. What possible explanation could she give if discov-ered outside a dead man's cabin? Or worse, inside it?

Seconds stretched, then Eloise straightened, throwing her a brief, dazzling smile. 'We're in!' Grabbing Flora by the elbow, she yanked her inside, closed the door and twisted the latch. 'Let down the blinds!'

The blinds fell to the ledge with a sequential dull thump, then Eloise flicked the light switch, flooding the room with a sulphurous yellow glow.

A mirror image of Eloise's, Parnell's stateroom was bereft of any signs of human habitation, which, Flora reminded herself, was hardly a surprise.

'You try the bureau,' Eloise ordered, advancing on the wardrobe, where she dropped into a crouch. 'I'll look in here.'

Flora felt a stirring of excitement as the top drawer slid open on silent runners, though it lay empty except for a few sheets of blank notepaper which bore the *Atlantic Transport Line* logo. What did $3,000 look like anyway?

'Anything?' Eloise whispered from her kneeling position in front of the wardrobe, replacing an obviously empty valise.

'Not yet.' Having searched the bureau, Flora moved on, but having run out of hiding places in the sitting area, moved into the bedroom and rifled through a chest of drawers. The top drawer contained a pile of card collars rolled together, while a lower one held some silk ties and several sets of underwear, all of which were frayed and discoloured. She opened the next drawer down, stuffed full of immaculate shirts.

Behind her, Eloise dislodged a row of shoes in the bottom of the wardrobe that fell in a series of soft thumps onto the floor. One bounced and came to rest beside Flora. She handed it back, noting the upper was highly polished but the sole looked thin and worn. The contrast appeared incongruous, as if the late Mr Parnell was all front and no substance.

'I'll take a look in the bathroom,' Eloise said. 'You stay here and search.'

Flora gave a silent nod as a pasteboard folder dropped to the floor from between a pile of shirts she had taken from the drawer. It lay open to reveal a sepia-coloured photograph. Flora placed the pile of shirts on a nearby chair and retrieved the folder, releasing a folded sheet of newsprint that fluttered soundlessly onto the rug.

Her attention was drawn to the photograph in her hand, of a darkly handsome man and a delicate, pretty blonde who wore a wide smile of uninhibited happiness.

A loud rattle of the doorknob froze Flora in place. Panicked, she thrust the photograph into the bottom of the drawer, dumped the pile of shirts on top and slid the drawer closed. Only then did she see the square of paper that had fluttered to the floor and with an impatient tut, she scooped it into her pocket and ducked down, her every nerve on edge as the doorknob rattled, louder and with more persistence.

Eloise's head appeared around the bathroom door, one finger pressed to her lips.

'Darling,' a high-pitched female voice came from outside. 'That's not our cabin. We're three doors farther down.'

A muttered curse followed the release of the doorknob and the brace of footsteps moved away, accompanied by soft feminine laughter.

Eloise tiptoed to the door, pulled back the side of the blind with two fingers and peered onto the deck. Turning to Flora she mouthed, 'They've gone.'

Flora released a held breath, a hand pressed to her bodice, beneath which her heart thumped painfully.

'We'd better go,' Eloise whispered. 'Did you find anything?'

Flora shook her head. 'There's no money here, not even small change.'

'Damn!' Eloise flicked off the light. 'What a waste of time.' Easing open the door, she checked both ways before beckoning Flora to follow.

They ran back to Eloise's cabin, where Flora slammed and locked the door behind them both as if they were being chased. They sat on the rumpled bed and collapsed into fits of nervous giggles like hysterical schoolgirls.

'I've never done anything like that before,' Flora said when she stopped for breath, a pillow hugged to her chest.

'What a dreary life you lead.' Eloise wiggled backwards onto the mattress.

'Possibly,' Flora bridled. 'However, yours will be somewhat less dramatic with your money out of reach. Where does that leave you now?'

'I'm not what you'd call broke exactly, but honestly, I could kill Frank for—' She broke off and flushed prettily. 'I mean, if he hadn't fallen down that companionway.' She wrapped her arms around her bent legs, her chin resting on top of her knees. 'Don't mention this to anyone, will you, Flora, but something doesn't seem right about Frank's accident.'

Flora stiffened. 'What doesn't seem right?'

'That's just it.' She hunched her shoulders almost to her ears. 'I don't know. Falling down staircases wasn't Frank's style. Pushing people down them, now that's more like him.' She stretched her arms luxuriously, yawning. 'Anyway, thanks for your help, Flora. I'm sorry we didn't find anything.'

'Which must strike you as odd.'

'Odd?' Eloise's black lashed fluttered once. 'In what way?'

'Bun-Mr Harrington, told me Mr Parnell won a considerable amount of money at cards last night.'

'He did?' A frown appeared between her perfectly arched eyebrows. 'How much of a considerable amount?'

'Over $2,000, maybe more.'

'No!' Eloise bolted upright. 'The sneaky bas—' Words appeared to fail her, and sighing, she dropped her chin back onto her knees.

'The reason I mention it,' Flora went on, 'is because that money wasn't in his stateroom either. He didn't have a chance to lodge it in the ship's safe as the purser's office was closed at that time of night. So either he gave it to someone, hid it, or it was stolen.'

'And we've looked in all the likely hiding places.' Eloise gave a dismissive 'tsk' through her lips. 'Frank didn't trust banks either so I doubt he would have planned to give it to the purser.' Her head jerked up again, pinning Flora with a hard stare. 'You think he was killed for the money?'

'I couldn't say, but as it isn't here...'

Eloise shook her head. 'I can't imagine anyone on board taking such a risk. It's small change to most of them.'

'Not necessarily. An ocean liner is a great leveller. Once on board we can be whomever we wish.' Flora recalled the state of Parnell's shoes. 'After all, did you know I was a governess when we first met?'

'Not at all. It wasn't until Mrs Penry-Jones said – well never mind what she said. Besides, she didn't speak directly to me, more in my presence. Women like her don't talk to actresses. Ah counted myself lucky she asked me to pass the mustard at dinner.'

'Exactly what I mean. Anyone can buy a first-class ticket, everything else can be invented to suit their purpose. Maybe Mr Parnell wasn't what he said he was?'

Eloise slid off the bed and stood, her arms crossed at her waist. 'Look, Miss Governess, I don't know what you're implying, but ah haven't invented or stolen anything.'

'I wish you'd stop being so defensive,' Flora cut across her. 'I wasn't referring to you.' Unless her judgement was faulty, Eloise wasn't a killer.

'You said you weren't happy with the manner of Mr Parnell's death, well nor am I. I believe someone killed him.'

Panic entered Eloise's blue eyes. 'Ah don't know anything about that. Ah want to get back what is rightfully mine, nothin' else. If you spread talk like that, before you know it, I'll be the one accused.'

'But surely—'

'No, I mean it.' She dragged Flora to her feet by one arm in a surprisingly firm grip for someone with such a slight frame. 'Thank you for helping me tonight, but I'm not being accused of murder.' She propelled Flora out onto the deck where a cool wind tugged at her skirt.

Before the door closed, she heard Eloise whisper, 'Not again.'

8

MONDAY

After a surprisingly restful night, Flora was up and dressed, pouring hot tea from the pot brought by the stewardess, when Eddy stumbled into the sitting room.

'You look tired, didn't you sleep well?' She untucked a corner of his cardigan that had caught in his trousers.

'I had a strange dream, about Meely.' He stifled a yawn. 'I was six again, and she took the ladder away from my tree house when I was still inside.' He rubbed his eyes with both hands. 'I dreamed she left me there for days, not just until suppertime, which was what really happened.'

'How ungenerous of her. I take it you forgave her? In your dream I mean?' Flora knew all about strange dreams, but this one didn't sound too disturbing. In response to his sleepy nod she continued, 'Now, have you and Ozzy any plans for the day?'

'Not really.' Eddy flopped into a chair. 'We've played all the deck games and seen as much of the ship as the crew will let us. We tried to sneak into the engine room, but some burly chap in an overall ordered us out.'

'I should think so. I hope you won't try that again. It's dangerous down there.'

'Jolly hot too.' Eddy scratched his head and yawned. 'The other boys are still talking about Mr Parnell's murder. Have they got any ideas as to who did it?'

'Have you been worrying about Mr Parnell's death, Eddy?' Flora asked gently.

After what happened the previous night, she could so with some reassurances herself, but right now Eddy was her main concern. Knowing this moment was bound to come, she was prepared to offer reassurances she hoped were convincing, though her own doubts loomed as large as ever.

'Whatever for?' Eddy said. 'It's exciting to think a madman is throwing people down staircases. Ozzy says I won't have to buy any tuck for a month with a story like that to tell at school.' His eyes widened as an idea struck him. 'Maybe Ozzy and me could hide behind a winch or something and catch him at it when he selects his next victim?'

'Don't you dare, and you shouldn't joke about such things.' Flora's cup rattled as she handed it to him. 'Besides, who exactly is saying Mr Parnell was killed deliberately?'

Eddy's lower lip trembled. 'I didn't make it up, Flora, honestly. Giggles told the second officer he thought it wasn't an accident.'

'Who is this Giggles? One of the other boys?'

'It's what everyone calls Captain Gates, because he's always laughing.'

The name suited the man, with his sparkling eyes and animated features that spread into a smile at the slightest provocation. The passengers certainly seemed to like him and clamoured to be invited to dine at his table.

'Yes, I suppose so. Although I trust you'll always address him as Captain Gates, and nothing else?' Flora concealed her worry behind brisk authority. Bunny was right in that the boys on board were going to make the most of this and any attempt to keep them quiet was doomed, so she might as well find out what was being said. 'What exactly *did* the captain say?'

'We were in one of the lifeboats and heard him quite clearly.' Eddy swiped a biscuit from the tray and took a bite.

'What were you doing in a lifeboat?' Flora pushed aside all thoughts of the captain.

'Playing pirates.' His grimace showed he regarded the question as ridiculous. 'He was talking to that German chap with the moustache. "The matter warrants further investigation," were his exact words.' Eddy spoke through a mouthful of biscuit. 'That means he thinks it was a murder, doesn't he?'

The mention of the German sent Flora's thoughts racing in another direction. How was he involved? He reached for the plate of biscuits again, but Flora got there first and moved it out of his reach, and though he scowled at her, offered no protest other than a soft sigh.

'What was Mr Hersch's response to that, Eddy?' Flora forgot her initial thought to pursue the misuse of the lifeboat for the time being.

'Dunno. He mumbled something, but Ozzy kicked my shin at that point and I had to shift position.'

Eddy glanced up at the mantel clock and gasped. 'Blimey, it's nearly time for breakfast, and I'm not completely dressed.' He slurped half his tea in one gulp, then headed for his room.

'Eddy!' Flora gasped. 'Since when do you use words like that?'

He turned back with his hand on the bedroom doorknob and shrugged. 'Ozzy says it sometimes.'

'It's a profanity, which I'm certain would be frowned upon at Marlborough.'

Eddy murmured something unintelligible just as the door closed with a bang, but Flora chose not to ask him to repeat it.

Perhaps it was a good thing he was off to boarding school.

* * *

Bunny was seated alone at their table when Flora entered the dining room for breakfast. He gave their combined order to the waiter, with whom he exchanged views on the continued good weather and their current speed.

Flora contributed no more to the conversation but a vague smile and drummed her fingers on the table until the waiter left.

'Well,' she asked Bunny when the man was finally out of earshot, 'aren't you going to ask me about Eloise?'

'What's to ask?' He swallowed a mouthful of coffee, setting the cup back into its saucer with a click. 'She was semi-conscious when I left. I assume you settled her in bed and left her to sleep it off.'

'Not quite, she—' Flora broke off as the waiter returned with a gleaming silver coffee pot, fidgeting as he fussed with the crockery and inquired if they desired anything further.

'You seem edgy,' Bunny said when they were alone again. A tiny crease appeared between his brows as he gave her some thought. 'Did something happen after I left last night?'

Flora told him, his face turning from mild interest to an incredulous stare as the story progressed.

'Are you serious?' he demanded when she had finished, his voice dropping to an angry whisper. 'How could you have been so reckless?'

Several heads turned in their direction and she shushed him. 'It all happened so quickly, I didn't have time to argue. Eloise practically dragged me along.'

'I'm not the one to whom you'll have to make your excuses if you're found out.' He spread a piece of toast with butter, adding after a pause. 'There was nothing there, you say?'

'No money, but there was a photograph of a man and a woman in amongst his shirts. I didn't have time to study it closely, because we were interrupted, but—'

'You were discovered?' The toast froze halfway to his mouth, a drop of melted butter dripped onto the tablecloth.

'Don't panic.' She waved him away. 'It was only a couple who had come to the wrong stateroom. They went away again. No one saw us.'

He exhaled slowly through pursed lips and relaxed back in his chair. The relief on his face made her want to wrap her arms around him to reassure him he had no reason to worry on her account. It was a strange sensation, similar to the protectiveness she felt towards Eddy, but somehow different.

'Do you have the photograph?' he asked.

'What?' She slanted a sardonic look at him beneath her lashes. 'Add theft to my litany of crime?'

'No, of course not, I simply—' He dropped the toast back onto his plate.

'Can you be sure it wasn't a picture of Eloise and Parnell? They might have been closer than she admitted.'

'I'm positive.' She hunched closer. 'The man in the photograph was taller and far more handsome. Oh, and he had a moustache.'

'Like roughly a third of the male population,' Bunny murmured.

'Here's another question then. Why does Eloise dye her hair an unflattering black? It dulls her vibrant looks, which as an actress, I imagine is the opposite of what she would want.'

'I expect actresses do it all the time to suit their roles.' He took another bite of his toast and chewed.

Flora fiddled with her napkin, mainly to give her something to do with her hands to stop her slapping him. Why did he have to contradict everything she said?

'Flora?' he said, slowly after a moment. 'You realise that had Eloise taken the money, and been caught, you would have been an accessory to theft?'

'The money was Eloise's, so that's not like—' she broke off. 'Oh. I couldn't prove that, could I?'

'Exactly. And it worries me that you took her word for it.'

He was right. That was exactly what she had done, believed every word Eloise had told her; an actress, who had already fooled her once by convincing her she was drunk. The fact Bunny had also been taken in didn't make her feel much better either.

'It didn't sound like a lie at the time.' Aware her excuse sounded feeble, Flora fell silent as the waiter slid a plate under her nose that contained a triangle of yellow smoked haddock that glistened beneath a layer of melted butter, a perfectly round poached egg on top. Until that moment she hadn't realised she was hungry, her mind having been too preoccupied with Eloise and their adventure, interspersed with the croaky voice outside the dining room. She had studied the voices of everyone around her closely since it happened, hoping someone would give themselves away, but thus far no one had even made her think twice. She trickled vinegar onto her fish, then caught Bunny's expression of horror and frowned. 'What?'

'Are you actually going to eat that?' He wrinkled his nose and peered at her plate.

'I certainly am.' She had always loved the piquant taste of vinegar and put it on everything. Well almost. 'Could we return to our original subject, Eloise couldn't have known Parnell was going to die.' She loaded her fork with flavoursome fish and brought it to her lips, trying not to moan with pleasure as she chewed the first mouthful. 'She's not convinced it was an accident, either.'

'Then she should take her concerns to the captain. Why do you care if it was murder or not?' Bunny lowered his voice as passengers filed into the dining room. 'You didn't even know the man.'

'Maybe not.' Flora twirled her empty fork. 'I simply hate being told what to do by men who think they have all the answers. Officer Martin, the captain, even Dr Fletcher's dismissive sneer irritated me. They seem to think because I am a girl, I have no common sense or intelligence.' She stabbed the poached egg viciously with her knife, breaking the yolk that leaked in a pool over her plate.

'Governess, or emancipated woman? Which are you, Flora Maguire?' Bunny winked at her over the rim of his coffee cup.

'Maybe both.'

A warm glow spread upwards from her stomach, which she fought down. She refused to let that smouldering look affect her. He probably wasn't even aware he did smoulder.

'What about the cash Parnell won at cards?' Flora said, composed again. 'Eloise didn't know about that. That money should have been in his stateroom, but there was no sign of it.' She was about to dip a piece of bread roll into the runny egg yolk on her plate, but thought better of it.

'Or she said she didn't. Everyone was talking about Parnell and the card game. She might have learned of it at any time during yesterday.'

'I hadn't thought of that.' Though Eloise's reaction when Flora had mentioned it seemed genuine.

'His winnings could have been on his body when he was found.' Bunny chewed a piece of bacon thoughtfully. 'If so, Captain Gates would have lodged it in the ship's safe without telling anyone.'

'I suppose that's possible.' Flora summoned an image of Dr Fletcher going through the dead man's pockets and sighed as her theory began to fall apart.

'So where does this take us?' Bunny asked, when she remained silent. 'Perhaps Eloise thought he would lose her money at the card table and refused to give it to him. They argued and he ended up at the bottom of those steps?'

'But he didn't lose,' Flora said. 'He won.'

'The other night he did, yes. But gamblers always think they'll win. That's why they're gamblers.'

'I don't believe Eloise is either a thief or a killer.' Flora forked more fish into her mouth. 'She's a young woman alone who has to make the best of her life because she has no one else to do it for her.'

'How do you know she's alone in the world? Is that what she told you?'

'No, not in so many words. It was an impression I got.' Her fork hovered above her plate as she considered the question. 'Bunny,' she began, judging this was the right moment to tell him about the incident outside the dining room, 'something very odd happened last night.'

'I know it did. You became a burglar.'

'No, not that. Last night, I—' She gasped, and clamped a hand to her mouth as creeping dread crept into her chest. 'I've just remembered! We didn't fix the lock shut on Parnell's door after we left.'

Bunny groaned. 'Tell me you're joking.'

She shook her head, wincing. 'Do you think anyone will notice?'

'Probably, but there's nothing you can do about it now.' His gaze slid past her shoulder, and he cleared his throat in warning.

Flora turned her head just as Cynthia approached, looking stunning in yellow silk that clung to her slender figure.

'Aren't you two the early birds,' she cooed in a fair imitation of one herself. 'Here, and I thought I was the first.'

'The sea air makes me hungry.' Bunny stood while Cynthia took her seat.

Gerald and Monica appeared, squabbling their way from the door, but within five feet of the table, their sour expressions had transformed into

identical smiles, as if a switch had been pressed. At times, they were incapable of being more than a handclasp away from each other, while at
other times they appeared positively hostile.

Flora reached for her coffee, frustrated the moment had passed and
annoyed with herself that Bunny was bound to find out about the croaky-
voiced man at some stage. When he did, he would think she was deliberately keeping secrets from him.

The dining room filled rapidly for breakfast, with Mr Hersch the next
to arrive, followed by the Cavendishes, who arrived hand in hand, then
followed by an exuberant Miss Ames, attired in her characteristic
mismatch of colours. Mr Crowe sidled in unnoticed, until Flora spotted
him helping himself to coffee from a pot at another table, too impatient to
wait for their own waiter to arrive with theirs. Soon the steady stream of
new arrivals dwindled to ones and twos, but with still no sign of Eloise.

'She's probably sleeping it off,' Gerald said when he caught Flora
staring at Eloise's empty chair.

'I suppose so.' Flora gave him a weak smile, although it wasn't the
condition of Eloise's head that concerned her.

The waiter removed Flora's empty breakfast plate, leaving her to linger
over coffee and observe her fellow diners in search of something which
might give her some clue as to who might have a nature cold enough to kill
a man, and threaten women in corridors.

Cynthia sat on one side of Mr Hersch and picked at a bowl of fruit,
while Miss Ames occupied the other. This morning she wore a lime
green blouse under a cobalt blue jacket with mutton leg sleeves. She
reminded Flora of a parakeet as she nibbled alternatively at two pastries
with slightly protruding teeth. The older woman and the beautiful girl
made a strange trio with Mr Hersch, whose penetrating eyes beneath
thick, arched silver brows viewed the world with wry amusement. He
kept both women entranced with stories about voyages he had been on;
his ability to pay attention to a beautiful woman and a plain one with
equal charm, a skill Flora could never have guessed at but couldn't help
admiring.

As with all genuinely clever men, Hersch made no attempt to demonstrate his intellect, giving considered and equal responses to their every

remark, no matter how banal. He even managed to coax a genuine laugh from Cynthia.

Flora tried to imagine his voice reduced to a hiss, but failed. If he wished to hurt someone it would be in face-to-face combat, not shoving a drunken man down a flight of steps in the dark. Which also meant he wasn't likely to hide behind pillars and whisper threats either. Then she remembered, Hersch was already with Bunny and Cynthia at the dining table when she arrived last night, so it couldn't have been him, not unless he possessed the gift of being in two places at once. The constant thinking and re-thinking gave her a headache and she was still no wiser.

'Do you happen to be acquainted with Mrs Moreland's school in Bath, Miss Maguire?' Monica's question distracted Flora. 'We hope to send our girls there in the autumn.'

'Really, Monica,' her husband said with barely concealed irritation. 'Flora doesn't have an intimate knowledge of every educational establishment in the county.'

'I don't, I'm afraid,' Flora said gently, softening Gerald's response. 'I live at least fifty miles from Bath. Though I may know someone who might. I'd be happy to write and ask them for you.'

'That's most kind of you, my dear.' Monica's gracious smile transformed into a frosty glare she directed at her husband. 'I've heard such good things about it and their fees are higher than anywhere else.'

Gerald jumped slightly, but whatever he was about to say to this remark, he abandoned, plucked a toothpick from the silver pot on the table and chewed it into shreds.

'Does Gerald seem overly nervous to you this morning?' she whispered to Bunny once Gerald's attention turned to a gentleman at a nearby table.

'He does actually.' Bunny topped up his coffee and offered to do the same for her. 'Not like him, is it? But then he is married to Monica.'

'Perhaps her character is such *because* she is married to him,' Flora retorted, accepting the offer of coffee.

'Hester!' Mrs Penry-Jones snapped, making Flora jump. 'You know I don't like sugar in my coffee.

'I'm dreadfully sorry, Mrs Penry-Jones, I quite forgot.' Flushing, Hester summoned the waiter, who replaced her employer's cup with a fresh one.

Flora tried not to look, her sympathy for Miss Smith almost painful. She wondered if anyone had thought to ask Hester how she felt about Parnell's death?

'How are you feeling, Miss Smith, after the events of yesterday?' Mr Hersch's amiable smile expertly diffused the awkward moment. 'The death of a fellow passenger?' His question voiced Flora's thoughts so closely, she stared, though she had to content herself with his profile as just then, he was not looking her way.

'I–I think it was a dreadful thing to happen.' Hester pushed her fried egg into mush with her fork. 'Not that I was acquainted with the gentleman.'

'He wasn't a gentleman!' Mrs Penry-Jones snorted. 'He was a weak, vacillating man with no ambition. Bound to come to a bad end.'

'That's a somewhat harsh judgement on so short an acquaintance,' Flora said, impulse overriding her discretion.

'It's quite obvious!' The old lady sniffed. 'I was there when he persuaded a room full of strangers to gamble for high stakes on first meeting. Vulgar man.'

'Indeed he did, much to my cost.' Gus Crowe broke off from eating to remind them.

Flora groaned inwardly at his bald admission. Surely if were guilty he wouldn't be so ready to let everyone think so? Or was it bravado on his part, because most of the table were at the game and knew how much he had lost.

'Still looking for villains, Flora?' Bunny gave her a playful nudge, breaking her silent contemplation.

She was about to deliver a pointed retort but thought better of it. He was right and thus far she could detect no guilt among the company, only a few unpleasant character traits.

'Are you sure you didn't know him, Mrs Penry-Jones?' Gerald spread a bread roll with butter as he talked. 'I could have sworn I saw Parnell being admitted to your suite the night he died.'

'Don't be ridiculous!' The old lady's eyes narrowed with outrage. 'You must have been mistaken.'

Hester released a dismayed gasp as she fumbled the glass lid of a jam pot, leaving a smear of apricot conserve on the white tablecloth.

Gus Crowe smirked and handed her a napkin, leaving her to attempt to clear up the sticky mess, while the old lady fastidiously removed the dish from Hester's reach with a long-suffering sigh.

'Had anyone knocked at Mrs Penry-Jones's suite, I would certainly have heard it,' Hester said, coming to her employer's defence.

Mrs Penry-Jones threw Hersch a look of triumph, whilst ignoring Hester's attempt at support.

'Possibly.' Gerald wiped his fingers on his napkin. 'It's difficult to tell whose stateroom is whose. All the doors look the same.'

'If that is what you saw, Mr Gilmore.' Mr Hersch fixed Gerald with a hard stare. 'Why did you not inform the captain?'

'What makes you think I didn't?' Gerald held his gaze and the two men stared each other down. Gerald capitulated first, though Hersch appeared to have no answer to this, saved from further questioning by the arrival of Max.

'Couldn't find my cufflinks,' he explained, when Cynthia scolded him for lateness. 'Looked everywhere, but they aren't in the suite.'

'Not the ones I gave you for a wedding present?' Cynthia's eyes narrowed.

Max flicked up the back of his jacket and sat. 'No, not those. The emerald ones.' He held up one sleeve, which sported a flat, gold oval. 'Had to wear these instead.'

'You probably packed them in one of the trunks that have been put in the hold. I'm sure they'll turn up.' Cynthia waved him away.

'I had them last night in the smoking room. I went to wash my hands so the cards wouldn't stick, and had to roll up my sleeves, so—' He broke off and pasted on a smile. 'You're probably right, my love. They'll turn up.'

'Is the meal not to your liking, Miss Smith?' Mr Hersch asked gently. 'You've hardly touched your breakfast.'

'The eggs are undercooked.' Hester pushed her plate away with a tiny grimace of distaste.

'My head is pounding this morning.' Mrs Penry-Jones rose from the table, pausing theatrically until all eyes were on her. 'I'll return to my suite and lie down. No, Hester, don't get up. Finish your breakfast.'

The gentlemen's chairs scraped back, and, with the hesitant gait of someone with arthritis, she limped past a steward who scrambled to hold open the door.

'Your employer appears more upset about a death on board than she would have us believe, Miss Smith,' Mr Hersch observed as the gentlemen resumed their seats.

'Not at all.' Hester returned his benign look steadily. 'She's notoriously unsentimental.' Colour returned to her cheeks and her cat-like eyes sparkled. Suddenly she looked, if not pretty, but softer and more animated.

'Does Mrs Penry-Jones have family?' Monica asked, apparently eager to take advantage of the lady's absence.

'Her husband was a lawyer in upstate New York,' Hester replied without hesitation. 'He died years ago. I believe she was married before, but they lived in Baltimore then.' She paused to summon the waiter with surprising confidence, demanding her congealed eggs be replaced. 'She claims acquaintance with everyone,' she went on when she had everyone's attention again. 'But most of the names she mentions are long dead.'

Cynthia choked on her coffee, returning the cup to the saucer with a firm click, her knuckles as white as the china in her hand.

'As for what you saw, Mr Gilmore' – Hester turned a coy look on him – 'I could have been wrong about Mr Parnell. I sleep quite heavily, so he might very well have called on Mrs Penry-Jones.'

Flora frowned. Hester's blatant contradiction seemed odd. And why would she imply her employer had been lying? Then again, she could simply be a trouble maker. Hester certainly behaved differently when Mrs Penry-Jones wasn't present.

'Excuse me.' Cynthia rose abruptly, her face pinched. She threw her napkin onto the table with the force of someone issuing a challenge to a duel. 'I've remembered something important I must do.' Without meeting anyone's eyes, she turned and marched out of the dining room.

'I ought to go and see if she's all right,' Max said with a sigh, rising more slowly.

'Honeymooners, eh?' Gerald chuckled when the pair were out of sight. 'Never know what's likely to upset 'em.'

'How would you know, Gerald?' Monica sniffed.

'I wonder what Max said to upset Cynthia?' Bunny whispered. 'Her face was like thunder.'

Flora frowned, unsure whether it was Max who was the cause, or something else entirely.

9

On the saloon deck that afternoon, Flora watched Eddy partner Ozzy in an enthusiastic game of *Chalking the Pig's Eye*, offering encouragement when he lost and praise when he scored a point. The sound of her name being called brought her head up to where Bunny waved from the promenade deck above her. He pointed with a finger at his own chest, then down at her in a gesture inviting himself to join her.

At Flora's nod, he performed a 'thumbs up' gesture, pushed back through the crowd, and a moment later, emerged again on the lower deck. Flora watched with possessive affection as he made his way towards her, offering polite smiles and greetings to fellow passengers as he passed.

'How is Eddy getting on?' he asked on reaching her.

'He does have a remarkable aptitude for guessing where he should enter his mark.' Flora said, conscious of the pressure of his upper arm against her shoulder.

'Look, he's done it again!' She nodded to the blackboard which stood mere feet away, the roughly drawn shape of a pig traced in white chalk. 'That's his third high score.'

'Hmmm...' His sceptical tone brought her head round to face him. 'That could be because his blindfold is thinner than Ozzy's.'

'I hadn't noticed that actually.' Flora narrowed her eyes. Bunny was right. Eddy's blindfold was a thin strip of navy blue chiffon, too thin to obscure his sight. 'I'll have a word with him later on the subject of fair play.'

'Best keep it to yourself if I were you.' Bunny chuckled lightly. 'By the way, I was about to pay a call on Matilda, would you care to join me?'

Flora hesitated, her desire to spend time with Bunny vying with her responsibility towards Eddy. 'That's kind of you, but I need to ensure Eddy is suitably occupied.'

'He appears suitably occupied to me, and quite happily so. I think he won that game.'

'Perhaps, although maybe I need to spend more time with him. I'm conscious of having left him too much to his own devices lately.' Now they were virtually alone, she gathered her courage.

'There is a reason for my being so cautious. It's because someone approached—' She looked up to see Eddy bounding towards her. 'Never mind, I'll tell you later.'

The longer she left telling him about the man outside the dining room, the harder it became, though she couldn't very well do so in front of Eddy.

'May I go and listen to Mr Gilmore's new gramophone?' Eddy bounced on his toes in front of her. 'It's one of those new ones which plays discs instead of cylinders.'

'Father has a recording of "When Johnny Comes Marching Home",' Ozzy added, joining him.

'Do say I may, Flora!' Eddy pleaded.

Flora hesitated, torn between denying Eddy a treat and a need to keep him close.

'That sounds wonderful, doesn't it Flora?' Bunny ignored the hard look she slanted at him. 'I wouldn't mind hearing that myself sometime.'

'Come now, Flora,' Monica chided. 'The boys would enjoy it. Gerald and I will even take them into tea later, how about that?'

'Well, Flora?' Four pairs of eyes viewed her expectantly.

A movement from the corner of her eye distracted her before she could answer. Captain Gates had passed on her right and strolled towards the companionway to the deck above.

'If Mrs Gilmore is agreeable, Eddy, you may listen to the gramophone.'

Flora turned to Bunny. 'I'll come and see Matilda with you another time. Right now, there's something I must do. Please excuse me.'

Accompanied by a despondent 'as you wish' from Bunny and enthusiastic thanks from Monica and both boys, Flora headed for the staircase lobby and climbed the stairs to where Captain Gates stood talking to Dr Fletcher. She had tried to reassure herself that her fears of croaky-voiced assailants who hid in alcoves were totally unfounded and that she and Eddy were perfectly safe, but she knew she shouldn't ignore what happened outside the dining room, for Eddy's sake if not for her own.

The thought persisted that if she found it difficult to tell Bunny, then perhaps she should tell someone in authority. Without a proper description it was unlikely they could do anything about it, but keeping it to herself was a heavy burden. She hovered on the fringe and waited for a suitable lull in the conversation, then almost left it too late, when, without warning, Captain Gates nodded curtly to Dr Fletcher, turned and pushed through the door onto the outside deck.

Flora was about to follow, when Dr Fletcher intercepted her. 'Is there something you wanted, Miss Maguire?'

'Um... I wish to have a word with the captain.' Flora bounced on her heels as she watched her target disappear rapidly down along the deck through the window.

'Anything I can do? He's a busy man, you know.' The implication the captain was too exalted to talk to her showed in Dr Fletcher's world-weary expression.

'Well, all right.' She took a deep breath, aware what she about to say might sound odd in the clear light of day, but surely the ship's doctor was also a senior member of the crew. Maybe he had enough status to take whatever action was appropriate?

'Last evening, a man approached me outside the dining room. Well, I assume it was a man, but I didn't see him, or her. But he – or she – delivered a warning.'

'What sort of warning?' Dr Fletcher folded his arms and regarded her down his nose.

'That I should not ask questions about Mr Parnell's death. Well, that's not exactly what was said, but I assume that's what was meant, it wasn't that specific. However, it was implied that people are lost from ships all the time.'

'And so they are. What exactly *did* he say, Miss Maguire?'

'That, um... I should leave well alone. And before you ask, no, I didn't recognise his voice. Or maybe her voice,' she trailed off, knowing by his face he had already dismissed her as either mistaken, or over dramatic.

'I see.' He turned away to acknowledge a regal-looking couple who sauntered past.

'I thought the captain should know,' Flora persisted. 'Bearing in mind a man has been killed.' She sensed his attention had drifted away and wished she hadn't sounded so vague.

'Mr Parnell died as the result of a fall,' he interrupted her, regarding her with a mixture of resignation and false sympathy which must have taken him years to perfect. 'I understand you were distraught at finding the body, though perhaps you have allowed yourself to dwell too much on the incident. As for whispered threats, well, they could simply be your fertile imagination.'

Flora counted backwards from ten. 'I wish you wouldn't keep accusing me of being distraught in a tone you might use for "unhinged". I didn't imagine the threat, Doctor. It was quite real, and menacing.' She put emphasis on the last word, attracting attention from several people who traversed the lobby.

The doctor smiled at them in an I-have-this-under-control way, and once they had passed by, he grasped her arm and guided her firmly into a door recess. 'Forgive me, Miss Maguire, but you do appear somewhat agitated. Would a sedative help?'

'No, it would not, and—oh, never mind.' She rolled her arm out of his hold as it occurred to her she was wasting her time. 'I only ask that you relay my message to the captain. He'll understand its importance, even if you don't.'

'Certainly. If that's what you wish.' He clicked his heels, then left through the same door the captain had used moments before.

Flora stared after him, while several uncomplimentary adjectives about officers, and men in general, lined up in her head. Even if he chose to pass on her concerns to the captain, would he do so in the light-hearted, patronising way he had used just now?

She should have followed her own instincts and told Bunny first. He might have dismissed her too, but he would have done so in a more polite way. She wouldn't make that mistake again.

* * *

Flora paused beside Eloise's stateroom on her way along the deck; the blinds were drawn and there were no sounds of life from inside. She moved away and was about to unlock the door of her suite when a shadow detached from a nearby pillar and walked towards her. She tensed instantly, but turned to see Mr Hersch's kind smile, and chastised herself for being so jumpy.

'Miss Maguire.' He raised his fedora an inch above his head then replaced it on his salt and pepper hair. You look a little harassed, if I may say so.'

'Maybe I'm still a distraught female with nothing to think about but the state of her nerves?' Flora replied, not bothering to hide her frustration.

'I see someone has ruffled your sleek feathers, my dear. Would you care to share your disquiet with a sympathetic ear?'

'I'm sorry, I don't mean to be flippant.' She strolled to the rail and rested her hands on the polished top, her gaze on the horizon. A line of ragged grey-white clouds floated in a pale blue sky as if warning worse was to come. However, the weather had been so mild since she boarded, she forgot all the stories she had heard about storms in a North Atlantic spring.

On the saloon deck below, the Entertainments officer was organising a group of children in a boisterous game of quoits on one site and badminton the other.

'I tried to tell the captain something, but Dr Fletcher persuaded me to tell him instead, and now I wish I hadn't... Oh, never mind, it's nothing really.'

'I suspect it's a great deal more than nothing, Miss Maguire.' He cocked his head to one side. 'If it's something to do with the late Mr Parnell, I might be able to help.'

Flora doubted it, but the idea was tempting. 'May I ask you something first?'

'Of course, what is it?' He narrowed his eyes against a fine spray of salt-water blown into their faces by wind, the sky suddenly heavy with sagging clouds.

'What is your interest in Parnell, Mr Hersch?'

'Very much the same as yours, my dear. An innate sense of justice for the victim.' He slanted a downward look into her eyes and held it. 'Let's say, I have some experience in these matters.'

'I'm not sure if you are naturally enigmatic or are keeping something from me. Whichever it is, I have to tell you I find it quite annoying.' She turned away but instead of the reprimand she expected, Mr Hersch laughed, a full blown, genuinely amused laugh that rolled through his chest.

'My, my, you are indeed angry today. I'm sorry if I have added to your chagrin, my dear. To compensate, I'll tell you the latest on our late friend.' Without waiting for her response, he went on, 'Captain Gates feels Mr Parnell's death might not have been accidental.'

'Oh.' Her eagerness dissolved into disappointment. 'I'm afraid my young charge has pre-empted you. He heard you talking to Captain Gates when he said the same thing.'

'I see.' He nodded slowly. 'Have you recruited the young man as your spy?'

'I don't have to. He's quite capable of rooting out things on his own. I would be interested to know why though.'

'Simple, my dear. You were quite right about the wound to Parnell's head, the lack of blood and the lividity. He didn't die where he was found.'

'How interesting.' Pride puffed up her chest a little. 'And what did the good doctor say to that?'

'What could he say when the evidence was clear.'

'Indeed. Now that you've been candid with me, Mr Hersch, I will tell you what I told Dr Fletcher.' He evidently had the captain's confidence, and he was much nicer than the doctor. 'Yesterday,' she began slowly, 'someone accosted me outside the dining room.' She related all she could remember about an encounter she would rather forget, but could not, while he remained silent, his head down and poking repeatedly at one of the rail supports with his toe.

'Those were the exact words?' he asked when she had finished, his frown deepening.

She nodded, grateful he had not asked if she had imagined it.

'Did you believe him?'

'Dr Fletcher dismissed the whole thing as my state of mind, but—'

'No, Miss Maguire. I asked if *you* took this man's threat seriously?'

She licked salt from her lips, her eyes narrowed against the wind. 'He unsettled me enough to believe he might hurt me.'

'Have you said or done something which would make this person think you know more than you should?'

'I don't think so. The entire table discussed Mr Parnell's accident over luncheon, but I doubt I said anything which would warrant a threat.'

'Who else have you told about this person?'

'Only Dr Fletcher. He agreed to relay the details to the captain, but he treated me like an hysterical female, so I have my doubts.'

'Fletcher is a difficult man to read, with a somewhat inflated view of his own abilities. The captain, on the other hand, is very experienced. I'll mention it to him myself if you wish.'

'Thank you, I appreciate that. I didn't know whom to tell. Or even if I should.'

'You're talking to *me*.'

'Yes, I know, but—' She hoped she didn't sound self-pitying.

He cut her off with a slight gesture of his hand as a middle-aged couple passed by. When they had moved out of earshot, he said, 'I suggest, that for the time being, it would be wise to make everyone believe you have acceded to this person's wishes.'

Why hadn't she thought of that?

'Tell me,' Hersch went on, 'what did you think about Miss Smith's behaviour at breakfast?'

'Hester?' Flora blinked, disarmed by his unexpected change of subject.

'Well, she doesn't appear to like Mrs Penry-Jones much, which makes me wonder why she remains in her employ.'

'I've seen worse masters and less respectful servants.' Hersch's sigh conveyed long experience of studying his fellow man. 'Perhaps Miss Smith views a few sharp remarks a fair exchange for a life of material comfort?'

'Possibly,' Flora replied, convinced whatever advantages Hester enjoyed would never really be hers, merely an illusion of affluence.

'Has anyone else on board engendered your mistrust?' he asked after a moment.

'Not really. Cynthia doesn't like Hester Smith, and she and Max whisper together a lot, but that's hardly surprising for honeymooners.' Flora ran through a list of names in her head. 'Miss Ames asks lots of questions, but that ties in with her being an author. Mr Crowe is arrogant as well as grasping, what my father would call a "freeloader". He appears to relish other people's disagreements too. Even encourages them.'

'I've noticed that myself.' He ran a thumb and forefinger down either side of his moustache, a gesture he used when thinking. 'And what does Mr Harrington think of your theory about Mr Parnell?'

'He listens, but he's not convinced.' Flora pushed thoughts of Bunny to the back of her mind. He confused her enough without discussing him with a third party. She anticipated telling him she had been right about Parnell with a glow of triumph, but it occurred to her Mr Hersch might demand discretion in exchange for his revelation.

'Mr Hersch, if the captain has doubts, why hasn't he instigated a search of Mr Parnell's stateroom?'

'That's an interesting suggestion, Miss Maguire. What do you expect him to find?' He held her gaze steadily.

Flora hesitated. His eyes were too knowing, too far seeing, and she wasn't adept enough in deception to keep it from him for long.

'Something among his belongings might shed some light on the reason for his death. Documents perhaps, a letter, maybe?' She daren't mention the photograph, it was too specific. She would end up confessing to burglary if she wasn't careful.

'I would ponder that theory, if I were you, Miss Maguire.' A smile pulled at his lips without revealing his teeth. 'You might be required to explain it by someone who will not accept dissembling.'

'I'll bear that in mind.' Flora exhaled slowly, aware her cheeks felt hot. 'If someone did kill Mr Parnell, how will we find out who it was?'

'That, I do not know, but if we wait, I feel sure the killer will make a mistake and reveal himself.'

'Just that? Wait?'

'Where could a murderer go? We're in the middle of the Atlantic.' He touched two fingers to his hat, inclined his head and strolled off along the deck.

Flora didn't find this at all reassuring, although he hadn't dismissed her croaky-voiced man as a figment of her imagination. Hersch's mention of having 'knowledge in these matters' was an indication he was interested in finding out what had happened to Mr Parnell.

* * *

Tuesday

After an early breakfast, spent in the company of a subdued Gus Crowe, who complained at heavy losses the night before at cards, and Miss Ames who spent the entire meal comparing Thomas Hardy to some obscure Victorian writer Flora had never heard of, she spent the morning in her suite, re-arranging her wardrobe and putting Eddy's scattered belongs away. He arrived during the process and pulled everything out again with the explanation that he wanted to show Ozzy a box of Napoleonic toy soldiers his father had presented him before they left.

Having seen him off again, and with nothing else which needed her attention, she strolled the saloon deck, exchanged pleasantries with a few other passengers and occupied a steamer chair where she read a whole chapter of *Northanger Abbey* without interruptions. She closed the book and glanced along the deck, where Gerald was organising a noisy game of shuffleboard with several young boys, among them Ozzy and Eddy.

She watched for a while, but gently declined Gerald's invitation to take a turn.

'Have you seen Mr Harrington this morning?' Flora asked. 'He wasn't at breakfast. In fact, our table was almost empty.'

'We were up late today, so we ate breakfast in our suite. The Cavendishes did too, as the steward delivered theirs at around the same time. As for Harrington, I believe he went to check on his motor car.' Gerald pushed his panama to the back of his head. 'He mentioned the straps had worked loose or something.'

'I should have known, thank you.'

'What ho.' Gerald lifted a hand in acknowledgement of a shout from his son. 'Looks like my turn again.' He loped away, waylaid at the edge of the small crowd by a woman in a hat so wide, Flora couldn't see her face, but the way in which Gerald spoke, his hand on her arm and his face tilted close to hers indicated she was attractive.

Ozzy appeared at Gerald's side and tugged at his jacket flap, and with a final, lingering caress of the woman's hand, he backed away and joined the game. The woman remained on the sidelines as the game progressed, her face still hidden by the brim of her hat. Flora speculated on whether or not Monica knew the lady, but had come to no conclusion when a burst of familiar male laughter attracted her attention.

She glanced up to where Bunny strolled along the upper deck beside an extremely pretty blonde girl Flora did not recognise, who skipped beside him, twirling a bag on a cord on her wrist, her face turned up to his as she talked.

Disappointment conjured a bitter taste in her mouth and she stepped smartly beneath the deck canopy so they wouldn't see her as they passed. She waited until their voices no longer reached her, then turned and strode in the opposite direction, muttering a curt 'excuse me' to a couple who barred her way, ignoring their surprised protests as she shouldered past.

Once inside the suite, she slammed the door hard, hurled her jacket onto a chair and strode to the bedroom and threw herself onto the bed, one arm flung over her head. Once the initial rush of anger had receded, common sense prevailed and she chastised herself for stupidity. What did she expect? Charming young men from good families did not take up with governesses. How stupid of her to believe she and Bunny had some sort of connection, when it was plain he was only being kind.

The bugle sounded for luncheon, and unprepared to witness Bunny flirt with his blonde companion, Flora stubbornly remained where she was. A shaft of light drew patterns on the ceiling as occasional footsteps, laughter and the odd murmured comment came from outside; though no knock came at her door, and eventually, the deck fell silent.

* * *

Flora woke, disoriented, easing up on an elbow, and groaned. The clock on her bedside stood at after four. Half the afternoon had gone, and having missed luncheon, she was ravenously hungry. Throwing off the coverlet, she washed her face and hands before swapping her creased skirt and blouse for a pastel, flower-print dress with a high collar and mutton leg sleeves.

In the sitting room, Eddy and Ozzy had come and gone, their occupation evidenced by a half-finished game of snakes-and-ladders beside an empty packet that once contained garibaldi biscuits. Out on the boat deck, the line of steamer chairs were filled with dozing or reading passengers, but neither Bunny nor the blonde girl were amongst them.

In search of something to eat to still her growling stomach, she headed up the grand staircase to the library, at the top of which Gus Crowe stood talking to a crewman.

Flora paused on the half-landing, conscious their discussion was becoming less a talk and more a lecture, delivered by Crowe and accepted with occasional, subservient nods by a sailor who was little more than a boy. Finally, Crowe wagged a pointed finger beneath the crewman's nose, and marched away. Flora was about to follow, when Crowe halted, his gaze fixed on the door that led to the upper promenade deck that gently swung closed. From that angle, she couldn't see what had caught his attention, but Crowe continued to stare through the door's window for long seconds as if pondering his next action. Then he seemed to make up his mind, straightened his shoulders and pushed through the door onto the deck.

Flora hitched her skirt and ascended the remaining stairs, but before she reached the top, she collided with the same crewman Crowe had been talking to, who was now on his way down.

'I'm so sorry, Miss.' He pressed his back against the wall to let her pass, his frowning expression altering in an instant to abject apology.

'That's quite all right.' Flora took in a pair of troubled eyes that peered out from beneath close-cut sandy hair before she continued on to the library, where the same steward who had attended her last time greeted her at the door.

'Would you like tea, Miss?'

'Thank you. I'll be over there.' She indicated the sofa she had occupied on her last visit. Before she reached it, Bunny's face appeared round a white-painted pillar.

'Thought it was you.' He peered at her over his spectacles. 'Had the same idea myself. Why don't you join me?' His heartbreaking smile made her stomach lurch as she imagined him directing that same gaze at the girl she had seen him with earlier. The image hurt too much, so she pushed it away, nodded in agreement and waited as he shifted sideways to make room for her.

'Miss Maguire will take her tea here,' he instructed the steward.

'Those cakes look nice.' She debated whether or not she dared order a plate of her own and devour them all, but decided against it and instead, watched as Bunny poured tea for them both from his original pot, handing her a full cup.

'You don't use this, do you?' he said, moving the sugar bowl out of her reach.

She shook her head, unaccountably touched that he had remembered. 'It's a pity about the books not having arrived in time before we sailed. I had hoped to give Eddy some work to do in preparation for school.'

'Talking of Eddy. I heard he and the Gilmore boy persuaded the purser to let them see the wheel house this afternoon. I imagine that would add to his education every bit as well as a book.'

Flora lifted her cup and smiled at him over the rim. 'Eddy is determined to see everything there is to see on this ship, he's so impressed at the fact it's so new. I hope the purser kept a close eye on them.'

'Forgive me if you feel I'm intruding,' Bunny said as the waiter returned and placed a small plate of finger sandwiches on the table. 'You seem agitated where Eddy is concerned. Has he given you reason to be worried about him?'

Flora returned her untasted tea to the saucer. 'Actually, there is something I've been meaning to tell you. The other night, I was accosted by someone outside the dining room.'

'Accosted?' His brows lifted into his hairline. 'By whom?'

'That's the problem, I don't know. But whoever it was warned me to leave well alone.'

'Good grief, how dare they? And leave what alone?'

'I can only assume it had something to do with my asking questions about Mr Parnell's death. Or someone overheard me saying I didn't think it was an accident.'

'Well, yes but even so.' His mouth opened and closed as he floundered. Then his features hardened, his eyes glinting behind his spectacles. 'If I find out who the fellow was, he'll regret it.' He stirred sugar into his tea vigorously with a minute silver spoon. 'Menacing ladies is not to be tolerated.'

'Brave talk, Mr Harrington.' Flora felt a rush of pleasure, immediately supressed beneath the knowledge Bunny was simply being himself. A kind young man who was generous to everyone. Including pretty blonde girls who liked to flirt with him.

'Excuse me, but I was boxing champion at school.' He crossed one ankle over the other, revealing an expanse of sock. 'If it happens again, or anything like it, I hope you'll refer it to me.'

'I did tell Dr Fletcher and Mr Hersch, who promised to tell the captain, so maybe they have dealt with it already. But thank you for your concern.'

'In that case I sincerely hope it has been, though I wish you'd mentioned it before.'

'I did try, but, well, the moment never seemed right. The longer I left it, the more I began to believe I was imagining the entire thing.' The relief at having unburdened herself settled on her like a warm blanket. She helped herself to a sandwich and took a bite, savouring the crisp cucumber with piquant salmon, to which the kitchen had added exactly the right amount of vinegar.

'I like a girl with a proper appetite.' Bunny watched her finish the sandwich. 'Not like these silly society "gals" who push everything away with distaste. So false.' Bunny addressed a passing waiter, one finger pointed to the nearly empty plate. 'Could we have some more please?' The man bowed and disappeared.

'I imagine you know quite a few society girls.' She tried to sound casual, but her throat constricted, making her voice high.

'Too many,' he murmured into his cup. 'Here, have one of these.' He offered her the cakes that had caught her eye on arrival.

She accepted without being asked twice and took her first bite of a vanilla slice, relishing the combination of cream, sweet icing and strawberry jam on her tongue. In no time at all the cake was gone, and she eyed the rest hungrily. Dared she take another?

Following her gaze, Bunny lifted the plate and held it out towards her. Flora hesitated and he laughed. 'Go on, I know you want one.' He waved the plate slowly from side to side an inch beneath her nose. 'Besides, it will appear greedy if I do, and I hate eating alone.'

'You were alone when I arrived,' Flora reminded him. 'And if I'm not mistaken, about to consume the entire contents of the tray by yourself.' She held her breath, hoping he wasn't going to say he was waiting for someone.

'That's different. Now go on, I can't eat while you watch.' Flora obeyed and he continued, 'Tell me about yourself.' He sat back and folded his slender hands across his midriff.

She licked cream from her fingers, giving her time to construct a suitably fascinating answer, but failed. 'My life is quite ordinary, I'm afraid. I've spent most of it in the schoolroom of a country mansion in Gloucestershire.' She dropped the remains of her second cream slice back onto her plate. Somehow it did not taste quite as exquisite as the first.

'What made you become a governess?' Bunny finished his in three mouthfuls, then wiped his fingers theatrically on a napkin.

'It wasn't so much a choice, more a transition. My father is Lord Vaughn's head butler, all of whose daughters were educated by governesses. Lord Vaughn doesn't believe in girls attending school. I was the same age as the youngest, Lady Jocasta, so I joined them in the schoolroom. Lady Vaughn had Eddy late in life and when I was eighteen, it seemed a natural progression for me to become his governess.' She lifted her chin proudly. 'In fact, you could say I've been educated far above my station.'

'It doesn't appear to have done you any harm.'

Flora smiled in agreement. She'd felt privileged to have shared a schoolroom with the earl's children, played games with them in the Capability Brown gardens, and rode ponies across the fields. What she didn't mention, was that when the Vaughn girls dined in a room where painted cherubs graced a ceiling two storeys high above an Adam fireplace, Flora ate with her father in the butler's pantry, a candle between them to lift the gloom of the half-basement.

'When Eddy goes to Marlborough,' she forced her thoughts back to the present, 'my duties will be confined to school holidays. I've begun teaching the daughters of gentlemen in the village for extra money. I'm cheaper than boarding school, and anyway, I quite enjoy it. The money is useful. I've saved quite a bit.'

'What are you saving for?'

'My future I suppose, whatever that is.' Flora frowned. No one had ever asked her that before.

'You don't have something you want to do? Or are you content living in someone else's house and teaching other young girls to become ladies?'

She stared at the congealing cream on her plate, the thought never having occurred to her before. She had always regarded Cleeve Abbey as her home. And yet – a distant memory lingered in the back of her mind, of a time where home was a room with a black-leaded range and a scrubbed pine table where the door opened into a sunny garden that threw a pool of sunlight onto grey flagstones. The scene was mixed with distress which mingled with the coppery smell of blood and the scrape of wool on her hands. Images too vague and elusive to put a name to, but before she could make sense of them, a shadow filled her head.

'Are you all right, Flora? You've gone pale.' Bunny plucked her hand from her lap, her fingers sandwiched in his; a touch that was comforting and exciting at the same time.

'Too much cake, perhaps,' she said, her voice high and brittle. Embarrassed, she snatched her hand out of his, then when his eyes filled with hurt, wished she hadn't.

'You've mentioned your father to me, but not your mother. Why is that?'

'She died.' Flora shrugged. 'At least, that's what I've always been told.' She attempted a laugh but it fell flat. 'I mean, I've never seen her grave, and whenever I broach the subject with Father, he changes the subject. He's Ulster Scots and quite, well – private. He has the ability to avoid direct questions with such subtlety, you don't even realise, then the moment passes and you cannot ask again.'

'What's Ulster Scots?'

'I'm surprised at you, Mr Harrington.' She tucked in her chin in mock surprise. 'Don't they teach history at Marlborough?'

'They tried, but I dozed off sometime between the Wars of the Roses and the Repeal of the Corn Laws. I was more interested in the sciences.'

'That's a lot of history you missed. Anyway, in the seventeenth century,' she began, in the same way she would deliver one of Eddy's lessons, 'the Scots Border Reivers were banished to Ulster as punishment for their raiding farms, cattle stealing and other dastardly deeds. Over the next hundred years or so, one of my ancestors married a Maguire, which makes me a mixture of Scots and Irish.'

'From what little I gleaned from the perpetual drone of my history master, those border raiders had a hard life, with little choice but to steal other people's livestock to survive.'

'A generous view, but not everyone was a victim.' Flora sighed.

'Was your mother never mentioned when you were younger?'

'Once, when I was about twelve, I heard the housekeeper say "that poor Lily Maguire" in a tone that implied something dreadful had happened to her.'

'You never discovered what it was?'

'No.' Flora stared at her lap. 'No one would have satisfied a child's curiosity about something whispered in hallways. I have dreams about her though, all the time. Disjointed, frightening dreams where I know she's hurt and I cannot help her.' She turned to face him. 'I've never told that to a soul before. Not even my father.'

'Has it occurred to you,' he began, jiggling his foot, 'that your obsession with Parnell's death could stem from unresolved questions about your mother?'

'It's not an obsess—'

'No, don't interrupt.' He held up a hand. 'Maybe you look for complicated explanations for straightforward things?'

'I thought we agreed there was more to Parnell's death than a freak accident. What changed your mind?' Flora bridled at the fact he doubted her – again.

'You're avoiding my suggestion about your mother.'

'I'm sorry,' she murmured, not knowing quite what she was apologising for. 'I'm accustomed to pretending whatever happened, didn't.'

'Perhaps you need answers so you can make peace with it. With her. Then perhaps those dreams might stop.'

'Maybe.' Flora frowned, recalling her father's haunted gaze whenever her mother was mentioned. She pressed a finger into the crumbs on her plate and carried it to her mouth, uncomfortable with the conversation but unsure as to how to change it. 'I can't really remember her, apart from one scene that repeats in my dreams like a stage play.'

'Then use it,' Bunny said gently. 'Strip it of the dread and the panic that makes you shy away from that image and remember exactly what you saw.' He leaned closer and picked up the teapot, the view of his exposed neck between his collar and hairline strangely sensuous.

'What, now? This minute?' Her hands shook and she buried them in the folds of her skirt, though not quick enough for Bunny.

'Not if it makes you uncomfortable. Wait until you're alone, and in control.' He poured more tea for both of them. 'What do you intend to do when Eddy no longer needs a governess, even for holidays?'

Flora shrugged. 'I could never see a life beyond Cleeve Abbey.'

'I couldn't imagine leaving Winterbourne, either.' He helped himself to another sandwich. 'I had to face a different sort of life when my father died. Daunting in many ways, yet I'm glad it happened.'

'Glad your father died, or you had to sell the family jewels?'

'The second premise. I took my privileged, sheltered way for granted, living on an income I hadn't earned, but with no real idea of how the world worked. Then I came to realise the society parties, shooting house weekends and the social round I was brought up to think important didn't matter at all. Besides, I meet far more interesting people these days.' He lifted the bar of his glasses with one hand and adjusted them on his nose. 'You, for instance. That's worth missing a hunt ball or two.'

She lifted her teacup to her lips in an effort to hide the blush that threatened. At the same time, she told herself he wasn't making a declaration. For her to read something into his words would confuse him, and she had already revealed too much of herself.

'Where did you grow up?' she asked when she could trust herself to speak.

'In Surrey,' he replied, apparently happy to indulge her. 'A lonely, only child with an absent father who travelled a great deal, and – oh my goodness.' Bunny twisted his wrist, indicating his watch. 'Is that the time? The dinner bugle will go in less than an hour.'

'To be honest, I don't think I can face dinner after all this.' Flora surveyed the array of empty plates on the table in front of them, on which sat smears of cream among a scattering of crumbs. The thought of more food made her feel slightly sick.

'You could be right,' Bunny said, rising, one hand extended to help her up. 'How about I call at your suite in about an hour? We could take a walk on deck to work off all that whipped cream, then have a coffee in the bar later on.'

'As long as you think your friend won't mind.' The second the words were out she regretted them. Warmth crept into her neck, but the only emotion in his face was bewilderment.

'Who?' He guided Flora into the staircase lobby, frowning as if trying to recall whom she meant. Then his face brightened. 'Oh, her. Why on earth should she?'

'No reason.' Flora shrugged.

'She asked to see Matilda, but I seriously doubt she was interested in engines. Halfway through an explanation on horsepower and suspension, she asked if we could sit together inside. I told her she wouldn't be able to see the engine from there, but—'

'Are you making fun of me?' Flora's voice was hard but she couldn't help the broad smile that crept into her face.

'No – well, just a little.'

'What did you say to – um?' She couldn't bring herself to ask the girl's name in case it made her too real.

'Oh, I prattled on about the engine until she got bored and gave up. She stormed off actually. Called me a boorish, insensitive ninny.'

'Instead of which, you are actually a calculating ninny.' She clamped her lips together, trying not to laugh as he hunched both shoulders in a depreciating shrug. 'I'll be ready in an hour.'

On her way back to her suite, Flora scolded herself for having almost spoiled their lovely afternoon with her stupid jealousy.

10

Flora kept Bunny waiting for a full minute before answering his ring at the suite door, gratified to see his start of admiring surprise when he took in her appearance.

They climbed to the tiny bar on the upper promenade deck, where he held out a chair and bade her sit. Conscious of how her neckline dipped in front, Flora adjusted her shawl around her shoulders, aware his gaze lingered on the rhinestone ornament in her hair.

'Have you given any more thought as to what I said earlier about those nightmares you have about your mother?' Bunny asked, lowering himself into the chair beside her.

'I wasn't aware I had discussed my dreams with you in any detail, much less referred to them as nightmares,' she said, bemused by the way he restarted conversations they had left off hours before, yet enjoying the challenge of having to think fast to keep up with him.

'That's true. But I'm a good listener, and I'm observant.' He slanted a sideways look at her, too quick for her to read the emotion behind it. 'Did I exaggerate?'

'No, you didn't.' She glanced away, mildly uneasy. 'Therefore, because I cannot solve the mystery of my own mother's death, you think I turn my attentions to the enigmas of strangers?'

'Something like that.' He offered her a plate of almond biscuits, laughing when she feigned horror at the sight of more food. 'I have an amateur interest in the work of a man named Sigmund Freud who has some interesting theories about how our minds work.'

'The Austrian doctor who hypothesizes the existence of libido?' Flora stifled a giggle when he slopped coffee into the saucer while pouring. 'I do know what the word means.'

'Oh, er, of course, I would never suggest otherwise.' He set down the coffee pot and eased his collar away from his throat with one hand, though his eyes held surprised admiration. 'What a surprising young woman you are, Miss Maguire.'

'I like to think so.' She accepted his compliment along with her coffee cup. 'Lord Vaughn was given a copy of a book, *The Interpretation of Dreams*, which was published last year. Lord Vaughn is a friend of the publisher, who doubts it will sell so the book isn't widely available yet. Anyway, my father has read it and, in his opinion, Freud's ideas are thin excuses for unhealthy sexual practices amongst relatives.'

'Your father discussed his ideas with you?' Bunny's eyebrows appeared to have taken up permanent residence halfway up his forehead.

'Of course. He's quite a reactionary. Though I haven't yet convinced him to approve of my joining a suffragette club.'

'And, um – what do you think?' Bunny cleared his throat nosily. 'About Freud I mean, not the suffrage movement.'

'I'm not convinced.' She decided to stop teasing him, though his discomfort delighted her. 'He ascribes most female ailments to hysteria, no matter what the symptoms. I doubt his male patients receive such casual dismissal.'

'Hmm, I shall have to examine his theories in more detail. However, I do believe talking through your dreams might help you.'

'My mother's death isn't a problem, only the circumstances. I believe she was attacked by someone.'

'Then you must ask your father what happened, or risk never being at peace with the past.'

'You don't know my father. I doubt he would give me a straight answer. Instead, he'll prevaricate until I give up.'

'Give him some credit, Flora. You're an adult now. Maybe he's been waiting for you to ask.'

'Possibly,' Flora said, still uneasy with the conversation, relieved when the door opened to let in a stream of passengers, laughing and chattering as they spread into the room.

Gerald and Monica arrived first, followed closely by Max and Eloise, then Mrs Penry-Jones, who accepted a chair from Max with a condescension that would have shamed Lady Catherine de Bourgh. The lack of seating in the small bar on the upper deck necessitated a reorganization of chairs, which the men allocated to the ladies, leaving the gentlemen to perch on stools. The activity gave Flora time to count heads, noting everyone from their table was present apart from Cynthia and Mr Hersch.

Max's head bent close to Eloise as they talked, her hand straying occasionally to caress his arm. Mrs Penry-Jones glared at them with eagle-like intensity from her chair opposite, matched only by Hester's sulky glare. Max glanced up and caught the old lady's eye, gave a self-conscious start, and slid his arm from beneath Eloise's grasp. He cleared his throat noisily and leaned backwards, putting another foot of space between them.

'What did I say about honeymooners?' Bunny nodded at a disconcerted Max. 'Poor chap cannot talk to another lady without everyone passing judgement.' He tapped Flora's arm. 'Here's the blushing bride now. Let's see if she notices.'

'Of course she'll notice,' Flora said. 'If you think otherwise, you don't know women very well.'

Cynthia paused on the threshold, her gaze roaming the room until it alighted on Max, then switched to Eloise with such malice, Flora could almost feel the heat.

'Ah, I see you are quite right.' Bunny coughed and looked away as Max muttered something to his companion, then rose to greet his wife, leaving Eloise isolated but undaunted at her table until Gus Crowe sidled into the vacated seat uninvited.

Flora had made several calls at Eloise's stateroom during the day, all of which had gone unanswered. On the rare occasions she had seen her on deck, she always contrived to disappear into the crowd before reaching her.

'I must have dropped my tiepin somewhere.' Max rummaged through his pockets before taking his seat 'The catch is loose, so it's probably my own fault.'

'Is it valuable?' Miss Ames asked, her jaunty walk across the room to join them sent the pink bows she had attached to her upswept hair bobbing like butterflies.

'I suppose so, it's set with a rather exquisite diamond.' Max turned to where Gerald scoured the floor around the table.

'It's not there, old boy. Take my word for it. I'll ask the barman to keep a lookout.'

'Don't fuss so, Max. It's only jewellery.' Cynthia waved an unconcerned hand in his direction 'At least, that's what you're always telling me.' She exchanged a knowing look with Monica, who rolled her eyes in silent sympathy.

Once settled, Max ordered coffee and drinks for everyone, while Gerald's insistence he share the tab was garrulously declined, as was Bunny's offer to cover the next round.

Flora tried to catch Eloise's eye, but after several attempts, Eloise shifted her chair so her shoulder was turned in Flora's direction.

'I knew it!' Flora's sharp nudge dislodged Bunny's elbow from his chair arm. 'She *is* avoiding me.'

'Maybe she's embarrassed about that evening?' Bunny suggested.

'I doubt that. Eloise isn't easily embarrassed,' Flora said, ignoring his oblique criticism. 'She won't escape me that easily.' Eloise's parting words when Flora had left her stateroom stayed with her. That she wasn't going to be accused of murder – again.

Gus Crowe glanced up and saw Flora looking at him. She looked away but not quick enough to miss his inclined head and reptilian smile that didn't reach his eyes.

Flora wrinkled her nose in distaste and was about to make a disparaging remark about him to Bunny, but he was deep in conversation with someone at the next table.

'He knows Frederick Lanchester, the inventor of the disc brake.' Bunny broke off to inform the others, including Flora in his enthusiasm. 'The man who invented the electric starter.'

She adopted a suitably enraptured expression, though he might have been speaking a foreign language for all she understood. Instead, she listened to one of Monica's anecdotes about the four-year-old twin daughters they had left at home. It seemed Gerald had refused point blank to let 'Monica's darlings' accompany them on their trip, with the excuse they were too young to appreciate it, let alone behave in a civilised manner. Monica ended her charming story – though one which would only appeal to other doting mothers – with an ostentatious dab at her dry cheeks with a lace handkerchief.

'No waterworks tonight, please.' Gerald grimaced. 'We'll be back with the little harridans within the week. Then you'll complain you never get a moment to yourself, despite having a house full of servants.'

'I don't expect a mere man to understand a woman's maternal feelings.' Monica threw him a glare cold enough to freeze lava. '

'Have you any children, Mrs Penry-Jones?' Miss Ames asked, distracting attention from the Gilmores' burgeoning spat.

The old lady's sharp gaze flicked to her questioner over a pair of rectangular pince-nez. 'I had a son, once.'

Flora waited for more, but no further explanation was forthcoming.

'How sad,' Miss Ames also seemed eager to hear more. 'Though nature tends to soften the blow with time, don't you find?'

'I do not.' Mrs Penry-Jones sniffed. 'Nor should one comment on another's misfortunes unless acquainted with the circumstances.' She rose unsteadily to her feet, setting the stool behind her into a precarious wobble. 'It's quite stuffy in here and too crowded. I think I'll retire.'

Hester scrambled to her feet, stopped in her tracks by her employer's long-suffering sigh.

'Really, girl, I wish you wouldn't bob up and down whenever I move. I'm quite capable of returning to the suite alone. I shan't require you until the morning.' Manoeuvring with her stick, she caught an arriving passenger on the shin, and almost tripped the steward who sprang forwards to assist her.

'Oh, dear, I seem to have upset her.' Miss Ames said once the door flapped shut on the old lady. She dropped two cubes of sugar into her coffee with a shrug. 'Funny old thing.'

'Mrs Penry-Jones is rather too fond of grand exits,' Gerald quipped, earning him a glare from Monica.

'It's still a shame about her son.' Flora turned an enquiring look on Miss Smith that she hoped would invite gossip, but Hester's attention remained squarely focused on her tiny glass of brandy.

'Perhaps her pain is too raw to speak about.' Cynthia pinned Hester with a look filled with dislike, which Hester appeared not to notice. Instead, she turned a flirtatious look on Mr Crowe, which did not sit right on her plain features. If she was trying to make him think she was attracted to him, it was a poor show.

'You promised me a game of poker,' she called to him across the room. 'I'm free now if you have the time?'

Nodding to Eloise, who was busy chatting to a gentleman to her left, Crowe sidled over to their table. 'Always happy to oblige.' He delved into a pocket and withdrew a pack of cards.

'The first rule of gambling for money, Miss Smith,' Mr Hersch's round tones with its hint of an accent interrupted their conversation, 'is never trust a man who uses his own cards.'

Flora's head jerked up in surprise, for she had not noticed him arrive. Her gaze slid to the brown envelope he tucked hurriedly into an inside pocket of his jacket.

'My advice,' the German continued, taking the chair vacated by Mrs Penry-Jones, 'would be to ensure the pack is unsealed in front of you.'

'Are you accusing me of underhand dealings?' Crowe's handsome but sly features suffused with colour.

'Not at all,' Hersch said, unruffled. 'Though I doubt the lady is in your league.'

'I'm not quite such a novice as you might think, Mr Hersch,' Hester said, her eyes narrowed.

'If you intend to make a game of it, Crowe, I'll join you for a hand or two,' Gerald said.

Crowe rubbed his hands together and gestured to Eloise his intention to move to a table that had become vacant moments before. Gerald offered Hester his arm, and the pair joined him, both emptying their pockets of change onto the table.

Monica threw her husband a long-suffering look, before she continued her conversation with Miss Ames.

'Do you mind, Cyn?' Max pleaded, flicking glances at the card game.

'Of course not, darling,' Cynthia gushed, although her smile did not reach her eyes.

Flora's gaze slid again to Eloise, who hunched over her untouched glass as she ran her pendant absently along the gold chain round her neck. Then she snatched her bag from the table and rose, shouldering her way through the crowd round the bar without a word to anyone.

'Excuse me. I won't be a moment,' Flora whispered to Bunny before hurrying after her.

11

Flora entered the lobby in time to see the door to the ladies' powder room swing shut on Eloise. Following her inside, she stepped into a subdued haven of pink and gold, where elaborate gilt mirrors graced the walls. Intricate crystal bottles containing perfume, lotions and fragrant soaps had been piled into porcelain dishes, along with piles of fluffy towels set at intervals along a marble-topped counter that ran beneath the mirrors. Apart from a uniformed attendant in a corner who sat reading a book, Eloise was the only occupant. She stood before a wide mirror, her chin jutted forward as she applied an unnecessary coat of lipstick.

'Oh, hello, Flora,' she said as if surprised to see her, before continuing what she was doing. 'Where have you been hiding?'

'I'm not the one who's been hiding.' Flora slapped her velvet clutch bag onto the counter. 'You've been avoiding me.'

Eloise pouted, her hand which held the lipstick halted in mid-air. 'I thought you and your young man preferred some privacy to get to know one another.' She turned back to the mirror, smoothing her lower lip with a finger.

'He isn't my young man. Bunny's simply been very kind to me since—'

'Kind? You shouldn't be so modest.' Eloise returned the lipstick to her bag, withdrew a tiny sheet of oiled paper and applied it to her lips. 'The pair of you have been inseparable since we left New York.'

Flora's immediate rush of pleasure dissolved as common sense reasserted itself. 'I think he's attentive to any woman he meets. He's been brought up that way.' At the same time, the idea of Bunny as her beau appealed.

'Ah know infatuation when ah see it.' Eloise pouted at her reflection. 'Those delicious glasses are quite appealing, don't you find?'

Flora pushed away from the wall and stepped closer. 'I would rather know about your young man, not speculate on mine.'

Eloise's eyes darkened for half a second before she gave a decisive shake of her head.

'I don't have one. My career is too important to me. Besides, what man would be willing to traipse round the theatres of the world after his wife?'

'Who said anything about a wife?' Flora said, triumphant when Eloise's face paled.

'Don't you find these electric lights unflattering?' Eloise's gaze flicked to the attendant in a silent plea for discretion. 'Too stark for me, but then I suppose it's cleaner than gaslight. All that sticky soot ruins everything.'

The attendant took the unspoken cue and disappeared through a door marked 'Private'.

'Now, will you kindly tell me what this is all about?' Eloise demanded.

'The night we searched Mr Parnell's cabin, I found a photograph in his shirt drawer.'

'Really? What sort of photograph?' Eloise plucked a bottle of perfume from the counter. Her voice remained casual, but as she removed the stopper her hand shook.

'One with you in it.'

Eloise's chin jerked up and her lips parted.

'Your hair is darker,' Flora went on before she could contradict her. 'And your make-up more elaborate, but I'm right, aren't I? It was a wedding portrait.'

Eloise gave a dismayed cry and the bottle slipped from her hand, spilling perfume onto the counter. A cloying smell of roses filled the air and she lowered the bottle to the vanity with a clunk; miraculously it stayed intact.

'I suppose you think you've been very clever.' Her face drained of expression, and she gave an awkward shrug. 'I was married once, what of it?'

'Then you won't mind if I tell Mr Hersch where to find that photograph?'

'Why would you tell *him* anything?' Confusion clouded her features. 'What's that German got to do with it?'

'He's been asking questions about Mr Parnell. He and the captain.' Flora pushed her advantage, 'They aren't happy about how he died.'

'What?' A sharp movement of Eloise's hand sent her open evening bag onto the floor. A circle of gold rolled along the carpet and came to rest beside Flora's shoe.

Flora bent and retrieved what she saw was a thick gold bracelet.

'Give that to me!' Eloise plucked the bracelet from Flora's fingers, too late to prevent her having read the inscription engraved on the inside.

To E on our Wedding Day, T.

'I'd forgotten about this.' Eloise rolled it in her fingers. 'I should have thrown the thing overboard when—' she broke off on a ragged breath. 'Do you trust me, Flora?'

'That's a big thing to ask after all the lies you've told me.'

'I *am* asking.' Eloise's bravado drained away, leaving her white and trembling.

'Then I was right.' A flush of triumph widened her smile. 'It *is* you in the photograph with the man who gave you that.' She indicated the bangle. 'What are you afraid of? Mr Parnell is dead, he can't show it to anyone.'

'It's complicated. And now that German is asking questions, you say?'

'He is, mostly about Mr Parnell's death.' Eloise's fear still seemed out of place. Or was Flora being naïve? 'He hasn't asked about any money if that's what's worrying you.'

'It isn't that.' Eloise's delicate features crumpled. 'It wasn't meant to be like this. If he sees that photograph the game will be up. I have to get it.' Desperation burned in her eyes, she opened and shut the clasp with rapid clicks until Flora itched to snatch it away.

'Mr Hersch is only trying to discover who killed your friend. There's nothing sinister in his questions.'

'Frank wasn't a friend.' Eloise snorted. 'I hadn't even met him until after Theo died. He turned up at a café across from our apartment block one morning when I was upset and scared. He was sympathetic, or he pretended to be.' She retrieved her bag, jammed the bracelet back inside and snapped the metal catch shut. 'Parnell most probably wasn't his real name.'

'You can trust me. Tell me what happened.'

'Theo was quite a bit older than me. We eloped, which shocked everyone, but that didn't matter to us.' Her breath caught. 'We were meant to be together. Then quite suddenly, he... he died.'

'Oh, I'm so sorry, that must have been awful for you.' Flora instantly regretted her harshness.

'It was.' Eloise shuddered. 'The worst part was when the gossip began, implying that I had something to do with it.'

'With his death, you mean?' At Eloise's nod, she went on, 'Did the police think you were involved?' *So that was what she meant by 'not again'...*

'If they did, they never indicated as much to me.' Eloise twisted the bag in her hands. 'Although others weren't so unforgiving. Then the letters started.'

'What letters?'

'I received two letters from a lawyer.' Eloise swallowed. 'The first saying that Theo's family were challenging his estate. He hadn't made a new will after our wedding, you see, so by law everything came to me. The second one said they were unhappy with the coroner's verdict of death by natural causes. They were going to have him exhumed and his death investigated. They said I would probably be prosecuted for killin' him.' Her face crumpled and she released a sob. 'As if losing Theo wasn't bad enough, they wanted the world to think I had murdered him. That's when I panicked, emptied Theo's safe and booked passage on this ship.'

'But if you hadn't done anything, you would have been exonerated.'

'Don't be naïve, Flora. They're rich, and I'm, well I'm an actress.'

'Couldn't you reason with his family?'

'I've never met them, and didn't want to once the correspondence began. They wouldn't want to hear what I had to say. They'd made up their minds I was after Theo's money.'

'You told Parnell what you planned?'

Eloise nodded. 'That was my first mistake. He told me he could get me a part in *School for Scandal* in London, and would come to England with me. It was the perfect way out, so I jumped at it.'

'Sounds a bit contrived to me,' Flora said.

'I see that – now.' She braced both hands on the counter, her face inches from the mirror. 'He pretended to be my friend, then that first night on board he was so different.' She stared into the glass as if she didn't recognise herself. Was she imagining what she used to look like without the flat black hair and heavy make-up?

'What changed?' Flora asked gently.

'Money, I imagine.' She plucked a linen square from a pile on the counter and dabbed at each eye, careful not to smudge the heavy make-up. 'Isn't it always?'

'Mr Parnell demanded money from you, or he would have you arrested.'

That was what their argument had been about on the first night.

'Frank claimed he had evidence I had done it.' Her head jerked up and held Flora's gaze in the reflection. 'I would never have hurt Theo."

'What sort of evidence?' Flora eyed the door marked 'Private', hoping the attendant wouldn't return too soon.

'He wouldn't say, but promised to destroy it if I paid him.'

Flora rolled her eyes, knowing Eloise would never have been free of such a man, no matter how much money she gave him. 'Where does Mr Hersch come into this? Why are you afraid of him?'

'I'm not sure. I assume he's either working for the lawyer who sent me those letters, or the police. That photograph is the only thing that can link me to Theo now Frank is dead. I can disappear in London, but whilst I'm on this ship, the German could still cause trouble for me. I—I promise I'll tell you everything, if you just help me get that photograph.'

Flora suspected Mr Hersch already knew Eloise's real identity, but kept silent so as not to distress her more than she was already.

'All right.' Flora's anger had turned to exasperated sympathy. 'But we can't try and get the photograph tonight. Everyone will be returning to their staterooms about now. There's also the possibility someone had noticed we didn't lock his stateroom door when we left either.'

'I had forgotten about that!' Eloise clenched her fists at her sides. 'We were in something of a hurry to leave, if I recall. Perhaps no one has noticed. How about we try tomorrow, before breakfast?' She stepped closer, the gold flecks in her eyes clearly visible. 'Now, where exactly did you see that photograph?'

* * *

'You've been gone a while,' Bunny observed when Flora returned to the bar with Eloise.

Before Flora could think up an excuse, Eloise interrupted, 'Little accident in the powder room with some perfume. Flora was kind enough to help me.'

'I wondered what that delicious scent was.' Gus Crowe slid between them, his oily smile in place. 'I thought you had abandoned me.'

'Your poker game didn't last long, Mr Crowe.' Flora looked to where Gerald, Max and Hester still played.

'The stakes got a little rich, even for me.'

'Would you be a prince, Gus, and buy me a brandy?' Eloise pouted and ran a finger along his jaw.

Crowe's lascivious smile disappeared and his face suffused with a look of raw panic.

'Worry not, Crowe,' Gerald said from the table behind them, evidently having overheard. 'We're Max's guests this evening, all drinks are gratis.'

'In that case.' Crowe whispered something to Eloise which made her giggle, then arm-in-arm the pair headed for the bar.

'Will Eloise never learn when it comes to men?' Flora murmured, nodding her thanks to the waiter who slid a fresh cup of hot coffee in front of her. While she pondered on the mystery of what attracted one person to another, a shadow fell across her lap. She glanced up to where Mr Hersch bent over them.

'Might I buy you both a drink?' He dragged a stool forwards and strad-dled it.

'Oh, er, most kind of you,' Bunny said. 'But I think Max has—'

'Please, I would rather,' Hersch cut across him and summoned a waiter.

'I'm quite happy with my coffee, thank you,' Flora said.

'I'll have another brandy, provided you make it a small one,' Bunny said.

'I see you are busy forming interesting alliances, Miss Maguire.' Hersch glanced at Eloise and Crowe, just as Mr Crowe grabbed a large handful of cigarettes from a box on the bar and rammed them into his pocket. Eloise had turned her gaze on Mr Hersch's profile with such intensity, Flora wondered he didn't feel it. Eloise made a moue of distaste and twisted in her seat, removing Hersch from her line of vision.

'I was wondering if you had learned any more since our discussion, Miss Maguire?' Hersch brought Flora's attention back to him.

'Not really,' Flora lied, busying herself with her coffee cup.

'I have a question for you, sir.' Bunny lowered his voice so even Flora barely heard him. 'If no one on this ship knew Parnell, who could have a reason to kill him?'

Hersch tugged at his left earlobe, before answering. 'I'm confident someone else, apart from Miss Lane was acquainted with Mr Parnell before this voyage.'

'Is one of them Mr Gilmore, by any chance?' Bunny threw Flora an apologetic glance, adding, 'Something which occurred on that first night has been troubling me.' He pushed his glasses up his nose before continu-ing. 'Although it might not be relevant—'

The low chatter around them was interrupted by a gale of harsh laughter from Crowe, followed by Eloise's girlish giggle as the pair availed themselves of Max's generosity.

Flora's glance strayed to the brash man who literally rubbed shoulders with the simpering girl, the source of their common interest still a mystery.

'Go on, Mr Harrington.' Hersch brought Flora's attention back to their conversation.

'Gilmore said something to Parnell at dinner,' Bunny said. 'I didn't hear what it was, but Parnell turned white. He went really still, as if he had received an unexpected shock.'

'You mentioned that to me before,' Flora said slowly, 'though you didn't put it quite like that.'

'No, well. I didn't want to cast aspersions.' He touched the bridge of his glasses with a finger. 'It wasn't anything to do with me either, but since then—'

'Yes, I understand.' Hersch slowly stroked his moustache. 'Did Mr Parnell respond to whatever was said?'

'The dining room was noisy and I had young Eddy at my side chattering away, so I didn't hear what they said.' Bunny shrugged an apology. 'Parnell then went red in the face, an aggressive red rather than embarrassment I thought.'

'And Mr Gilmore?' Hersch took a sip of his brandy, his expression neutral as if the subject was only of mild interest to him.

'He brushed it aside with "Sorry, I got it wrong" sort of things. It can't have been that important as they both joined the card game later on. Parnell was the sort who seemed to annoy people easily. He even managed to upset Mrs Penry-Jones' companion that night too.'

'Hester?' Flora interjected, unable to stop herself. 'You saw them together?'

'Well, not in a romantic way. It was nothing really, just a minor altercation outside the reading room.'

'Even so,' Mr Hersch looked from Bunny to Flora and back again. 'Anything you saw could be important. A killer is loose on this ship don't forget.'

'Yes, yes I see that. I didn't see much.' Bunny frowned as if trying to remember. 'Parnell had his back to me and Hester looked cross. They were hunched in a corner, so I doubt they even saw me. Then the lobby began to get busy and they went off in different directions.'

'It doesn't sound much,' Flora said, disappointed. 'He could have trodden on her toe or something.'

'That's why I didn't mention it.' Bunny split a look between them. 'I take it Miss Smith has an alibi?'

'In fact, she does.' Hersch swirled the remaining brandy in his glass. 'Quite a strong one.'

'There you are then,' Bunny said, defensive. 'It didn't occur to me that Hester being annoyed might mean anything.'

'Hester is always annoyed.' Flora sniffed, glancing to where the subject of their conversation sat with Miss Ames, both sipping delicately at tiny glasses of some brown concoction. 'Like Cynthia Cavendish was annoyed with Parnell when I saw them together?'

Hersch's eyes narrowed. 'You didn't mention that to me, Miss Maguire.'

Flora groaned inwardly. 'It was the day we boarded, and well, Cynthia dismissed it when I broached the subject. Said he had collided with her and she gave him a set down. Then he was found dead so I forgot about it.' *Sort of.*

'I see.' His unblinking gaze made her squirm. 'Thus, within hours of boarding, Parnell had angered three ladies of different ages, social classes and marital status?'

'Doesn't sound as if the man was very popular with women,' Bunny said.

'Indeed not,' Hersch mused, mostly to himself.

'Are you going to tell us where *you* were before breakfast on Sunday morning, Mr Hersch?' Flora asked, emboldened by Bunny's reassuring presence.

'Good point,' Bunny said, folding his arms.

Hersch split a smile between them as he took a sip of his brandy. Flora thought he wasn't going to answer for a moment, then he gave a tiny nod, drained his glass and placed it on the table in front of him. 'I summoned the purser at six thirty with a request to lodge some papers in the ship's safe. He obliged, though I doubt he was very happy about it.'

'I don't suppose you'll tell us what sort of papers?' Flora asked.

'You assume correctly, young lady. I was with the purser in his office when a crewman arrived, saying Parnell had been found dead. That was at a little after seven o'clock. Now, I'll take my leave of you both.' He rose from his stool with the economic grace of a man used to a lifetime of physical activity. No groans of effort, nor the easing of stiff joints, though he must have been at least sixty. 'Goodnight, Miss Maguire, Mr Harrington.

Might I ask that if either of you discover anything else of interest pertaining to this matter, that you let me know?'

'I–I suppose so,' Flora replied, while Bunny murmured an assent.

She followed the German's progress through the double glass doors onto the deck, uncertain why he would make such a request. He paused at the rail and withdrew a cigar from his inside pocket which he fingered as he stared out to sea.

'I wish I knew why Mr Hersch is so interested in who might have wanted Parnell dead.'

'He could well say the same thing about you.' He leaned closer, his breath warm on her cheek. 'There are usually only three reasons for murder. Money, love, jealousy, or to hide another crime.'

'That's four.' Flora's gaze went back to the panoramic window, where Hersch stood talking to another passenger at the rail, a cloud of smoke hovering between them.

'Have you noticed he always manages to obtain more information than he gives away?' Bunny said, following her gaze.

'Why summon a purser so early in the morning? It's a bit unusual, don't you think?' Flora said.

'Not really.' Bunny appeared to give the matter some thought. 'Hersch strikes me as a man who wouldn't hesitate to drag a minion from his bed to do his bidding.'

'In which case, maybe Parnell did the same and lodged the money Eloise gave him in the safe after all?'

'Only the purser or the captain are in a position to know that, and I doubt they'll tell us. What about Gerald?' He nodded to where Gerald sat with Max and Hester. They had recruited a fourth player to take Crowe's place, with piles of silver at each place.

'Had you paid more attention to what Gerald said to Parnell that night, it might have told us something,' Flora answered.

'Sorry, but I'm no good at eavesdropping.' His brow lifted. 'Are you?'

Flora chose not to answer him. Then an image of something that occurred earlier returned. 'Of course. It was a telegram!'

'What was?'

'The envelope Mr Hersch put into his pocket earlier. He had received a telegram.' *But from whom? Was Eloise's suspicion correct and he did indeed work for her late husband's lawyers? Had he informed them that Eloise was involved in another death?*

'Good luck persuading him to tell you,' Bunny said. 'Although I can't see Gerald killing Parnell, even if he didn't think much of him.'

'It doesn't make sense he would do so on the first night of a voyage either. Not when he will be trapped for over a week.' Flora stiffened. 'Perhaps it was an accident?'

'Haven't you been working to prove it *wasn't* an accident?' Bunny gave a dismissive snort.

'No. I mean Parnell wasn't supposed to die. The fact he did has made things complicated for whoever did it. He's panicking. Which could have been why he threatened me. He isn't sure who knows what and is trying to cover his tracks.'

'Which rules out Gerald, he's cleverer than that.'

Flora couldn't help but agree. Perhaps because she liked Gerald. The man obviously adored his son and he had been especially kind to Eddy too. Yet on the other hand, she didn't like the way he talked to his wife. Monica might be abrasive and over-emotional at times, but she didn't deserve the cruel edge of his tongue. Especially not in public. 'I cannot help wondering who our German friend is working for,' she added.

'What makes you think he's working for anyone?'

'Something Eloise said, but she's scared and may have twisted things.'

'It seems Hersch has persuaded you that everyone's word is suspect in this affair but his own.'

Flora's coffee cup froze on its way to her mouth. 'Are you saying I'm wrong to trust him?'

'Not that exactly. But it could be exactly what he wants.'

Her stomach did a sickening lurch. Had she accepted everything Mr Hersch had told her too readily? It was possible. After all, what better way to distract her than appearing to be as eager as she to discover the truth? Then again, it wasn't Hersch who had growled at her outside the dining room. Or was it?

'Flora,' Bunny spoke her name in the slow, contemplative way he did when putting a thought together, his arm draped across the back of her chair inches from her shoulder. 'Why did Hersch ask us to bring information to him? Why not the captain?'

'I don't know.' Flora frowned. 'He told me he had examined the body as well.'

'Really?' Bunny shifted his glasses slightly on his nose. 'Why did he do that? And more interestingly, why did Captain Gates allow it?'

12

WEDNESDAY

The next morning, Flora woke to dramatically changed weather where a
low leaden sky smothered the sun. A malevolent wind howled around the
ship as if seeking a way in, while the deck rose and fell, taking Flora's
stomach with it. Her ablutions took longer than usual, with one foot
braced against the basin to steady herself as bottles on the shelf above the
sink slid to one side, then changed direction without warning and threatened to topple onto the floor.

Four days of unsteady floors and flat horizons had made her long for
the familiar smells of grass, earth, even manure. The clop of horses'
hooves and the swish of tree branches in the wind were preferable to the
stark loneliness in the creak of bulwarks, or the wind's mournful howl as it
sang through the winch lines.

Struggling into her corset, it occurred to Flora that if she ate any more
cream cakes, she would be pounds heavier by the time they reached
England. However, the thought of breakfast made her mouth water, so she
decided abstemiousness could wait.

In the sitting room, Eddy greeted her with raised eyebrows and an
exaggerated study of his wristwatch.

'I know I'm late,' Flora forestalled what she assumed was a cryptic
remark. 'I didn't sleep particularly well.' Images of being caught in

Parnell's cabin had plagued her sleep, making the night less than restful. The deck did a sharp dip sideways, sloshing Eddy's tea onto the carpet. 'Maybe we're in for a real storm.'

'I do hope not.' Flora righted herself again, her gaze going to the fine spray that battered the windows, then back to the tray at Eddy's elbow. 'And you'll have no room for breakfast if you eat all those biscuits.'

'Can't help it.' He grinned. 'This sea air makes me ravenous. I'd better not be late either, or Ozzy will snaffle all the sausages.'

'Be careful, Eddy,' Flora called after him, debating whether she should accompany him.

'Be careful of what? A bit of wind?' He snatched his jacket from a chair and made for the door.

Flora hesitated, unwilling to tell him what was really worrying her. 'The deck will be slippery, make sure you hold onto something.'

'Don't fuss, Flora. I know my way round this ship quite well now.' He beamed at her seconds before the door banged shut behind him.

Almost immediately, a muffled knock announced the arrival of Eloise.

'I thought that boy would never leave.' She stomped inside the room without an invitation, a shawl wrapped tight round her shoulders. 'It's freezing out there. Are you ready?'

'I suppose so.' Flora tied a scarf round her head and followed Eloise into a salt-tinged wind that plastered her skirt to her legs.

Her second foray into burglary proved a lot less stressful than her first, in that all she was required to do was to pace the covered deck outside Parnell's stateroom while Eloise made her search. Guilt made her feel conspicuous, but was offered no more than a polite, 'good morning,' or a casually delivered, 'blustery weather, isn't it?' from tightly muffled passengers who hurried past on their way to the dining room.

'Did you find it?' Flora demanded when Eloise finally emerged.

'It's not there!' She grabbed Flora's arm and dragged her the furthest point beneath the canopy away from the worst of the wind.

'You must have!' Flora hissed. 'I didn't lie to you. It was there.'

'Did I say you had?' Eloise snapped. 'Frank's stateroom has been emptied since we were last there. His clothes are all gone.'

'What are you going to do?' Flora asked.

'There's nothing I *can* do, but hope no one challenges me before we reach London.' She glanced past Flora's shoulder, gripping her upper arm in warning.

Flora turned her head to where Bunny approached more slowly than normal. He kept close to the suite doors, his shoulders hunched against the wind.

'My, you look handsome today, Mr Harrington,' Eloise greeted him as he drew level, and peered up at him through her sweeping lashes. 'But then you always do.'

Had Bunny not flushed a deep red, Flora might have been jealous. How had such an attractive man not learned to handle compliments with grace, even contrived ones?

'Good morning, Miss Lane, Flora.' He pushed his glasses further up his nose with a middle finger. 'I came to see if you were up to breakfast in this rough weather. Not everyone takes it in their stride.' As he spoke, a gentleman rushed past them, a handkerchief clutched to his mouth.

Eloise backed away. 'I don't mind the wind, but the food on this ship is too rich for my girlish figure, so I'll make do with coffee in my stateroom.'

'Eloise!' Flora aimed a pointed glare in her direction, but with a brief wave through the gap in her door, she closed it on Flora's protests.

'Did I interrupt something?' Bunny asked.

'It doesn't matter,' Flora said through gritted teeth. She slipped her arm through his and drew him in the direction of the dining room. 'I'll catch up with her later.'

* * *

'Are you sure you want to sit out here?' Flora asked Bunny for the third time since he had suggested the idea over breakfast.

With a firm hand in the small of her back, he guided her onto the saloon deck, where passengers scurried past them, their backs to the bulwarks to avoid being showered with salt spray from a choppy sea.

'Why not? Look, the Gilmores are game.' He nodded to where Monica and Gerald occupied steamer chairs set in the shelter of the main superstructure. 'Hersch and Gus Crowe are here too. C'mon, Flora, you can't back out now.'

'All right,' Flora muttered, grabbing onto a winch line, the metal slick sharply cold beneath her fingers. 'But I warn you, if it gets too bad, I'm going back in.' She flopped into her steamer chair with bad grace, wishing she had remained in her suite.

A door banged behind them, announcing the arrival of Max, his arm round Cynthia's waist as they slowly edged towards the line of steamer chairs, wrapped from head to toe in a beige fur coat with a matching hat that could never have been mistaken for anything but real fur.

'How did I let you talk me into this, Max?' Cynthia tottered across the slick deck, giving small shrieks as the odd wave landed on the edge of the deck.

'Rubbish!' Max wrapped his overcoat tighter round himself. 'It's no worse than a walk on Brighton beach in November. Character-building.'

Cynthia didn't look convinced, her cheekbones highlighted with angry colour as she took the chair Max had dragged into line for her.

In a calf-length mink coat which might have conceivably survived the early half of the last century, Miss Ames bustled to join them, her arms splayed to keep her balance. At the end of the row, Mr Hersch resembled an amiable polar bear in his white fur coat that reached to the floor, a matching hat pulled down over his ears.

Eloise ignored the steamer chairs, and braving the wind she stood at the rail, her head thrown back and her long jacket flaps spread behind her like wings. She laughed at the waves that sent a shower of salt spray over her, calling encouragement to others to join her, though no one did. Flora watched her, bemused at her change of mood. She had been frantic to get that photograph back, but now she seemed unconcerned at the thought someone else might have got there before her.

Or had she had lied about finding it after all, and didn't want Flora to know?

She shook her ungracious thoughts away, reluctant to believe Eloise had deceived her – again.

'This Atlantic air is certainly exhilarating.' Mr Hersch pulled his fur hat down to his eyebrows, a scarf covering the lower part of his face leaving only his eyes visible.

Gus Crowe huddled on the chair beside him, shivering in his raincoat and thin trousers.

Taking pity on him, Flora handed him the spare blanket from beneath her chair.

'Thanks, awfully.' Like a small boy offered a treat, he grabbed it to his chest as if it were a lifebelt. 'Ankles getting a bit chilled, what?'

A steward staggered along the line of chairs, a tureen of hot bouillon balanced precariously on a tray. He paused in front of Bunny, one foot hooked round the metal support to prevent him sliding across the deck, and expertly poured the flurry of orders thrown his way.

Bunny scraped his chair closer to Flora's with a screech of wood, handed her a full cup from the tray and took one for himself. Accepting it gratefully, she held it briefly below her chin, allowing the savoury-smelling steam to warm her face. The steward moved on and served Monica, whose chocolate-coloured fur coat boasted a fur-lined hood in a lighter colour which made Flora envious. Her own wool coat was heavy, but uncomfortable when wet, so she hoped the sea wouldn't get any rougher. Even Bunny was wrapped in a sheepskin coat with a wide fur collar and matching trim along the edges. Her gaze swept the line of chairs, and the thought occurred to her that with so many pelts on display, they might have had raided a zoo.

'Now tell me,' Bunny said from the chair which still bore Eddy's name. 'Why do you keep staring at Eloise? Has she annoyed you again?'

'She's such an enigma, I wish I knew what she was thinking. One minute she's terrified and the next she doesn't have a care.'

'Excuse me, I'm going to get my fur muff,' Monica said, squeezing between their chairs. 'These gloves aren't warm enough,' she explained, though Flora hadn't asked. 'Won't be a moment.' With a firm grip on her hood, she headed back to her suite, her head bent into the wind.'

'Go on, you were saying,' Bunny prompted when she had gone.

'Eloise told me she was married, but that her husband died.'

'Really?' His reaction was satisfyingly astonished. 'She just came out with it?'

'Not at first. She dropped a bracelet and when I saw the inscription, she explained. Well part of it. I got the impression they hadn't been married long, but I don't know the details.'

'Flora,' Bunny lowered his voice in warning, 'don't you think you're taking this investigation business too far? We all have something we don't wish to world to know. If all Eloise has to hide is a photograph and a bracelet, she's doing better than most.'

'Eloise said Parnell blackmailed her into giving him the money.' She chose not to mention their second foray into Parnell's cabin, unwilling to have that conversation again.

'Money that hasn't been found,' Bunny reminded her.

'Granted, but she gave it to him because Parnell claimed to have evidence that Eloise had killed her husband.'

'Did she? Kill him, I mean?'

'Parnell or her husband?'

'Both. Either. Goodness, Flora, are you saying Eloise murdered Parnell to stop him revealing she had killed her own husband?'

'I don't know what I'm saying. She promised to explain everything, but now she's avoiding me again,' Flora muttered into her bouillon. 'I could help her if she was honest with me. I wouldn't judge her.'

'If you insist on sympathising with suspects, you'll never be a detective,' Bunny said, his low chuckle making her insides melt, just as a sound to her right brought her attention to where Gerald glared angrily at Gus Crowe across Monica's still empty chair, his cheeks and nosed flushed an enraged red. 'What exactly do you mean by that?'

'I thought Parnell was a friend of yours, that's all I said. If I was wrong, I apologise. No need to get tetchy.' Crowe's smirk revealed more triumph than apology.

'If your intention is to get me into strife with the captain, Crowe, you're out of luck,' Gerald snapped. 'Parnell and I met once. It was years ago and under unfortunate circumstances. I hardly recognised the man and he used a different name.'

'What business did you say you're in, Gilmore?' Gus Crowe's hooded eyes were like slits, as if he knew something no one else did.

'I didn't.' Gerald's mouth curved into a superior sneer, and he tossed back the contents of his bouillon cup in one swallow.

'What's that dear?' Monica returned, apparently having heard the tail end of their conversation. She eased back into her steamer chair, the muff perched on her lap like a sleeping cat. 'He's in shipping now, aren't you, dear? He stopped dealing in property after that awful scandal—'

'That's enough, Monica,' Gerald scowled her into silence. 'I'm sure everyone here doesn't want to know our entire history.'

'I was only saying,' Monica sniffed and buried her nose in the cup Cynthia handed her.

Embarrassed looks ran along the line, while everyone sipped their bouillon and pretended not to have heard.

'Is anyone going to the dance tomorrow evening?' Cynthia raised her voice above the howl of the wind in a diplomatic change of subject.

'I haven't quite decided,' Miss Ames replied. 'It strikes me as disrespectful after a death on board.' She tossed the trailing end of her ancient fur stole over her shoulder, releasing a flurry of tiny hairs.

'Captain Gates thought it would be a good idea to reinstate it,' Mr Hersch said. 'He's more than aware what the death of Parnell has done for morale on board.

'Have you appointed yourself ambassador to the crew, Hersch?' Crowe asked, a sneer on his face; his nose and cheeks red from the cold, which made him less attractive than ever.

The German merely smiled, while Flora gave the idea some thought. She would have liked to attend, not least because Bunny would be there, but couldn't ignore the fact she had nothing suitable in her wardrobe for a dance, despite Amelia Vaughn's generous contributions.

'Well, *I'm* going.' Cynthia waved her bouillon cup in the air. 'I need something to cheer me up. I'm sure most of the other passengers feel the same.'

'I expect Eloise would agree with you.' Monica nodded to the lone figure of the actress at the rail. 'This business has spoiled the voyage for the young people. What about you, Flora?'

'Humph, disrespectful if you ask me,' Mrs Penry-Jones said before Flora could answer, her mouth puckered in disapproval. She resembled a

Russian babushka doll with her scarf hiding her hair and fastened tightly beneath her chin.

'At least the fancy dress theme has been abandoned.' Gerald's sanguine nature resurfaced after his brief spat with Crowe. 'Makes the prospect slightly more welcoming. Monica would have me decked out as a harlequin if I let her. Bobble hat and all.'

'Gerald!' Monica's tone conveyed hurt. 'You look quite dashing in that costume.' She turned to Flora. 'Well, dear. Will you be going?'

A sudden vision of Gerald's generous, six-foot frame in a diamond-patterned costume complete with pointed hat made Flora's mouthful of bouillon go down the wrong way. She took a rasping breath, which ended abruptly when Bunny obligingly slapped her hard between her shoulder blades. Recovering herself, she was about to respond, when Mrs Penry-Jones' round tones cut across her again.

'Not if she has any regard for the way things ought to be done. In my day, governesses did not attend the captain's dance.'

Flora hesitated, torn between acceptance and attracting more censure from that quarter.

'Say you will.' Bunny nudged her. 'I was hoping for at least one turn around the floor with you.'

'I don't have anything suitable to wear,' Flora said, embarrassed at this admission as much as the plea in Bunny's voice.

'That's what every woman says,' Max muttered with some bitterness.

'Come to our suite after lunch, Flora.' Cynthia leaned across Max's lap, her pixie face wreathed in a warm smile. 'I have heaps of dresses, and we are about the same size. I'm sure to have something which will suit you.'

'Tha–that's most kind, thank you.' Flora blinked in surprise, by both the offer and its source, while Bunny delivered a 'who would have thought it' look.

Cynthia gave an elegant little shrug, cast a swift sideways look at Mrs Penry-Jones and winked. 'Can't let the old folks have their way every time, can we?'

'Really!' Mrs Penry-Jones gave a pointed sniff before going back to her bouillon.

13

The pounding of feet along the deck announced the arrival of Eddy and Ozzy, both dressed for the weather in layers of jumper, overcoats and flapping scarves.

'What have you two being doing this morning?' Flora asked, reassured by the increased presence of the crewmen, who ushered passengers away from the slippery areas on decks and staircases, offering helpful arms to the less steady on their feet.

'Not a lot,' Ozzy answered for them both. 'The deck games have been cancelled because of the high winds.' He hunched his shoulders in dejection and scuffed the sole of one shoe against the deck. 'We don't know what to do now.'

'Have some hot bouillon,' Monica suggested, nodding to the steward who had halted a few feet away to serve a group of hardy passengers.

'Not hungry,' Eddy said, caught Flora's hard look and added, 'thank you, Mrs Gilmore.'

The boys ran to the rail, where Eloise welcomed them with a smile, a hand on Eddy's shoulder as she pointed out something on the horizon. Another ship perhaps? Eddy had both feet on the bottom metal support, while Ozzy propped his chin on the polished wood as the ship dipped and rolled on the choppy grey sea.

'Do be careful, Ozzy.' Monica's voice was edged with panic, just as a particularly large wave broached the rail further along the deck. 'He never gets seasick, you know. Such an excellent constitution.'

'Stop fussing, Monica,' her husband growled.

'Perhaps Mrs Gilmore is right, Eddy,' Flora couldn't help agreeing with her. 'You're too close and it's getting quite rough out there.'

As the words left her, a plume of spray leapt the rail, sending all three of them backwards with a combined shriek. Their mouths opened in shock, their hair plastered to their heads as they held their hands held out to their sides. Eloise joined in the excited, half-fearful screams of laughter, each of them indicating each other's soaked clothes and dripping chins.

Bunny left his chair and grabbed some blankets from a box beside the steamer chairs. He advanced on the boys and wrapped one round each of them, including Eloise. 'How about we order some hot chocolate to help you dry off?' he suggested, nodding to a second steward who was working his way along the line. 'Don't need to be hungry for that, do we, boys?'

Monica bustled between them with towels, which she used to dry the boys' hair

'I'll get that,' Mr Hersch offered. He dropped a pile of coins into the steward's hand, then enlisted the boys' help in the positioning of two steamer chairs before handing them large mugs of the steaming hot chocolate.

Eloise flopped into an empty steamer chair without bothering to check the label, dabbing her face delicately with a towel. 'Is there any hot chocolate for me? Not that I should, but this sea air makes banting incredibly difficult.' She lifted her feet onto the footrest, grinning like a schoolgirl.

Gus Crowe huddled miserably in his chair and ignored her.

Bunny gave a small sigh, pushed his glasses up his nose and waved for the steward to bring another mug.

'What's "banting"?' Flora asked no one in particular.

'No idea.' Gerald blew into his cupped hands.

'It's the limitation of refined carbohydrates to promote weight loss devised by a William Banting in the 1860s,' Bunny said, passing Eloise her hot chocolate.

'How knowledgeable you are, Mr Harrington.' Eloise giggled. 'I don't know what a carbo-whatever is, but if I follow the plan, I'll become more slender.'

'My mother uses it sometimes,' Bunny said in answer to Flora's unasked question. 'Besides, Miss Lane,' he inclined his head in Eloise's direction, 'I think you are quite slender enough.'

Eloise saluted him with her cup of chocolate, which Flora imagined must contain enough starch and sugar for the entire day.

'When my clothes begin to pinch I take herbal tea to suppress my appetite,' Cynthia said. 'I swear by it. If you wish... Eloise... I could bring some to your stateroom later?' Cynthia stumbled slightly on the name, as if she had to think about it.

Eloise stammered her thanks, echoing Flora's surprise at Cynthia's new-found generosity.

'Perhaps Cynthia's had an epiphany as to the equality of all God's creatures,' Bunny whispered, his breath warm on Flora's cheek. 'She normally ignores Eloise, or shoots daggers at her with those beautiful eyes of hers.'

'She's not exactly been my best friend, either,' Flora murmured, just as a woman huddled into a voluminous coat with her head down rushed past them without an acknowledgement.

'Did you see that?' Monica waggled her head at the woman's retreating back. 'She completely ignored us! That's happened several times recently. Anyone would think one of *us* killed Mr Parnell.'

'Who says he was killed?' Gus Crowe looked up sharply from his bouillon, but relaxed back again when no one responded.

'Most likely that lady didn't know what to say,' Monica ventured. 'It's human nature to avoid what we regard as a threat.'

'What's that sailor doing up there?' Max pointed to the open bridge, where a young sailor was wrapped in a sou'wester and stared through a telescope.

'Trying to keep warm, I imagine,' Crowe mumbled.

'I don't envy any of the crew up there on a bridge open to this weather,' Max turned his head, indicating the capped heads of the crew above the canvas sheets that surrounded the bridge, the men's collars pulled up to their ears and hats jammed down.

'Keeping a watch for icebergs,' Gerald said, ruffling Ozzy's hair. 'We're on the southerly course, so I doubt we'll see any *bergy bits* in these waters.'

'Papa!' Ozzy ducked away in mock annoyance and patted his hair down again. Watching them, Flora's heart twisted at the man's easy affection for his son; one which Eddy would benefit from with his own father, but which happened rarely.

A wave jumped the rail, covering the deck with icy saltwater that swirled and sucked through the gap below the bottom rail. The deck tilted, sending the tray of empty bouillon cups into a sideways slide, which were caught by a sprightly steward.

'The weather is deteriorating, I'm afraid.' Officer Martin halted beside them, a hand clamped on his cap that glistened with spray. 'We're heading into a nor'easter, so I advise everyone go back inside.' As he spoke, the wind sent a burst of rain against the weather cloths around the open bridge with a loud hiss.

'Is it a real storm?' Eddy's face lit with childish glee.

'Is it dangerous?' Eloise asked, gazing up at the sailor from beneath her lashes.

'It is, Miss.' Officer Martin offered her his arm. 'As I said, it's best I get you inside.'

'Well, help me up, Gerald,' Monica snapped, looking askance at Eloise's flirtatious acceptance of help, possibly because it was not directed at herself.

She made two attempts to rise from the steamer chair, falling back again both times as the deck pitched.

Sighing, Gerald hauled her to her feet, handing her to Officer Martin who had returned to help.

'It's a while until luncheon,' he shouted over the wind. 'How about Eddy comes back to our suite?'

'If you're sure that wouldn't be an inconvenience?' Flora narrowed her eyes as fine spray stung her face. An empty steamer chair crashed into the one Monica had just left, sending Flora's chair several feet closer to the rail.

'I'll get them to the dining room in time for luncheon.' Gerald threw an arm around each of the boys and the three hobbled across the deck like competitors in a three-legged race.

Cynthia struggled to stay upright, encumbered by her heavy coat and several blankets. Max wrapped an arm around her, the pair locked together as they staggered toward the safety of the interior.

Bunny paused at the open door to the lobby, his gaze strained in the direction of the aft deck.

'Aren't you coming inside?' Flora stepped backwards as a sheet of salt spray landed two feet away.

'I'm going to check on Matilda first,' he shouted, his hair blown vertical by the wind. 'Make sure she's tied down.'

'Couldn't you ask a crew member to do that?' Flora shouted back, fighting to stay upright on a deck that tipped sharply to one side. Other passengers streamed past and she found herself forced by the rush into the staircase lobby where she stopped to brush water from her coat. When she looked through the window again, Bunny had gone.

Crowe stooped to retrieve a book left on a chair by a gentleman in a caped overcoat. The man's retreating back was still visible on the stairs above, but Crowe made no effort to call out to him, and instead, slid the book into his pocket.

Flora sighed, asking herself again why Eloise spared the odious man any of her time.

* * *

Flora's finger had barely grazed the doorbell of the Cavendish suite before it was flung open by a bright-eyed Cynthia who had changed into a fine wool suit in a rich emerald green to suit the colder weather. 'There you are!' she cried, as if she had been lurking in wait. 'Max has gone out for a bit to do whatever it is men do, so we have the place to ourselves. I was about to order coffee.' She fluttered to the fireplace where she gave the bell an enthusiastic push.

'That would be very welcome.' Flora dithered on the threshold before entering, feeling a little like Gretel about to enter the witch's house. The suite was a mirror image of Flora's own, but immaculately tidy, with not one personal item in evidence. Had she stumbled in there by herself, she would be hard-pressed to place anyone in the rooms.

'We keep our things in here.' Cynthia led her into the unoccupied second bedroom, where the bed had been removed, the space taken up with four steamer trunks stacked on their sides. Their front sections stood open to reveal a bank of drawers on one side and rows of gowns, skirts, blouses, undergarments, shawls, scarves and petticoats on the other.

'See if there's anything here which catches your eye.' Cynthia waved her arm in a wide arc. 'This is such fun, just like school.'

Flora almost told her she didn't know what that was like, having never attended one, but refrained for fear of sounding self-pitying.

'You have some beautiful things here, Cynthia.' Her fingers caressed silk, merino wool, muslin and chiffon in pastel shades of primrose, lilac, cornflower blue and ecru, with equal awe. Even the Vaughn girls didn't own so many things, the younger ones not above wearing their sisters' hand-me-downs.

'My trousseau,' Cynthia said airily. 'I left most of it behind, though I had to buy a heavier coat than I imagined I would need.'

'Was this your first visit to New York?' Flora asked, pulling out a blue dress she decided was too dark and replacing it.

'I was born there, actually.' Cynthia leaned against the door frame and examined the fingernails of one hand. 'Mama divorced my father when I was ten. Or he divorced her, I never did find out the reasons behind it. Not something one talks about with one's parent. Mummy married an Englishman not long after, so I was brought up in London.'

'Is that why you decided on New York for your honeymoon?' Flora kept talking, self-conscious that she trawled through another woman's clothes while the owner watched.

'Something like that. Though I wish Max had not announced the fact we are newlyweds to the shipping line. Since the moment we stepped onto the *SS Marquette*, for the outbound journey we've been gawped at like specimens under glass.'

'Don't you like being the centre of attention?' Flora discarded an eau-de-Nil muslin gown as being pretty but too insipid for her skin tone.

'It isn't that. New York was spoiled for me by—' she broke off at the rattle of crockery. 'Ah, here are our refreshments.' She poked her head round the door frame and called to the unseen steward. 'Just leave it on the table, would you?'

An evocative aroma of fresh, brewed coffee and the chink of cups floated out of the sitting room, followed by the suite door closing again.

'What about this one?' Cynthia unhooked a silk gown the colour of poinsettias from the nearest trunk. She frowned, her lips puckered. 'No, it's not your colour.' She returned it to the rail and leaned her hip against the door, her arms folded. 'I don't suppose you've heard any more about that man who died? What was his name? Parnell?' She hesitated on the last word too long for it to be a convincing memory lapse.

'Why do you ask?' Flora pretended to examine a cream silk gown with coral trim, suspecting Cynthia had been working up to this question since she had arrived. The thought struck her then that it might also have been the sole reason for inviting her.

'Merely idle curiosity.' Cynthia picked at a cuticle. 'Some of the passengers have been talking, and well, it seems there may have been something odd about it after all.'

'Really?' Flora asked, feeling Bunny would have been proud of her acting ability. 'What sort of thing?'

'That Mr Parnell may not have fallen.' The hunted look in Cynthia's eyes intensified. 'Max thinks someone will have informed the newspapers.' Her hand on the door frame tightened until her knuckles showed white.

'A death on board is bound to be newsworthy,' Flora said. 'Especially if the killer is caught. In which case the police will have to be involved.' Her use of the words 'killer' and 'police' had the desired effect. Cynthia's pigeon wing eyes darkened to slate, taking an effort to compose herself. 'Do you like that one?' She indicated the peacock blue gown in Flora's hands. 'That colour makes me look pasty, but flatters your complexion beautifully. Do try it on, though I'm sure it will fit.'

Flora obeyed, luxuriating in the feel of the silk as it slipped over her slight curves down to the floor. The fitted bodice was covered with gauzy lace where the silk showed through, and the skirt billowed out a little at mid-calf level.

'It's lovely, Cynthia, thank you.' Flora twisted and turned before a cheval mirror, admiring the way the silk, shot through with silver, caught the light.

'My pleasure.' Cynthia preened. 'I'll have it pressed and sent to your suite in time for tomorrow. Get changed now and we'll have that coffee.' She patted Flora's arm, before disappearing into the sitting room.

Returning the gown to its hanger, Flora retrieved her skirt from where it was draped across one of the trunks. She fastened the row of side buttons and smoothed down the folds, halted by a crackling noise from the pocket. Frowning, she withdrew a crumpled piece of paper with the *New York Times* banner printed across the top. Its presence confused her at first, until she realised it was the one that had fallen from Parnell's drawer when she and Eloise searched his stateroom. She had shoved it into her pocket when the doorknob rattled and forgotten about it. The headline 'Bridegroom Van Elder Is Dead' snagged her attention, and intrigued, her gaze scanned the print quickly.

New York Mar. 7 1900

The marriage last Saturday evening of Theodore van Elder of this city and Miss Estelle Montgomery, of New York, which was a great surprise to their friends, was followed this evening by the sudden death of Mr Theodore van Elder from acute gastritis. The fact that he had not been in good health for some time, and that the friends of the couple knew nothing of their engagement, made their marriage all the more surprising.

Mr van Elder was a well-known man about town. Miss Montgomery was his second wife. A child by his first wife is heir to a fortune. Mr van Elder's mother is wealthy. Miss Montgomery was to have been the guest of honour at the theatre party last Saturday evening, but she surprised her friends by dropping in upon them just as they were about to start for the theatre and informing them that she had wed Mr van Elder.

Since the evening of the marriage, Mr van Elder, on account of sickness, has scarcely been able to leave his apartment. Mr van Elder was over forty years of age and originally from Baltimore, but recently engaged in business in New York. His widow is but twenty-three and a beautiful woman.

Reaching the end, she looked up from the page, her thoughts whirling as she put possible faces to names in her head.

'Flora?' Cynthia called from the sitting room. 'Your coffee will get cold.'

'Er—coming.' Flora thrust the paper back into her pocket and went to join Cynthia.

14

Flora read the newspaper clipping again back in her own sitting room, staring at the stark print long after she reached the end. Her thoughts whirling, she was vaguely aware of the slap of horizontal rain that lashed the deck outside, accompanied by the scream of the wind. Convinced the obituary referred to Eloise and her late husband, she tried to put the pieces together in her head. That Eloise had changed her name came as no surprise, though the fact her husband had died less than a week after their secret wedding sent chills through her. No wonder his family were suspicious – anyone would be – and had engaged lawyers.

Did a question remain as to how Theo had died? Because if it *was* gastritis, then why was Eloise convinced she was about to be accused of murder? So certain, in fact, she left the country with only the things she could carry to avoid it. And if her late husband's lawyers had employed Mr Hersch, what did he know which could be used against her?

That Parnell kept the clipping gave credence to Eloise's claim he had tried to blackmail her, but which also begged the question that the evidence he spoke of could exist as well.

She recalled the raised voices on her first night on board and tried to picture Eloise battering Parnell with an ashtray, but somehow the image felt wrong. Parnell had been taller than Eloise and far stronger. Unless she had taken him by surprise. In which case, how did she get his body out of the stateroom and down to the deck below?

With these questions and others circling her head, it took a moment or two for her to notice a repeated knocking at her door. The sound persisted as her progress across the room was hampered by the fierce bucking of the ship. Finally, she flung the door open to reveal Bunny.

'I thought you were never going to let me in.' He shouldered sideways through the narrow gap, smoothing his wet hair back with cupped hands. He removed his steamed-up glasses and wiped the lenses with a handkerchief produced from a pocket.

Flora fetched a towel from the bathroom, their hands connecting as he took it from her. She drew hers back sharply, hoping he did not notice the impeding blush that prickled her skin. 'Is the storm getting worse?' Flora asked, self-conscious he might think her gauche if she coloured at every innocent contact, though at times she caught the sparkle in his eyes that implied he felt it too.

He nodded. 'Looks like it, though Matilda is secure, thank goodness.' He emerged from under the towel, still giving his scalp a vigorous scrub. 'Everything all right? You seem distracted.'

Silently, she handed him the clipping. 'Read this.'

He handed back the towel without speaking, and took the page from her.

'The night Eloise and I searched Parnell's cabin—'

'Broke into,' he corrected her.

'Yes, all right then, broke into. That fell onto the floor with the photograph I mentioned.'

Bunny scanned the paper swiftly then he looked up, his expression unfathomable. The deck lurched, rain sluicing the window like a hosepipe being aimed at the glass. Bunny staggered, steadying himself with a hand on the back of a chair. Flora grabbed the door to stop herself sliding into him.

'Perhaps we had better sit down, or we'll fall down.' Flora lowered herself into the nearest chair, waving him into one opposite. The deck lurched sharply as he sat, so he fell the rest of the way.

'I've never heard the names van Elder or Montgomery before.' He paused and narrowed his eyes. 'Unless...'

'Surely you've made the connection by now.' She twirled her hand in a circular motion as encouragement.

'Oh. I see.' His eyes widened. 'Eloise is this Estelle van Elder, formerly Montgomery.' He shrugged. 'You were aware she was a widow.'

'Widowed five days after the wedding.' She tapped the page he still held in his hand. 'I need her to explain that, and everything else she's been hiding since we came aboard.'

'That might not produce the result you wish for,' he said gently. 'If Eloise thinks you're nosing too deeply into her affairs, she might complain to the captain. It's not as if you have the authority to question people.'

'I doubt it. She's too scared at being found out. But you do have a point.'

'As I recall, I have quite a number of points, but you always manage to circumvent them.' He flicked the paper with a finger. 'It says here he was over forty years of age and his widow is twenty-three. That since the evening of the marriage, Mr van Elder did not leave his apartment. That implies all sorts of shenanigans right there.' Bunny made to hand the clipping back to her, but when she dismissed him, he folded it in half and slipped it into an inside pocket of his jacket. 'I'll hang onto this for a bit then. Shall I?' he asked unnecessarily.

'We mustn't jump to conclusions.' Though she was aware it was an attempt to cover the fact she had had the same thoughts herself. Ones she was loath to harbour about Eloise. 'I know it looks bad, but—'

'But what? You hardly know the woman.'

Flora was about to remind him that she didn't know him either, but left the words unspoken. Instead, she said, 'Eloise, or Estelle, or whatever her name is, thinks Mr Hersch is working for the van Elder family.'

'Maybe he is,' Bunny said. 'I warned you to be wary of that man. He might look like an amiable old uncle, but I suspect there's more to him than that.'

'He's not that old.' Nothing about Mr Hersch had made her distrust him thus far, though she was beginning to wonder whom she could trust on this ship. No one seemed to be what they claimed.

'I don't see what we could do, although...' Bunny paused and stroked his chin.

'What?' Flora urged.

'A friend of mine is a reporter for the *New York Times*. I could ask him to discover what he can about this Theodore van Elder chap, including the circumstances surrounding his death. In the meantime, I suggest we don't say anything to anyone.'

'Even Mr Hersch?'

'Especially him. We've no idea what's he's up to, or why.'

Flora chewed her bottom lip, torn between her promise to the German, and her wish to stay in Bunny's favour. Finally, she nodded. 'All right, I won't say anything.'

'Come on then!' Bunny heaved himself to his feet and made his way to the door.

'You want to go to the telegraphy office now? In this?' Flora waved at the darkened window which showed a slate grey, lowering sky and an angry sea.

'Why not? Most of the passengers are holed up in their staterooms.' He braced the door open with his hip while Flora fetched her coat, then led the way out onto the promenade deck.

'Who would care if we sent a telegram anyway?' Flora said, as a blast of salt spray stung her cheeks and the stiff wind plastered her skirt to her legs.

'Most people wouldn't,' Bunny shouted above the scream of the wind. 'Though the killer might.' He released the door behind them, which slammed into its frame with a deafening bang.

'I hadn't thought of that,' Flora murmured.

* * *

Bunny's knock on the wireless room door was answered by a fresh-faced crewman with damp hair whose brass name plate identified him as Seaman Crofts. Flora thought he looked vaguely familiar but couldn't quite place him.

'You're lucky to catch me, sir, Miss.' He ushered them inside and leaned a shoulder against the door when it threatened to spring open again. 'I was seeing to the bells, and have just this moment got back.'

The cramped room held an oversized wooden desk sat below a rack of tightly packed shelves, the atmosphere permeated with the aromas of dust, ink, paper and wet wool.

'What were you doing to the bells?' Flora raised her hand to adjust her disarranged hair but gave up when she saw there was no mirror.

'Muffling them. Bells on board ship are considered bad luck as they signify funerals.'

'I thought they were essential to sound the watches?' Bunny said, frowning.

'Yes, sir, that's true. But if they ring of their own accord, as in a storm, it means somebody is going to die.' His youthful face showed complete acceptance of this superstition. 'The deck bell was clanging away like a good'un in this wind.'

Flora had no time for omens or superstitions, preferring to rely on practicality combined with a keen sense of her own survival. The look she exchanged with Bunny told her his philosophy ran along similar lines.

'I want to send a telegram,' Bunny said, hiding a smile. 'To the offices of the *New York Times*.'

'That's a newspaper, sir.' The crewman dragged a pad of paper towards him, his expression changing from eagerness to wary suspicion. 'You're not a reporter are you? Because the captain said I wasn't to send details of the death of that passenger to anyone—'

'No, not at all,' Bunny reassured him. 'This is a personal matter I wish treated with the utmost privacy.'

'As you say, sir.' Crofts gave a curt nod, apparently satisfied, and wrote down the words Bunny dictated.

'There's no mention here of the gentleman who died,' the sailor said when he had finished. 'So I don't reckon it can do any harm. Pounds or dollars, sir?' He scribbled a few symbols on a scrap of paper before handing it to Bunny.

'Oh, er, pounds if you don't mind,' Bunny replied. 'I don't have any American currency left.'

'Then that's twenty-two words, sir, at eight shillings four pence for ten words. The signature is included, so that will be sixteen shillings eight pence.'

'Can't you put it on my account?' Bunny asked, frantically searching his pockets.

'I'm sorry, sir.' Crofts didn't look in the least regretful. 'All wireless telegraphy charges are strictly pre-paid.'

'Well, I'm not sure I—ah!' Bunny withdrew a pound note from an inside pocket and handed it over.

Flora waited as Seaman Crofts counted out change from a cash box into Bunny's hand, her attention caught by a sheet of notepaper on the desk, and at the top was written:

Telegraph Request – Urgent

Carl Hersch's name was beneath and the word 'SENT' in sketchy block capitals was scrawled across it.

'How does the telegraph machine work?' she asked, feigning interest in the contraption on the desk in front of them.

Seaman Crofts launched into a lively description of the wireless telegraphy machine, made up of three cylinders of various sizes joined by cogs and strips of metal above an ivory and black keyboard that resembled a small pianoforte.

'Um, I see, most interesting.' Paying cursory attention to the combination of metal, wood and wires, Flora squinted at the words on the page with Mr Hersch's name on which read:

Montana Land Deal 1890

Followed by the words:

Herein requested list persons...

Her view of the rest of the writing was cut off when the sailor slid his elbow over the page.

'Sorry.' Flora took a step back. 'I didn't realise it was confidential. I was just fascinated to see how it was done.'

'No bother, Miss. My fault for not putting the papers away.' He shuffled the sheets into a rough pile, while Flora stared at the top one with longing and wished she had been more discreet.

'Time to go, Flora,' Bunny said from behind her.

She turned to leave, then halted when she remembered where she had seen the sailor before. 'Excuse me, but didn't I see you talking with Mr Crowe on the stairs yesterday?'

'I speak to most of the passengers at one time or another.' He bent his head to a pile of papers again, his cheeks flushed.

'I'm sure you remember this one. He was being unpleasant, wasn't he?' she asked, drawing an enquiring look from Bunny. 'He does have an unfortunate manner sometimes.'

'Um – well, he was a bit cross.' A sheen of sweat appeared on the sailor's forehead. 'We settled the matter, so I doubt you'll find he has any complaints.'

'I'm sure he doesn't.' Flora adopted a sympathetic smile. 'You must have to deal with all sorts of people in your job.'

'I do, Miss. Now if you don't mind, I have to get on.' He indicated Bunny's telegram in front of him.

'Of course, and we must get along to luncheon.' She grabbed Bunny's arm and hustled him into the lobby.

'What was that all about?' Bunny asked, when the door closed behind them.

'I'm not sure.' Flora tapped her teeth with a fingernail. 'It could be nothing at all. Then again...'

* * *

The wind continued to howl as Flora made her way along the interior corridor, grateful for Bunny's steadying arm keeping them upright. In the lobby outside the dining room, they paused to allow a stream of unsteady diners through the doors ahead of them.

'What's that chap doing?' Bunny pointed through the window onto a deck barely visible through a wall of spray that crashed over the rail.

'Where?' Flora peered through the mist, where she could just make out the figure of a man in a long overcoat. Bent almost double, he struggled to plant one foot in front of the other on the steeply angled boards. 'He's making for the aft deck.'

Flora grabbed for the handrail as the crest of a running wave lifted the floor beneath her feet, hovered, then plunged the ship downwards again, taking her stomach with it.

Another wave, even bigger this time rolled over the rail. The man on deck staggered, glanced back once over his shoulder, his white face suffusing with terror as the water rushed towards him. At the last second, he made a grab for the rail on the steps up to the promenade deck, but his hand closed on thin air as the wall of water crashed over him, obscuring him completely.

'Stay here!' Bunny commanded, flinging open the outside door.

'No! Bunny. It's too dangerous!' Flora called into the wind, aware with a sinking dread that he couldn't possibly have heard her.

Cold water slammed into her eyes and her skirt billowed out like a sail, her shawl whipping painfully round her shoulders. She would be blown off her feet if she stayed there, leaving her with no option but to heave the door shut again.

Water dripped from her hair as she stared through the glazed part of the door to where Bunny waded through knee-high seawater, using fenders, winches and even chairs as handholds. Her gaze jumped forwards to the struggling man, who, with nothing to hold on to, was being pulled towards the rail in the grip of fast-flowing water as it was sucked back into the sea.

A loud creak sounded from the far side of the deck as Bunny's motor car slid inexorably across the boards towards both men, its canvas cover billowing in the wind, the straps trailing behind it like streamers. Flora gasped in horror as the deck tilted to the starboard side, and the metal monster gathered speed. The creak and squeal must have alerted Bunny, for he gave the moving car one hesitant look before he plunged past it, straight for the half-submerged man.

A rush of tender admiration tinged with fear tugged at Flora's chest at what it must have cost him to ignore his beloved motor car and go to the man's aid. Another wave submerged them both beneath a giant grey hand that threatened to pluck them from the deck. Together, they rolled sideways, dragged towards the gap below the bottom rung, where nothing but empty air stood between them and the ferocious sea. The deluge swirled and receded from the boards, leaving the two stranded figures huddled against a massive circular winch riveted to the deck.

Flora's breath caught and she mouthed silent bargains with God for Bunny's safe return, aware that a crowd had gathered behind her in the lobby, issuing murmurings of dismay and horrified gasps. A line of sailors, clambered down the outside companionway, their heads down against the wind and rain which reduced their progress to agonising slowness.

'He's got him!' someone behind Flora yelled.

Flora's chest tightened as her gaze flicked back to Bunny. The deck levelled out on the next wave, and he hauled the man upright by his collar. The man clutched his right arm to his chest as if it were useless, the other hooked round Bunny's neck. The next wave fell short and in the brief respite, the pair limped and staggered towards the lobby door.

Behind them, the motor car came to a shuddering rest against a pile of folded steamer chairs jammed tight against a lifeboat.

Crewmen surrounded them and dragged them into the lobby where the man collapsed, his sodden clothes forming a wide, wet pool on the floor.

'Be careful with him!' Bunny braced a hand against the wall as he heaved in laboured breaths. His glasses were gone and his hair hung in dark rats' tails on his forehead and neck, his drenched jacket clung to his shoulders, accentuating his muscular build.

Weak with relief, Flora pushed her way through the group who clustered round him and threw her arms round his neck. Freezing moisture leached through the bodice of her blouse, but she clung on, inhaling the male scent of him, mixed with the wind and salt, her throat clogged with relief and grateful tears.

'Hang on now, Flora.' Bunny gave an embarrassed laugh. 'It's all over now. No need for theatrics.' He disentangled her hands and held them down at her sides while his gaze swept the row of faces around them.

'Sorry, I—' A thrust of disappointment streaked through her chest and she stepped back, her possessive pride dissolving like mist. He was right, she had no claim on him, making it presumptuous of her to be so demonstrative. The one consolation being that he was alive. 'You've lost your glasses,' was the only thing she could think of to say.

'Drat, those were my favourites too.' He peered out to the storm-ravaged deck with a bemused expression, as if somehow he could detect the lost spectacles.

Gerald pounded his back in a loud, wet slap, distracting him, while Gus Crowe murmured, 'Good show, old man.'

Flora tugged her coat round her to cover the damp patch on her skirt, as if she could hold in her mortification at what she had just done. She had hugged him, in public! No wonder he had shied away from her! Her instinct was to apologise, but his focus had turned entirely on the rescued man who now lay on a stretcher slung between two sailors. A lady bent over him, only partly visible through the throng of people, one of his hands sandwiched in both of hers.

'Darling,' she cried piteously. 'Can you hear me? Please say you can hear me.'

'I doubt it, ma'am,' a crewman answered. 'He's barely conscious, I'm afraid. We'll get the doctor up here in a trice to see to him. He's a lucky chap, we nearly lost him overboard.'

The woman lifted her head, and Flora released a shocked gasp. 'Bunny, that's Cynthia! The man you rescued was Max.'

'Really?' Bunny blinked, then with mock seriousness, added, 'I must have been too busy trying not to get swept overboard to notice.'

'Was that sarcasm, Mr Harrington?' Flora snapped. How could he make jokes when seconds before she had been terrified he was about to die?

'I knew you were smart.' Bunny choked on the last word and lowered his head, overcome by a bout of coughing.

'You'd better see the doctor too,' Flora said, concerned. 'I read somewhere that swallowing seawater can be dangerous, and you were in it for a while.'

Bunny nodded, but waved her away. 'When I've made sure Max will be all right first.' He moved away and conducted a brief, one-sided conversation with Dr Fletcher, while the crewmen carried the stretcher with Max along the corridor, Cynthia tottering awkwardly alongside.

The drama over, the crowd dispersed towards the dining room, one or two lingering behind to pat Bunny on the back and murmur praise.

'What was Max doing out there in such heavy seas?' Flora asked, when she and Bunny were alone in the middle of the lobby.

'He most probably didn't realise the danger,' Bunny said. 'Not everyone is an experienced sailor.'

'You will see Dr Fletcher, won't you? Just in case?' Flora pleaded, hoping he wouldn't dismiss her. What was it with men and doctors? Neither her father nor Lord Vaughn would ever call one voluntarily.

'Later.' He cast a myopic glance at the empty deck that a few moments before had been tilted at forty degrees and beneath several feet deep in freezing sea water. 'My priority right now is to make sure my motor car is still in once piece.'

'You're not going back out there?' she asked, horrified.

'The wind's dropping and we aren't pitching quite so much. I can't leave it too long or she'll bash herself to pieces out there. I'll see if any of the crew are willing to help.' He gave her an awkward pat on one shoulder, then loped off along the internal corridor that run through the entire ship to the aft deck.

A stone settled beneath Flora's breastbone as she watched him disappear round a corner.

The thought struck her that Bunny might have been right about Max being an inexperienced sailor, but if so, why had he been heading for the aft deck, when the dining room lay in the opposite direction?

15

Only the most stalwart of the passengers turned up for the late luncheon, which consisted of sandwiches and coffee arranged in the dining room. Neither Eloise nor Hester had put in an appearance, and eating became a balancing act as plates and cutlery skittered across table tops, the ensuing embarrassment covered by uneasy laughter.

Bunny's bravery and Max's lucky escape became the main topic of conversation, however, Dr Fletcher's pronouncement that his injuries were little more than a wrenched arm and concussion proved something of an anti-climax.

'Probably didn't realise how powerful a rogue wave could be,' Gerald said in response to a question someone posed as to what Max was doing outside. He swiped a ham sandwich from a tray, pointing it at the group of animated young boys at the far end of the room. 'The storm doesn't appear to have spoiled their appetites.'

Miss Ames' mouth puckered in distaste at the group of children who darted between the tables.

'There's Ozzy! Yoo-hoo, Ozzy, darling!' Monica's high-pitched wail made Flora wince, while, red-faced, her son hid behind Eddy.

A ship's officer called for quiet, and when the general chatter had died down, announced what everyone already knew, in that the wind and rain had dropped, but outside activities were still hazardous. When he informed them that the bridge tournament would go ahead after luncheon as scheduled it was greeted by light clapping and a wave of sighs.

'That's something anyway.' Gus Crowe's face visibly brightened.

'I doubt they'll be playing for money,' Gerald warned.

'Not even a little side bet, my friend?' Crowe gave a knowing wink.

Gerald didn't reply, at which Crowe narrowed his eyes, one finger placed against his nose. 'Ah, I get it, the little woman wouldn't approve, eh?'

Monica scrambled to her feet, carefully avoiding Crowe's gaze. 'Flora, dear, there's a musical recital planned for this afternoon with a gramophone every bit as good as Gerald's. Ozzy would love to go and I suggested Eddy attend as well, if you approve of course. It will keep them occupied whilst we attend the bridge tournament in the library.'

'Perhaps I could take them?' Flora suggested. It would be a good excuse to stay away from Bunny, and it wouldn't do her any harm to spend some time with Eddy. Not that he would notice her presence if a gramophone was involved.

'They will be supervised by a reliable group of grown-ups.' She regarded Flora with her head on one side. 'He'll be quite safe, you really shouldn't worry.' Her words were accompanied by a discordant scraping back of chairs as the passengers made their way out to the staircase lobby.

'That's very kind of you, Mrs Gilmore. I've been a bit distracted lately.'

'I had noticed, my dear, and think nothing of it.'

'Do you think I'm being overly protective?' Flora picked at a button on her sleeve. She couldn't quite forget those menacing words that voice had whispered to her outside the dining room, or consign them to no more than an empty threat.

'A little, my dear.' She covered Flora's hand with her own for a heart-beat before pulling away. 'However, it merely shows how conscientious you are, which cannot be considered a bad thing. I wish I had a treasure like you for my girls.' A speculative gleam appeared in her eyes. 'I don't suppose you would think of leaving your current employment?'

She replied with only a silent smile, although with Eddy going off to Marlborough next term, she would be virtually redundant.

'I'm only delighted Ozzy has found such a congenial friend. Will you be joining us in the library for bridge?' Monica asked as they stepped onto the promenade deck.

'I'm not sure yet. I don't even play.'

'Huh, as if that matters.' She flapped a dismissive hand. 'Better than staying alone in your suite.'

Flora thanked her again, having agreed to think about the bridge idea before they went in different directions. Perhaps Monica was right and it was better than being alone? Though how was she was going to face Bunny after that episode in the lobby? Regret mixed with longing as she recalled the feel of his chest pressed against her bodice and his cold breath on her cheek.

* * *

At a few minutes before three, Flora joined a group of both familiar and unfamiliar faces gathered in the library, where sofas and armchairs had been pushed against the walls, the space occupied by an arrangement of card tables, each containing four chairs. Flora took the empty chair beside Monica, who was quick to reassure her that Eddy and Ozzy were looking forward to their musical afternoon, and Gerald had agreed to collect them at teatime.

'That doesn't give him much time for bridge,' Flora observed.

'Oh, he isn't keen. He'll play one game and then give up and look for something more entertaining.' She patted his arm on the table. 'Won't you dear?'

Gerald beamed at Flora in response, then addressed the surrounding tables. 'Anyone care to wager who'll turn up after that gale?' He nodded to where Mrs Penry-Jones sat a few feet away. 'I'll lay evens on Miss Smith coming to the tournament,' he lowered his voice to a whisper. 'She was quite a star at poker last night. Took a hundred dollars off me.'

'Did she indeed?' Flora was alerted to a different side of the feeble companion.

'I'll accept that bet, old man.' Crowe swept two glasses from a tray borne aloft by a passing waiter, one of which he set before Gerald. 'Didn't see her at luncheon. Perhaps she's got her head over a bowl at this very moment.'

'Thank you, but I didn't want a drink,' Flora said sarcastically, pleased to see Crowe look embarrassed.

'How indelicate of you, Mr Crowe.' Miss Ames inhaled sharply through narrowed nostrils. 'She could be suffering. Seasickness is exceedingly unpleasant.'

'Just a little joke, you know.' Crowe reddened, and eased his collar away from his neck.

Flora hid a smile, noting how crass Crowe was with the male passengers but reverted to an embarrassed schoolboy when chastised by a woman. She gave the rapidly filling room a searching glance, but thus far there was no sign of Eloise. Banting or not, she must have been ravenous by lunchtime.

'I see the weather hasn't affected you, dear lady?' Gerald addressed Mrs Penry-Jones as if she were deaf, though she occupied a table not six feet away.

'I never get seasick.' She sipped from one of the glasses handed to her by a waiter, then peered at it, her nose wrinkled. 'Hester, on the other hand, turned positively green earlier and had to lie down.' She moved her cane from one side of her chair to the other, catching Crowe sharply on the ankle. 'I doubt she would miss a game though. She's quite an enthusiast where bridge is concerned.' He drew his foot rapidly under the table, apparently too proud to rub it in company, despite the fact it must have hurt. Gerald smirked, but Crowe scowled back, most likely because he was already down on their wager.

'I hope our young hero is fully recovered without any long-term effects?' Gerald changed places and took the empty seat beside Flora.

'That was valiant of him to go after Max like that,' Miss Ames said.

'Foolhardy if you ask me.' Crowe caught Flora's hard look, adding, 'But very brave.'

'Ah, here he is now.' Gerald indicated to where the crowd had parted to allow Bunny through.

He had changed his clothes, his hair darkened by water slicked back behind his ears. He worked his way towards them, hindered by a volley of back-slapping from those around him and hearty congratulations for a job well done.

Flora's stomach did a strange flip as the memory of his muscled chest pressed against hers flooded back. Her pulse quickened and she pretended to be absorbed in something Monica said.

Perhaps she should have obeyed her first instinct to remain in her suite with a book, but as the time for the tournament grew nearer, she was inexplicably drawn to their exclusive group. The atmosphere on board had undergone a subtle, but noticeable change in the last three days, especially in the dining room.

Enthusiastic greetings and the swapping of places to chat went on at the other tables as normal, though few ventured near Table No. 6, as if those who had shared the victim's last evening were tainted by Parnell's death.

There was also the possibility that if she denied herself the ship's company, she might miss a vital clue as to who killed Parnell, or of discovering whether Eloise's fears were valid or not.

'I persuaded one of the crewmen to help me get Matilda back under canvas,' Bunny said when he reached them. 'Odd how she managed to shake loose from the straps which were secured tight when I checked them earlier. No damage though, thank goodness.' He accepted a glass from a waiter of what looked like fruit punch, but which probably wasn't. 'Has anyone found out how Max is?'

Flora sneaked a sideways look at him and away again, but his expression held only warmth, and no embarrassment.

'I imagine he's tucked up in bed with his devoted bride in attendance.' Gus Crowe gave a knowing wink.

'Did I hear you say earlier that you don't play bridge, Flora?' Monica asked, her nostrils narrowed in distaste at Crowe's insensitivity.

'I'm afraid I don't,' Flora replied. 'Is it difficult to learn?' She had no real interest in the game, but she wasn't going to admit Bunny was her main reason for being there, despite what had happened between them in the lobby.

'It's similar to whist.' Gerald picked up a pack of cards and proceeded to shuffle them. 'Each player takes a turn as dummy. A trump suit is chosen and players bid the number of tricks they expect to achieve with their hand, and whether they wish to have a trump suit or no trump.'

'You must follow the suit of the player who starts,' Monica added. 'If unable to do so, you can play any card.'

'Exactly,' Bunny joined their conversation, grinning. 'Thus the trick is won by the highest trump, if there are trumps. Points are also awarded for honours, and—'

'Enough!' Flora lifted both hands in surrender, wishing she hadn't asked. 'All these rules are giving me a headache.'

'It will make more sense when you begin playing,' Monica said.

'Or maybe not.' Bunny cast Flora a sideways look she pretended not to see.

'Didn't I say she would never miss a game of bridge?' Mrs Penry-Jones muttered darkly, her gaze on the door.

Flora glanced to where Hester eased between the chairs as she made her way towards their table a wave of scent in her wake which struck Flora as being too heavy for her. She couldn't recall having noticed her wearing scent before, but the thought didn't last as when Gerald held out a chair for Hester, he extended his other hand behind her back, into which Crowe slid a folded banknote with a roll of his eyes.

Gerald held the note up to the light, squinted at it ostentatiously, then pocketed it.

'Quite a character that Gerald, isn't he?' Bunny said, *sotto voce,* his head ducked towards Flora. Then before she could respond, his smile dissolved into a frown. 'Look, Flora, about earlier. I didn't mean to—'

'Please don't worry about it,' she waved him away, her cheeks burning. 'I would sooner forget about it if you don't mind.' She wanted nothing of the sort but recoiled at the idea of having her indiscretion discussed in company.

'*I* don't want to forget,' he insisted in a fierce whisper. His expression changed to concern and he leaned closer. 'Is something wrong? You keep staring at the door.'

'You know what's wrong,' she whispered back. 'But that's not what is worrying me right now,' Flora lied. 'Eloise wasn't at luncheon and she's not here now.' Flora voiced the worry that had nagged at her all morning. 'She's avoiding me again.'

'There's not a great deal you can do if she's reluctant to talk about it.'

'We had an agreement.' Rising, Flora skirted the table, glad to be escaping Bunny's intense stare. 'I'm going to find her. I won't accept any excuses, either.'

'Flora!' Bunny called out, but she ignored him.

'Never mind her, Mr Harrington.' Mrs Penry-Jones' stentorian voice accompanied the loud drum of her fingers on the tabletop. 'Are you going no trumps, Monica?'

* * *

Flora's angry footsteps took her as far as the bottom of the stairs leading to the promenade deck. She slowed to a halt and leaned her back against the wall, her eyes closed as she recalled Bunny's stern expression when she had thrown her arms round his neck. She had embarrassed him, and now she was herself embarrassed.

Well, he could have his wish. She would be nothing but coolly polite to Mr Bunny Harrington for the rest of the voyage.

Pushing away from the wall, she shoved roughly past an elderly matron who blocked the door to the promenade deck, uncaring of the outraged, 'Well!' that sounded from behind her.

The wind still sang through the winch lines, but outside Eloise's stateroom, the rain had reduced to little more than a light drizzle, which failed to penetrate the deck canopy.

Flora gave the door a determined rap with her knuckles, then immediately did it again, but no sound came from inside.

'Open the door, Eloise,' she muttered, then louder, 'you've avoided me for long enough!' She rattled the door handle, but it refused to turn.

She blew air between pursed lips and peered in at the window beside the door, but the blind was pulled down, leaving only a small gap at the bottom where it had snagged on something.

Flora crouched lower, her hands cupped round her eyes to block out her reflection in the glass. 'Eloise!' she called in a harsh whisper through the thick glass.

At first glance, the room looked empty, apart from an upright, deep green ladies' boot that poked out from behind the partition. Knowing Eloise's messy habits, she assumed it had been thrown there in a careless moment, but a closer look revealed the row of buttons across the arch were fastened – with a foot inside it.

A trickle of dread squeezed her chest. She backed away slowly, glancing to left and right in search of help, but the deck remained deserted.

Rhythmic footsteps from the boat deck sent her to the rail where the purser crossed the boards below her.

'Excuse me,' she called out to him in panic 'I need your help urgently.'

His smile of welcome faded as he bounded up the outside companionway, reaching her in a few strides. 'What's the problem, Miss?'

'There's something terribly wrong with my friend. Do you have a key to these staterooms?' Anticipating her request would be met with a caveat about company policy, Flora grasped his arm and pulled him resolutely towards Eloise's door.

'I–I'm not sure I ought to simply barge in. Perhaps she's sleeping, or er... entertaining?' His brows lifted in apology as he gave the door a tentative knock with his knuckles.

'Don't you think I've already tried that?' Flora gritted her teeth, her fists clenched at her sides. 'Look, I wouldn't ask if it wasn't serious. I'll wait out here if you insist. All I ask is that you take a look.'

He appeared about to say something but then changed his mind, showing he was weakening.

'Please!' Eloise's door stayed firmly shut and with every second that passed, her greatest fear crystallised, knowing had she been all right, Eloise would have heard the commotion by now.

With a resigned sigh, the purser rummaged in a pocket, withdrew a key and unlocked the door that gave with a sharp click.

Forgetting her promise, Flora pushed past him, then came to an abrupt halt at the end of the bed.

'Hey, Miss, I can't just let you in, I have to—' He halted behind her and released a shocked breath. 'Oh, my.'

Eloise lay on her back on the floor, her arms flung outwards from her sides. Between her neckline and mid-thigh was a harsh, bright scarlet splash against the cream silk of her dress. Her unnaturally black hair formed a cloud of curls round her head, her vivid blue eyes open, but seeing nothing; devoid of pain or even surprise.

Flora's heart filled her chest and something thick and fuzzy stuck in her throat. Her stomach heaved and the cabin tilted around her.

'Don't look, Miss.' Strong hands pulled her backwards, though his words seemed to come from underwater.

Her knees crumpled as his order came far too late. She hung onto his arm to keep herself upright, her gaze fixed on the splash of red that grew and filled her vision.

This couldn't be happening. It had to be one of her dreams and she would wake soon, shivering and tearful.

'Is everything all right, Mr Willis?' a tentative male voice called from behind them, followed by a shocked gasp.

'Fetch the doctor, would you, Brady?' The purser wasted no time. 'Then inform both the captain and Dr Fletcher.'

Heavy footfalls marked the man's retreat as the purser gripped Flora's upper arms and hustled her back out onto the deck where the wind tugged at her skirt. 'Miss, I have to lock this door again until the captain arrives. Shall I send for a stewardess to stay with you?'

'Bunny,' Flora murmured his name as a reflex.

'Who, sorry?'

'Mr Harrington. He's at the bridge tournament.' The deck spun and she grabbed an upright support to steady herself. Bile rose into her throat and despite a salt-tinged wind rushing past her face, she couldn't breathe. She broke away from the purser and ran along the wet deck until the metal bars of the rail bit into her thighs, halting her. She gripped the polished wood top so hard, her fingers cramped in protest. The pain came as a welcome distraction, though not enough to still the words that echoed in her head: *Eloise is dead.*

16

The angry sea had settled to a gentle swell beneath a sky filled with the soft blues and pinks of a late spring afternoon, as if the fury of the skies had expended all its energy in the violence that took place in Eloise's state-room. The wake of the ship stretched behind them in a surging white line towards the horizon as the wind tugged Flora's hair across her face.

She had no idea how long she stood there, her gaze fixed on the frothing water until her breathing slowed and the urge to scream dissolved.

'Calmer now?' Bunny asked gently, the whoosh of the silk lining of his jacket strangely loud as he slipped a protective arm round her shoulders.

She didn't respond, though she sensed he had been close by for some time.

He tucked a strand of her hair behind her ear, his fingers brushing her cheek, the touch making her want to bury her face in his neck, but she resisted in case he rejected her again; that would be too much to bear.

'How could anyone do something like that to Eloise?' She squeezed her eyes shut, as if she could banish the images in her head.

'The captain is inside her stateroom with Mr Hersch and Dr Fletcher.' Bunny massaged her shoulder with one hand. 'Their combined efforts should catch whoever did this pretty quickly.'

'Huh!' Her anger surfaced again. 'Faint hope of that. At least this time no one can call it an accident.' *This time? How much more tragedy could occur on one short voyage?*

'Dr Fletcher wants you to take this.' He held up a small brown bottle with ridges on the side, twisting it round in his fingers. 'It's a sedative. For the shock, he said.'

'That's the last thing I need right now,' she snapped, annoyed with herself for taking her temper out on Bunny.

'It's all right to cry, you know.' He slipped the bottle into his pocket, and leaned his elbows on top of the rail, his shoulders hunched.

'I'm too angry to cry.' She swiped a hand across her cheek that came away dry. 'Eloise believed no one could touch her if she kept her identity secret. But she was wrong.' She straightened. 'Did you say Mr Hersch was with the captain in her stateroom?'

'Yes. It appears our German friend is actually a detective.' Bunny adjusted his glasses on his nose with his free hand. 'A Pinkerton's detective, no less.'

'I've never heard of them.' Flora sighed. 'Though I should have guessed something of the sort. He has a unique way of prising things out of people without giving anything away himself.'

'The agency is quite famous in America.' Bunny stepped closer. 'And talking of prising things, we might have some explaining to do about the van Elders?'

Flora frowned. 'You were the one who told me to keep the newspaper clipping quiet until after we had heard from your reporter friend in New York.'

'Well, yes, but I had no idea Eloise was dead when we sent that telegram.'

'Was she? Dead, I mean. What time did we return from the wireless office?'

'Difficult to say, around twelve forty-five, or one o'clock maybe. Then we had that drama with Max which must have taken about twenty minutes. After that, you went into luncheon and I arrived a little later.'

'That's about right.' Flora paused, thoughtful. 'I went back to my suite to change before coming to the bridge tournament, and – oh dear, this sounds as if we're trying to get our story straight.' She gave an embarrassed laugh that tailed off into a sob.

'Well, we are in a way. As for the clipping, you waited three days before you showed it to me.'

'I genuinely forgot about it,' Flora hissed as a couple strolling the deck passed by, only to pause in front of Eloise's door, murmuring to each other. She waited until they had passed on before adding, 'Are you implying Eloise's death is somehow my fault?'

'The reverse, actually.' His arm drifted to her shoulder and tightened. 'Nothing either of us did or said would have made any impact on the outcome. Someone wanted Eloise dead for reasons of their own.'

Flora bit her lip hard as her guilt refused to be banished so easily. She pressed a clenched fist against her mouth and spoke into her fingers. 'I could have confronted Eloise with the clipping, insisted she tell me the whole story.'

'Maybe she had no intention of telling you anything. Have you thought of that?'

'I would have convinced her,' Flora said, not quite believing it herself.

'Even so, if Parnell was blackmailing Eloise, the obituary doesn't tell us why someone would want to kill them both.'

'No, no, it doesn't.' Flora sighed. 'Maybe Parnell tried to kill Eloise?' Flora tried to make sense of her muddled thoughts. 'But she managed to fight him off and he died instead.'

'Then who killed her?'

'I don't know.' Her voice came out as a frustrated whine. 'But maybe she was right in that Mr Hersch was employed by the van Elders to expose Eloise.'

'Which he didn't do.' Bunny brought his free hand down on the rail with a thump. 'Which is exactly why we must examine only the facts, not fit them to our theories.'

'Now you sound like Mr Hersch.'

'Do I? I've always wondered what it would be like to be a detective.' She turned a bemused expression on him and he added, 'Before I discovered motor cars, that is.'

He moved his arm from her shoulders to her waist, easing her away from the rail. 'You need to sit down, preferably with some hot sweet tea to help with the shock.'

'That sounds good – oh!' She brought a hand to her mouth. 'Eddy!'

'Gerald said they couldn't keep this latest death from the boys, so he is going to break it to them together after the recital.'

'It's so kind of him, although I feel I ought to do it. I've absolved my responsibility for Eddy to too often lately.'

'Maybe it's best coming from Gerald. You know what little monsters young boys can be. They'll probably demand details, and you're in no state to deal with that.'

'Details,' Flora said under her breath. 'I knew there was something odd about it.'

'Odd about what? What are you talking about, Flora?'

'Eloise. There was plenty of blood this time, I could hardly look away, but it wasn't until just now I realised I couldn't see what caused it.' Her hand came down on his arm in a gentle shake. 'There was no weapon.'

'Don't think about it now. Leave it to the captain and Mr Hersch. Look, Flora,' he lowered his voice, though there was no one close enough to hear, 'I might have chosen the wrong time to talk about this, but when you hugged me this morning, I—'

'It's perfectly all right.' Flora rolled her shoulder out of his hold, her back stiff. 'I understand. It was presumptuous of me and won't happen again.' How could anything be normal between them after this?

'That isn't what I meant. Flora please allow me to explain.'

She flung away from him unwilling to listen, stomach knotting as the colour red flashed before her eyes.

Images flashed through her head of the day she had first met Eloise on deck. How they had giggled together on Eloise's bed after they had broken into Parnell's stateroom. Even their revealing talk in the cloakroom took on a piquant quality now she knew it would never be repeated. Uniquely female moments of camaraderie Flora had rarely experienced in her life.

'Why don't we go to the library?' Bunny suggested. 'The bridge tournament will have broken up by now.'

Flora shook her head. 'I'm just not prepared to sit over tea waiting to be summoned by the captain for another of his formal interviews. I need to talk to him, now.' Her gaze strayed to uniformed crewman posted outside Eloise's stateroom.

'He's not there,' Bunny guided her away from Eloise's door. 'I saw him leave a few minutes ago with Hersch.'

Flora turned and marched to the far end of the deck. Ignoring the astonished faces that turned in her direction, she erupted into the interior lobby and made for the stairs.

Bunny's footsteps sounded behind her, but she didn't stop until she reached the upper promenade deck and halted on the landing, searching for a clue as to where to go next.

'Where is it?' she demanded, panicked.

'This way, opposite the library.' He pointed to a door marked 'Captain', moved past her and gave it a sharp knock with his knuckles.

A mumbled 'come in' came from the other side, and Flora entered the L-shaped cabin no larger than a stateroom with a spectacular double aspect view of the ocean she was too heartsick to appreciate.

Captain Gates occupied a swivel chair at a leather-topped desk, with Mr Hersch and Officer Martin, all of whom leapt to their feet at the sight of her.

'Ah, my dear Miss Maguire.' The captain adopted a sympathetic expression which was not his usual façade and didn't suit him. 'How are you feeling now?'

She took a second or two to catch her breath, which came in shallow gasps after her run up the stairs. How should she be feeling? She had discovered two dead bodies in the space of a few days, and now Eloise was dead. Murdered, in the most horrible way.

'I apologise, Captain,' Bunny said, following her in. 'Flora is very upset, but determined to speak with you.'

Tempted to tell him she could speak for herself, Flora decided against it. Bunny had been nothing but kind and he didn't deserve her harsh tongue.

'How are you holding up, Miss Maguire?' Hersch asked, peering into her face.

'Calmer,' she murmured, unable to bring one single question into her mind. Those she could summon were ridiculous. '*Who killed Eloise?*' and

'*What are you doing about it?*' being the most prominent. 'Are you really a detective?' was the only thing she could think of to say.

'I am, my dear,' he said gently. 'I apologise for not confiding in you. However, the information was not mine to give.'

'What does that mean?' Bunny snapped, his irritation equal to Flora's.

'Captain Gates and I were about to speak with you, so it's expedient you arrived here together,' he replied, making no attempt to explain. 'Which is how you have spent most of this voyage, is it not? Together.'

Flora groaned inwardly. Not only had she shamefully neglected Eddy in her quest to prove she was right about Parnell's death, now the entire ship must be gossiping about her and Bunny.

She could hear them now. '*Did you know that little hussy governess has set her cap at that nice Mr Harrington? And two bodies she has found now. If that doesn't tell you something about her, I don't know what does.*'

How could she ever face the other passengers again?

Her cheeks flamed, which made Hersch smile. 'I don't mean to imply anything, my dear, but your mutual attachment has not gone unnoticed.' He directed her to the last empty chair in the cramped room, leaving Bunny to hover in between.

Officer Martin withdrew his ubiquitous notebook from his pocket and resumed his seat, his pen poised over a page.

Flora almost laughed aloud, but suppressed it in time. Apart from the location, the scene was so redolent of Sunday morning, she might have stepped back several days.

'Here we are again, eh?' Hersch appeared to read her thoughts. 'Before we begin, I would ask that neither you nor Mr Harrington discuss what you saw in Miss Lane's stateroom with the other passengers.'

'Why?' Flora clenched both hands in her lap. 'The entire ship will be buzzing by dinner.'

'The death itself will likely become common knowledge, though the circumstances can be withheld. The crew have put out word that a maid came upon the body during her duties.'

'I didn't see anything,' Bunny said, defensively. 'The purser told me what had happened.'

'What about Gerald Gilmore?' Flora asked. 'Bunny – I mean, Mr Harrington, said he arrived soon afterwards?'

'He has also agreed to co-operate,' Captain Gates said. 'Mr Hersch is of the opinion the killer may reveal himself if we know more than he does.'

'Like baiting a trap?' Bunny said, his voice sharp.

'In a way.' The German inclined his head. 'We also need to know where everyone was at the exact time Miss Lane was killed.'

'And how,' Flora added.

'Beg pardon, Miss Maguire?' Hersch asked.

'How was Eloise killed? There was no weapon that I could see. Did you find one in her stateroom?'

Captain Gates exchanged a look with the German, while Officer Martin kept his head down as he wrote in his notebook.

'She was stabbed,' Hersch conceded after a pause. 'And no, we have not yet found a weapon. Now, if you would kindly tell us exactly where you were this afternoon, my dear.'

'Most people were in the library at the bridge tournament.' Bunny's eyes widened as he looked from the German to Flora. 'Surely you don't think Flora had anything to do with it?'

Flora smiled at this bizarre suggestion. As if she could do something so brutal to any human being, especially lively, fun-loving Eloise? But then, Hersch didn't know her, did he?

'I think we can assume Miss Maguire is not involved.' Hersch lowered his rear end onto the corner of the desk, his arms crossed over his chest. 'Mr Harrington, perhaps you could give us your version of events from the time you last saw Miss Lane?'

Flora listened with barely restrained patience during Bunny's ponderous account of their visit to the wireless room. He made no mention of the telegram they had sent, his rationale being that Flora wanted to see how a wireless telegraphy machine worked.

'An odd time to make a visit, after all, the storm was still quite fierce then,' Hersch observed, splitting a look between them.

'Let me ask *you* a question,' Flora said in an effort to distract him. 'Did you happen to find a large sum of money, or maybe a photograph in either

Mr Parnell's or Eloise's staterooms? I assume you instigated a search of them both?'

Officer Martin's pen stilled and Captain Gates cleared his throat.

'Why would you ask such a specific question, Miss Maguire?' Hersch fixed her with an enquiring look.

Flora held her nerve and refused to explain. 'Well, did you find anything?'

'No sum of money has come to light, nor any photograph.' During the removal of Mr Parnell's personal effects.' Hersch didn't meet her eyes, as if he was embarrassed by her insistence.

'The clipping,' she whispered to Bunny.

'What?'

She looked up and back, meeting his eyes at which he gave a start. 'Oh yes of course.' He hunted through his pockets in turn until he found the small sheet of newsprint that he placed in her open palm.

'I'm guessing you've seen this before.' She handed the piece of newsprint to Hersch.

He removed a pair of oval spectacles from his pocket Flora had never seen him use before and put them on. He scanned the page quickly without expression, then handed it to Captain Gates, confirming that this too was not a surprise. 'Where did you get this?' He removed the glasses slowly, swinging them gently.

'I have an explanation.' Flora attempted a smile. 'Though not a particularly good one, so if you don't mind, I'll save it for another time. Besides, it's not as if we share total honesty. Is it, Mr Hersch?'

'I suppose I asked for that.' Hersch tapped the arm of his glasses against his bottom lip. 'I won't press you. For the moment.' The threat he would do so later was implied. 'Why you think this obituary has something to do with Miss Lane's murder?'

'I didn't see the clipping until this morning, but Eloise had already told me her husband's name was Theo, and he had died. But not the circumstances. I didn't realise the relevance then. I still don't. Then there was the bracelet.'

'What bracelet?' Hersch's eyes sharpened.

Flora looked from the German to Officer Martin and back again.

'Eloise had a gold bracelet with an inscription that said, *"To E on our Wedding Day, T."'*

'We found no bracelet.' Hersch flicked another look at the captain.

'You must have. It was in her bag, the evening one with an embroidered rose.' Restless, Flora half rose, though there was no room to pace with five adults occupying the cramped cabin, so she relaxed back onto the chair again. 'It's a plain, gold band about half an inch thick with a safety chain. I told you about it.' She twisted in her seat to include Bunny.

He nodded. 'She did mention it. I can verify that.'

'Did you actually see this bracelet, Mr Harrington?'

'Well, no, I—'

'I didn't imagine it!' Flora snapped. 'Whoever killed Eloise must have taken it.'

Officer Martin resumed scribbling.

'Don't be too distressed, my dear.' Mr Hersch patted Flora's shoulder, the gesture reminiscent of a favourite uncle. 'We only discovered her a short time ago. Perhaps, when we put Miss Lane's belongings together?' He left the thought hanging.

'Of course.' Flora released a long breath. 'I'm sorry if I was overly emotional.' How could she explain to them that even after three days, she had formed a bond with Eloise? 'Perhaps I'll return to my suite now and order in dinner for Eddy and myself. A quiet evening might help my nerves.'

'I'll escort you back to your suite,' Bunny grasped her elbow gently and assisted her gently to her feet.

'Miss Maguire,' Captain Gates interjected. 'If it's not too arduous for you, we would rather you carried on as normal. You might hear something in the dining room; a detail that would not be revealed in an interview situation.' He laced his hands together on the desk in front of him. 'It would also be wiser if you do not reveal you were the one who found her?'

'Am I an integral part of your investigation now?' she asked, a brow raised in challenge.

'You always have been, my dear,' Captain Gates had added in his half-amused way.

17

'Eddy is fine,' Bunny assured Flora for the fourth time as they approached the dining room. 'He's much happier being with Ozzy and the other boys.'

'He was quite reserved earlier,' Flora said. 'Which makes me think he's more upset than he appears. He liked Eloise.'

'He didn't really know her.'

'It seems none of us did.' Flora recalled vividly the scene that morning on the deck. Eloise and the boys splattered by a giant wave and the way they had screamed with laughter and leapt about, soaking wet but without a care. Eddy would remember that.

'Still, it's unsettling for a child.' She directed a nod at the steward who bowed them into the crowded dining room. 'I hope there won't be any unkind gossip about how Eloise's choice of profession decided her fate. People can be quite cruel at times and I couldn't bear that.'

'If the conversation gets too gruesome, I'll redirect it.' Bunny squeezed her hand that rested on his forearm.

'No, don't do that.' Flora examined her courage and resolved to face what was necessary. 'Mr Hersch is right, we might hear something interesting.'

The Gilmores, Miss Ames and Gus Crowe, Mrs Penry-Jones and Hester all occupied their customary seats at the table by the time they arrived, though Mr Hersch, and Cynthia had yet to appear.

Flora halted, staring.

'What is it?' Bunny paused beside her.

'Three people weren't at the bridge tournament. Mr Hersch, Cynthia and Miss Ames. Max wasn't there for obvious reasons, and Hester came later and—' her gaze slid to Mr Parnell's empty chair, set beside Eloise's. A shudder went through her and she straightened her shoulders and continued to the table, where Bunny held out her chair.

'How can he possibly guarantee our safety?' Miss Ames demanded loudly. 'He's no idea who the killer is.' She had abandoned her rainbow hues for a slate grey skirt and white blouse, both of which accentuated her sallow complexion.

'Who is 'he', Miss Ames? Bunny slid Flora's chair closer to the table.

'Why, the captain of course.'

Conversation resumed, but was slow to gain momentum, becoming forced in places while responses to bad jokes were overly enthusiastic.

Gerald and Monica avoided each other's eyes, while Gus Crowe lounged carelessly in his chair, but even he barely spoke.

'I'm surprised to see *her* here tonight.' Bunny nodded to where Cynthia made her way slowly to the table, stopping now and then in response to comments she either returned with a brief word or waved away. Poised and lovely as ever, Flora judged her to be slightly diminished somehow, her eyes red-rimmed beneath a thicker than usual layer of make-up.

'She likes to make an entrance, doesn't she?' Monica whispered, loud enough for Cynthia to hear. She had barely sat before Miss Ames asked in an almost funereal voice, 'How is your poor husband, my dear?'

'In some pain still, and very tired,' Cynthia replied, with the air of a tragic heroine. 'He was asleep when I left.' The waiter slid a salad in front of her which she poked desultorily with no apparent appetite.

'Sickrooms can be very wearing, can't they?' Miss Ames fiddled with a necklace of jet at her throat. 'However, we cannot simply sit here and make no reference to what has happened. Miss Lane sat right here with us mere hours ago.'

Mrs Penry-Jones cast a vague gaze at her companion. 'We don't trouble ourselves with the affairs of such people, do we, Hester?'

'No, Mrs Penry-Jones.' Hester's cheeks pinked, but her hands remained steady.

'It's not as if we can get away from this murderer in our midst.' Monica's voice held slight panic. 'I mean, in a hotel we could simply leave, but here—'

'No, we couldn't.' Gus Crowe poured himself a glass of water and set the jug down with a thump. 'We would all be under house arrest in a hotel. The police would insist on it. We're all suspects after all.'

Captain Gates rose from his table at the far end of the room, a glass in one hand and a knife in the other which he clinked together to call for quiet.

'Chap's behaving as if we're all at a wedding,' Crowe snarled, attracting hard looks from their neighbours and a critical 'tut' from Mrs Penry-Jones.

'As you must all be aware by now,' Captain Gates said, making a valiant effort to instil gravity into his tone, but he still looked as if he was about to announce a concert or a singalong, 'Miss Eloise Lane was found dead this afternoon in her stateroom.' A wave of nods and low murmurs greeted his words, some turning to Table No. 6 in silent accusation. 'This event casts doubt on the previous demise of Mr Frank Parnell, but as yet, we are not certain the two incidents are connected.'

'Jolly unfortunate if they're not,' Gerald scoffed.

'The crew and myself are doing everything we can to apprehend the person or persons responsible, assisted by a gentleman from the Pinkerton's Detective Agency.' The murmurs and nods increased in pitch at this interesting element, until Captain Gates called for quiet again. 'Mr Carl Hersch has made himself available for anyone who has any pertinent information about either the death of Mr Parnell, or Miss Lane. In the meantime, we hope you will report any suspicious behaviour among your fellow passengers.'

'They expect us all to spy on each other now, do they?' Cynthia's eyes flashed with annoyance. 'As if I don't have enough to cope with, now I shall have to watch every word.'

'Why? What have you got to hide, my dear?' Monica's enquiry was said with bland innocence, but made Flora wonder what was behind it.

'Don't be ridiculous,' Cynthia slumped in her seat and turned away.

'Hush,' Miss Ames snapped. 'The captain is still speaking.'

'We believe these incidents to be isolated, and therefore wish to assure you everyone will be perfectly safe on board for the rest of the voyage. Thank you.' He smiled and bowed in response to a flurry of hand-clapping before he resumed his seat.

'Was anyone aware that German fella was a detective?' Gerald broke the heavy silence that had settled between them. 'Came as a surprise to me, I can tell you.'

'Why will no one tell us what actually happened to poor Eloise?' Miss Ames' voice rose. 'That nice young second officer would only say she had been discovered dead in her stateroom.'

'I heard she was strangled.' Monica pressed a hand to her throat. 'What with Mr Parnell possibly being murdered too, at this rate we'll all be slaughtered in our beds.'

'Don't be melodramatic, woman, Parnell wasn't murdered.' Gerald signalled to the waiter to bring him another drink, though he had barely touched his food. 'If one listens long enough to shipboard gossip, you'll hear Eloise was bludgeoned, poisoned, drowned and possibly suffered a heart attack.' He glanced at his wife's plate, sighing. 'Monica, dear,' he dragged out the words in barely restrained annoyance, 'what is the point of picking mushrooms out of a beef stroganoff?'

Monica grimaced, but continued to discard the offending items onto the side of her plate.

Flora picked at her poached salmon, the fork in her hand trembled on its way to her mouth, but she set it down, the contents untasted. Sadness bunched beneath her ribs. How could they talk about Eloise in the same breath as mushrooms? Although maybe Mr Hersch was right and allowing everyone to gossip was a good thing. It could also explain why he wasn't here.

'Racy ladies, these actresses.' Gus Crowe waved his fork in mid-air. 'Perhaps it was an assignation that went wrong.' His gaze swung to meet Gerald, returning his scowl with a slow wink.

Gerald shoved his plate away from him with such force, his wine glass threatened to topple over. He caught it just in time and muttered an apology, his face flaming. Muttering something inaudible to Monica, he stood and with a curt not and murmured, 'Excuse me,' then strode to the door.

'What's wrong with Gerald?' Flora whispered to Bunny. 'And where's he going?'

'I don't know.' Bunny stared after him. 'Perhaps he's more upset about Eloise than he said, though he hardly knew her.'

'Someone knew her well enough to kill her. Why not Gerald?'

'It's not that. Crowe goaded him just then. I would like to know what he meant.'

Flora ground her teeth in mute anger, but was for the moment trapped. Theatrical exits weren't de rigueur for governesses, besides, she owed it to Eloise to stay and discover what she could. Instead, she fumed silently at the callous way Crowe spoke of a woman he professed to be attracted to.

'Somewhat inappropriate, old chap.' Bunny appeared to sense Flora's discomfort and frowned at Crowe across her lap. 'Miss Lane is barely cold.'

'Sorry.' Crowe gave a light-hearted shrug but didn't seem at all apologetic. 'Didn't mean to offend and all that.'

'Mr Crowe could have a point.' Hester focused on the slice of meat she brought slowly to her mouth. 'Miss Lane did exhibit over-familiarity with the officers. Maybe it was one of them?'

Flora frowned, having never seen Eloise behave with more than friendliness towards everyone, except perhaps Gus Crowe, which was still a mystery. The man was certainly not attractive, had an oily, ingratiating way about himself, and he made no attempt to hide an underlying sleaziness.

'My stewardess,' Miss Ames began, pausing to ensure everyone was listening, 'told me in confidence that Miss Lane was found lying on her bed, quite blue and with her tongue hanging out of her mouth.'

'There, you see, strangled.' Monica turned a triumphant gaze on Miss Ames, who nodded sagely.

Flora's hand tightened on her glass until she was in danger of breaking it, then jumped when Bunny nudged her. Gossip had already twisted the truth to fit more salacious appetites, but if she could bear it a while longer some nugget of truth might emerge.

'Flora, could you pass the water jug?' Bunny asked, more she suspected to distract her than anything, as when she handed it to him he leaned close. 'You're doing fine,' he said, squeezing her hand on the tabletop.

Hersch's previous comment that their companionship had not gone unnoticed prompted her to slide her hand from beneath his. She reminded herself not to study his face too intently when he spoke, or return his brief, concerned smiles with betraying ones of her own. Such behaviour would confuse him and do nothing for her already tainted reputation. Governesses had to be like Caesar's wife: above reproach.

'What are you smiling at?' Bunny said. 'Have you thought of something?'

She shook her head. 'No, it's not important.' Frowning, she caught the tail end of something Hester said to Cynthia.

'...Eloise's cabin this afternoon, Mrs Cavendish?' Hester's voice was falsely subservient. 'You were bringing her some herbal tea, if I recall?'

Cynthia jerked her fork, smearing mustard onto the tablecloth. 'I–I did, yes. But there was no answer to my knock. The commotion on the deck below distracted me, and when I realised it was Max down there, I—' She halted as if she had come up against some mental image that was too horrible to bear, and shook her head to dismiss it.

Hester went back to her food, apparently unmoved. Was her apathy a case of a plain woman who could not bring herself to regret the passing of a pretty one, or something else?

'I suppose now he's Gates' best buddy, he's too grand to eat with us any more.' Crowe nodded to the figure of Mr Hersch as he came through the door. 'Oh no, my mistake, here he comes. Watch what you say, everyone.'

'Apologies for my late arrival.' The German's amiable gaze settled briefly on each face in turn as he took his chair.

'You missed the captain's speech,' Bunny said, swivelling his chair slightly to make room.

'Are you really a Pinkerton's detective?' Miss Ames asked before the German's rear had connected with the seat.

'I didn't miss it exactly,' Hersch smiled at Bunny. 'In fact, I helped him prepare it. And yes, dear lady,' he inclined his head. 'I am indeed.' He eased backwards to allow a waiter to place his entrée in front of him.

'You might have been a bit more forthcoming,' Crowe snapped.

'I agree,' Miss Ames added. 'We would have felt much safer had we known you were on board.'

'Don't see how.' Mrs Penry-Jones demolished a bread roll into crumbs on her side plate. 'We still have two dead bodies and no idea who the murderer is.'

'Everyone on board will be investigated fully in due course.' Mr Hersch held each of their gazes in turn. 'The perpetrator will be discovered, I assure you.'

'You think the murders were committed by the same person?' Bunny asked.

'We cannot be sure, but for the moment, yes. I'm sure things will be clearer when we reach England and the proper authorities are involved.'

'Are you suggesting it was one of us?' Mrs Penry-Jones looked up sharply. 'Most of us here were playing bridge when she was found. Except Cynthia of course, she was with dear Max who was being tended by the doctor.' She turned a burning gaze on Flora. 'Come to think of it, Miss Maguire, you left the library in something of a hurry. Where were *you* all afternoon?'

Flora frowned, not so much at her accusatory tone, but the reference to Cynthia's husband as 'dear Max' when she couldn't recall them ever having a conversation.

'I can vouch for Miss Maguire's movements, Mrs Penry-Jones,' Bunny answered for her, the words, 'not that they are any of your concern' hovered in the air.

'I'll wager you can.' Crowe gave a knowing chuckle.

Miss Ames supressed a smile, though not quick enough to conceal the glint of mischief in her eyes. 'I don't play bridge, in case anyone is interested. I was in my stateroom, writing.'

'Miss Lane was with us on deck before luncheon,' Monica said, then added quickly, 'she was in excellent spirits. Then the storm worsened and an officer warned us to go back inside. I don't recall seeing her after that.' She looked up to see Gerald had returned to the table, his expression much calmer than when he had left.

'We all know what Max was doing later on,' Gerald said, apparently having heard the last comment. 'Trying not to drown.'

At Cynthia's wince, Gerald leaned towards her as he took his seat. 'Forgive me, my dear. I meant nothing by it. One needs to keep a sense of humour about such things.'

'You're right.' Cynthia dabbed her lips delicately with a napkin and gave him a shy smile. 'Max wasn't badly hurt after all. I have a lot to be grateful for.'

'Huh, what was he doing out there in the first place?' Mrs Penry-Jones snapped as she gestured to Hester to pass her the butter.

'I saw Eloise just before luncheon.' Crowe gave up his attempt to attract a waiter and filled his wine glass himself. 'At least I think I did. It was a girl in a cloak with a hood similar to the one I've seen her wear.'

'Are you sure?' Miss Ames quizzed him. 'In which case you must have been the only one.'

'Really?' Crowe swept the table with a half-embarrassed glance. 'Oh well, I didn't see her in the dining room, but then it was a buffet and everyone was moving around a lot. The storm was still raging too, so...' Having instilled doubt, he left the words hanging.

'I saw her on deck on my way to the bridge tournament,' Hester volunteered, flushing as all eyes turned towards her. 'She was at the rail, just staring out to sea.'

'In that storm?' Gerald snapped. 'A tiny thing like Eloise could have been washed overboard.'

'I–I may have been wrong in that case,' Hester said. 'She was quite a long way away and I wasn't wearing my glasses. Though at the time I was convinced it was her.'

Flora slanted a sideways look at Hester, unable to remember having seen her wearing glasses.

Gerald raised a conspiratorial eyebrow at the detective. 'Ah, but Eloise didn't drown, did she?'

Hersch didn't react to this remark let alone respond to it. He simply carried on eating his stroganoff without getting any sauce on his moustache.

'Enough of this murder talk.' Crowe tossed his napkin onto the table beside his plate. 'It's like a morgue in here. I've lost my appetite. If anyone is in the mood for poker, feel free to join me in the smoking room.'

* * *

Flora stood silent at the rail beside Bunny as they stared out to sea, where the evening mist split like curtains being pulled aside to reveal a sea as dark as oil. His ability to sense when she wanted to talk, or when she preferred silence was a rare skill, and one of the things she liked about him. If only she could forget that impulsive embrace as completely as he evidently had.

A rising moon lit a cloud bank to pearly grey, while the wind struck a note in the rigging. The steady whoosh of the sea far below soothed her nerves, though could not banish the parade of images that marched through her head. The worst ones, like Eloise lying dead, she drove down, while she examined the less disturbing ones more closely: Eloise's smiling face as they sat on her bed after they invaded Parnell's stateroom, the palpable fear in her eyes when Flora had told her about the photograph. She hadn't wanted the German to see it. Why? To keep her marriage to Theodore van Elder a secret? But if, as she thought, Mr Hersch was working for her late husband's family, it wouldn't make any difference. Or was her fear not based on logic, and she was convinced that even without evidence they could make her life unbearable?

'Why was Gerald so jumpy with Crowe this evening?' Flora asked, still searching for reasons and the questions to go with them. 'Gerald usually treats him like an annoying insect, but something rattled him for him to go storming off like that.'

'Have your powers of perception let you down on this occasion?' Bunny leaned an elbow on the rail and twisted towards her.

'What do you know that I don't?' Flora narrowed her eyes at him.

'Gerald has developed a *tendre* for a certain lady in a stateroom on the stern saloon deck.'

'A serious one?' Flora's eyes widened. 'Not Eloise? I heard him once refer to her as a pocket Venus.'

Bunny shook his head. 'Not her, and I doubt it's more than a mild flirtation.'

'As far as you know,' Flora said. 'Maybe Gerald did have a similar flirtation with Eloise. One which went wrong when she threatened to tell Monica.' Flora's thoughts took flight. Maybe not all Gerald's secrets are innocent. Monica could be abrasive sometimes, but she was a kind, motherly woman with no malice in her. Or were Gerald's flirtations simply that, harmless and short-lived?

'Rumour says the lady in question enjoys his admiration, but has no wish to pursue it.' Bunny's upper arm pressing against hers. 'Apparently, she has set her sights on a certain wealthy widower who lives in Manchester.'

'How do you know all this? Have you been listening at doors?'

'Like you, I have begun to regard our fellow travellers through suspicious eyes.'

'You've persuaded me that men enjoy gossip every bit as much as us women.'

She tugged her shawl tighter as a salt-tanged breeze raised goose bumps on her arms. Perhaps this dalliance of Gerald's should be no surprise. Monica had a kind heart, but her social climbing and penchant for an expensive lifestyle must be a burden on any man, no matter how successful.

Bunny shook his head, frowning. 'I doubt Gerald is our man. A roving eye doesn't necessarily lead to worse crimes.'

'I suppose not. It also means we didn't learn anything new tonight, did we?' she said, disappointed. A sudden sharp gust of wind swept the deck and Flora shivered.

'You're cold, perhaps we should keep moving.' He offered his arm and they set off again along the deck in comfortable silence before halting outside her door where he turned to face her. 'We must trust Hersch to live up to the Pinkerton Detective Agency's reputation.'

'What do you know about Pinkerton's?' Not that she cared. It was enough for her then to be the entire focus of Bunny's attention. His face was inches from hers, and even in this low light, the sprinkle of freckles across his nose were clearly visible.

'Pinkerton was a Scotsman.' He removed his glasses and gently polished them with a handkerchief as an aid to thought, another habit she was growing used to. 'In the 1850s, his agency guarded President Lincoln on his way to his inauguration in Baltimore. They even foiled an assassination attempt.'

'That sounds more like muscle for hire,' Flora said.

'Indeed. For years they were regarded as strike-breaking thugs, employed by businessmen who objected to their employees making demands about their working conditions.'

'What did that have to do with solving crimes?'

'Very little.' He held the spectacles up to the electric light on the bulkhead, checking them before putting them on. 'Then in the 1870s, the president of the Philadelphia Railroad feared the activity of the coal mine trade unions would reduce his profits. Pinkerton's agents were employed to infiltrate a mining organization called, coincidentally, the "Molly Maguires", and as a result, over twenty members were executed.'

'My goodness, that's awful.'

'Perhaps, but the "Mollys" weren't entirely innocent. They contributed to the violence, so it was justice of sorts. After that, employers threatened with union action paid Pinkerton's to disrupt their meetings. They didn't spare the sap, either. A lot of heads got broken in the process.'

'And Mr Hersch works for them?' At his nod she continued, 'He doesn't strike me as a thug.' Flora jerked her chin back as a thought occurred to her. 'You're trying to distract me, aren't you?'

His gaze met hers and held. 'Is it working?'

'You're a nice man, Mr Harrington.'

'I try. I'm also truly sorry about the way I reacted when you hugged me earlier. No, don't look away, I know you're embarrassed, and I made it worse by my behaviour. I was taken by surprise, but in an agreeable way. I really liked it.'

'B–but I thought—'

'I know what you thought,' he whispered, his arm gently encircling her waist. 'I had hoped our first embrace wasn't going to take place in public while I was soaked to the skin, and gasping for air like a landed fish.'

First. He said first.

Her stomach did a strange but pleasing lurch, but too embarrassed to ask what was expected of her now, she eased away, preparing to offer polite thanks and a formal goodnight. Before she could speak, he placed both hands on the wall on either side of her shoulders, pinning her in place with a smouldering look. She could hardly breathe as he stared into her eyes in an unhurried way as if he enjoyed simply looking at her.

Without warning he brushed his mouth across hers in a feather-light touch that ended before it really began. He eased back a few inches, his gaze roving her face again. When his mouth pressed on hers a second time, he was not tentative, or light, but confident, even possessive.

Having never kissed anyone in passion before, Flora had no time to worry whether her reaction was appropriate or not. Instinct took over and her arms moved of their own accord to encircle his neck. The pressure of his mouth increased under hers, his touch becoming insistent, even fierce. His breathing quickened, and when the tip of his tongue flicked over her bottom lip, her nerves jumped.

Oblivious to the deck around her, Mr Hersch's cheery, 'Goodnight, Miss Maguire, Mr Harrington' sent them springing apart, though the detective didn't so much as pause in his brisk stride down the deck.

'I–I had better—' Flora stammered, certain he could feel her heart thump against her chest.

'Um... yes, yes of course.' Bunny dropped his arms and retreated, ducked his head, and jammed both hands into his pockets. 'Well, good-night then.'

She searched for an excuse to call him back, but the sight of Eddy's grinning face with his nose pressed against the window glass changed her mind.

18

THURSDAY

'I fail to see how a treasure hunt can possibly be considered frivolous and thus insulting to the dead, whereas a dance is not,' Monica complained as she and Flora watched the boys play an enthusiastic game of shuffleboard on the saloon deck below. 'It's too bad, when my Ozzy was so looking forward to it. He's excellent at puzzles.'

'Eddy is also disappointed, although he changed his mind when they announced the horse racing will go ahead this afternoon,' Flora said.

Despite Flora's incipient worry, Eddy had slept well the night before, followed by a pre-breakfast conversation where she reassured him Mr Hersch had everything in hand. She took refuge in the understanding that children were resilient; safe in the knowledge that however bad things became, they would be shielded from the worst of life's tragedies by the grown-ups.

'My boy's not on form at the moment, you know.' Monica's sharp features softened in concern. 'These deaths have affected him badly.' She clamped a hand onto her hat and waved. 'Oh look, Ozzy just scored a point.'

Flora's eyebrow rose as she watched Monica's sensitive boy leap in the air, screaming at the top of his lungs.

'It doesn't count!' Eddy shouted above his friend's delighted cries. 'Anything above fifty is subtracted. Don't you know the rules?'

Ozzy's shoulders slumped visibly, though he accepted defeat magnanimously and returned to stand behind Eddy so he could take the next shot.

'It appears,' Monica leaned closer, lowering her voice, 'that the steward had to chastise the boys at dinner last night for exchanging lurid details of poor Eloise's death. All conjured from their boyish imaginations of course. We wouldn't dream of telling Ozzy what really happened.'

'Do *you* know what happened to Eloise?' Flora asked, immediately alert.

'Well, no, not really,' Monica faltered. 'Although most murders of pretty girls tend to be throttling, don't they? At least it's so in novels.'

Flora nodded, but chose not to contradict her.

'I'll escort the boys to luncheon myself,' Monica insisted. 'One cannot be too careful with dangerous people about.' She glanced over Flora's shoulder and smiled. 'Not that you will be lonely, my dear, for here comes your beau.'

'No, actually, he isn't my—' Flora broke off when she realised Monica was already halfway down the deck and unlikely to hear her.

Bunny halted beside her and withdrew a brown envelope from an inside pocket and handed it to her, his expression grim. 'This was waiting in my cabin when I returned from breakfast.'

'From your reporter friend?' Flora took the slip of paper gingerly, though reading it proved a frustrating exercise as the corners kept curling in the wind on a quest to escape her fingers.

Confirm Theodore van Elder born Baltimore 12th April 1859, died 15th Feb. 1900. Leaves wife, Estelle van Elder, and child from previous marriage. Father deceased 1880, mother believed still living. Only other family member known, Marlon van Elder born 1865 — arrest record held by New York Police for various misdemeanours, including issuing valueless cheques and minor fraud. Aliases include Joseph Ellerman, Frank Ellerman, Frank Parnell. Whereabouts currently unknown.

'Not unknown any more.' Flora handed it back to him. 'Marlon van Elder is at this moment lying under a sheet in the doctor's office.'

'So it seems.' Bunny refolded the page.

'What it doesn't tell us, is his exact relationship to Theodore. Was he a brother, a relative by marriage? And why was he travelling with Eloise?'

'Flora,' Bunny's voice held a warning note. 'You're going to have to consider the possibility that Parnell and Eloise killed Theodore van Elder, and they were escaping the country.'

'He was blackmailing her. Why would he do that if they were in it together?' She shook the thought away, refusing to contemplate she had been so wrong about Eloise.

'Greed? A falling out of villains, maybe?' Bunny replaced the telegram back in its envelope.

'Eloise was as much a victim as Parnell.' Flora couldn't bring herself to call her Estelle, she would always think of her as Eloise. 'I wish we had told Mr Hersch everything sooner.'

'That would have been an interesting conversation.' Bunny cleared his throat, addressing a spot a few inches over her head. '*Mr Hersch, about that clipping I stole from the dead man's cabin when I was looking for a large amount of money with the girl who was herself murdered yesterday. I—*'

'All right, I see your point.' Flora gestured for him to stop. 'What do *you* suggest?' She worried the side of a thumbnail with her front teeth.

'Well, I—' he broke off and glanced past Flora's shoulder. 'Oh, look out.' He gave a low groan and tucked the envelope back into his pocket, patting it.

Flora turned to where Cynthia strolled the deck in a peacock blue dress with a matching coat that enhanced her grey eyes.

'How is Max coming along?' Flora asked as she came to a leisurely halt beside them.

'Bruised and sore, poor dear.' Cynthia's face relaxed in relief. 'He has no memory of why he was out on deck in that storm, and I shan't badger him.' The implication that no one else should either went unspoken. 'I'm so glad the dance is going ahead tonight. It will give us all a welcome distraction from this awful business.'

She stroked Bunny's forearm with a manicured hand. 'You must promise to dance with me, Bunny, because no one else will. Max will come too of course, but his arm won't be healed enough to dance with me. No doubt the other passengers will mutter about me if I take the floor with another man, but I do love to dance.'

'I'll be happy to, Cynthia,' Bunny said. 'What about you, Flora?'

Flora hesitated. 'I haven't made up my mind yet. I'll think about it.' The prospect of leaping round a dance floor didn't seem right somehow with Eloise lying dead in the doctor's office.

'Of course you'll be there.' Cynthia levelled her clear gaze on Flora. 'You cannot possibly waste that gown, it looks wonderful on you.' Her pretty face lit at the clear note of the bugle announcing luncheon. 'Oh good, I'm quite famished, though I've done nothing all morning except pour tea and plump Max's pillows. It must be this bracing sea air.' She turned on her heel and tripped across the deck with a backwards wave.

'It's as if Eloise never existed,' Flora said, mildly repulsed.

'They were hardly friends, though I admit, I didn't take Cynthia for the callous sort.' He patted his pocket where the telegram lay, 'I'll give this to Hersch straight away. We don't want him thinking we're keeping any more secrets now he has an official investigation under way.'

'Good idea, and I know I said we hadn't learned anything last night,' Flora said slowly, 'but didn't Cynthia admit she went to Eloise's stateroom with some tea yesterday afternoon?'

'I seem to recall she did, but there was no answer to her knock.'

'So she says. Cynthia has lied before, remember, when she claimed she had never met Parnell.'

With Bunny's reassuring form close to her side as they walked to the dining room, something about the telegram niggled at the back of her mind but remained elusive. Then she conjured Bunny's kiss the night before in her head, hoping it would be repeated, and soon, but not quite knowing how to create the right circumstances.

* * *

Flora's post-prandial walk brought her to the saloon deck, where she stood to admire the foam-topped waves crest and fall in the distance. She took her allotted steamer chair with her name in elegant script on a pasteboard label, dragging it along the boards so it was apart from the militarily spaced line of similar chairs. A glance upwards sent a dull burning sensation in her chest, reminding her that the exact point on the deck above was where she had met Eloise on their second day at sea.

A shadow fell across her outstretched legs. 'Good afternoon, Miss Maguire,' an accented voice dragged her from her sad musing. 'May I join you?'

She shielded her eyes with a hand. 'Good afternoon, Mr Hersch, and please do,' she replied, unsmiling.

'Oh, my dear, are you still brooding about the unfortunate fate of Miss Lane?' Ignoring the other steamer chairs, he dragged out a folding wooden seat from a pile set beneath the companionway, shook it open with an expert hand and crouched on the slats.

'Does that surprise you?' Flora resumed her contemplation of the sea.

'Are you not joining the ladies today?' he asked, ignoring her question.

Flora looked to where Miss Ames sat further along the row with Hester, while Mrs Penry-Jones commanded the attention of two older ladies who had formed her small coterie since boarding.

'Not today. I could do without having to endure Mrs Penry-Jones's comments about governesses with ideas above their station, or actresses getting their just desserts.'

'Don't let her bother you, my dear. People like her belong in the past. You should embrace the modern age, like Mr Harrington, for example. Now there's a young man well-equipped to tackle this new century with that horseless carriage of his.'

'I'm sure he'll succeed in his world.' Despite herself, Flora's possessive pride rose in her chest.

'His world? Why not yours too?' At Flora's shrug he went on, 'If you would take my advice, I suspect your pride is getting in the way of a meaningful friendship with that young man.'

'We move in very different circles.' She aimed for pragmatism but knew she failed, her cheeks burning as she recalled he had caught them kissing outside her door. 'He's used to a more sophisticated company.'

'How interesting,' he stroked a finger and thumb down either side of his moustache as he talked, 'that it's the working classes who cling most tenaciously to that maxim.'

He didn't speak for a moment, as if giving her time for the thought to sink in, the only sound between them the whoosh of the sea, the only sensation the gentle rise and fall of the ship as it cut through the waves.

'It must have been a dreadful shock, seeing Miss Lane like that?' he said after a moment.

'Indeed it was.' She tried to banish a sudden, shocking image that invaded her head. 'The purser hustled me out before I could take a proper inventory of her stateroom.'

'Is that your way of asking me to tell you what we found?'

'If you feel so inclined.' Her lips twitched but she fought the urge to smile.

His eyes slewed sideways, regarding her with a calculating gaze. 'If I didn't know better, I might imagine I'm being manipulated, Miss Maguire.'

Flora allowed herself a tiny smile. He always used her full name when he teased her. She quite liked it.

'What I can tell you,' he went on, 'is that despite the disarray in her stateroom, there was no sign of a struggle, therefore I assume—'

'Eloise knew her attacker and let him into her room willingly,' Flora finished for him.

'Exactly. Therefore, it was someone she had no reason to suspect.'

'A member of the crew, perhaps?'

He cleared his throat, as if his next words required a certain gravitas. 'What we do know is she received three deep stab wounds; two just below her ribcage and one in her right breast. All inflicted with a thin, straight-bladed knife.'

Having not expected such candour, Flora fought down a wave of nausea. 'Three stab wounds. Someone must have really hated Eloise.' *Or wanted to make sure she kept quiet.* 'But you still haven't found a weapon?'

'No. And I assure you a thorough search was carried out.' He twisted his hat between his splayed knees.

'Thus the killer took it with him, or you didn't find it, because it didn't look like a weapon, so it was overlooked.'

'An interesting idea, Miss Maguire.' His eyes when he glanced up and

held her were filled with surprised admiration. 'If Pinkerton's ever decide
to employ women again, I wouldn't hesitate to recommend you.'

'Again?' Flora asked. 'Has there ever been such a thing as a lady
detective?'

'Indeed, yes. There was an infamous one during the Civil War, the
American one that is. Kate Warne was Allan Pinkerton's mistress.'

'I suppose that's one way to get a job.'

Hersch chuckled. 'She was a very effective agent. Then there was Hatty
Lawson and Rose Greenhow; all effective information gatherers, from
what I understand.' His use of the term implied the women were merely
busybodies and gossips, character traits assigned to most women and
hardly flattering.

'Did they actually uncover any crimes?'

'Absolutely. Kate Warne uncovered an assassination plot on Lincoln
before that infamous theatre incident, and Rose moved in illustrious
circles thus was able to pass information about Bull Run to Jefferson
Davies. I believe you could join their ranks if you chose, my dear.'

'So Pinkerton's don't employ women any more?'

'Not since old Pinkerton died. His son didn't approve, so the practice
ceased when he took over. A shame really, I consider ladies a great asset
for uncovering that which is hidden.'

Was that a direct compliment to herself or was he simply reminiscing?

'There's something you might be unaware of,' she began. 'Eloise gave
Mr Parnell $3,000 the night he died.'

'Is that so?' he drew the words out slowly, his mouth twitching slightly,
whether in annoyance or scepticism she couldn't tell.

'I didn't mention it before, because—'

'You felt your observations were being treated as trivial?' His penetrating gaze made her squirm. 'Under what circumstances did Miss Lane
reveal this information to you?' Flora opened her mouth, but he silenced
her with an upraised hand. 'Perhaps I don't wish to know all the details,
and no, we didn't find any money in either stateroom.'

'Was Theodore van Elder murdered?'

Had Flora not been watching for the small start which greeted her
words, she would have missed it.

'The coroner's report in New York said he died from a gastric complaint.' He inclined his head to greet a middle-aged couple who sauntered by, though his gaze did not return to Flora.

'Which doesn't answer my question,' she insisted, not fooled by his mock-innocent expression. 'Who hired you, Mr Hersch?' She doubted he would answer, but it was worth a try.

He raised his hat, smiled and inclined his head, but just when she thought he was about to answer her, he glanced along the deck and frowned.

'Isn't that young Ozzy Gilmore coming this way? He looks a bit harassed.'

Ozzy sidled towards them, a hesitant look on his face, the fingers of one hand twisting a corner of his cardigan. 'Miss Maguire, have you seen Eddy?' he asked while he was still several feet away.

'Isn't he with you?' Anxiety mingled with dread, knotting Flora's stomach. 'When did you last see him?'

'About an hour ago.' Ozzy's eyes darkened with fear at Flora's tone. 'He–he said he had something to do and would see me later.'

The threat issued the other night came back to her like an echo. Her heart skipped and she drew a sharp breath. She started to leave her chair but Mr Hersch restrained her with a hand on her arm.

'Don't panic, Flora,' the German squeezed her hand, conveying that he understood her alarm. 'It will be fine, you'll see.'

'I would rather we found him, Mr Hersch. And quickly,' Flora insisted, turning back to Ozzy. 'Did he say where he was going?'

Ozzy hesitated, his gaze going to a point further along the deck. 'Oh here's Mama and Papa, maybe they know where he is.' Ozzy broke away from her and rushed towards them.

Flora rose to her feet, urging them to move faster as Monica and Gerald had paused to listen to their son's garbled explanation of what he and Eddy had been doing since luncheon.

'The boy can't get into much trouble on the ship.' Gerald's amiable laugh irritated rather than reassured as he strolled closer, exhibiting no signs of panic. 'The crew always keep an eye out for inquisitive youngsters going where they shouldn't.'

'I'm sorry to fuss,' Flora said when they reached her. 'But I really need to find him.'

'Yes, of course.' Monica bent so her face was inches from her son's. 'Ozzy, dear. Where did you last see Eddy?' Her firm but soothing voice contrasted with Gerald's casual one. 'He might need us, you see.'

'Don't frighten the lad, Monica,' Gerald glared at her. 'I'm sure the boy is fine.'

'If I knew I'd be in trouble I wouldn't have said anything,' Ozzy mumbled into his chest. 'I don't know where he went, he didn't tell me.'

'You aren't in trouble,' Mr Hersch said reasonably. He guided Ozzy to the stool he had occupied earlier, sat him down gently and crouched in front of him. 'What were you talking about just before he left? It might help us discover where he is now.'

'Not sure.' Ozzy scratched his head as if it might prompt his memory. 'He was annoyed when we got chucked out of the engine room the other day. Maybe he went back to get a proper look?'

'He wouldn't have, would he?' Flora split a frantic look between the two Gilmores. 'I warned him not to try that again.'

'Really, Flora.' Gerald's concerned frown deepened. 'There's no need to be so upset. He can't have gone far. You stay here with Monica, we'll go and look for him.' He gestured to Hersch, and the two disappeared through the door to the interior of the ship.

Mrs Penry-Jones and her companion had already left, but the commotion brought Miss Ames from her chair. She bustled to Flora's side, a look of concern mixed with curiosity on her face.

'Boys are so inquisitive at that age,' she said when Monica had explained the situation. 'I'm sure he'll be fine, Flora dear. Let me ask the steward to bring you a nice cup of tea.'

Flora did as she was told like a puzzled child, but couldn't banish the fear something bad had happened. Eddy was as mischievous as the next child, but Flora had instilled in him that he wasn't to wander off on his own into dangerous places, or even safe ones, without telling someone. For him to leave his best friend for over an hour was out of character.

Flora didn't notice Hester Smith had joined them until she spoke. 'Mrs Penry-Jones dropped her reading glasses here somewhere. Ah, here they are.' She pounced on a slim ivory-studded case beneath a nearby chair. 'Is something wrong, you all look quite worried?'

'Young Eddy has gone off on an excursion into the bowels of the ship,' Monica said. 'The men have gone to find him.'

'I do hope he's all right.' Hester's brown pebble eyes settled on them each in turn. 'Some nasty accidents happen in those places. A friend of mine's brother was an engineer and he was very badly scalded once when a valve blew—'

'Thank you, Hester, that's quite enough!' Monica cut her off just as the steward arrived with a tray.

Monica fussed about arranging a folding table and had the tray set on top, where she fiddled with cups and saucers. 'Now drink this tea, Flora, you're shaking.' She pushed a cup of steaming brew in Flora's hands. 'Though I'm sure there's nothing to worry about. I expect he's found another friend to play with, and lost track of time.'

Hester fidgeted under the weight of Monica's hostile stare, until she finally took the hint and left.

'Stupid woman,' Monica muttered as Hester returned to Mrs Penry-Jones's circle.

Ozzy made to rise but she wagged a finger at him. 'You stay there, and don't say a word unless you remember something.'

'Anyone would think *I* lost him.' Ozzy hunched, his arms folded, his sulky expression half hidden by a hank of wayward fair hair.

Gus Crowe appeared from nowhere and propped an elbow on the back of Flora's steamer chair, his free hand drawing circles in the wood with a fingernail. 'Heard young Eddy's gone missing. Miss Smith is quite right though, those companionways are slippery and it's mostly in darkness. Hope he hasn't taken a tumble.'

'Do be quiet, Crowe!' Miss Ames snapped. 'You're not helping the situation.'

Flora's nerves tightened until they threatened to snap. She should have gone with Gerald and Mr Hersch, not that she could have done any good, although it might have been better than being the focus of all these disapproving stares. Obediently she drank her tea, though it was the last thing she wanted. However, it seemed to calm Monica, who was oblivious of the waiters who had removed the cloths from all the tables and stood around, fidgeting.

'Miss Maguire?' The German returned, his hands braced on the table. 'I ran into Bunny Harrington on deck, who has joined the search. Eddy wasn't in the engine room, so he and Gerald have gone to search the public rooms. He wanted you to know.'

'Thank you.' Flora breathed slightly easier as images of escaping steam and hot furnaces left her head. 'Did they say where they were going?'

'Eddy is familiar with the upper deck, so they'll try there first. I'll go and assist them, but I assure you someone will let you know the minute he's found.' He pushed himself upright and turned to leave.

Ozzy's fierce expression reminded Flora of something and she called him back, 'Mr Hersch!'

He paused and looked over his shoulder.

'The boys like to play pirates. Maybe you could check the lifeboats?'

Hersch nodded and left.

'Ozzy?' Monica drew the word out slowly. 'What's this about pirates and lifeboats?'

'Now I *am* in trouble,' Ozzy muttered, and slumped lower in his seat.

Flora stood the inaction for a full ten minutes before she pushed herself to her feet. 'I know you're all being kind, but I can't just sit here.'

'What do you hope to do, my dear?' Monica's puzzled features indicated the idea of doing anything more constructive had never occurred to her.

'I have to go and look for him.'

Grabbing her bag and shawl, she pushed through the door to the interior lobby, taking the elegant oak staircase to the promenade deck two at a time, ignoring the odd looks and impatient huffs of middle-aged ladies who made disparaging remarks about the young as she shoved past them.

Outside again, she found Gerald and a crewman had propped a short ladder against a lifeboat, while Bunny had climbed to the top, the canvas peeled back to look inside.

'Any sign of him?' Flora called, shielding her eyes with one hand.

'No!' Bunny called back, grasping the sides on his downward climb. 'We've only checked a couple so far.'

'Not here either!' Mr Hersch climbed the ladder that leaned against the lifeboat behind and unhooked the canvas covering. He shook his head at the sailor who held the ladder, then stepped off the fender onto the deck with surprising agility for an older man, slapping dust from his hands as he approached her. 'Are you sure there's nowhere else you can think of where he might go?'

Flora cast her mind back to her last conversation with Eddy that morning. 'He was looking forward to listening to the Gilmores' gramophone. But that's in their suite.'

'Which is the first place Gerald looked after the engine room.' Bunny jumped down the last two steps of the ladder and came to her side. 'What else is he interested in?'

'Your motor car.' Flora's throat burned.

Bunny bent his head close, his breath warm in her ear. 'Don't worry, Flora. We'll find him.'

Her eyes welled and she nodded, hoping he was right. She wished she had told him about the threat, but some part of her had refused to believe it was real. With Max's near death and Eloise's murder, a whispered voice in a corner had diminished in importance. She had convinced herself it meant nothing and neither she nor Eddy could be touched.

Now she had put Eddy in danger, for which she should never forgive herself.

'There are a few storerooms and empty areas on the lower deck,' Mr Hersch's voice broke into her thoughts. 'We'll take a look there next.'

'What about the other lifeboats?' Flora asked, wiping a tear from her cheek.

'I've set the crew to searching those.' Hersch indicated where two sailors had propped a ladder onto the lifeboat on the opposite deck.

They filed through the door into the interior rooms of the structure, past the communal bathroom and down three flights of stairs into an uncarpeted hallway lit by a symmetrical row of electric lights. Pipes ran along the ceiling above their heads and plain wooden doors ran down both sides at intervals, the grind and roar of the engines loud enough for them to shout. Gerald and Bunny moved along the row, opening each one alternately, assisted by a steward with a bunch of keys who obligingly unlocked each one.

'Why is everything under lock and key?' Flora demanded, impatient by the time they had peered into the sixth room in a row which held little but packing cases and foodstuffs stacked on rows of shelves. 'There's nothing much down here.'

'Stowaways,' the steward said without looking at her. 'Security has to be top class to keep them out.'

As they turned a corner, Flora heard a faint but repeated sound above the engine's low roar. She cocked her head and grabbed Bunny's arm. 'Listen!'

'I can't hear anything,' Gerald said. 'Everything echoes down here.'

'Bunny held up a hand for silence. 'It's coming from along there.' He pointed to the far end of the hallway, where growing closer, the noise turned from a faint indistinctive sound to a muffled yell and an occasional thump from behind a door. 'What's in here?' Bunny pointed.

'The darkroom, sir. It's only used when a passenger wants some photographs developed.'

'Get it open, man!' Bunny instructed.

The steward rattled the pile of keys in search of the appropriate one, then flung the door open, revealing a dishevelled and dusty Eddy who blinked as the light hit his face.

'I've been banging and calling for ages!' Eddy said, his face contorted in anger. 'Where have you been?'

'Eddy!' Ignoring his grubby state, Flora threw her arms around him. 'Are you all right?'

'Steady on, Flora.' Eddy shrugged her off and scrubbed at his head with one hand, yawning.

'What happened, young man?' Mr Hersch asked from behind them.

'I told you he was merely up to some jape,' Gerald said, openly relieved.

'I wanted to see how photographs are developed,' Eddy explained, brushing dust and wood shavings from his blazer. 'I've never seen it done before and the door was open, but no one was about to show me. I was going to leave, but the door slammed behind me and when I tried to open it again, it was locked.' He licked his lips and squinted up at Flora. 'I'm hot and thirsty. Could I have a drink of lemonade?'

'We'll get you one in a moment,' Bunny answered for her. 'Eddy, how did the door shut and lock all by itself?'

He shrugged. 'The key was in the lock when I got here so I went in. Then it closed and I heard the lock turn. I called out but no one heard me.'

'Or they did and ignored you.' Flora murmured burying the rest of that thought. 'Maybe the deck tilted and it closed the door?' she said instead, tightening her arm round Eddy's shoulders, unwilling to let go of him.

'This door wouldn't lock on its own,' Mr Hersch insisted. He closed then opened it twice to demonstrate. 'It requires a key, and there was none in the door when we arrived.'

'I shouted and shouted,' Eddy said, as if he was angry at having been ignored, 'then got tired, so I sat down for a bit. I must have fallen asleep and when I woke up, I started banging on the door again. That's when you got here.'

'The photographer's assistant must have locked the door thinking the room was empty, sir,' the steward suggested, evidently reluctant that any of the crew might be blamed.

'Would you enquire if anyone had photographs developed within the last couple of hours?' Bunny asked him.

'I will, sir, but,' he shuffled his feet, 'the assistant has been known to forget about the key and leave it in the door. The photographer is always telling him about it.' At Bunny's sigh he rushed on, 'But no one comes near the darkroom normally. There's nothing there anyone would want.'

'Nothing but inquisitive small boys,' Gerald said.

'It's not a very large room, they would have seen him,' Flora said, though she was too relieved to argue the point, and hugged Eddy tighter, ignoring his protests. 'You should have told someone where you were going. Who knows when you might have been found?'

'Well, at least until the next person had a photograph to develop,' Gerald said and shrugged when they turned to stare at him.

'I'm sorry, Flora,' Eddy said, contrite. 'I'll take Ozzy with me next time.'

'No you won't.' Flora gave him a tiny shake. 'You aren't to come down here at all. Ever.'

19

Once everyone had been thanked for their efforts and an account of Eddy's minor adventure related to the ladies who had remained on deck, Flora took Eddy back to the suite to change his clothes and give him the lemonade he had demanded four times in ten minutes.

Even Mr Hersch joined the general consensus that it was no more than a youthful prank that had ended well, while Bunny was the only one who understood her fears, but even he expressed an aside that in this case, she might have been mistaken.

'Shutting him in a storeroom is hardly the same as pushing him over-board,' was his reasoning.'

Flora had winced at the idea, but did not argue, though a niggling doubt remained. A prank maybe, but a deliberate one intended to scare her. And Eddy.

Her suggestion to Eddy that he sit quietly with a book until teatime, he greeted without protest.

'Does it have to be a book?' Eddy asked, yawning. 'Could I read one of the copies of *The Strand* you brought down from the library?'

'Oh dear, I should have taken those back. Remind me to do so when you've finished.' She flicked through the last edition from the previous year, checking to see if the content was suitable. 'There's a story here about seven dragons by Miss Nesbit which should keep you occupied while I go and have a bath.' Her skin felt itchy from her walk through the bowels of the ship and dust motes clung to her hair.

'Ooh, yes.' He took the magazine from her and settled in an armchair in the sitting room with a glass of lemonade beside him.

'I'm not sick, Flora,' he had offered in protest to her suggestion he read the story in bed.

'You won't go off again without telling someone, will you, Eddy?' she called to him through the open door while pulling the pins from her hair. 'I know you were fine this time, but I cannot ask Mr Hersch, Bunny or Gerald to come running after you. We might not find you so quickly another time.'

'There won't be a next time, Flora, I promise,' Eddy said with a sigh. 'And it wasn't exactly quick, either. I was banging on the door for ages and ages.'

'I know you think I'm fussing, but I only want to keep you safe.'

'I'll tell you in future,' Eddy mumbled only just loud enough to hear. 'You don't have to keep going on about it.'

Satisfied, she closed the bedroom door, went into the bathroom and turned on the taps. As hot water gushed into the small tub, she threw a generous handful of lavender crystals provided by the steamship company into the water.

She allowed the water to sooth her tense muscles until her fingers started to wrinkle. Once dried, dressed and with her hair carefully pinned up again, she emerged into the sitting room.

'You must be enjoying that story, Eddy, you've been very quiet. Would you like—' she broke off. The room was empty, the magazine lying open on the cushion.

'Eddy?' She checked his room, but he wasn't there either.

A familiar rush of dread squeezed a groan through her lips, just as she spotted a sheet of white paper on the bureau by the door, and on it was Eddy's handwriting.

Gone to see Matilda with Ozzy,

His name was scrawled at the bottom, then in smaller script:

This is to tell you where I am.

Sighing, she grabbed a shawl to ward against Atlantic winds and stepped out onto the promenade deck, where she was drawn to the rail by the clatter of footsteps and a baritone shout alerting her to a commotion on the saloon deck below.

'Come back here!' Bunny's voice called, just as Eddy appeared, running full pelt from beneath the superstructure, followed by Ozzy. Bunny gave chase, but collided with a strolling couple, and halted to apologise. By the time he had disengaged himself and moved on, the boys had disappeared. He raised a hand to his forehead and scanned the deck, then dropped both arms to his sides in resignation, turning back in the direction he had come.

Flora groaned, pushed away from the rail and descended to the deck where Bunny stood beside Matilda, the canvas pulled aside, and the ropes holding it secure lying like coiled flat snakes on the deck.

'Young rascals,' Bunny muttered. Having discarded his jacket on the bonnet he was in the process of rolling up his shirtsleeves.

'I take it you mean Eddy and Ozzy?' Flora said, reaching him. 'I'm so sorry, I cannot believe after what happened not two hours ago that he's up to mischief again.'

'Escaped again, did he?' Bunny pushed a casual hand through his fair hair and grinned at her over one shoulder. 'I caught them playing inside, so chased them off.'

'I'm so sorry. I thought he was still in the suite but he crept out leaving a note. Though he knows better than to go near Matilda unless you are with him.'

'Still getting yourself into a state about boyish antics, eh?' Bunny teased, nudging her gently.

'Don't tease me. I cannot help worrying about him. Someone must have known he was in that darkroom, what with it being so small, they couldn't have missed him.'

'Stop worrying about it, I used to do far worse than that when I was his age.' Bunny applied a spanner to a nut somewhere beneath the bonnet. 'I climbed a flagpole once, nearly killed myself getting down again.'

'I can't stop worrying. Suppose someone does wish him harm?'

'We'll make sure that doesn't happen.' He nodded to the motor car. 'Anyway, this wasn't your fault either. I suspect Ozzy was the ringleader in this case, and boys, as they say, will be boys.'

Flora cast a critical eye over the gleaming yellow paintwork, but nothing stood out as a source of Bunny's annoyance other than the disarranged cover. 'Have they done any damage?'

'A few footprints on the seats and sticky marks on the steering wheel.' He bent to peer inside. 'I cleaned all this earlier. Now I shall have to do it again.'

A movement from the corner of Flora's eye drew her gaze to where the boys hovered twenty feet away. When they saw her watching, they ducked behind a corner.

'I can see you there!' Flora called in her best governess tone. 'Now both of you, come out and apologise to Mr Harrington.'

Eddy shuffled forward. 'We didn't mean any harm, honestly.'

'It wasn't us, Miss Maguire,' Ozzy insisted, displaying the indignation of a child unaccustomed to being chastised. 'The ropes were already undone when we got here.'

'The cover had been pulled back too,' Eddy added.

'Even so,' Flora glared at them, 'neither of you should have—'

'What do you mean?' Bunny cut across her. 'I checked the canvas before luncheon, everything was secure then.'

'The door on the driver's side was open as well.' Eddy's courage returned and he crept closer.

'You're sure about that?' Bunny asked, frowning. 'This was how it was when you arrived?'

'Yes, sir!' both boys chorused.

Flora didn't know Ozzy well enough to judge his character accurately. Eddy, on the other hand, was more easily read, and she was sure he was being truthful.

'Well, if you didn't unwrap it, who did?' Bunny murmured, mostly to himself.

'Ah, got the motor out, I see.' Gerald called as he strolled towards them, resplendent in a white blazer, his straw hat tipped back on his head. Oblivious of Bunny's concerned frown, and the boys' subdued faces, he circled the contraption with an appraising eye, peering through the windows. 'I think I'll buy myself one of these when I get home. You don't see many in Reigate.'

'Oh, Papa, that would be super!' Ozzy threw Eddy a triumphant look.

'Actually I didn't get it out,' Bunny said, resigned. 'Though it appears someone did.'

Gerald eyed his son knowingly. 'Have you been messing about where you weren't supposed to, son?' He placed his hands on his hips and glowered in mock sternness, though his eyes glinted with the amused pride at his son's capacity for mischief. 'I'm surprised at you, young man.' he ruffled Eddy's hair. 'Getting into mischief so soon after your adventure.'

'I wasn't much.' Eddy poked the toe of his shoe against a wheel. 'And we weren't doing anything wrong, sir.'

'I don't suppose you saw anyone loitering about here earlier, did you, Gerald?' Bunny asked.

'I've been with Monica in our suite.' Gerald shook his head. 'I've not been near.'

'We didn't do anything!' Eddy protested, his pleading look going from Bunny to Gerald and back again.

'You know exactly what I mean.' Flora silenced him with a glare. 'And leaving me notes won't get you out of trouble either. Not after what we discussed.'

'Don't be angry with him, Flora,' Bunny interrupted gently, adjusting his glass which had dropped on his nose. 'I'm probably overreacting. It's just that these machines are rare and jolly expensive. There's always the fear my competitors might try to beat me to the English market by sabotaging this model and ruining my future plans.'

'Oh,' Flora said, dismayed. 'I didn't think of that.' First murderers on board, disappearing schoolboys and now saboteurs. How had she had imagined this voyage would be uneventful?

A few feet away Gerald had engaged both boys in a play fight that elicited frowns from some passengers who strolled in pairs along the deck, while others directed indulgent smiles at the game. He feigned surrender when Eddy sprang at him, then launched a half-hearted attack with one arm. Ozzy pitched in, brandishing a short wooden stick.

Flora watched, resigned, as Eddy threw himself into the game with enthusiasm. He didn't appear to have been affected by his brief imprisonment in the darkroom earlier. She wished he wasn't so ready to jump into the next adventure, but without frightening him, how could she prevent it? That's what boys were like, and truth be told she wouldn't want him to be anything else, though at the same time it made her realise how vulnerable that made him.

'Now, you two.' Gerald broke off to wink at Bunny before addressing the boys. 'If Flora will allow, what say we study the form before the horse racing? Might even win a couple of bob, eh?'

'With all that's happened I had forgotten about the racing.' Flora sighed, looking to where the crew had begun setting up the ropes at the other end of the deck.

Bunny grunted something unintelligible, muffled by the fact he was now bent double with his top half tucked inside the vehicle. He backed out and straightened. 'I had better get her wrapped up again first, then I'll join you.'

'See you there then.' Gerald wrapped an arm round each of the boys and guided them along the deck. 'Thinking again, Flora?' Bunny eased to her side as he wiped his grubby hands on a cloth.

'Yes, but it's not important.' She chewed her bottom lip. 'Actually, it is. Eddy slipped out when I wasn't looking. He left me a note, so I know he was trying to be considerate, but he has no idea how dangerous going off on his own could be. I can't lock him up in the suite until we dock, so what do you suggest?'

'Er, I meant to tell you before, but I slipped a few dollars to one of the stewards to keep an eye on him.' He cocked his chin at a young officer who hovered beside a winch. 'That chap there. He's very conscientious.'

'You did that?' She turned to stare at him, opened mouthed? 'Why?'

'Because I took that threat you received seriously. And I saw how frantic you were when Eddy went missing earlier.'

'That–that's really kind of you. I wish I had thought of it myself.'

'My pleasure.' He grinned, evidently pleased with himself. 'It wasn't entirely altruistic. If you felt Eddy was safe, you could spend more time in my company. I take it you've heard no more from our mysterious man?'

'No, nothing.' Touched by his thoughtfulness, guilt stabbed at her for her ridiculous jealousy earlier. 'Perhaps we should ask him what the boys did to your motor car?'

'Eddy was telling the truth. They didn't do anything.' She turned back to where he stood in his shirtsleeves. 'By the way, speaking of adventures, have you given any thought as to why Max was on deck yesterday in that storm?'

'It happened too fast for me to think anything. I was too busy trying to grab him before he was sucked under the rail.'

She tugged one end of the canvas sheet while he did the other. 'A gale is blowing, waves are breaking over the deck strong enough to knock someone off their feet. The luncheon bugle went five minutes before, but instead of using the interior corridors to get to the dining room, Max is outside, working his way between the winch lines in the other direction. Where was he going?'

'Give me a clue.'

'Think about it.' She slanted a sideways look at him. 'What is of interest on deck other than this?' She nodded at the motor car.

'Matilda?' He shrugged. 'It's possible, but she's been here under canvas all week. You cannot be sure that's where he was headed.'

'No. Which is why I intend to ask him.'

'But what about the horse racing? I thought—'

'They haven't finished arranging the deck yet, so I've got enough time before it starts. Keep me a seat will you?' She aimed a brief wave in his direction and headed for the outside companionway up to the promenade deck.

* * *

'How nice of you to come,' Cynthia greeted Flora at the door to the Cavendishes' suite. 'Max is still a bit groggy from the sedative the doctor gave him, but he's more comfortable today.' Her overly cheerful voice continued into their bedroom where Max sat propped against a pile of pillows. Garbed in a gaudy silk bed-jacket over striped pyjamas, a wide bandage circled his head, and his left arm was tightly wrapped in a sling. Though his youthful pink plumpness had not yet returned, the deathly pallor which had driven Cynthia into hysterics had disappeared.

'I'm so glad you weren't badly hurt, Max.' Flora took the chair tucked into the narrow space at the side of the bed.

'Thanks to Harrington.' Max attempted a laugh that was cut off by a wince. 'Shoulder's deuced sore, but I'm on the mend.' He reached for a glass of water at his elbow, but before his hand connected with the glass, Cynthia grabbed it and held it to his mouth.

'C'mon, old girl, I'm not an invalid.' He grimaced and pushed her hand away.

'I keep thinking that you could have been killed!' she said, though there was no real emotion behind them. In fact, she sounded angry and her eyes remained dry.

'Well I wasn't, so stop fussing.' His sharp retort softened by a brief caress of her cheek.

'It's all so awful. I wish this business was over with.'

'What business is that?' Flora asked, still perplexed about how either of them were really feeling. Cynthia played the part of a distraught wife to perfection, but her eyes said something else. Max seemed irritable, even worried, his gaze darting the room.

'I meant this voyage of course,' Cynthia said quickly. 'The honeymoon, everything which sets us apart as a focus of common gossip. I want to get back to being simply Mrs Maximilian Cavendish.'

'It must have been terrifying for you, Max,' Flora said. 'Whatever made you go out in that storm must have been important.'

'Yes, Max.' A tiny crease appeared between Cynthia's perfectly plucked brows. 'You never did tell me what you were doing out there in that storm.'

Max split a look between them, and eased upright against his pillows. 'Actually, Cyn. I would really love some tea. I'm sure Flora would too. Would you oblige, darling?'

Flora was about to refuse, but his imploring look changed her mind. 'Er – yes, that would be very nice, thank you.'

'I'll summon a steward.' Cynthia nodded, rising.

'Actually, Cyn,' Max halted her at the door, 'Gerald borrowed my copy of *The Invisible Man*. He's an H.G. Wells enthusiast, apparently. Would you slip along to fetch it for me? I could do with something to read.'

'You didn't answer her question,' Flora said when they were alone.

'It was an accident.' A raised vein pulsed in his temple and he refused to meet her eye. 'I went for a stroll and misjudged the severity of the wind.'

'The crew had issued a storm warning, and ordered us all inside. Why did you take such a risk?'

'I'm aware this voyage has been difficult for everyone, what with two deaths.' He gave a long-suffering sigh. 'But you shouldn't read something into it.'

'Shouldn't I?' Flora waited. His eyes still roamed the room, full of angst. Even Eddy was more expert at dissembling than this man.

'Look, Flora.' He plucked at the bedclothes with his uninjured hand. 'You ought not to involve yourself in this business.'

'I *am* involved,' Flora said. 'I found Eloise's body.' The words were out before she could stop them.

'I–I had no idea.' His head jerked round and he met her gaze. 'I was told one of the housekeeping staff found her.'

'That's what Mr Hersch wants everyone to think.' Flora fidgeted, regretting her impulse. For all she knew, Max could be guilty. Then her gaze strayed to the sling and she changed her mind. 'I've already been threatened to keep my mouth shut, but things have gone too far.'

'Threatened?' His eyes hardened. 'By whom?'

'That's just it, I don't know.' Her stomach tightened as she spoke of something she thought she had suppressed until now. 'Look, I hadn't known Eloise long, but I was fond of her. Do you have any idea who killed her?'

'Why should I know that?' He slapped the coverlet. 'In fact, I wish I didn't know anything at all.'

'If it's something which would help the investigation, you must tell Mr Hersch.'

'Hah! Hersch. He's still trying to run things, is he?' His show of temper turned to derision. 'I would have thought he would have given up by now with his target dead.'

'Who would that be? Parnell or Eloise?' What did he mean by a target? Had Eloise been right in that Hersch was working for the van Elder lawyers? Had he been about to expose her as a murderess?

'Eloise Lane wasn't her real name,' he said, his eyes widening slightly when Flora didn't react. 'You knew?'

She nodded, but offered no explanation. He wasn't the only one who could be enigmatic.

'Did you kill Mr Parnell, or should I say Marlon van Elder?' Flora blurted, aware Cynthia would be back any moment.

'Where did you hear that name?' His eyes narrowed as he searched her face, but when she didn't answer he turned away in disgust. 'Of course I didn't kill him,' he snapped. 'That fool died falling down those steps. Probably drunk, knowing him.'

'But you did know him?'

'I didn't say that. I knew *of* him.'

'I'm getting tired of all these short answers, Max. What aren't you telling me?' She suspected a lot, but how to make him reveal it before Cynthia came back? 'What relation was he to Theo, Eloise's husband?'

'Be careful, Miss Maguire.' A flash of anger entered his eyes, turning them from vacuous blue to cloudy grey. 'Your meddling might cause more harm than you imagine.'

The door sucked open and Max expelled a relieved breath.

'Here you are, darling.' Cynthia set a loaded tray on the nightstand, her manicured fingers darting amongst the china like butterfly wings. 'Monica couldn't find your book at first, but it seems Ozzy had it under his pillow.' She placed a green leather-bound volume at his elbow, handed Flora a full cup then tipped three sugar lumps into Max's cup before placing it in his hand,

'Now, what have you two been talking about?' She perched on the side of the bed; the only free space left in the room as Flora occupied the only chair.

'I was just saying to Max.' Flora hid her frustration beneath a smile. 'How nervous the passengers are about the fact there's a killer on board.'

'Yes, of course.' Cynthia shuddered theatrically but her gaze sharpened. 'Has Mr Hersch discovered anything new?'

'If he has, he isn't sharing it with me. It's only a matter of time though, what with two murders to solve.' Flora studied their faces, certain the answers lay in this room.

'Two?' Cynthia's smile turned stale round the edges. 'Mr Hersch thinks Mr, er, Parnell was murdered as well?'

'He's thinks they are connected, yes. And despite the captain's announcement at dinner last night, he's not convinced they were committed by the same person.' Flora wasn't sure where the thought came from but, it suddenly made sense.

Max's hand jerked and hot tea splashed onto his bare arm below his sling. He gave a sharp cry, which brought Cynthia to her feet, dabbing at the wet stain with a napkin, and murmuring in distress.

'It's all right, Cyn.' Max waved her away. 'You got most of it.' He massaged his forehead with his free hand. 'I'm sorry to be so unsociable, Flora, but I get tired easily, what with the pain and all that. I could do with some sleep.'

'Of course, darling.' Cynthia fussed. 'Let me get rid of this, then I'll see you out, Flora.' She re-loaded the tray and manhandled it into the sitting room.

Left with no choice but to leave, Flora rose. 'I hope you'll feel better soon, Max.'

Flora was about to follow Cynthia, but at the last second, Max thrust out his hand and grabbed her arm, bringing her attention back to his face. His eyes were open, clear and intense.

'Take my advice, Flora. Don't get pulled into this. Nothing good will come of it.'

'Pulled into what?' Flora whispered urgently, aware they risked being heard by Cynthia. 'What did you do?'

'I can't explain. If only Cyn had listened to me at the beginning, but she's a loyal girl, you see.' His gaze drifted past her shoulder just as Cynthia reappeared. He dropped Flora's arm as if it were hot, and relaxed onto his pillows with a sigh.

'Poor dear, he didn't sleep well last night.' Cynthia closed the door and drew Flora into the sitting room.

'How is all this drama affecting you, Cynthia? Hardly an ideal honeymoon.' Flora took in her darting eyes and the paleness of her skin beneath a layer of face powder.

'Me?' Cynthia issued a high-pitched laugh that bordered on hysteria. 'What could possibly be wrong with me? It's poor darling Max who got hurt.'

* * *

Flora joined the line of spectators gathered to watch the horse racing on the saloon deck, where hemp ropes had been strung on wooden posts marking the course. Several of the more youthful members of the crew wore caps with matching coloured bands across their shoulders, each of whom straddled broomsticks on which had been attached papier mâché horses' heads.

Lines of excited children hung over the rails on the upper decks as she made her way to the bench seats set out for spectators, her gaze settling on Eddy in relief that for once he was where he was supposed to be. Gerald, Monica and Ozzy sat on the far side of him, while Bunny beckoned to her from the other.

'How's Max?' Bunny whispered as he reached him, shifting aside to make room for her, his upper arm grazing hers.

'I'll tell you later,' she whispered back, pushing aside the puzzling interview she had just had, she leaned forward and smiled at Eddy, who grinned back at her. For now, she was intent on enjoying the warm afternoon where she didn't have to think about violence and death for a while.

'If this isn't to your taste,' Bunny nodded to the lines of 'horses' gathered at the end of the course waiting for the orders to be off, 'we could go to the concert in the dining room?' When she shook her head, he said, 'What about the art exhibition? Every old biddy on board has been painting away this week. Even Mrs Penry-Jones. Mostly bowls of fruit from the kitchen and seascapes, but they aren't bad.'

'No, I'm quite happy here, if that's all right with you.'

'It's more than all right, Miss Maguire.'

They exchanged smiles, which she liked to think had become their secret code that said each other's company was all they required, for now. Flora had even come to terms with the fact Eddy's escapade in the dark-room could have been what everyone said – a boyish prank with no real harm done. Though there was still the mystery of the man outside the dining room.

She was about to broach the subject of Max, when Eddy shouted her name. 'I'll explain later,' she whispered, as Eddy left his seat and joined her, his straw boater tipped back on his head.

'Tease me, why don't you?' Bunny murmured, half serious, making her laugh.

'I'm backing *Arthritis* in the *Seasick Hurdle*,' Eddy said, waving a slip of paper in her face.

'Placing real bets at your age?' Bunny blinked in feigned shock though his smile remained in place.

'It's only twenty-five cents a time, which is about a shilling.' Eddy pulled a mildly disgusted face. 'And it's only a game, I shan't develop the gambling bug.'

'I should hope not.' Bunny delved into his trouser pocket. 'What do you reckon on *Count de Money* in the *Lowbrow Handicap*, or shall I lose my shirt?'

'Lose, I think,' Eddy replied. 'His rider is that paunchy fellow in a yellow cap over there, see?'

'Hmm. perhaps I'll just stick with *Steam Hammer*. His rider looks sprightly enough.'

'That's Captain Gates' horse.' Eddy spoke with the calm authority of someone who had researched their subject. 'Well, not a real horse, natu-rally. A hobby horse. Anyway, each one is sponsored by an officer or a passenger.'

'How many races are there?' Flora asked.

'Six, with six horses per race.' Bunny tipped a pile of small change into Eddy's hand. 'Here, put this on for me, would you?'

'Right-o.' Excitement brightened the freckles across his nose and he raced away, the coins clutched tightly in his hand.

'Must we watch every race?' Flora fanned her face with her programme, regretting having refused the art exhibition, which would at least be cooler. 'It's getting hot out here and it's already noisy.'

'Where's your sense of fun?' Bunny nudged her. 'At least the atmosphere among the passengers has lifted a little after the gloom of the last few days.'

'It's not over though, is it?' she said sadly, though not wishing to spoil the afternoon, added, 'Besides, I'm an English rose who doesn't much like the harsh sun. It creates freckles.'

'Hmm, you could be right.' He gave a start, both hands held up in surrender. 'I meant about the noise and the heat, not the freckles.'

'Forgiven.' Flora conceded, then with more warmth, 'How about we watch the first race, then go to the library for tea? I doubt Eddy will notice. And besides, I have something—'

'—to tell me, yes, I got that. Look, they're getting ready for the off.'

The loud report of a starting gun was followed by squeals of encouragement as the 'horses' set off. Spectators hollered for their favourite, whilst children screamed in delight as the orderly line rapidly deteriorated into a shoving, closely bunched, pile of bodies.

When the first hobby horse fell rather than crossed the line, the deck erupted in an enthusiastic roar from the men and a round of polite clapping from the ladies.

'That was energetic!' Flora fanned her face rapidly, aware strands of hair were plastered to her forehead. 'I enjoyed that more than I had anticipated.'

'I don't have to come, do I?' Eddy frowned at her when she explained she and Bunny were going for tea. 'There's another five races yet.'

'As long as you behave yourself and do what Mr and Mrs Gilmore tell you, they have said you can stay with Ozzy.' Having said her goodbyes to the others, she took Bunny's arm and made their way up two flights of steps to the upper promenade deck. The muffled sound of far-off cheers reached them as they stepped into the calm of the deserted library. A steward gave a surprised start, surreptitiously stubbed out a cigarette in a tin plate, and tucked it beneath a pot plant before approaching them with a smile of welcome.

'Quiet day?' Bunny's mock-innocent gaze slid to the pot plant then back at the steward, who flushed.

'Tea for you and the lady, sir?' He covered his embarrassment with a bright enquiry.

'Thank you, yes. We'll be over there.' Bunny indicated a trio of red leather chesterfield sofas in an alcove visible from the door, the same ones they had sat on during their last visit.

'Now, what was it you wanted to tell me about Max?' Bunny asked when the loaded tea tray occupied the table between them. 'By the look of your face he had something interesting to say. Have you solved both murders and now know everyone's secrets?'

'Don't tease, this is important. Max knew Eloise wasn't called Eloise and he also knew Marlon van Elder and that Mr Hersch was working for the van Elder family.'

'Max told you all that?'

'Not exactly. Max let something slip which confirmed he knew Hersch was on board because of Eloise. At least I think that's what he meant.' Bunny's expression displayed only scepticism. 'You don't look very surprised.'

'No, really. I am. I was just thinking. But where does that lead us? Did Eloise kill her husband or not?'

'Not sure yet, although I'm sure I would have got more out of him if Cynthia hadn't come back.'

'You think Cynthia doesn't know?'

'Max certainly didn't want her to overhear us talking, but surely, if he knew, then she must as well. Although,' she paused as doubt intruded, 'perhaps he simply didn't want her to know he had told me.'

'That's a bit convoluted for me.' Frowning, Bunny lowered the teapot onto the tray. 'Did you find out what Max was doing out on the deck in the storm?'

'I asked him that, but he avoided the question. I was thinking about this van Elder family while we watched the race. I believe there are more of them on board, it's the only thing that makes sense.'

'Well, don't keep me in suspense.' Bunny handed her a full cup. 'Explain.'

'I think, Cynthia is the daughter of the late Theodore van Elder.'

'How did you come to that conclusion?' Bunny paused with two lumps of sugar held over his cup.

'Am I right in thinking the obituary I found is still in your pocket?'

'It is.' He patted it as if to reassure himself.

'If you recall, it says Theodore van Elder had a child from a previous marriage who was an heiress to a fortune. I think that is Cynthia.'

'But isn't she English. Van Elder was an American wasn't he, from Baltimore?'

'Her parents divorced when she was young. When her mother remarried, they moved to England and Cynthia went with them.'

'Goodness, Miss Maguire, you have been busy.' Bunny sat back in his seat, one ankle crossed over the other as he stirred his tea. 'Where are you going with this?'

'Actually, not very far. I have a theory though.' She wiggled backwards in her seat and prepared for a detailed discussion. 'Say Cynthia believed Eloise killed her father, so she hires Pinkerton's, who send Hersch to get some evidence against her. When Eloise comes aboard, Hersch came too.'

'What was Marlon van Elder's role in all this?

'Ah, now I'll assume they chose him because Eloise didn't know him. He told her his name was Parnell, but we know he was one of the van Elders. I'm not sure of his precise relationship. A brother or maybe a distant cousin?'

'Which is irrelevant now as the man is dead. Bunny mused. 'What we have is Cynthia and Max, together with Marlon van Elder set out to prove Eloise had killed her husband, Theodore van Elder? Hmm, seems they must have had some evidence to back that up.'

'Which Parnell claimed to have, although Eloise was adamant she didn't kill her husband.'

'Then who killed Parnell, I mean Marlon van Elder? Max?' Bunny's bemused expression showed he didn't expect an answer.

'I did consider that, but what reason would he have?' She eyed her tea but left it untouched, unwilling to interrupt her train of thought. 'And unless he deliberately tried to drown himself, he couldn't have killed

Eloise. I'm not sure why yet, but I think they were killed by two separate people.'

'Which makes everything more complicated.' Bunny studied the ornamental glass ceiling which threw a kaleidoscope of jewel colours onto the floor. 'Marlon van Elder was hardly a respectable member of the family, judging by the list of aliases and charges listed in that telegram I received. Although he could still have been in league with Eloise in the killing of her husband. Maybe he got greedy about the money, so she killed him.'

'Then who killed her? Apart from Max, there's only Mr Hersch and Cynthia.'

'I doubt Cynthia could have done it.' Bunny snorted.

'Why, because she's beautiful?' Flora threw him an oblique look. 'If she believed Eloise had murdered her father—'

'A father she had likely not seen since she was a child.'

'Is that relevant? Family is family.'

Bunny glanced up, his eyes narrowed at something beyond the double glazed doors to the lobby. 'Looks like we aren't the only ones seeking refuge from the horse racing.' He cocked his chin. 'Isn't that Mr Hersch with the captain?'

'Yes, it is.' Flora followed his gaze. 'And that's Gus Crowe with them. What's going on?'

'I would have thought he'd be watching the horse racing. Not like Crowe to miss a chance to run a book on the side when there's gambling to be done.' Bunny returned his cup to the tray, straightening. 'Oh, watch out. They're coming in here, and none of them look particularly happy.'

20

'Is this absolutely necessary?' Crowe demanded, his raised voice tinged with panic. 'I've already answered all of your questions.'

'I'm aware of that, Mr Crowe.' Captain Gates gently patted Crowe's shoulder as they moved into the library. 'Mr Hersch merely has a few things he wishes to clarify.'

'Well, make it snappy.' Crowe impatiently shrugged him off. 'I don't intend to waste time repeating myself.'

'This looks as if it might be interesting,' Bunny's breath felt warm against Flora's ear. If she hadn't been so intrigued by what was happening in front of her, she would have relished his closeness more.

Flora nudged him into silence, her head cocked to hear every word.

Crowe approached the seat Hersch indicated, his gaze darting around the room until it halted on Flora and Bunny. With his rear hovering above the chair he halted, demanding, 'What are they doing here?' His frown deepened to suspicion.

'Ah, Mr Harrington, Miss Maguire. I didn't see you there.' Hersch's affable smile betrayed no surprise at their presence. 'Surely you don't object, Crowe. After all, it's simply routine.'

'What?' Crowe started. 'And suppose I do object?' He dragged a hand-kerchief from a pocket and wiped his forehead.

'What exactly do you object to if, as you say, you're an innocent man?' Mr Hersch eased backwards as the steward lowered the tea tray onto the table in front of them. After which he and the captain ranged themselves in chairs on either side of Crowe.

Flora held her breath, hoping she and Bunny weren't about to be dismissed, but instead, Mr Hersch beckoned to them. 'Perhaps you would like to join us? You might find this interesting.'

'Well, I'm not sure if that's app—'

'Thank you, we would love to.' Flora dragged Bunny to his feet and propelled him towards their table. 'She took the sofa opposite Mr Crowe, who glared at her. Bunny sighed but joined her.

'Well as long as this is quick.' Crowe drummed his fingers on the chair arm, issued a bored sigh and fidgeted with his shirt cuff.

'Told you,' Bunny whispered. 'He'd rather be gambling.'

Flora clamped her lips together to prevent a smile and waited, convinced she was about to hear something startling.

'Weak stuff, this American tea.' Captain Gates stirred the contents of the teapot vigorously with a spoon. 'I might be a naturalised American citizen, but there are some things I still miss about the old country, and this is one of them.' He clicked the lid back on the pot, then poured the steaming liquid into three cups before unhurriedly adding milk.

'Could we get on with it?' Crowe snapped, refusing the cup held out to him with an angry shrug.

Flora agreed. The tension was painful, though she kept silent.

'Let's return to the first night on board, Mr Crowe,' Hersch said. 'When I believe you lost a sum of money to Mr Parnell at cards?'

Flora looked from the captain's benign smile to the German's triumphant one, then back to Crowe's tense features, the scene reminding her of two smug cats playing with a trapped mouse.

'I told you that when you questioned me the first time.' Crowe's jaw hardened. 'I wasn't the only one, either. Parnell cleaned up that night, as you well know. It doesn't bear repeating.'

'Maybe it does, simply for my own purposes, you understand.' The detective stirred sugar into his tea, then offered the bowl to the captain, who politely declined. In turn the captain offered a plate of biscuits round the table including Flora and Bunny in the gesture.

Bemused, Flora accepted a biscuit she didn't want, enjoying their by-play which was clearly designed to keep Crowe off balance. Crowe was suffering too as he fidgeted with his shirt cuff, released it with a sigh and ran a hand through his hair, his knees jiggling.

'What did you do when you left the card game, Mr Crowe?' Hersch sipped his tea, grimaced and reached for the sugar bowl. Using the tiny silver tongs, he dropped another sugar lump into the cup.

'How do you expect me to remember after so long?' Crowe laughed as though the question was a joke but betrayed his tension when he eased three fingers between his neck and his collar. His eyes darted between Hersch and the captain, sliding over Bunny as if he were of no interest. He lifted his hands from the arms of his chair and let them fall back again. 'I–I think I stood at the rail for a while and smoked a cigarette.'

'You think, or you did?' The detective's spoon clicked rhythmically against the china, his steady gaze on Crowe's face. 'You also said that you saw Mr Parnell going into Hester Smith's cabin.'

'Did I? Ah, yes, I remember now.' Crowe rolled his eyes. 'Look, we've already been through all this.' He pushed a hand through his hair, cutting grooves into the liberally applied pomade. 'It could have been that old biddy's cabin, I cannot say for certain. What difference does it make?' He tugged up his sleeve and ostentatiously peered at his watch. 'I really don't see the point of this, so if you don't mind, I'll be going.' He slapped his palms against the arms of his chair and pushed himself to his feet.

'Sit down,' the German ordered, his voice a growl.

'Why the devil should I? You've no right to interrogate me,' Crowe blustered.

Flora swallowed. She gave Bunny a half-fearful glance, but he only shrugged. Flora was about to interrupt, when the door swung open again and Officer Martin entered with another crewman Flora recognised as the wireless operator. Crofts strode forwards as if he was on a parade ground, coming to an abrupt halt beside the captain's chair where he performed a curt double step and stared straight ahead, his cap tucked beneath one elbow.

Crowe froze in a half-crouch, his lips bloodless.

'This looks like an interesting new development,' Bunny whispered. 'Crowe seems about to faint.'

Flora shushed him, her confidence in the German fully restored.

'This young man has an interesting story to tell,' Hersch helped himself to a biscuit from the tray, demolishing it in one mouthful.

'Seaman Crofts?' Captain Gates addressed the crewman. 'Do you recognise this gentleman?'

The sailor flicked a look at Crowe and away again, then went back to studying the wall. 'Yes, sir, he's Mr Augustus Crowe.'

Crowe stood and took a step toward the door. He gazed around the library as though he weighed up the chance of escape and decided it might be futile. 'Now, look here!' Beads of sweat appeared on Crowe's brow and he held himself rigid, betraying his fear. 'Are you going to take the word of a kid against mine?'

'It depends entirely on what the kid says, Mr Crowe.' Hersch gestured for Seaman Crofts to continue.

Crowe shrugged, with a hint of his earlier bravado and sank onto his seat.

Flora bit her lip to hide a smile, admiring of the detective's calm handling of the situation. Whatever the sailor had to say would definitely not be a waste of anyone's time. She settled back in her seat and prepared to enjoy what happened next.

'Well, sir.' The sailor cleared his throat. 'Mr Crowe asked me to deposit some banknotes in the ship's safe.'

'Was there anything unusual about this request?' Hersch asked with all the confidence of someone who knew the answer.

A flicker of fear entered Crowe's eyes and he hunched further into his seat, but this time remained silent.

'No, sir, except—' Crofts swallowed. 'He paid me ten dollars to change the date on the receipt slip to that of the day we sailed.'

'You didn't think that strange?' Hersch persisted, still not looking at Crowe.

'Not at the time, no.' Crofts' confidence seemed to grow at the captain's calm acceptance of his answers. 'I didn't connect it to the man who died.

Not then. Everyone accepted it was an accident until Mr Hersch told me Mr Parnell had been murdered.'

'Now, see here, I don't have to listen to this.' Crowe's tone was threatening, but his lower lip trembled as if he was on the verge of tears.

'And how much did Mr Crowe lodge in the safe?' Captain Gates asked, ignoring Crowe completely, who had reverted to massaging his forehead with the fingers of one hand.

'Five thousand dollars, sir,' Seaman Crofts replied. 'Three thousand in large banknotes with the banker's ribbon still on them. The rest was loose, in smaller denominations.'

'Got him,' Bunny chuckled.

Flora gasped. While she and Eloise had searched Parnell's cabin, Crowe had already taken the money. Then a thought struck her. Had Eloise known?

'Quite a coincidence,' Hersch said with menacing calm. 'The exact amount Mr Parnell was alleged to have in his possession on Saturday evening.'

'You may go, Crofts.' The captain inclined his head in curt dismissal.

Seaman Crofts threw him a fearful glance, turned and almost ran from the room, closely followed by Officer Martin.

'Damn you, you've got it all wrong. Crowe flung out of his chair but between the table and the two men there was nowhere for him to go. 'Surely you don't think I killed Parnell? Crowe protested as the two crewmen left the library. 'I'm not going to stay here and listen to nonsense.' He made a feeble attempt to leave, but Bunny and the captain blocked his way.

Flora's eyes widened as Crowe raised his fists as though he would attack one or both of them, then thought better of it.

Hersch slammed him back into his seat. 'Don't attempt that again, Crowe, and mind your language in front of a lady.'

Flora released a held breath and smiled in thanks at Hersch.

'You bloody vultures!' Crowe spat as the door closed on the two crewmen. 'I may have taken the money, but I didn't kill the man!'

'Language, Crowe,' Hersch warned, tugging down the front of his jacket as he relaxed back into his seat.

'Look,' Crowe rubbed both palms back and forth along his thighs, 'I admit I was angry at having lost so much money to Parnell on the first night. It might have been small change to him, but to me – well, sums like that don't come easily. I followed him back to his cabin, hung about outside and smoked a cigarette. I had no firm plan then, but needed to think.'

'Go on,' Hersch prompted.

'The Gilmores walked by while I was standing there. Then Parnell went into that companion's room.'

'Hester Smith?' Flora blurted. 'He went inside? Are you sure?'

Hersch cast her a brief sideways look that demanded silence, and Bunny gave a low hiss.

'Sorry,' Flora muttered, annoyed to be silenced like a child when she was the one who had fought to get anyone to believe her? Especially Bunny.

'Actually, no, I'm not certain it was Hester's.' Crowe's knuckles whitened on the chair arms and he blinked as if confused. 'Gilmore said he saw Parnell going into the old woman's suite, so maybe it was hers. Whichever it was, when he came out again he went into Miss Lane's stateroom. I didn't get that wrong, because she came to the door in her night things.' Crowe snorted. 'Quite pally, they were too.'

'You didn't mention that detail in your original account of that night,' Hersch observed.

'I was hardly going to admit I was hanging about outside Parnell's cabin, was I?' His laugh was harsh and bitter. 'I wasn't certain the Gilmores saw me either, but as it turns out they hadn't.'

'Then what did you do?' Captain Gates asked.

Crowe slid a sly look at Flora and away again. 'I assumed Parnell and Miss Lane would be together for the rest of the night. I waited for a bit, then went into Parnell's cabin.'

'You broke in?' Officer Martin asked.

'It wasn't locked.' Crowe shrugged. 'Parnell had stashed a wedge of banknotes in a shoe in the bottom of the wardrobe. Far more than he had won at the card game, so I—' he broke off and ran a shaky hand through his hair, making it stick up in greasy spikes.

'What happened then?' the captain asked.

'Well I–I took the money of course.' Crowe threw up both hands to convey that anyone would have done the same thing.

'I gather something went wrong?' Hersch prompted.

'It certainly did.' Crowe's eyes sharpened in recollection and he glared again at Flora. 'Parnell came back. I opened the door to leave and there he was. He looked as shocked as me.'

Flora squeezed closer to Bunny, growing increasingly uncomfortable beneath his hard glare, as if he blamed her for his plans going awry.

'What did you do?' Hersch's voice had dropped as he offered gentle prompts.

Now Crowe had begun telling his story he didn't look inclined to stop.

'What do you think? He attacked me. I threw a punch, and we scuffled for a bit. I thought he was stunned when he hit his head on the washbasin in the bathroom.' He gave a short, cynical laugh. 'I'm surprised no one heard the noise. I tell you I acted in self-defence, so you can't pin any murder on me.'

'What about the ashtray?' Flora asked. 'The one you hit him with.'

'What ashtray?' Crowe stared at her in accusation. 'No, I told you. He hit his head on the washbasin.'

Flora resolved not to speak again. Not because Hersch or the captain kept looking at her, but because Crowe did. And his stare was almost painful.

'It stands to reason you needed to get rid of the body,' Hersch said gently. 'Is that when you threw him down the companionway?'

'No! I didn't throw him anywhere. That's not how it went!' Crowe's eyes flashed with anger and a tiny bead of spittle appeared on his lower lip. 'I left him lying on the stateroom floor – alive! The next morning, when Dr Fletcher said he had died in a fall, I–well I kept quiet.' His thin lips curled into a sneer, as if congratulating himself on his ingenuity at having turned the situation to his advantage. Then he turned a burning gaze on Flora. 'Everyone believed me, except you, Miss Busybody Governess.' His voice lowered to a hiss.

The sound brought back a half-buried moment of clarity for Flora.

'It was you!' She gasped. 'You threatened me outside the dining room!'

She watched Crowe's face prepare for denial, but realising he was found out, turned it into a sly grin. 'You locked Eddy in the darkroom as well didn't you?'

Bunny issued a sharp protest which trailed off in a growl. For a split second, he looked as if he might launch himself at Crowe, but was held back by a quick, hard look from Captain Gates.

Flora's chest tightened at the thought of these last wakeful nights, afraid for both herself and Eddy due to this insipid little man. She clenched her fists in her lap to prevent her leaping up to slap him.

'It wasn't deliberate, and only meant to frighten you off.' Crowe fidgeted in his chair, tension drawing furrows in his brow. 'I saw him wander away on his own and go down into the hold. The key was in the door and I locked it on impulse. I would never have hurt you or the lad.'

'Pity we didn't know that at the time,' Flora said, though something told her Crowe was holding something back. What did he think she knew?

'Look' – temper flared in Crowe's eyes – 'I robbed Parnell. I hold my hands up to that, but his death was an accident.'

'Even if you were correct,' Hersch said, 'and Mr Parnell had somehow managed to stagger to that companionway in search of assistance, and fallen, that still makes you guilty of manslaughter.' He let the information sink in, before asking, 'Why did you kill Miss Lane?'

'I didn't kill her!' Crowe's head jerked up, his eyes frantic. 'I had no reason to want her dead.'

'Miss Lane's stateroom was next door to Parnell's. Maybe she heard you fighting with him and threatened to reveal your part in his death?' Hersch said. 'Or perhaps,' he went on when Crowe failed to answer, 'you and Miss Lane came to an agreement?'

'Did she suggest you share the haul with her in return for silence?' Hersch's words fell into the heavy silence.

'Eloise saw you arguing with Seaman Crofts,' Flora said, incredulous, recalling Crowe's start of fear in the staircase lobby. 'She saw you through the window and guessed what you had done.'

The blood left Crowe's face until his complexion resembled milk. 'She–she badgered me about the money, said she knew I had got it and wanted her share. She agreed not to stir things up if I split it with her when we reached London. That the situation would suit us both.' He pinned Flora with a pleading stare. 'When I saw you and Eloise had become friendly, I thought she had told you about our – arrangement. I'm no killer. Especially not a woman or a kid! I had to make sure you'd keep quiet until we docked. I meant to scare you, that's all.'

Crowe fisted his hands and brought them down on his knees. 'Then the next thing I know, she's dead. That shook me, I can tell you.' He directed a panicked look at Hersch, then the captain. 'I swear I didn't kill Eloise. I had no reason to.'

'I tend to disagree.' Hersch said, his eyes hard. 'You had no intention of splitting that money with her, so picked your moment and got rid of her. When you knocked on her stateroom door that afternoon I imagine she let you inside in all innocence.'

'That's not what happened, I—'

'You can tell your story to a judge, Crowe.' Hersch cut him off. Had his moustache been long and curly, Flora imagined he would have twirled it. 'You'll remain confined to your stateroom until we reach London. There you'll be handed over to the authorities.'

He strode to the door, beckoning to the sailors who stood sentry outside. The pair marched into the room and arranged themselves on either side of Crowe.

'Aren't you forgetting something?' Crowe rose shakily to his feet, but summoned enough defiance to shrug off the sailor's hold. 'I didn't commit any crime in England, we were in international waters.' The sailor refused to be beaten and grabbed his arm again, shoving it firmly behind his back while the second sailor secured his other arm. Crowe struggled between them, his shin caught the table and rattled the crockery, but he was held fast.

'On an American-owned ship,' Hersch reminded him. 'I imagine the British will send you straight back to New York to stand trial.'

'We'll see about that!' Crowe threw them all a final sour look, but the fight seemed to have gone out of him and he offered no further protest as the sailors shoved him out the door.

'Good work, Hersch.' Captain Gates tugged down his jacket, his habitual smile firmly in place as he swung his head towards the sofa where

Bunny sat with Flora. 'I'll see you later at dinner then. Miss Maguire, Mr Harrington.' He replaced his cap, touching the peak in salute on his way out. 'Is that all it was?' Flora asked, mildly disappointed as the door flapped shut. 'A fight over money which resulted in the death of a man?'

'Which, as you may recall, was my first theory,' Bunny said.

'You don't have to be so smug about it.' Still uneasy, Flora chewed her bottom lip. 'I'm still not convinced that Mr Crowe stabbed Eloise.'

'She was blackmailing him,' Bunny added, as if that explained everything.

'He's an unpleasant thief, but I believed him when he said he was no murderer. Parnell attacked him first, and Crowe defended himself. Eloise was a tiny thing and easily overpowered. Are you asking me to believe he brought a knife to her cabin with that in mind?' She shook her head. 'I don't accept that.'

However, it explained why Eloise had been so calm, almost happy during that morning during the storm. It had occurred to Flora at the time that she had lied to Flora about Parnell's cabin being empty and had found the photograph. With that safe and the money from Parnell in the offing, she must have believed this had solved her problems. Then why was she killed?

'Don't give the man too much credit, Miss Maguire.' Hersch rocked on his heels, a self-satisfied grin on his face. 'Killers often become more violent if they think they have got away with one murder. They invariably maintain their innocence to the end too.'

Flora searched for something that might make a dent in his self-confidence, then something occurred to her he hadn't yet answered. 'Apart from Eloise's stateroom, where else did he go that night? Mrs Penry-Jones' or Hester's?'

'I don't see that it matters now.' Hersch swept a biscuit from the plate in front of him and bit into it.

'Or it could matter a lot,' Flora murmured. 'Eloise lied about Parnell having argued with her that night.' She tapped her top lip with a finger. 'Who else was lying? Crowe or Gerald Gilmore?'

'My money's on Crowe.' Bunny followed Hersch's example and took a biscuit too, chewing thoughtfully.

'Maybe neither of them.' Hersch brushed crumbs from his jacket. 'It was the first night, so perhaps no one was sure about whose cabin was whose.'

'We need to find out.' Panic lifted Flora's voice an octave. 'We dock at Tilbury in two days, after which everyone will disappear into their own lives and you'll never catch him.' Her stomach knotted at the thought that whoever had done such a terrible thing to Eloise might escape justice.

'This affair has been an ordeal for you, Flora.' Hersch rose to his feet, held out both arms and shot his cuffs, apparently pleased with himself. 'I hope you can put it behind you and relax for what remains of the voyage.' He gave her shoulder a fatherly pat before following the captain out.

'Well, that made for an interesting afternoon.' Bunny tucked a hand beneath her elbow and drew her to her feet. 'How much of it should we reveal to the rest of the company at dinner do you suppose?'

'None of it.' Flora hooked her bag over one arm and straightened her skirt. 'We'll let Hersch do that, I'm notorious enough as it is. Did you happen to notice that at no point did our detective or the captain reveal that Frank Parnell and Eloise Lane weren't their real names?'

'I didn't, actually. Is that significant?' He swiped another biscuit from the plate and bit into it. 'Maybe he's simply protecting the identity of his clients?'

'Maybe.' Flora fell into step beside him as they emerged onto the deck, replaying the interview in her head. Despite the captain's logic and the German's conviction, she still couldn't see Crowe as a cold-blooded killer, and whoever had murdered Eloise was certainly that.

21

Bunny arrived exactly two minutes before their agreed time to take her to dinner, a broad smile of surprised admiration telling her all her efforts had not been in vain. She had vacillated all afternoon, then decided it would be a shame to waste the chance to wear Cynthia's gown, which made her confident she could compete with the other passengers. The evening was almost warm, so instead of taking the interior corridor, they strolled across the deck towards the dining room, pausing to admire the dramatic sunset from the rail.

'You aren't nervous about this evening's dance, are you?' His arm grazed hers, the touch of his soft dinner jacket sliding over his muscles made her shiver. 'I mean, you can dance?'

'No, of course not – I mean yes I can dance, I'm not nervous and I am rather looking forward to it.' She kneaded the delicate purse in one hand, crushing it. 'Although there are times I wish Lord Vaughn had sent me home on a different ship, one with no murders on board.'

'How did Eddy enjoy the horse racing?' Bunny laughed, changing the subject.

'He arrived back at our suite with a pocket full of coins I chose not to ask about. Not that Lord Vaughn would object if he knew. He's not averse to a day at the races himself.'

'I'm glad you felt confident enough to leave him alone tonight.'

'I didn't.' Flora winced. 'That steward you hired is bringing Ozzy over to our suite for the evening. He'll sit with them then put him to bed.'

'With Crowe safely locked up in whatever passes for a brig on this vessel, I doubt you'll need him now.' Flora gave him a sharp look and he shrugged. 'Oh well, I might as well get my money's worth.' He winked, then pushed open the door of the dining room bathed in electric light, savoury food smells and the clink of crystal glass and low tones of music from the palm court orchestra.

'You look very elegant, my dear,' Monica said as Flora and Bunny took their seats. 'I wish I had the colouring for dramatic hues, but pastels suit me better.' She indicated her peach-coloured gown with its tight-ruffled bodice.

'I wish you did too.' Gerald's appraising gaze slid up and down Flora's costume. 'I hope you'll allow me a dance after dinner, Flora?'

'Of course, Mr Gilmore, I'll look forward to it.'

'I thought we had ventured past the formal by now,' he said, mildly affronted. 'Do call me Gerald, after all this is not your average sea voyage.'

'Please don't talk about – well – you know what, again,' Monica waved a lace handkerchief across her face. 'Let's enjoy a lovely evening without that.'

Gerald rolled his eyes at Flora over her head, murmuring, 'Yes, dear.'

The atmosphere of the room was charged with excited chatter and an air of anticipation, and a hysteria born of relief, which Flora attributed to the fact everyone believed the killer was under guard.

'I hope there won't be any of that Vaudeville music this evening.' Mrs Penry-Jones eyed the quintet orchestra with suspicion. 'Too low-class in my opinion.'

'Really?' Bunny pinned her with a challenging stare. 'And I was hoping you would partner me in one of the new jazz dances, Mrs Penry-Jones?'

'I'll thank you not to goad me, young man.' Her evening bag hit the table with a thump, though her pebble eyes twinkled with flirtatious amusement.

It seemed no woman was safe from Bunny's charm.

Miss Ames swung a scarlet wrap over one shoulder, the sequin-encrusted edge missing Flora's face by a half inch. She plucked two glasses of transparent purple liquid from a tray and handed one to Mrs Penry-Jones.

'Do try some of this, it's quite delicious.' She giggled and downed half the contents of her own glass. 'It tastes just like damsons.'

'Indeed it does,' Mrs Penry-Jones said after her first sip, frowning into the glass before she gulped the rest. 'Goodness, it's hot in here.' She flapped an ostrich-feather fan rapidly in front of her face, the glass held out to Hester. 'Get me another one of these fruit cups, would you?'

Hester obeyed with an annoyed pout, her severe bun putting Flora in mind of a bad-tempered Jane Eyre.

'That isn't a fruit cup, is it?' Flora whispered behind her fan to Bunny.

Bunny winked. 'Not even close.'

His gaze met hers and held, creating a sweet, tingling sensation that started somewhere deep in her belly and spread into her chest doing odd things to her nipples. Memories of their kiss remained, and hope lingered that their closeness might continue once the voyage was over.

Flora dragged her eyes away and turned to where Cynthia made her entrance, looking serene in an apricot gown trimmed with ecru lace, a simple line from bodice to hem, and pretty lace cap sleeves. Her champagne-coloured hair was drawn up onto her head in loose curls which exposed her swan-like neck. A crewman wheeled a bath chair alongside her in which Max sat, still wan-looking and with a square plaster on his forehead replacing the bandage; his sling-wrapped arm supported on a cushion on his lap.

'I love Astrakhan Caviar.' Cynthia read from the menu card, then slid it into her evening bag. She caught Flora's gaze and giggled, 'A souvenir of the most dramatic honeymoon ever. Maybe I'll ask the captain to auto-graph it.'

'Why weren't *we* invited to dine with the captain?' Monica said in a harsh stage whisper, nodding to where Captain Gates held court to a table full of smug-looking passengers. 'We're as important as anyone else on this ship.'

'I don't know why they call him Giggles,' Gerald said in an undertone, making no attempt to answer her complaint. 'Haven't seen the fella laugh for days.'

'Hardly surprising,' Miss Ames chided. 'Two deaths are hardly going to look good on his record.'

A sudden, swift depression engulfed Flora, before a voice in her head whispered that Eloise would have been the first to encourage her to enjoy herself.

'Who would have taken that Crowe chap for a double killer, eh?' Gerald held up his empty champagne glass as a summons to a passing server. The man bowed, swapped it for a full one and bowed again before melting into the crowd.

'If a man is ruthless enough to bludgeon another man to death for money,' Hester said, 'he's hardly likely to baulk at stabbing a defenceless woman.'

'I hate the word, bludgeon.' Cynthia gave an exaggerated shudder. 'It conjures such horrible images.'

'I never liked him. He always struck me as the sleazy type.' Miss Ames peered into her glass as if disappointed to find it empty.

'I thought Mr Crowe was a charming man.' Monica twirled the ice chips in her glass. 'A little rough around the edges maybe.'

Flora was about to point out that neither fact made him homicidal but kept her thoughts to herself.

'What happens now the killer has been apprehended?' Miss Ames asked no one in particular.

'The police in London will have questions of their own, I imagine,' Gerald replied. Hester's ubiquitous tapestry bag slipped to the floor with a resounding thump. She bent to retrieve it, but had barely replaced it on her lap again before it fell to the floor again.

'Do stop fidgeting, Hester!' Mrs Penry-Jones glared at her.

'Sorry, Mrs Penry-Jones,' she simpered, her flush deepening.

As the meal progressed, conversation moved by mutual agreement away from murder, until the tables were cleared away and the orchestra opened the dancing with a lively tune Flora didn't recognise.

'How about the quadrille?' Bunny whispered.

'Lovely.' She lifted her chin in mock offence and took his outstretched hand, though was not prepared for the surge of awareness that swept over her as his hand closed possessively round hers, as if it belonged there.

Bunny led her onto the dance floor where they made up the set of four couples in a square. In seconds, the music filled Flora's head as she changed partners and returned to her own pairing with Bunny in the formation again. The need to concentrate dispelled the tensions of the last few days among a swirl of colour, light and noise as the fiddlers worked the melody into a noisy crescendo.

Instead of returning to their table at the end of the dance, Bunny slipped his arm round her waist as the strains of 'A Bicycle Made for Two' filled the room.

'Look over there,' he whispered in Flora's ear. 'I suspect Gerald is taking his leave of his shipboard romance.'

She turned her head to where Gerald danced with the young woman she assumed must be the same one he was talking to at the deck game.

'Poor Monica?' Flora whispered. 'Do you suppose she knows?'

'If she does, she's making an excellent job of feigning ignorance. Or maybe she's aware his attachment is only temporary, and once home she can rein him in again.'

'That's too worldly for me,' Flora sniffed. 'I expect husbands to be devoted. To the exclusion of all others.'

'In your case, that wouldn't be difficult.'

All of a sudden inhaling became difficult as his hand shifted to her back, his head lowered until his temple rested against her cheek. Her chin grazed his shoulder as they swayed around the dance floor, the weight of unspoken words pulled between them. 'Don't you think you're holding me too close?' she whispered once they had covered half the floor.

'Possibly, but I rather like it.'

She pressed her cheek against his shoulder, where she fitted so naturally, it was as if they had done the same thing many times. She wanted the evening to last forever, with Bunny's hand spread across the back of her waist, and the warmth of his jaw beside her cheek as the room revolved in a kaleidoscope of light that leapt and blurred.

The music changed and Bunny relinquished her to a hovering Gerald, though not without reluctance. 'Not too upset by this murder business, are you, my dear?' Gerald asked. She gave a non-committal smile, her focus on her feet to prevent them being trampled, Gerald being an enthusiastic rather than a skilled dancer. 'Nice girl, I thought,' he went on when she didn't answer, gripping her harder, though it was a fatherly touch rather than a suggestive one. 'Must make the whole mess difficult for you when you seemed to like her.'

'I did.' Flora responded, hesitating to explain her misgivings about Gus Crowe being in custody.

'Not boring you, am I?' he asked with the confidence of a man who cannot imagine doing any such thing.

'You're not a boring man, Gerald. In fact, you are quite a surprising one.' She slanted a flirtatious look up at his face, pleased when his smile went stale round the edges.

'Can't think what you mean by that, my dear.' He cleared his throat, then apologised when his toe grazed her instep.

'No harm done then,' Flora said. 'And I didn't mean to put you off.'

When the tune ended, she thanked Gerald politely, then left him in the middle of the floor staring after her with a perplexed frown on his face. By the time she located Bunny, the next dance had begun and he was partnering Cynthia, who laughed up into his eyes as he twirled her around the floor.

Max was also watching them, his gaze on his wife with a fierce pride tinged with sadness. Did Max, like her, feel he didn't deserve someone so dazzling? Or was he plagued with thoughts of misdeeds as yet unrevealed? Flora shivered, but didn't have time to brood, as a young man from California approached her and requested the next dance.

She had hardly returned to the table before Mr Hersch claimed her, which gave her momentary dread, though he surprised her by managing the two-step with remarkable grace for a big man, handing her back to Bunny with a flourish when it ended as if that was where she belonged.

The hardworking quintet made a valiant effort with 'After The Ball'.

'I don't know about you,' he whispered into her hair when the last notes had faded away. 'But I could do with a sit down and a drink.'

'Good idea.' Flora slipped her hand into his quite naturally, pulling him gently towards their table, where Cynthia and Max sat with Miss

Ames and a very flushed Mrs Penry-Jones, none of whom seemed eager to leave, though around them tables had begun to clear, waiters collected glasses and the band began to collect up their instruments.

Gerald had returned to the table where he sat holding Monica's hand, which drew an enquiring glance from Bunny.

'Guilt,' Flora whispered, at which Bunny nodded and ordered fresh drinks, slipping the waiter a banknote to avoid being told they were packing up for the evening.

'Gone to the powder room,' Mrs Penry-Jones said when Flora's gaze lingered on Hester's empty chair. 'Though why such a plain woman needs to spend so much time in front of a mirror escapes me.'

Flora merely smiled, recalling the heady perfume Hester had worn the other day. Perhaps expensive fragrances were the woman's weakness?

'Y'know, it strikes me,' Gerald mused, as if he had turned the question over in his head all evening, 'that Crowe chap didn't have it in him to murder a gel.'

'He robbed her, didn't he?' Monica snapped, resuming her seat, apparently catching the tail end of the conversation. 'Sounds simple enough to me.'

'Maybe too simple,' Max murmured.

'That's what I think,' Flora couldn't help herself. 'I don't believe Crowe killed Eloise either.'

Max reached for his glass, but fumbled it, and instead sent it toppling sideways.

Cynthia's hand shot out and caught Max's glass, though not quickly enough to prevent a spray of amber liquid onto the pristine white tablecloth. 'Can't we simply forget about all that for one evening?'

'Sorry.' Max gave his wife a sideways look before going back to working his way through a plate of petit fours left in the middle of the table. 'It's a nasty business all round which has got out of hand.'

Cynthia slowly wiped drops of whisky from her hand, but did not respond.

'I agree with Cynthia.' Gerald brought his hand down hard on the tabletop, making Flora jump. 'Accept what everyone else has, that Crowe was a cold-blooded killer.'

'Maybe, but—' Flora halted when Bunny's hand gripped hers on the table, a plea in his eyes.

'Let's not ruin this delightful evening by bringing up all that business again. Crowe is in custody. It's over.'

'I didn't bring it up! Gerald did.' Flora bridled, annoyed he was treating her like some vacuous female who needed instructions on how to think. She grabbed her bag from the table. 'Excuse me, but I promised to say goodnight to Eddy.'

'It's nearly midnight!' Bunny's impatient sigh accompanied the scrape of her chair as she rose. 'He'll be asleep by now.'

Ignoring him, she strode from the room, her angry footsteps propelling her across the deserted lobby and through the double doors onto the deck. Taking a deep breath of salt-tinged air, she set off across the boards.

A thick layer of fog drifted in off the ocean, softening the electric lights to a misty glow, the thrum of the engines beneath her feet a constant background sound.

The ship's bell rang the hour with a muffled gong just as the moon broke through a bank of cloud in a milky ball, pushing through the grey vapour, only to be swallowed again, throwing the deck into darkness.

The scene in the dining room replayed in her head as she walked. How dare Bunny try to control her into silence? He had no right to censor her opinions, and if he wasn't prepared to accept she had a mind of her own, they weren't suited at all. Though something else scraped at her brain she couldn't shake. She had missed something, though what and where escaped her. She had seen it clearly at the time but allowed it to slip past her without understanding what it meant.

Preoccupied, it took her a moment to realise that the suite door stood slightly ajar. She pushed it wider with one hand, her breath held as she flicked the light switch, bathing the room in light. She gave the empty room a swift glance, then tiptoed to Eddy's door, easing it open on oiled hinges. The night light on his bedside table created soft yellow arc that threw the corners into shadow. Eddy must have heard her as the mound of covers lifted and he propped himself onto one elbow.

'Flora?' He scratched his head and blinked. 'Is something wrong?'

'I'm sorry. I didn't mean to wake you, but the suite door was open.'

'The stewardess must have left it like that.' He eased upright and wrapped his arms round his bent knees. 'Did you have a good time?'

'It was a lovely dance, I—' She broke off at a dull thump that came from the sitting room behind her.

'What's that?' Eddy's eyes rounded as he slid from beneath the covers.

'Stay there!' She held up a hand and backed out of the room. The door to her bedroom stood open where she was certain it had been closed when she entered. Her head swivelled to the main door to the deck just as the flap of a full-length cloak disappeared through it.

A lance of fury sliced through her chest, and without thinking, she launched herself after the intruder.

'Flora!' Eddy's voice, both fearful and exasperated, called after her.

22

Flora's feet thumped across the deck, propelled by raw anger that someone had dared enter their suite while Eddy slept. Her feet were already sore from dancing all evening but she pounded on, each step vibrating through the thin soles of her dancing shoes.

Just as the thought struck her that the intruder couldn't have got far, she caught sight of a figure gliding through the mist ahead of her, appearing as a dark outline in the swirling mist, only to disappear again immediately.

She rounded the corner and hurtled onto the port side, where the deck stretched before her, empty but for a line of sulphurous lights burning on the bulkhead. She paused, her nerves alert for footsteps, or the sound of a swinging door, but all she heard was the persistent rumble of the ship's engines several decks below.

Her gaze searched the line of blank doors beneath bulkhead lamps, their yellow glow dulled into blurry halos by the fog. She was alone. Frustrated, she banged her clenched fist against the rail and flung away, striding back the way she had come. When she reached the top of the companionway where the metal steps dropped below her feet into a soup-like mist, panic bunched beneath her ribs. Halting, she glanced around but saw nothing, only an empty deck.

The hairs on her neck rose and a shiver ran through her, as if a vengeful spirit had passed close by. Then came a grunt to her left, followed by a rough, painful shove between her shoulder blades that launched her forwards into empty air.

She groped for the handrail, but missed, the sensation of falling making her stomach lurch sickeningly. The deck came up to meet her like a black wall, and she slammed against the boards, the air expelled from her lungs in a painful rush.

She lay still, trying to breathe, but her ribs would not obey. Her heart hammered as she anticipated footsteps that meant whoever had pushed her was on their way to finish her off. Seconds passed slowly, during which an image of the jagged gash on Parnell's head came back to her. She closed her eyes but panic built as she still could not take in a breath.

She started to feel dizzy, but heard nothing, while her own voice in her head screamed at her to calm down and breathe.

Slowly, her chest moved and she took in a gasp of air, then a larger one, until her shallow, rapid breathing settled into a more regular rhythm.

With slow, tentative stretches, Flora moved her toes, then her ankles, until with measured, stiff movements, she pushed herself gradually up onto an elbow.

'Miss! Miss!' a youthful male voice shouted. 'Are you all right?' A pair of uniformed legs ending in regulation shoes filled her vision. Judging him one of the crew, and hopefully benign, she lifted her head to where his silhouette stood out against scudding clouds and wisps of fog that made her head spin.

'Did you see him?' Supporting herself on her palms, she eased into a crouch, surprised when there seemed to be nothing broken.

'See who, Miss?' The crewman leaned down, tucked his shoulder into her armpit and hauled her upright.

'The man who pushed me.' Flora tested her weight on the sole of her left foot that sent a nausea-inducing pain through her leg. Hopping onto her right foot, she leaned against the sailor, grabbing the rail for support on her other side.

'I saw only you, Miss. Took quite a tumble, you did.' He took in her gown and grinned. 'That party punch carries a bit of a wallop, doesn't it? No wonder you were a bit shaky on those steps.'

Incensed, Flora stiffened but was too shaken to argue. Besides, she had only had one glass, or was it two?

'Thank you, but I'm neither drunk nor dead.' Pain and his implied insult made her snap. She leaned both forearms on the rail and bent forwards, fighting dizziness.

'I was sure you were going to end up like—' he broke off mid-sentence. 'I'll send someone to fetch the doctor, shall I, Miss?'

'Would you take me back to my suite first? Then if it isn't too much trouble, fetch Mr Harrington? He's probably still in the dining room.' She visualised Bunny drumming his fingers on the table, checking his watch every few seconds. The thought comforted her – a little.

Despite the sailor half carrying her up the steps to the promenade deck, their hop and pause technique made their progress frustratingly slow, hampered further when the crewman stopped to instruct a passing colleague to fetch Bunny. When they finally reached the upper deck, the sailor manhandled her inside the suite, apologising profusely when her injured foot glanced off the door frame.

'What happened, Flora?' Eddy stood at the open door to his bedroom, his eyes wide and frightened. 'I–I stayed here like you said.'

'Now, young sir,' the crewman clucked like a schoolmaster, though he couldn't have been more than five years Eddy's senior, 'give the lady a chance to catch her breath. She's had a little fall.'

'I have not had – oh, never mind.' Flora gritted her teeth and cast a longing look at the closed door of her bedroom but abandoned that plan and lowered herself into the nearest chair.

Why was someone in their suite? Crowe was under lock and key in his stateroom. Everyone must have known she was at the dance, but surely they had not come to hurt Eddy?

Bunny appeared at the door, his breathing fast and shallow as if he had run all the way from the dining room. 'A crewman said there had been an accident!' He entered the room, closely followed by the crewman who had been sent to fetch him, and crouched beside her, all knees and elbows as he attempted a hug but withdrew when he realised there were two pairs of eyes watching them.

'That's what they always say.' Flora glared at the crewmen, neither of whom appeared to be doing anything useful.

'Did that man hurt you, Flora?' Eddy hovered at her shoulder.

'What man?' Bunny's stern gaze went from Flora to Eddy and back again.

'I was pushed down the companionway,' Flora said, narrowing her eyes at the sailor's sceptical look, though Bunny's shocked face was more satisfying. 'You might suggest a search, though I doubt it would do much good now.'

'Did you see this man, Eddy?' Bunny asked, his gaze flicking to the young sailor, who shook his head.

'We both heard him,' Eddy insisted. 'He was in the sitting room. Flora went after him.'

'He was real!' Flora slapped her skirt, then winced at the sudden pain that jarred her ankle.

'The doctor is on his way, sir,' Flora's young helpmate said at Bunny's shoulder.

'Good. Thank you, but I can handle it from here.' He ushered the crewman to one side, where they conducted a brief, one-sided conversation before returning to her side.

'They'll take a quick look around the decks to see if anyone is still about,' Bunny said, returning to where she sat. 'But they cannot accuse anyone found admiring the night ocean of having attacked you.'

'It's not as if I could describe him, either.' Flora propped her head in one hand. 'I should imagine several people have long cloaks, which is all I saw.' Her initial anger dissipated as she began to see things from a bystander's view. Like the sailor who helped her, everyone would assume she had been at the punch bowl and simply lost her footing.

Dr Fletcher stepped into the minor chaos in his white dress uniform, all brisk efficiency and terse questions about where her foot hurt, the answer to which was everywhere, and where had it spread, which seemed to be everywhere as well. Apart from a sharp gasp at his rough handling of her foot, she remained stoically silent.

'I doubt you've broken your ankle, Miss Maguire,' he pronounced on completion of his examination. 'Sprained most like. I'll bind it for you. Keep it elevated until the swelling goes down. And get lots of rest.'

He delved into his ubiquitous black bag, withdrawing a familiar brown bottle she had last seen Bunny put into his pocket.

Dr Fletcher smiled as if he read her mind, pouring the contents into a tiny glass. 'You refused my ministrations before, but I insist you take this. It will help you with the pain and allow you to sleep.'

Flora eyed the murky brown liquid with distaste, then held her breath and tossed it to the back of her throat, swallowing it in one go. 'Ugh! That's bitter.'

'There's a good girl!' The doctor hefted his bag into one hand. 'I'll come back in the morning to check on you. Goodnight, Miss Maguire, Mr Harrington.' The pause between their names held a multitude of speculation, but Flora was too weary to protest.

'He's annoying,' Bunny said when the door closed behind him.

'Papa says it's compulsory for medical men.' Eddy sat draped over the opposite chair, his leg swinging. 'Optimism and a patronising manner is their stock-in-trade.'

Flora swallowed repeatedly in an effort to rid herself of the medicinal taste, then attempted a smile, short-circuited as a wave of nausea enveloped her. 'Oh, dear. I think I'm going to be sick—'

Bunny moved incredibly fast for a man who had been in a half-crouch beside her a moment before. In seconds, he shoved the porcelain bowl from her dresser into her hands.

The wave of sickness passed without any visible result. 'It's gone. But thank you anyway.'

'My pleasure.' Bunny removed the bowl, placing it on a nearby table.

'I didn't hear the intruder come in.' Eddy said, dismay clouding his features.

'It's not your fault.' Flora patted his hand absently. She didn't want to think about what might have happened if she hadn't returned at that exact moment.

'C'mon, old man.' Bunny guided Eddy back to his room. 'It's getting very late. Back to bed with you so you can get some sleep.'

Eddy issued a half-hearted protest, but allowed himself to be led away.

'He's trying to be brave, I can tell,' Flora said when Bunny returned.

'It could have been worse.' He perched on the arm of the chair. 'He might have come face to face with this chap.'

'I'm so glad he didn't.' Flora shifted in her chair, groaning when pain shot through her hip.

Concern darkened his eyes, as he clapped his hands on his thighs and rose. 'Someone will have to help you into bed.'

'It isn't going to be you, Mr Bunny Harrington. I'll get the stewardess to do it.'

'I wasn't offering, as it happens.' He pushed his glasses further up his nose by the bridge, and pressed the bell beside the mantle.

Returning, he squatted beside her chair, his face inches from hers. 'I want to apologise for my short temper earlier. I should never have spoken to you like that. It's just that, well we were having such a lovely time at the dance and for a little while I wanted to forget about death and – well, you know.' He gave a light shrug. 'I was enjoying your company immensely. Was that selfish of me?'

'No, I was too. You're forgiven, if I am for storming off like that.' It occurred to her then that if she hadn't, she wouldn't have found the intruder at all. Then what would have happened?

'You did scare me though. When I heard they had found you at the bottom of the companionway, I thought—'

'That I was lying dead on the deck like Mr—'

'Not a bit like Mr Parnell,' he interrupted. 'He went down quietly, whereas you, my dear girl, never will.' He raised one sardonic eyebrow to show he was only joking as he tucked a blanket round her. 'I'll make sure a crewman remains outside this suite tonight.' He placed a cushion behind her head. 'Then I need to report to our detective friend.'

Flora didn't comment on what Mr Hersch was going to say about her latest escapade. Her future at Pinkertons didn't look too promising if she wasn't capable of apprehending one intruder.

'I'm going to be black and blue in the morning,' she said through a yawn. 'I can feel the bruises erupt as I sit here.' Her tongue felt thick in her mouth, her words a slurred mumble as the sedative took effect. 'Tell me one thing before you go.'

'What's that?' He ducked his head close to her face as if he had trouble hearing her.

'What *is* your name?' Despite her attempt to keep them open, her eyes fluttered closed and she could no longer see his face.

'It's Ptolemy.' The embarrassed laugh in his voice sent pleasant ripples into her stomach, though she was convinced she must have misheard as her head started to float gently. She didn't have the energy to ask him to repeat it, and when the stewardess arrived to help her out of Cynthia's gown, Bunny had gone.

23

FRIDAY

Flora clenched her bottom lip between her teeth and lifted her swollen ankle gingerly onto the foot stool Eddy had thoughtfully, if noisily, kicked across the room toward her.

'Does it hurt much?' He crouched on the floor at her elbow, his eyes sharp with concern. 'Shall I stay here and keep you company?'

'Yes, to the first question, but no to the second. You'll be bored, and besides, all I need is a pot of the stewardess' best coffee.' She kept her voice light-hearted for his benefit, but the memory of a hard shove at her back and the sickening sensation of falling brought the previous night back in full force.

Her drug-induced slumber hadn't lasted long and pain had woken her in the early hours. She spent the remainder of the night in a futile attempt to get comfortable, but even the weight of the bedclothes sent a dull ache into her hip that radiated downwards into her thigh and knee and her right ankle was swollen to twice its size. She had lain, restless and impatient waiting until daylight poked through her blinds, then rose and begun the awkward task of dressing, which took far longer than normal.

'I heard you and Mr Harrington talking last night,' Eddy said. 'The sailor said you fell, but I told him over and over you were pushed, but he just laughed and said something about fruit punch'.

Flora's heart sank. 'Maybe I was wrong as it all happened so fast. Anyway, he's not about to come back.'

'I don't believe you. I know when you're fibbing and you weren't last night.' His eyes narrowed but with dismay rather than anger. 'That man did hurt you and how do you know he won't come back?' He dropped his chin onto the arm of her chair and stared up at her, an appeal in his eyes.

'Well, I don't, of course.' Flora hesitated, aware she had failed to keep him out of harm's way, with or without Bunny's steward and the vigilance of the Gilmore's. If he wasn't safe inside their suite, where would he be? She didn't want to lie to him, but didn't want to frighten him either.

'If either you or Ozzy are worried about anything you see or hear, all you have to do is shout for a crewman.' She was about to mention the one Bunny had hired would always be close by, but Eddy would be the first to remind her he hadn't been there when the intruder arrived.

Eddy pushed a hand through his wayward hair, reminding her she must remember to get it cut. The temptation to keep him with her all day was strong, but that was neither fair nor practical.

The Gilmores had sent a get-well card together with a note promising to keep an eye on him until she was mobile again, though it was obvious from its tone they didn't feel it was necessary.

That terrifying moment just before her foot stepped into thin air kept returning. She *was* pushed – but by whom?

'I'm glad Mr Harrington is looking after you.' Eddy picked at his sleeve, self-conscious. 'I... I think you look really good together. Even better than Meely and that Vanderbilt chap.'

Flora's hand stilled in the process of smoothing his hair. 'I'm glad you like him. He's a kind man and a welcome friend for the voyage.'

'That isn't what I meant. You're quite old now, Flora, it's time you had a beau.'

'Indeed?' She slapped his shoulder lightly, torn between laughter and pique. 'Thank you for the advice, young man, I'll give it due consideration. Now off you go to breakfast before it's all gone.'

'In a minute.' Eddy's teeth worried at his lower lip. 'I have a confession to make.'

'You're an Anglican, Eddy, you don't make confessions.' Her clumsy attempt to make him smile failed miserably as his bottom lip quivered.

'Well, I need to this time,' he persisted. 'It could be my fault you got hurt.'

'Why would you think that?' She eased her upper body in search of a more comfortable position, but then wished she hadn't when pain flared in her ankle.

'Ozzy and me' – he hunched his shoulders and stared at his hands – 'well, we found this thing in Mr Harrington's motor car. I'll show you.'

Before she could ask what he meant, he had scrambled to his feet and disappeared into his room, reappearing again seconds later with a flat stick about a foot long, made of dark wood that he held reverently in both hands.

Flora took it from him, the wood smooth, almost waxy to the touch, a vague memory intruding, of the boys with Gerald as they played a game on the deck, but the image remained indistinct.

'We found it stuffed down the back of the seat,' Eddy said. 'Ozzy said we should take turns looking after it. Is this why the man came to our room last night? He wanted this back?'

'I'm not sure.' She weighed it in her hands, where a gold strip of metal cut through the polished wood a third of the way down. 'It looks foreign, Oriental maybe. What are these marks carved into it?'

'I didn't notice that.' Eddy peered at it. 'Looks like some sort of cuneiform writing.'

'It looks well made, whatever it is.' She let the object drop to her lap. 'This doesn't belong to you, Eddy, and could be valuable. We must find out to whom it belongs.'

'We weren't going to *keep* it.' Eddy's voice rose slightly. 'Not forever, anyway. We didn't know what it was at first, which is why I brought it to you. I thought you should see what it does – look.'

He held the stick at either end and tugged it gently. The end slid off smoothly, revealing a thin steel blade that tapered into a point at the top.

'It's a knife,' he said unnecessarily.

'So I see.' With far more care than she had used previously, she took it gently from him, making sure the sharp blade came nowhere near her skin. 'When exactly did you find it?' The possibility that it belonged to Bunny made her heart race. She held her breath, hoping Eddy would disabuse her, but why else would it be in his motor car?

'Yesterday, before dinner.' He hunched his shoulders in the nonchalant shrug employed by boys when they know they have done something they shouldn't, but prefer not to explain. 'It wasn't there on Tuesday.'

Eddy dropped his chin, suddenly sheepish. 'Am I in trouble?'

'Not now you have owned up. Off you go to breakfast, Eddy. I'll deal with this.' Then she noticed something she hoped Eddy had not; where the blade met the hilt was a reddish-brown stain that looked very much like dried blood. Was she holding the weapon used to stab Eloise?

And what was it doing in Bunny's motor car?

* * *

Having reminded Eddy for the third time that finders are most definitely not keepers, Flora sent him off to breakfast in the company of a steward, with express instructions to go straight to the Gilmores' suite afterwards.

Alone again, and with the blade safely re-sheathed, Flora debated what to do. Her first instinct had been to tell Bunny, but suppose it *was* his? She shook the thought away as ridiculous. Bunny wasn't a killer.

A quick glance at the mantle clock told her it was still forty minutes to the breakfast bugle. Tucking the knife under her jacket, she let herself out onto the deck.

Her halting walk to the port side of the promenade deck took a frustratingly long time, and when she finally reached the correct stateroom, a dull, persistent throbbing radiated up her thigh.

She leaned her shoulder against the door frame and rang the bell, fretting. Bunny's stateroom was two doors away, and she hoped he wouldn't go to breakfast early and see her. She didn't want to have to explain, and the fewer people who knew about the knife the better. The door swung open, and Mr Hersch's imposing figure filled the frame, his brows drawn together in an enquiring scowl.

'Good morning, Flora.' A fleck of shaving foam clung to his skin below one ear, and his tie was undone. His gaze slid to her tightly bound ankle and the slipper that was the only footwear she could fit over it. 'Should you be on your feet?'

'I'm sorry to bother you this early, but there's something you should see.' She clamped her arm tight against her jacket, where the knife pressed into her side.

'You'd better come in.' He scanned the empty deck both ways before stepping aside.

Flora made for the nearest chair and lowered herself into it with a relieved sigh.

'Forgive me for failing to put in an appearance last night.' Mr Hersch dabbed the foam from his face with a towel he then draped over his shoulder. 'Officer Martin reported your er, mishap to me but assured me you weren't badly hurt. I assumed questions could wait until this morning.'

'I hardly expected you to come rushing to my side, though I must ask...' The knife clicked against her ribs and she swallowed before continuing. 'Do you believe I'm suffering delusions? That I had one glass of punch too many and imagined someone pushed me down those steps?'

He held her gaze unflinching for long seconds as he fastened his collar studs, wiped his hands on the towel, and discarded it onto a chair. 'No, Flora, I do not.'

Satisfied, she withdrew the knife from inside her jacket and held it out.

He took it from her without speaking, subjecting it to an intense, unhurried study.

'Eddy and the Gilmore boy found it.' Flora filled the silence. 'It's a—'

'A Korean ceremonial dagger.' He slid open the two ends as if he had done the same thing a hundred times before. 'A particularly nice piece.' He closed it again with a click.

'You've seen it before?'

'I've seen one like it. This one's quite old. Valuable too, I imagine.' His gaze lifted to meet hers. 'Where did young Eddy get it?'

'In Mr Harrington's motor car.' She let the implication settle in. 'Take a closer look at the blade.'

He flicked her a swift enquiring glance before he obeyed, frowning. Then gave a slow, thoughtful nod. 'Blood. Do I take it you believe this is the weapon you think was used to kill Miss Lane?'

'Don't you? Then whoever did it hid the knife in the motor car. And before you ask, I doubt Bunny had anything to do with it. The killer simply used the motor car as a convenient hiding place.'

'Do you have any theories as to who that might have been?'

'Not a clue, though I doubt it was Gus Crowe. Where would he get a ceremonial dagger?' He straddled the arm of a chair, the knife held loosely between both hands where it resembled nothing more dangerous than a wooden stick.

'Where indeed,' he mused, his brows lowered in thought. 'Miss Maguire, Flora, I apologise if you thought I did not take you seriously in the library yesterday.' He tapped the knife against the palm of his other hand. 'In fact, you were right, there is another killer on board. My inquiries are not yet over, but I'm getting close.'

'That's something, I suppose.' Flora shifted in the chair in an effort to get comfortable, releasing a low groan when the ache in her hip flared. Her satisfaction at being right would come later, when she wasn't so uncomfortable.

'Are you in pain, Flora?'

'I have some colourful bruises, but the discomfort is easing,' she lied. 'It's a shame so many people have touched that knife. We might have got a fingerprint from the blade which could prove who used it on Eloise.'

'Fingerprint?' Hersch's brows lifted in amused surprise. 'You know of such things?'

Flora glared at him, insulted. 'Sir Francis Galton attended a house party at Cleeve Abbey last year. He's a fascinating man, we had quite an enlightening discussion.'

'Galton? The British anthropologist?' Hersch's eyes widened.

'Charles Darwin is his cousin,' Flora added, unable to resist the chance to show off a little. 'Sir Francis published a book on the subject. Did you know that no two people in the entire world share the same fingerprint?'

'As a matter of fact, I did. However, even Pinkerton's has yet to establish them as a reliable method of identification. No court in the land would accept them as evidence.'

'No, I suppose you're right,' Flora said, disappointed. 'We'll have to think of another way.'

'We?' He placed the knife on a table at his elbow and sat back in his chair, the fingers of both hands linked together over his stomach. 'Flora,' he began, his rare use of her given name dragging her gaze to his face, 'if I reveal something, I trust you'll keep it to yourself?'

She nodded, her throat dry in anticipation.

'The van Elder family—'

'—Employed you to follow Eloise and find evidence against her.' The expression of startled astonishment on his face almost made up for all his secretive behaviour thus far.

'How did you know?'

'Eloise told me she had her suspicions, though they weren't conclusive. She was too afraid to approach you in case you intended handing her in to the police.'

'Actually, that's not quite—' he broke off at the look on her face. 'I'm aware Parnell claimed to have such evidence, which is why she gave him the money.'

'Then you *were* hired by Cynthia Cavendish?' The fact Eloise hadn't lied about everything made Flora feel her faith in her had been justified.

A glint of surprise lightened his eyes, but was gone in a second. 'That information is confidential. As is whatever evidence I might have uncovered in the course of my enquiries.' His smile hinted at a greater amusement he had no intention of sharing with her.

'Why must you be so evasive after everything that has happened?' Flora's jaw clicked in temper. 'Don't I have a right to know? After all, someone tried to kill me last night.'

'I'm aware of that, my dear, but you must admit you have put yourself in his way.'

Flora squirmed, acknowledging the truth of his remark, but still she refused to be treated like an annoyance, or worse, a useless female. 'Why won't you tell me what you really think?'

Hersch tucked a hand beneath Flora's elbow and tugged her gently to her feet. 'I think, that if I don't leave now, I will miss my breakfast.'

'There's something else before you throw me out,' Flora snapped, hopping on her good foot, her arm braced against the door frame. 'You ought to ask Max Cavendish why he was on deck that day.'

'Mr Cavendish suffered a concussion which has affected his memory.'

'Rubbish. If you believe that, you're more easily deceived than I thought. He's keeping something back. He told me not to involve myself in his business.'

'Can you be more specific?'

Flora hesitated. 'Well, actually it's not so much what he said. But I'm sure he's protecting Cynthia, but from whom or what I don't know.'

'Return to your suite and rest that foot.' He stepped back and closed his door, leaving her standing there with her mouth open.

By the time Flora reached her sitting room, her ankle throbbed painfully. She slumped into the chair and scratched the area of itchy skin she could reach inside the bandage, going over what Hersch had said, and more importantly what he hadn't revealed. The van Elders could easily have had something to do with Eloise's death, but if the German was on their payroll, would he be prepared to expose them?

Then she remembered she had left the knife in the German's stateroom and released a frustrated groan.

24

The stewardess set Flora's morning tea in front of her, then straightened sharply when the doorbell sounded. 'That's most probably the doctor, Miss Maguire.' She rubbed both hands down her apron. 'I'll let him in as I leave.'

'How is the ankle this morning?' Dr Fletcher's cheery greeting was in stark contrast to Flora's mood. 'You should have slept well last night with the help of my sedative.'

'It helped, but every time I moved, the pain woke me.' Nor had her early morning jaunt to Mr Hersch's cabin helped either.

'I have something a little stronger which might help.' He set his leather bag on the low table in the middle of the room and rummaged inside. 'Although wouldn't you be more comfortable in bed?'

'I'd rather not. I hate lying in bed during the day.' Ignoring his disapproving frown, she submitted meekly to having her temperature taken, followed by another painful manipulation of her ankle.

'The swelling isn't as bad as I thought, but you do look peaked this morning and your eyes are dull. Are you sure you didn't hit your head when you fell?'

'I did not fall,' Flora replied, her words distorted by the six-inch long thermometer he inserted under her tongue. 'I was pushed. I cannot remember whether I hit my head or not. I had rather a lot to think about at the time.'

'Hmm, any nausea, headache or dizziness?' He held her wrist lightly in his fingers and peered at his watch.

'All three, actually, but I'll get over it. Especially if the person who pushed me is found.' She caught his sceptical look beneath the concerned façade. 'You don't believe me, do you?'

'Let me put it this way.' His ingratiating smile put Flora's teeth on edge. 'In my experience, young females can be particularly fanciful when not kept busy. And you have been running around this ship making some startling claims during this voyage.' He tipped some of the contents from a small brown bottle into a tiny glass and held it out, removing the glass tube from her mouth with his other hand.

'What claims? I haven't said anything that Mr Hersch hasn't.' She took the glass from him and downed the cloudy liquid in one swallow, shuddering as the bitter taste hit the back of her throat. 'Besides, I must have discovered something important to unsettle our killer. And I don't mean Mr Crowe, either.'

He released a derisive chuckle while examining the readings on the thermometer under the light. 'Mr Crowe is most certainly the culprit, and he will face the authorities when we reach England.'

'You've accepted he killed Mr Parnell then?' Flora frowned. 'Didn't your report state he died in a fall?'

'Uh, well, I couldn't do a full post-mortem, so perhaps I was mistaken. Besides, he killed that young lady, didn't he? The actress?'

'Parnell was an opportunist thief, not a cold-hearted killer.' The urge to display her superior knowledge was strong. The memory of the telegram she had seen on Seaman Croft's desk rose into her head, but she wasn't sure why. 'He had something to do with Montana, I think. Or was that Gerald Gilmore?' Her head spun and the details slipped frustratingly out of reach.

'That friend of yours, the German who turned out to be a Pinkerton's man' – his eyes narrowed, making them appear closer together than they already were – 'has been asking a lot of impertinent questions.'

'Hardly impertinent. He's only trying to unearth the truth, and between us we've managed to—' she broke off as the dizziness returned.

'Are you sure you wouldn't be better off in bed?' He placed a cool hand against her brow, which should have been pleasant, but wasn't. 'It might be the best place for you right now.'

'I'm sure. I only injured my foot. And would you ask Captain Gates to come and see me? I want to tell him what happened formally.'

'Don't concern yourself, my dear. The captain knows all he needs to about this affair.' His dismissive grin made her want to slap him. 'As your doctor, I suggest you concentrate on getting better. I'm still worried about your head. You appear to be rambling somewhat.'

'Do I?' Flora gave this idea consideration. He might be right. She did seem to be chattering away to no purpose. 'All right, I'll stop talking and let you do your job.'

'Now,' he began, all smiles now that she was doing as she was told. 'I want you to take another dose of this in an hour. Could you do that for me?' He placed the brown ridged bottle on the table with a firm click.

Flora grimaced. 'If I must, though it makes me groggy and I can't think straight.'

'That's what potassium bromide solution is supposed to do, young lady.'

* * *

Flora couldn't remember the doctor leaving; the pain in her hip was markedly dulled by the sedative, while the passing of time took on an unreal quality. She dozed and dreamed, woke then dozed again, and the next time she opened her eyes, Bunny was standing in front of her.

'I brought your breakfast.' He placed a loaded tray on the table in front of her.

Flora surveyed the array of sausage, fried eggs, bacon, fruit compote, toast and marmalade. 'I doubt I could eat half that, though the coffee smells good. Would you mind pouring me a cup?'

'How are you this morning?' He handed her a steaming cup.

'Sore, drowsy, definitely not myself.' She took a delicious sip of aromatic coffee and eased back in her chair. 'Did I ruin Cynthia's dress?'

'Not at all. Simply a few dirty marks the laundry are confident they can remove. This is hardly the time to worry about a dress.'

'I'm a woman. Clothes matter, especially when they aren't mine.'

'Dr Fletcher thinks you imagined that push, you know.' Bunny perched on the arm of the chair opposite and rested his forearms on his knees. 'He said I was to ensure you don't exert yourself for the next couple of days. He suspects you have a head injury.'

Flora dismissed him with a wave, judging the good doctor must be severely under-employed to create problems where none existed.

Flora picked desultorily at her food, resenting Bunny's critical eye observing her every bite. At the same time, a tiny voice in her head told her she should appreciate his concern instead of being annoyed by it.

'Did you notice if anyone was missing from the dance last night?' she asked after a moment, unable to remember herself where everyone was when she left the dining room.

'Not that I noticed.' Bunny stroked his clean-shaven chin thoughtfully. 'Mrs Penry-Jones got quite voluble on the fruit punch and had to be escorted back to her suite by a crewman.'

'Where was Hester when this was going on?'

'She had gone to be sick in the powder room and returned looking quite green. I suspect she had overdone the punch too, I imagine. Then Cynthia sulked when Max announced he was tired and insisted on leaving. Poor chap looked quite worn out.'

'What about Gerald and Monica?'

'Like me, they stayed until they turned the lights out.' He poured coffee for himself and stirred sugar into it. 'Miss Ames proved to be quite an accomplished dancer. Couldn't get her off the floor.'

'I had this strange dream last night,' Flora began as a memory resurfaced, 'where you told me you had been named after some ancient Greek.' She peered at him over the rim of her cup.

The rhythmic clink of his spoon halted. Slowly, he set it down gently in the saucer. 'Ah, you did hear me. No dream, I'm afraid. A whim of my father's. Ptolemy was Alexander the Great's boyhood companion at Mieza, you know.'

'No, I don't know. What's Mieza?'

'A sort of boarding school for Macedonian nobles. Alexander studied there under Aristotle.'

Flora cut up her sausage into small pieces, mainly to disguise the fact she hadn't eaten any, while speculating on how such a royal name got abbreviated to that of a small furry creature with oversized ears.

'Many believed that Ptolemy was Alexander's illegitimate half-brother.' Bunny balanced the coffee cup in one hand and plucked a slice of toast from the silver rack with the other. 'I like to think that's true, anyway.'

'Why didn't your parents call you Alexander? That wouldn't have raised any eyebrows.'

'They did, it's my second name.' He pointed his toast at her, eyes narrowed. 'I would appreciate it if we dropped the subject now.'

'As you wish.' She paused with her fork held in mid-air, a roundel of sausage clinging to the tines. 'You do believe I was pushed down those steps, don't you?'

'I'll admit I wasn't sure at first. No, take that look off your face. It's not beyond the bounds of possibility that your mind played tricks after everything that has happened. However, I lay awake last night thinking about it.'

'And what conclusion did you come to?' Flora held her breath. If he dismissed her again, she hadn't the strength to fight him. Her limbs felt heavy and his voice kept receding, then growing louder again. Even the room seemed to be moving, though she attributed that to the motion of the ship.

'I agree that Gus Crowe is a sneak thief, not a violent criminal who would stab a woman for a gold bracelet. Parnell died in a botched robbery.' He took a bite of toast and chewed thoughtfully. 'Incidentally, Hersch told me at breakfast that they had found the murder weapon. The one used to kill Eloise. He didn't explain as to what or where and cut me off when I asked.'

Aware of an uncomfortable buzzing in her ears and strange colours floating before her eyes, Flora decided to explain about the knife later, when her head was clearer. The fact it was found in his care still bothered her on some level.

'Tell me about your plans for your factory in England.' Apart from not wishing to discuss knives, the reason for her question escaped her. It wasn't as if she would be a part of it.

'My main problem is finding an engineering firm to make the parts.' He folded both hands over his flat stomach, his long legs stretched out in front of him. 'I'll have to manufacture every piece of the engine and body-work myself, of course, which will make production very slow. Then there's the travelling needed to show my designs to possible buyers at the show.'

'What show?' Flora asked through a yawn.

'There's an automobile show in Madison Square Garden scheduled for next November.'

'Isn't that where they hold those boxing matches?'

'It is, although other events are staged there too. The exhibition will last an entire week, sponsored by the Automobile Club of America.'

'There is a club for motor cars?' Flora asked, incredulous.

'Your scepticism wounds me, Miss Maguire. Motor travel is no temporary madness, I'm confident it has a long and illustrious future. There will be upwards of sixty exhibitors at the show in New York, all displaying at least thirty new autos.'

'So many? I had no idea.' Flora eased her neck from side to side, but it didn't help. She felt as though she were underwater.

'You aren't listening to me, are you, Flora?' Bunny chuckled, the sound of his hands slapping the arms of his chair bringing her eyes open with a snap. 'Before you fall asleep again, Dr Fletcher said I was to make sure you took some medicine.' He circled behind her chair towards the mantle, returning with the bottle and a small glass, which he filled and handed to her.

She took it with unsteady fingers, staring at it for a few seconds with dismay.

Bunny turned back to put the bottle back on the shelf and when his back was turned, she tipped the contents into the last inch of coffee in her cup. Licking her lips ostentatiously, she held out the empty glass. 'There. Now take it away.'

He hauled her upright, tucked his other arm behind her knees and swept her into his arms, then carried her into the bedroom. Flora tried to say something about wishing the circumstances were different for such a romantic display, but the words came out as an unintelligible slur. The effort to stay awake became too much, and she barely registered the click of the door before sleep claimed her.

25

Flora dreamed of a violent storm at sea, all black clouds, forked lightning and falling with stomach-churning speed into massive troughs, only to be heaved upwards again into a boiling mountain of water. The sky suddenly turned white and she fell to the floor with a thump in the kitchen with the black range that had been such a strong image throughout her life. The scene played out as it always did, with her tiny self as she crawled on a stone floor, her mother's skirt clutched in her hands. Then something new intruded.

Someone was calling her name, over and over.

With a groan of protest, she rolled her shoulder to rid herself of a disturbing weight that pressed down on her.

'Flora!' The voice came again, louder this time, followed by a violent shake.

She prised her eyelids open, bringing a hand to shield her eyes as stark daylight poked the tender spot behind her forehead. A blur of colour and shadows came into focus and turned into Bunny's worried face, which loomed inches above hers.

She jerked upright, narrowly avoiding a collision of heads. 'What's going on?' she mumbled, though it came out more like, "Wassgoingon". A shaft of pain sliced through her head and she palmed her forehead with a hand.

Bunny released a ragged sigh, then gathered her into his arms and held on tight, his hands seeking out the contours of her back. He pressed his lips against her left temple, rocking her gently.

Flora stiffened at first, confused, until his touch sent ripples of pleasure through her spine. 'Hmmm, that's nice,' she murmured, relaxing into him. Slowly, she opened her eyes, then froze at the sight of Mr Hersch at the end of the bed, Eddy next to him, both staring at her wide-eyed.

'How are you feeling?' Hersch's penetrating gaze searched her face.

'Fast asleep up until two minutes ago.' She wriggled out of Bunny's grasp and brought a hand to her hair, encountered a mass of tousled curls that were past repairing, and lowered it again. 'What are you all doing in my bedroom?' She hugged the coverlet up to her neck, despite that she was fully dressed beneath it.

'She's not sweating from what I can tell.' Hersch crept closer and peered at her, making the tiny space claustrophobic. 'No shivering or tremors. Her pupils look clear and are of normal size.'

Flora jerked her chin back, away from his searching gaze. 'Would someone explain—'

'How much of that sedative have you taken?' Bunny interrupted. He wrestled the coverlet from between her fingers, took her hand in his and searched her face. 'Don't scowl like that, Flora, this is important.'

'Well.' She forced herself to think. 'Dr Fletcher gave me some last night and again first thing this morning.'

'Did you take any more apart from the one I gave you?'

'Um, well actually, I threw that one away. It tasted bitter and I don't like the stuff. It made me feel as if I was floating.'

'Oh, thank God for your contrary nature.' The intense look in Bunny's eyes dissolved with his exhaled breath.

'Will someone please tell me what's happening?' Flora scooted further up the bed, the coverlet still clutched in both hands.

Bunny tugged the coverlet aside and pulled her gently upright. 'Come into the sitting room, and we'll explain.'

'I'll just settle this young man with Mrs Gilmore.' Hersch patted Eddy's shoulder and guided him out of the room. 'There, you see, Ed, old chap, she's perfectly fine. All that fuss about nothing.' His soothing voice receded as they left, followed by Eddy's half-hearted protest that he wanted to stay.

Monica Gilmore must have been waiting outside the suite door, for Flora heard her high-pitched greeting to Eddy, followed by an enthusiastic recital of plans she had in store for the afternoon, most of which seemed to involve food.

Reassured he would be looked after, and with Bunny's supporting arm round her waist, Flora concentrated on getting her stiff muscles to move into the sitting room, her eyes widening at the sight of not only Captain Gates, but Dr Fletcher and Officer Martin as well. The latter stood by the door, hands clasped behind his back as if on guard.

'To what do I owe the pleasure of this gathering?' Flora asked, conscious of her rumpled, sleep-heavy appearance.

'Don't joke, Flora,' Bunny's grip on her arm tightened as he lowered her into a chair. 'We were genuinely worried about you. And for good reason'

'However, we are very relieved to see you well, Miss Maguire.' Captain Gates inclined his head, the lines beside his mouth deeper than usual, his eyes lacklustre.

Flora wished she would smile again. She missed his smile.

Hersch plucked the brown bottle from the mantle and held it up. 'Is this what the doctor gave you, Flora?'

'It's bromide, to help me sleep.' She looked to the doctor for confirmation which was not forthcoming. Instead he avoided her eyes and stared at the floor.

'I don't think so, my dear.' Hersch dropped the bottle into his pocket. 'When we have this analysed in London, I suspect we'll find it's a strong concentration of laudanum. Well, Dr Fletcher?' He turned to face the doctor. 'How much of this did you intend her to take?'

Without warning, Bunny launched himself at the man, both hands encircling his throat as he snarled, 'You were asked a question! How much did you give her?'

The doctor's eyes bulged and he emitted a strangled gurgle as he tried to prise Bunny's hands from his neck without success.

'Bunny!' Flora started forwards in her chair. 'What *are* you doing?' She cast a pleading glance at the detective, but instead of intervening, he remained passive to one side.

Officer Martin looked about to step between them, but Captain Gates shook his head.

'I said, how much?' Bunny repeated, giving Dr Fletcher a rough shake.

'Four grains,' he croaked, his voice distorted. 'Four grains each dose.'

Bunny released him with a snort of disgust, flattened both hands against the doctor's chest and shoved him backwards with such force, he staggered against the bulkhead.

Fletcher righted himself again, a sneer on his mouth, though the hand he pushed through his hair shook.

'I don't even know what that means,' Flora murmured, staring at a red-faced Bunny, who fought to settle his breathing. Flora was more accustomed to his calm manners and gentle nature, so this burst of uncontrolled anger shocked her; that it was on her behalf was also strangely exciting.

'Six grains is a fatal dose,' Hersch said finally, one brow raised. 'The accumulation of that much laudanum over a twelve-hour period would most likely have killed you, Flora.'

'What?' Flora gaped. 'But that's ridiculous. Why would Dr Fletcher try to kill me?' Had the doctor pushed her down the steps? Is that why he was so keen to intimate she had imagined it?

'Care to enlighten the lady, Fletcher?' Captain Gates spoke for the first time.

'Yes, why don't you do that – Fletcher?' Bunny came to stand beside her chair, one hand caressing her shoulder.

The doctor's eyes flickered with doubt, but he didn't speak.

'Nothing to say, Doctor?' Hersch snorted. 'Then let me do it for you. Nine years ago, Mr Parnell was a major organiser of a fraudulent land deal in Montana.'

'Montana,' Flora repeated, sifting through the fog in her head. 'Why does that word mean something to me?'

'I sent a telegraph to a contact of mine asking him to unearth a list of people who lost money in that same venture,' Hersch continued. 'Their response came through this morning. Gerald Gilmore's name was there as having lost money in that deal. That first night on board, he recognised Parnell.'

Flora vaguely recalled Bunny mentioning something like that, then pushed the memory away and concentrated on what Hersch said.

'Dr Fletcher lost money in the same enterprise,' he went on. 'A lot of money. He also encouraged some of his patients to invest.'

'I didn't know it was fake!' Dr Fletcher interjected. 'I was swindled like everyone else.'

'Unfortunately,' Hersch went on as if he hadn't spoken, 'the good doctor was hounded out of his practice as a result. Unable to continue his career in an assumed name, so hiding was his only option. He took a position as ship's doctor to avoid the scandal.'

'You call *this* a career?' Fletcher gave the suite a slow, contemptuous look. 'Handing out plasters and tonics to rich, spoiled hypochondriacs?'

'What he didn't bargain on,' Hersch continued, getting into his stride, 'was that the man he held entirely responsible for his plight would turn up as a passenger on this ship calling himself Frank Parnell.'

'I certainly did not!' Fletcher growled. He adjusted his tie, though this struck Flora as more a nervous reaction. 'I spent years rehearsing what I would say if I ever saw him again. Then there he sat, throwing money around without a care. I lay awake half that first night, then rose early and went to his stateroom before I lost my nerve.'

'Did you expect him to apologise?' Bunny demanded. 'Or recompense you for your losses?'

'That's the last thing I expected, though I wanted him to know he had ruined my life!' Fletcher's gaze, cold and reptilian, slid towards Flora. He reeked of self-pity, making her wonder how she had ever imagined him attractive, let alone trusted him.

'What happened?' Hersch said gently, gesturing to Bunny for silence.

'Parnell came to the door with a towel held to a gash on his head.' Fletcher swallowed before continuing. 'Nothing serious, but it bled quite a bit. Said Crowe had attacked him. He even assumed that in a fit of remorse, Crowe had sent me along to see to him. When I told him why I was really there, he laughed; said I was simply an unlucky punter and should have got over it by now.'

'I can see why that would enrage you,' Hersch said. 'However, that doesn't explain how Mr Parnell ended up dead.'

'I'm not saying any more.' Dr Fletcher stared at him, a belligerent, superior stare that was also a challenge.

'I see,' Hersch mused. 'Then I'll speculate, shall I? Feel free to interrupt at any point.' Hersch jammed his thumbs into his waistcoat pockets, his feet splayed as if he was about to address a courtroom. 'Parnell's lack of remorse enraged you, so you picked up the first thing to hand, which happened to be a heavy brass ashtray. Am I right so far?'

Fletcher didn't react at first, then his mouth twisted as if the memory gave him a certain satisfaction. 'That gash was a darned sight worse when I had finished, I can tell you,' he muttered, so low, Flora had to strain to hear him.

'Then,' Hersch paced the room, stroking his chin. 'You cleaned the wound with a towel, then removed as much of the blood as you could from the bathroom. I should imagine it was almost six by then, when you knew the crew would be round to wash the decks. Hmm, not everyone would know that.' The detective raised a finger as he spoke, obviously enjoying himself. 'You waited in his stateroom until the cleaning crew had finished, then intended to throw him overboard. Isn't that right, Fletcher? After all, no body, no crime, eh?'

'You tell me.' Cruel pleasure poisoned his words.

'All right then,' Hersch continued, unperturbed. 'You dragged the body as far as the companionway, but something disturbed you. A passenger maybe, or a member of the crew? Whichever it was, you panicked and dumped it down the steps. You went back to collect the bloodied towel and the ashtray, because the maid noticed they were missing when she went in that morning. All you had to do was wait to be summoned and told a body had been found. How am I doing, Fletcher?' He grinned at the doctor, whose surly expression had not changed. 'Once the body was taken to your office, you stripped and washed it to ensure no evidence remained to contradict your report that he had died from a fall.'

Faced with the stark facts of what he had done seemed to dawn on the doctor. His arrogance dissolved and he shifted his feet, unable to meet anyone's eye.

'What did you do with the towel and the ashtray?' Bunny asked.

'I threw them overboard.' Fletcher snarled. 'Which proved more difficult than I anticipated. Whenever I left my cabin, a passenger would waylay me with a minor complaint. You'd be surprised how little free time the crew get aboard this ship.'

'I cannot comment on your conditions of employment,' Hersch sniffed. 'You'll have to take those up with the captain.' He slid a conspiratorial look in Captain Gates direction.

'I still don't understand why you tried to kill *me*,' Flora said. 'I never suspected you.'

'It would have come back to you.' Fletcher's lip curled as he spoke, contempt in every syllable. 'This morning, you mentioned that accursed land deal. It was only a matter of time before you told someone else, so to buy some time I swapped the bromide for laudanum. Another day and I would have been able to get off this wretched ship and disappear.'

'You weren't supposed to wake up, Flora.' The weight of Bunny's stare sent Fletcher back a pace, though his chin still jutted angrily 'Our good doctor had already prepared the ground about a possible head injury.'

'Which I didn't have,' Flora murmured. Tipping the medicine into her coffee was a momentary impulse. She could just as easily have drunk it to keep Bunny happy. Although had it not been for that awful drug, she wouldn't have been so voluble with Fletcher in the first place.

'I think we've heard enough.' Captain Gates gestured to Officer Martin to escort the doctor out, though Fletcher shrugged off the man's retraining arm with a harsh, guttural snort, and stomped outside to where two more crewmen waited.

The captain replaced his cap, tipped the peak at each of them, then followed.

'It never occurred to me it was him,' Flora said softly, still stunned. She glanced at Mr Hersch. 'Did you know all along he had been swindled by Parnell, or rather, Marlon van Elder?'

'No,' Hersch replied. 'I only received the list this morning by wireless telegraph. I was as surprised as anyone to see his name on it.'

'When I saw Mr Hersch and the captain drag Fletcher out of his office, I tagged along,' Bunny gently massaged Flora's shoulder as he talked. 'Never been so angry in my life.'

Flora smiled, glad of it, but it was a subject for another time. 'I wonder if Seaman Crofts is aware his telegraph machine has captured a dangerous criminal?' She rubbed her upper arms with both hands to still a shiver that wouldn't go away. 'And how did you know about the sedative?'

'Eddy told me,' Bunny said. 'We met on his way back from breakfast. When I asked how you were, he said you were sleeping and the suite smelled like a sweet shop. That's how I knew something wasn't right.'

Flora stared at him. 'What has that got to do with anything?'

'Cinnamon,' Hersch interjected. 'It's not used in the administration of bromide, but often mixed into laudanum to disguise the bitter taste.'

'I even insisted you take it.' Bunny shook his head, his face white. 'Thank goodness you defied me.' He sniffed ostentatiously. 'Come to think of it, it does smell a bit like a confectioners' emporium in here.'

Flora giggled, a sound too close to hysteria for comfort.

'I suppose doctors are the best qualified to kill people,' Flora said, as an image of Eloise broke through the cotton wool in her head. 'Dr Fletcher didn't kill Eloise though did he? She was stabbed.'

'That would make everything conveniently simple, wouldn't it?' Hersch sighed. 'But no, I think not. However, you may rest assured, the net is closing in.' He rubbed his hands together and backed towards the door.

Once he had gone, Flora became keenly aware of Bunny's presence. The fact he had been so angry at the doctor's actions thrilled her on the one hand, but a niggling thought scraped incessantly at the edge of her brain.

'Bunny? Do you happen to have an interest in antique oriental daggers?'

'I beg your pardon?' His brows drew together as he reached to tuck a strand of her hair behind her ear. 'Are you sure you didn't take more of that laudanum than we thought?'

'Nothing, just something that occurred to me.' She raised her chin to meet the angle of his gaze, searching for something in his eyes, but there was nothing to fear. There never had been.

26

Flora hobbled along the deck at Bunny's side, her coat buttoned to her neck, one arm tucked through his. The *Minneapolis* would dock at Tilbury the next afternoon, and she found herself counting each hour before she would have to say goodbye to him.

'I'm sorry to drag you out into the cold, but I needed some air after being in the cabin most of the day. Taking meals in the suite may sound like an unheard of luxury, but it palls after a while.'

'Cabin fever, I believe they call it.' He pressed her elbow into his side. 'I don't feel at all dragged. Should whoever attacked you reappear, I intend to be on hand to protect you.'

'I take it Dr Fletcher still insists he didn't push me, or that he killed Eloise?' The last she did not believe herself, but she wouldn't reject it completely until the truth was revealed.

'He will only admit to battering Marlon van Elder.' Bunny slowed his pace so she could keep up. 'Who, incidentally, used his real name for that land fraud.'

Flora bit her lip. The thought that whoever shoved her down the companionway still roamed the ship remained an uncomfortable one.

'That suggestion of yours for hot and cold compresses on my ankle worked well.' She eased closer, determined to relish every moment of their last day together. 'It still aches, but it's not unbearable.' When he didn't respond, she shook his arm. 'Are you listening?'

'Sort of, I was just wondering what was going on over there?'

'Where?' Flora followed his gaze to where Mr Hersch stood with the captain and two crewmen beside Mrs Penry-Jones' suite. 'Is something happening?'

'Possibly.' Bunny shifted his hold on her arm, pulling her in the reverse direction. 'Though whatever it is, they won't want us listening to a private conversation. Shall we go back?'

'Not on your life.' Flora carried on walking, though it was more of a hop and stagger. 'I'm going to find out what's going on.'

He capitulated with a sigh, though Flora suspected his reluctance was feigned.

'Good evening, Flora, Mr Harrington.' Mr Hersch greeted them with a tilt of his head at the suite door. 'How nice to see you out and about again, my dear.'

'Thank you. We were just getting some air.' She tried to peer round him but his bulk effectively blocked the door. 'Is something wrong?'

'Do feel free to make a party of it!' Mrs Penry-Jones's harsh voice reached her from inside. 'Come in, come in, the governess and her *inamorato* may as well witness my downfall.'

Flora directed an astonished look at Bunny, who blinked behind his glasses.

Mr Hersch stepped to one side, a hand extended as an invitation for them to enter.

'Are you sure we ought to?' Bunny asked, hesitant.

'Absolutely.' Flora risked a glance at Captain Gates, prepared for his dismissal, but he didn't react, so requiring no further encouragement, she pulled Bunny behind her as she limped into the suite.

Mrs Penry-Jones dominated the room from one of the ubiquitous wicker chairs with their plush red upholstery, her complexion pale but for two spots of red high up on her sharp cheeks; her back held straight, though her head wobbled on her thin neck. With one hand, she gripped her silver-topped cane propped beside her right knee, the other plucking nervously at a pleat of her skirt.

Max occupied another chair against the wall, the plaster on his forehead reduced to the size of a half-crown, his injured arm still strapped to his chest.

Cynthia paced the room, chewing a thumbnail, her slate grey gown matching her troubled eyes.

'Do sit down, Cynthia,' Max snapped, apparently at the end of his patience.

Cynthia broke off her restless pacing to look at Flora and Bunny, her gaze hardened as she turned it on Hersch. 'Are we a public spectacle now?' she demanded, making no attempt to sit.

'Where's Miss Smith?' the detective asked, ignoring Cynthia's question.

'I sent her to fetch me some tea to help calm my nerves at this dreadful intrusion,' Mrs Penry-Jones clamped her lips into a hard line.

'I shan't intrude long,' the detective said archly. 'I merely wished to ask if any of you has seen this before?' From an inside pocket he withdrew the knife Flora had left in his stateroom, slid the blade from its wooden sheath and held it up. 'I shall ask Miss Smith the same question when she returns.'

Flora may have imagined it, but though no one spoke, backs stiffened perceptibly.

'It belongs to me,' Mrs Penry-Jones said after a moment. 'My first husband brought it back from Korea thirty years ago.'

'I suspect it's considerably older than that.' Hersch returned the blade to its sheath. 'May I ask why you brought it with you on this voyage?'

She gave a mild shrug, her gaze sliding to Cynthia.

'Don't look at *me!*' Cynthia squeaked. 'The last time I saw that – that thing' – she waved her hand in Hersch's direction – 'it was in Grandmamma's vanity case.'

Cynthia's jutted chin, the superior gaze and the wagging finger were all Mrs Penry-Jones, but in a younger body. Flora bit her lip to prevent a smile, surprised she hadn't noticed before, but explained it away by the fact she had rarely seen them so close together.

'She's her grandmother?' Bunny whispered in awe, though he did not appear to require a response.

'Apparently so,' Flora replied with a smile, having no intention to admitting to him that she had only come to this conclusion since they entered the suite. But it certainly made sense.

'I keep that dagger for protection,' Mrs Penry-Jones continued as if Cynthia hadn't spoken. 'I didn't even know it was missing.'

'What about you, Mrs Cavendish?' Hersch turned to Cynthia 'Might *you* have used this to stab Estelle van Elder?'

Cynthia's mouth worked but no sound came.

'How could you, Cynthia?' Mrs Penry-Jones released a horrified gasp. 'We agreed! To seek justice for Theo, not bloody revenge. Why couldn't you have simply waited?'

'Grandmamma! How could you think such a thing?' Cynthia rounded on the old lady, her lovely eyes flashing with anger and a keen intelligence she seemed to have masked up until now.

'Would someone care to explain?' Captain Gates asked, bemused.

'I wish they would too,' Bunny muttered, confused.

'Don't you see? Everything makes sense' Flora said. 'I'd like to find out if Mr Hersch is about to blow their story apart, or give them all alibis?'

'What do you mean, how—'

Flora shushed him. 'Just listen.'

'It was all *her* idea.' Cynthia cocked her chin at Mrs Penry-Jones. 'No one was supposed to die!'

'We're every bit as responsible, Cyn,' Max began. 'If only we had let the authorities—'

'Shut up, Max!' Mrs Penry-Jones snapped. 'You don't have to say anything. You cannot be compelled to give evidence against her anyway. She's your wife.'

A look of patient sympathy crossed Max's slightly chubby face, before he reverted to resigned silence.

'For the benefit of Miss Maguire and Mr Harrington, allow me to return to the beginning.' Hersch closed the knife which he set on the low table in front of him with a sharp click. 'Earlier this year, Mr Theodore van Elder took, as his second wife, Estelle Montgomery, a woman considerably younger than himself.'

The old lady straightened slowly, as if gathering her dignity around her like a cape. 'That girl was nothing more than a scheming trollop!'

'However,' Hersch drew out the word in warning, 'a week after the wedding, Mr van Elder unfortunately died.'

'I told you that obituary was suspicious,' Bunny said with a snort.

'Exactly!' Mrs Penry-Jones pinned the detective with a triumphant glare.

The detective shook his head. 'The coroner's report stated Theodore van Elder succumbed to a bout of gastritis. There was nothing suspicious about his death.'

'Fiddlesticks!' Mrs Penry-Jones sniffed. 'My son was only forty-two. No, Estelle, or Eloise or whatever she called herself, persuaded him into a hole-in-the-wall wedding, only to murder him for his money.'

'They were married,' Flora said. 'She already had access to his money. Besides, to kill him within a week would have been too obvious. And who killed Eloise?'

'Mrs Cavendish?' Hersch raised an enquiring eyebrow in her direction.

'Are you accusing my wife of murder?' Max's furious gaze raked the detective.

'I'm quite capable of answering for myself, Max.' Two spots of red bloomed on Cynthia's porcelain cheeks as she waved him away. '*I* didn't kill Eloise.'

'No, Mrs Cavendish,' Hersch said slowly. 'I don't believe you did. After the stewardess helped you dress for the bridge tournament that afternoon, you called at Miss Lane's stateroom with the tea you promised her. The reason you received no answer, was because she was already dead.'

'There, you see, Grandmamma!' Cynthia flung at the old woman in triumph. '*Now* do you believe me?'

Mrs Penry-Jones did not respond, her knuckles whitening on the top of her walking stick.

'Is that why you all came on board together?' Flora was unable to help herself. 'To confront Eloise?'

'Of course! I wanted her exposed.' Mrs Penry-Jones narrowed her eyes at Flora. 'Which was Marlon's job, but he fluffed it.' Her disdainful sniff conveyed her lack of surprise at his failure.

'Marlon was my nephew by marriage, estranged from the family due to some disreputable behaviour I won't go into here.' She closed her eyes briefly as if the embarrassment was too much. 'After Theodore's tragic death, he came crawling to me, asking for a chance to redeem himself. I charged him with befriending Theodore's widow in order to discover how to make her pay for what she had done.'

'Then why engage Pinkertons?' The term 'belt-and-braces' jumped into Flora's head.

'Insurance.' Mrs Penry-Jones glared at her. 'When Marlon told me Eloise had booked passage for England, I couldn't risk her getting away before I could expose her. I had no idea he worked for the agency.' She waved her stick at Mr Hersch before bringing it down on the floor again with a thump.

'That's quite true,' Hersch said. 'I was engaged to follow Miss Lane to London and interview her there. I had no idea Mrs Penry-Jones or her granddaughter were on board.'

'You weren't meant to know!' Mrs Penry-Jones snapped, then her eyes glinted. 'And have you forgotten you work for me? I won't tolerate being questioned in this way.'

'The young lady's death ended our agreement, Mrs Penry-Jones.' Hersch brooked no argument. 'As a result of which I offered my services to Captain Gates.'

Mrs Penry-Jones grunted, but offered no response.

'Now if you don't mind, I'll continue for the benefit of you, Flora, and Mr Harrington,' Hersch said. 'Mrs Cavendish, how did you become involved when you reside in England and have done for the past fifteen years?'

Cynthia sighed, as if whatever fight remained drained out of her. 'Max and I were about to leave for Rome on our honeymoon when a telegram arrived saying Daddy had been murdered.' Her eyes brightening with unshed tears. 'I didn't know him that well, but he was still my father. We changed our booking and sailed to New York instead. Grandmamma was adamant the girl he married had killed Daddy, so Max and I agreed to help.'

Max gave a snort that implied his agreement had not been sought, but no one took any notice.

'On that first night,' Mrs Penry-Jones took up the story, 'Marlon told me he had obtained the evidence I needed. He was supposed to bring it to me the next morning, but he never arrived. When I heard he had been found dead, I thought—'

'That Eloise had killed him to prevent him doing so?' Hersch finished for her.

She nodded stiffly.

'I'm afraid he deceived you, dear lady.' The detective sighed. 'Marlon possessed no such evidence. We cannot know exactly what happened between him and Miss Lane, but we assume he convinced her to part with money in exchange for his silence.'

'That's what Eloise told me,' Flora said. 'I wondered at the time why she would agree to it if she wasn't guilty, but if she was being blackmailed by Parnell, it makes sense.'

She saw no reason to mention Eloise had tried to retrieve it from Parnell, much less her own part in that particular venture.

'Eloise had never met you or your family.' Flora glared at the old lady. 'She had no idea you were on board, but was convinced you had hired Mr Hersch.'

'If she was innocent, she would have had nothing to fear.' Mrs Penry-Jones sniffed.

'Don't you see? She must have been desperate, imagining she would never be rid of a family prepared to hound her across the Atlantic? She was right about one thing, you did hire Mr Hersch.'

'Not to intimidate her, merely to uncover the truth,' Cynthia added.

'Actually, those letters we sent were pretty intimidating, I—'

'Be quiet, Max!' Cynthia and the old lady snapped in chorus.

'If you believed that your stepmother killed your father, Mrs Cavendish,' Hersch asked, 'it's understandable you would wish her dead.'

'I did wish her dead,' Cynthia spat. 'Stepmother, indeed! She was a year younger than me.'

Flora experienced belated sympathy for Eloise, caught up in this twisted family. Recently widowed and with no one else to turn to, she had fled for a new life in another country. Then Parnell, a man who had pretended to be a friend, revealed that her husband's vengeful mother was on board issuing threats. Being offered a lifeline in exchange for money must have seemed not only attractive, but her only hope.

'And you, Mrs Penry-Jones, could you bring yourself to plunge a dagger into a young woman's chest?' Hersch asked.

'Most assuredly.' The old lady's eyes fluttered closed for a second. 'In my head I did so several times. But no, I didn't kill the girl. I wanted her to suffer for the rest of her life, and for the world to know what she had done. Dead, she provides me with no satisfaction.'

'Then who did kill Eloise?' Flora demanded.

27

Hester nudged the suite door open with a hip and manhandled a tray inside that Flora could tell at a glance held a good deal more than a solitary cup of tea.

'I'm sorry I was so long, Mrs Penry-Jones, but the kitchen didn't have any cucumber sandwiches left.'

She took in the now silent room with a slow sweeping glance, then with a dismayed cry, the tray of sandwiches, plate of cakes and crockery flew from her hands.

Mrs Penry-Jones let out a horrified shriek as the lid separated from the teapot, spraying her skirt with scalding liquid. Sandwiches and cakes went in one direction, the milk jug and crockery in another. A slice of smoked salmon splattered onto Cynthia's arm, eliciting a howl of protest, while Bunny backed against the wall, avoiding the trajectory of the hot water jug.

The sugar bowl had upended on the floor, bounced once on the carpet, before it rolled to a halt against the fireplace, leaving squares of white sugar scattered across the rug; the scene reminding Flora of a farce in a West End play. Hester appeared to have gone for full-out melodrama rather than simply letting the tray drop to the floor.

The mounting laugh which worked its way into Flora's chest was short-lived when she realised the one person who had made no effort to help bring order to the chaos was Hester herself. She had backed away before the tray did its devastating work and disappeared.

Flora rose unsteadily to her feet, signalling frantically to Mr Hersch, who was occupied with collecting debris from the floor. 'Mr Hersch,' she said again, bringing his head round to face her. 'Hester's gone.'

Uttering a curse under his breath, the detective ran for the door, followed by an equally disgruntled Captain Gates, who wiped cream from his jacket as he hurried out.

Cynthia picked her way over the scattered sandwiches and squashed cakes that littered the floor, and ran outside.

'Now what?' Max muttered, heaving himself awkwardly from his chair. He was about to follow, when Mrs Penry-Jones caught him on the shin with her stick.

'Where do you think you're going?' she snarled, raising both arms. 'Help me up. I'm coming too.'

Sighing, Max did as he was told, though with one useable arm, the process was seriously protracted.

'I take it you wish to go too?' Bunny asked, applying a napkin to remove a blob of chocolate icing from his trouser leg.

'Absolutely.' Flora limped out onto the promenade deck, gazing frantically around to see which direction the captain and Hersch had gone. There was no sign of Hester, but the clatter of heavy shoes on metal steps told her she had descended the companionway to the saloon deck.

Flora grasped the rail but Bunny gripped her elbow from behind, halting her. 'Oh no, you don't. You'll slip. Allow me.' He wrapped his arm round her waist, slid the other beneath her knees and swept her into his arms.

'What happened in there exactly?' Bunny asked as he carried her down to the bottom of the companionway with remarkable ease, while behind them Mrs Penry-Jones kept up a constant stream of fractious complaints to a slow-moving Max.

'Hester saw the knife,' Flora said. 'I knew it sounded wrong when I heard her at the dining table. I just didn't put it together until now.'

'Put what together?' He set her gently onto the deck, where the detective and the captain had halted ten feet away.

'She said,' Flora tried to remember exactly, '"If a man is ruthless enough to bludgeon another to death with an ashtray, he's hardly likely to baulk at stabbing a woman." Only a few of us knew Eloise had been stabbed.'

'Good grief! You mean Hester killed Eloise?' Bunny looked to where Hester had taken up position at the aft rail, both elbows hooked over the top, her full skirt billowing in the wind and her features in profile.

Max released an anguished, 'Oh, Lord,' as he joined Cynthia, who, leaned against his uninjured shoulder, her face white.

Several crewmen held back a group of spectators who had formed a wide semicircle around the woman at the rail.

Hester swivelled her head a quarter turn, raking them all with a dispassionate look; as if she didn't recognise them, or had dismissed them all from her mind as irrelevant.

Then her gaze snagged on Flora and held. 'What's *she* doing here?'

'She's concerned for you, Miss Smith, as we all are.' Hersch eased Flora backwards with an outstretched arm, then eased forwards again.

'You do know that Eloise didn't kill Theodore van Elder, don't you, Hester?' His tone conciliatory, as if persuading a child. 'I may call you Hester, mayn't I?'

'What does it matter? Nothing does.' Hester's low voice competed with the whoosh of the sea beneath the hull, while above them the wind sang in the winch lines. Hersch took a step closer, but Hester spotted him, stiffened and leaned back, her upper body balanced precariously on the rail. He halted, his hands held up in surrender.

'What are you doing, Hester, you stupid girl?' Mrs Penry-Jones demanded, her stick tapping a rhythm on the boards as she drew closer. 'Come away from there at once!'

Hersch frantically signalled her back, but she ignored him.

Hester's head whipped round to face her, eyes narrowed. 'Go away, you awful old dragon. If you hadn't demanded so much of him, he wouldn't have failed.'

'Who wouldn't?' Bunny said at Flora's shoulder.

'I think she means Marlon,' Flora replied.

'Of course I mean Marlon!' Hester shouted. 'He was my husband.'

'You're lying!' Mrs Penry-Jones said, indignant. 'Marlon was never married.'

'Of course,' Flora whispered. 'That would explain it.'

'Not to me, it doesn't,' Bunny said. 'What's she talking about?'

Flora stilled him with a finger to her lips, her head angled into his shoulder. 'Don't you males ever understand affairs of the heart?'

'We had it all planned,' Hester began, responding to her own inner voice. 'I was to take the position as his aunt's companion.' She sighed, her world-weary look intimating that had she known what a trial the exercise would become, she might have chosen to stab the old lady instead. 'Then, once Marlon was accepted back into the family, we would pretend to elope.'

'Ah, now I see,' Bunny said into Flora's hair. 'Parnell was her husband. Sorry, I got him muddled with this Marlon chap.'

'Marlon *was* Parnell. Oh, do pay attention,' Flora said, shushing him.

'But Marlon wasn't as clever as you, was he, Hester?' Hersch took half a step towards her.

'Get away from me!' She scooted backwards until her rear end protruded over the rail, her feet hooked into the metal bars.

'Why don't we discuss this rationally inside the suite?' His tone softened, became ingratiating.

'No!' Hester screamed. 'You're trying to trick me.'

Captain Gates whispered an instruction to a crewman that Flora had to strain to hear. 'Tell the chief engineer to slow all engines.'

The crewman slipped away and Flora looked up at Bunny, who shook his head. 'It won't help if she jumps. We must be doing sixteen knots and it's getting dark.'

Flora chewed her bottom lip but remained silent. She knew she couldn't move fast enough to stop Hester with her injured foot, nor could anyone else.

'He was weak,' Hester screamed, bringing Flora's attention back to her. 'Eloise convinced him she hadn't killed Theodore, but I knew the old woman wouldn't accept that. She would never let him back into the family.'

'What did you do, Hester?' Hersch made no further attempt to close the gap between them. This appeared to reassure her, and she continued to talk.

'I told him that we should at least get the money Eloise took from Theo's safe. It would help us start again back in New York. That night he went to her stateroom to say he would convince his aunt that she was innocent if she gave him the money. Then she could go to London and forget about the van Elders.'

'But you thought Eloise had killed him rather than hand it over? Why?' Hersch asked.

'I hung around Eloise's cabin the morning after he died, and heard that governess say she had heard them arguing.' She cocked her chin in Flora's direction. 'Eloise was the last person to see him alive. I thought she *must* have killed him.'

'Hester.' The detective kept his voice low, almost hypnotic. 'Tell us what happened.'

The ship dipped as a wave ran below the hull and Hester slipped.

A collective gasp went through the group of spectators, until Hester adjusted her grip, thus regaining her balance. The violence of the movement combined with the wind, had loosened the bun at her neck, leaving her honey-coloured hair to stream behind her.

She looked almost graceful sitting there, while behind her, slim fingers of dusk crept across a pink and orange sky that sported a lace overskirt of ragged clouds.

'Keep talking to us, Hester,' Mr Hersh urged. 'We need to understand.'

Her lip curled, as if she didn't believe him, but she began to speak again. 'When the officer sent us inside during the storm, I told Mrs Penry-Jones I was seasick and needed to lie down. Instead, I went to Eloise's stateroom.' A sly look entered her eyes at the memory. 'The silly madam ordered me out. She had no idea who I was and I didn't bother to explain, I just plunged the knife into her chest.' Her gaze clouded, as if she was unsure about the next part of her story. 'I think I did it more than once. She didn't even cry out, just stared at me as she slid to the floor.'

'What did you do then?' Hersch asked.

'I had to get the knife back to Mrs Penry-Jones jewel case before it was missed.' Hester blinked and shook her head. 'She was talking to someone,

I heard her through the adjoining door. The knife had blood on it, so did my dress, so I hid it in the motor car, then changed my clothes and went to the bridge tournament. I went back for the knife later, but those brats were playing in it.' Hester glared at Flora again as if she were solely responsible for her ruined plans. 'I tried to get it from that boy's room but—'

Flora gasped, and sensing her shock, Bunny tightened his hold around her as a salt-tinged gust of wind swept the open deck.

Hester shivered and despite the pain and fear she had experienced in the last twenty-four hours, Flora experienced a sort of sympathy for Hester. The invisible, plain girl whose circumstances had forced her into a life of subservience and humiliation. Then she finally meets a man who seems to genuinely love her, not caring that he's weak and incapable, because he was hers. Then their one chance to achieve a better life was taken in one violent act, leaving her with the prospect of carrying bags and running for smelling salts for the rest of her life.

It was enough to break most people.

A sudden impulse gripped her. She pulled away from Bunny, and she took a halting step towards Hester

'Flora? What do you think you're doing?' Bunny hissed. He made a grab for her but missed.

'You can't stay there forever, Hester,' Flora pleaded. 'It's getting dark and you must be cold in just that thin dress.'

'Why should you care?' Hester snarled, throwing her a look of disdain then back to the sea again. 'If you hadn't asked all those questions, he—' She broke off and inhaled on a choked sob.

'Marlon would still be alive?' Flora finished for her. 'No he wouldn't. He was dead before I cast doubt on what had happened. Eloise didn't kill him either.'

'I know that – now!' The wind pushed Hester's hair into her face. She took one hand off the rail to brush it back, unbalancing her. For a heart-stopping few seconds, she rocked precariously on the rail.

Cynthia gasped and Flora held her breath, but somehow Hester hung on.

'Flora, come back here,' Bunny instructed, but she ignored him.

'Even if you aren't cold, I am.' Flora took another step closer, her hand outstretched towards Hester, her palm upwards in invitation. 'Why don't we do what Mr Hersch suggested and talk about this inside? It isn't too late.'

Hester swivelled her head and met Flora's gaze, her thin lips quirked into a parody of a smile; like a cat who has spotted a friendly bird. Slowly, her hand lifted so that no more than a foot lay between their outstretched fingers. 'Isn't it?' she whispered, her gaze sweeping the row of curious spectators before coming to rest on Mrs Penry-Jones.

For long seconds, Flora thought she would take Flora's hand. Then something distant and primal entered her eyes.

Flora's breath caught as she knew what was about to happen but she was helpless to prevent it.

A triumphant smile spread slowly across Hester's face. She withdrew her hand, leaned backwards, and floated over the rail.

Mrs Penry-Jones released a long high-pitched scream.

Hersch groaned in frustration, while Bunny issued a loud curse. Max wrapped his arms around Cynthia, who buried her face in his shoulder.

A low murmur of dismay went up among the watchers, some of whom made a sudden but useless rush towards the rail. A line of crewmen spread out along the deck, bent over the rail while they searched the waves below, arms pointing and issuing orders to lower a lifeboat.

Flora froze, buffeted by the rising wind as her hand dropped nerveless to her side. Strong hands closed round her shoulders and she became aware of Bunny urging her backwards. She complied but barely acknowledged him.

She turned her head to where the captain stood, his brief headshake reiterating what Bunny had already said: they were travelling too fast and it was almost dark. If Hester had managed to survive the fall, there was the shock of the freezing water that would likely stop her heart. By the time the ship manoeuvred around and went back for her, she would most certainly have drowned.

Despite it all, Flora hoped they would try.

28

At Hersch's instigation, they reassembled in Mrs Penry-Jones's sitting room; each one of them silent and absorbed with their own disturbing thoughts. The devastation caused by the spilled tea tray had been cleared up; the Korean dagger repositioned on the mantle. A damp area of carpet evidenced a vigorous scrubbing, but otherwise the room looked untouched.

'I saw everything from the upper deck.' Mary Ames bustled into the room and plucked at Flora's sleeve. 'Has the captain ordered we go back to look for Hester?'

'I–I believe so,' Flora stammered. 'He's ordered a lifeboat lowered, but —' She shook her head, arms wrapped round her midriff.

When Hester realised what she had done, in that instant when the long fall to the sea began and there was no turning back, did instinct take over? Was she still conscious when she hit the water, and if so, did she fight to stay afloat in the freezing ocean, unable to catch her breath. Was she forced to watch in growing, numbing horror as the ship sailed steadily away from her?

'Flora?' Bunny's voice came to her as if from a long way off. 'Are you all right?'

She nodded, not trusting herself to speak.

'It's at times like this' – Miss Ames fussed over Mrs Penry-Jones, though the woman studiously ignored her – 'I feel the tragedies of life can be mitigated by portrayal in art.' She patted her pocket, where the outline of her notebook stood out. 'In this case, literary art.'

'She's going to put Hester's story in a book?' Flora whispered to Bunny. 'Can you imagine that?'

'It's quite a good plot actually.' Bunny shrugged. 'And we all have our own coping strategies.'

'Really?' She raised a cynical eyebrow at him. 'What was Hester's?'

'Maybe she couldn't face the prospect of dying at the end of a rope. It isn't a pleasant way to go.'

'And drowning is?' Flora murmured, not expecting an answer. Her ankle began to ache, which she contemplated using as an excuse to return to her suite.

Passengers had been running all over the ship during the last half hour and soon everyone would know what had happened. She didn't want Eddy to find out via shipboard gossip.

'Then this entire fiasco was for nothing?' Mrs Penry-Jones spoke, while fat tears carved lines in her face powder, hovered on her upper lip and dropped onto her clasped hands which resembled bundles of bones in her lap. 'Hester deceived me, too.'

'I'm afraid that's true, dear lady.' Hersch spoke with restraint, though Flora imagined he would have liked to say a great deal more had his innate good manners not prevented him.

Max comforted Cynthia, his uninjured arm across her shoulders while he whispered into her hair.

'Max,' Flora asked as something occurred to her, 'did you see Hester leave Eloise's stateroom after she... well, you know. Is that why you were on deck in the storm?'

Cynthia lifted her face from his shoulder and stared up into his face. 'Max?'

'I–I saw someone coming out of Eloise's room in a cloak just like the one I bought Cynthia in London.' Max blew air between his pursed lips 'It was obvious they didn't want to be seen, and I thought—'

'That it was me?' Cynthia said, aghast.

'No, I mean, well yes, maybe I did.' He licked his lips. 'I couldn't be sure. The storm was severe by then and the deck awash. Then the wave hit me, and Mr Harrington dragged me back.'

'You never told me any of this,' Cynthia pushed herself upright and stared at him.

'How could I? When I woke up to find out Eloise had been killed, I thought—' He massaged his forehead with his free hand. 'I knew you blamed her for your father's death. My first thought was to protect you. No matter what you had done.'

'Oh, Max.' Cynthia crumpled into his one armed-embrace. 'It *was* my cloak. I lent it to Hester, but I didn't kill Eloise.'

'I know that now,' he whispered. 'I feel terrible for having thought you capable of such a thing. I'm so sorry.'

'Don't be.' Cynthia ran her hand down his jaw. 'I should have insisted you tell me what you were doing outside in that storm, but I didn't want to hear it.'

Max's face paled. 'You thought *I* had done it?'

Cynthia's lips parted, whether to issue a denial or not, Flora couldn't tell. What damage had been done to their marriage with so much doubt she couldn't imagine, but the simple fact was, they would have to learn to live with it.

'I think we should go,' she whispered.

Bunny nodded, laced his fingers with hers and drew her to her feet, then helped her out onto the deck with the assistance of Mr Hersch.

'That explains how Matilda ended up on the other side of the saloon deck.' Bunny halted outside Flora's suite. 'Hester must have undone the straps when she hid the knife.'

'I cannot help feeling that had I linked Dr Fletcher with that land deal earlier, at least two people would still be alive.' Hersch released a sigh and stared sadly out to sea.

'You aren't responsible,' Flora said. 'Had Mrs Penry-Jones informed the agency they were travelling under different names, you would have known what was going on.' *Even so, she doubted he could have prevented Hester's malice towards Eloise – or Parnell's greed.*

Small groups of passengers had gathered at the rail, necks stretched and talking earnestly among themselves. A knot of sailors clustered round an empty lifeboat support on the promenade deck above them, their gazes trained out to sea.

'Have they found anything?' Flora asked.

'I doubt it,' Bunny sighed. 'But they have to go through the motions.'

'I'll leave you now,' Hersch said. 'Maybe we'll see each other at dinner, though somehow I haven't much of an appetite this evening.' He performed a polite bow and left them, his rhythmic footsteps receding along the deck.

'I didn't like to say,' Flora said when he was out of earshot. 'But I'm starving.'

'Me too,' Bunny chuckled, tucking his arm though hers. 'You were right, no one was who they pretended to be. A secret wife, a vengeful mother and a grieving daughter. Everyone can be whom they choose aboard ship.' He pushed open the door and ushered Flora inside. 'I shall have to listen to you more closely in future.'

'You never know, there might just be a time when you will do exactly that.'

'In a way, it's admirable that Max was prepared to protect his wife to such an extent,' Bunny said, making himself at home in the sitting room.

'I find it sinister that Cynthia will always remember her husband believed her capable of murder.'

'Hmm. In the same way is it romantic that Hester's passion for her husband turned her into a killer?'

'I don't think romantic is the right word.' Flora recalled that moment at the top of the companionway, and the vicious shove that had sent her to the bottom. In that second she had felt something inherently evil behind her.

'We arrive in London tomorrow.' Bunny nodded at a pinpoint of light that blinked in the distance. 'That must be the Eddystone Lighthouse.'

'Yes,' Flora sighed, though the prospect of home seemed less attractive than it might have done. Despite the trials and sheer terror of the voyage, the prospect of leaving Bunny, perhaps forever, knotted her stomach with dread. Although a small voice told her she would be relieved to get off this ship.

'I expect you're tired, so I'll say goodnight.' His hand slid down her arm, pausing to squeeze her hand. Something entered his eyes and for a moment she half expected him to kiss her again, but the moment passed. Instead, his gaze wandered over her face, pausing on her bottom lip, then he gave a cough, turned and walked away.

Flora watched him go, a hand braced against the door frame. When he reached the corner, she whispered, 'Goodnight, Ptolemy Harrington.'

'Is that you, Flora?' Eddy's voice sounded from the sitting room.

'Yes, it's me.' She stayed where she was for a moment, staring at the tiny blinking light as the ship carried her closer to home.

Eddy's face appeared round the door jamb. 'This steward they sent to sit with me can't play chess for toffee. I've beaten him three times already. By the way, what was going on down on the saloon deck earlier? He wouldn't let me look.'

29

SUNDAY

'Have you finished your packing, Eddy?' Flora called to him through his bedroom door.

'I did mine last night.' He wandered into the sitting room, buckling his belt over a hastily tucked in shirt. 'Can't wait to see Ozzy this morning. I'll bet he doesn't know Miss Smith was a real-life murderer.'

'I imagine his father will have told him. The entire ship must know by now.'

Flora had sat Eddy down before bed the night before and over cocoa and garibaldi biscuits, recounted a sanitised version of what had happened. Eddy had listened wide-eyed and silent until she got to the part about Hester's fall, her breath held in case he took it badly.

'Well,' he said through a mouthful of crumbs when she had finished. 'If she had survived and been picked up by the lifeboat, she would have been hanged anyway.' He had wiped a raisin from his upper lip and shrugged. 'Can you imagine what a spiffing essay I'll be able to write on "What I Did On My Holidays" when I get to school? No one will believe it!'

Flora would always remember that was the exact moment she knew Eddy would go on very well at Marlborough.

'Oh, bother!' Eddy's voice brought her to the present. 'I forgot to ask, how's your ankle?'

'Much better.' She flexed her foot to demonstrate. 'It still aches a little, but that's all. I recovered quicker than I thought.'

'You *are* going to see Mr Harrington again when we get home, aren't you?' He leaned against one of the wicker chairs and fixed her with a speculative stare so like his father's, she looked away, disconcerted.

'Doesn't that rather depend on what Mr Harrington wants?'

'What about you? What do *you* want?'

Flora paused in the act of transferring her vanity case to the pile of trunks lined up by the door. 'Maybe I should look further than Cleeve Abbey now that you'll be at Marlborough. I could take a position at a school in London, or go to Paris to teach English to French children.' Her heart lifted with new enthusiasm, her voice with it.

'You'll be alone,' Eddy said, despondent. 'Is that what you want?'

'I... I don't know. But whatever I do, I cannot rely on Mr Harrington, or any other man to make my happiness for me.'

'You'll always come home to Cleeve Abbey, though, won't you?'

'Possibly.' A smile tugged at Flora's mouth. Where else could she consider home? 'Now go and say goodbye to Ozzy. We'll be leaving soon.'

A look of abject horror crossed Eddy's face. 'Gosh, yes. I don't even have his address. See you later, then.'

The porter arrived and removed their trunks, after which Flora surveyed the empty suite, bereft now of the items which marked it as having temporarily been hers. Like her hairbrushes on the dresser and her negligee on the end of the bed.

The morning she had found Parnell's body seemed a long time ago now. So much had happened since then. What had Bunny said about stripping the emotion to lessen the impact of the past? She doubted she would be able to do it at Cleeve Abbey; no one at home had ever been willing to discuss Lily Maguire.

What had her mother done that was so reprehensible? Or maybe it was more about what had been done to her. Whichever it was, maybe Bunny was right, and it was time to find out for once and for all. Too much hurt was caused by secrets, as the Van Elders could attest.

Retrieving her valise from a chair, Flora stepped onto the promenade deck, where the discordant clamour of mechanical noise combined with the rumble of loaded trolleys being pushed across the deck. A line of carriages waited on the quayside for city-bound passengers.

She paused at the rail which gave her a view of the quayside, where a group of police officers stood beside a black closed carriage beside the gangplank. More of a black box on wheels with a metal grille in the rear facing door.

Gus Crowe emerged from beneath the superstructure, his hands shackled and flanked by two policemen. Heads turned as he appeared, and a low murmur went up amongst the crowd waiting to disembark.

Flora felt, rather than saw, Mr Hersch drift to her side. 'Viewing the results of your success, Miss Maguire?' he asked without rancour.

'Not at all. I think it's a tragic outcome for everyone. Especially Parnell, not to mention poor Eloise.'

'Indeed.' Hersch leaned his forearms on the rail, one foot on the bottom support. 'The charges against Crowe have been reduced to theft and common assault. We also discovered Max's tiepin and cufflinks hidden in his stateroom. And you were right about that bracelet by the way.'

'Oh?' Flora turned her head to look at him. His air of triumph that had prevailed the previous day had softened to resignation. 'You found it?'

He nodded. 'Amongst Hester's things. Why she took it is a mystery. The inscription would surely only serve as a constant reminder of how it was obtained.'

'I believe there was a more prosaic reason than that,' Flora said. 'She would most likely have sold it at her first opportunity.'

'What a pragmatic young lady you are, Miss Maguire.'

'I hope that was a compliment.'

'It was,' he said, grinning. 'There was no sign of any photograph by the way.'

'No. I didn't think there would be.' The morning of the storm came back to her, when Eloise raised her hand to the sea and dropped what looked to be confetti into the water. She had thought it was drops of water at the time, but now knew for sure what it was. At least Eloise was at peace when she died. A sort of peace anyway.

'Young Eddy looks none the worse for his adventures.' He indicated to where Eddy had joined the Gilmores and Ozzy further along the deck.

'Children are more resilient than we know. With their common experience, they will likely remain friends.' She smiled at Eddy as he chattered animatedly to Monica, accompanied by extravagant hand gestures.

'I wonder if Mr Gilmore will write to his new friend?' Hersch chuckled, pointing to where Gerald appeared to be searching the deck with his eyes for someone.

'Was I the only one who missed that, Mr Hersch?'

'I suspect that's why he volunteered to spend so much time with the boys? It gave him an excuse to be with the young lady without suspicions being raised.' He patted her shoulder gently. 'Don't feel bad, my dear. We'll make a detective of you yet.'

Bad didn't begin to describe what Flora felt at that moment. That Gerald was a good father and fond of Eddy only went part way to atone for using him as camouflage for a flirtation. She could only hope Lord Vaughn never discovered that she had exposed his son to dubious morals as well as a dangerous killer.

A flurry of activity commanded their attention to where two policemen appeared on deck, followed by the hunched figure of Dr Fletcher, his feet and hands in chains as he was escorted down the gangplank to the waiting van.

Flora could only imagine how he felt with a hangman's rope his only future as she watched him being shoved unceremoniously inside. Did he envy Hester's means of escape, or would he do anything to prolong whatever life he had left?

As the metal door slammed, Flora flinched, aware she would never know the answer to that question.

'I wonder what the future holds for Flora Maguire, the intrepid detective?' Hersch asked once the Black Maria had moved off.

'She's retiring without having reached her zenith. Too dangerous – and complicated.' She extended her gloved hand. 'It was a pleasure to meet you, but if you want any murders solved, I hope I will be the last person you think of.'

'Now that would be a shame.' He took her hand in both of his and squeezed before releasing her and raising his hat. 'It was nice meeting you.

Perhaps our paths will cross again.' Skirting her, he strolled slowly down the gangplank, ruffling Eddy's hair as he passed.

'Flora!' Eddy called from the end of the deck. 'Papa's carriage is here. They're loading our trunks right now.' He inserted a sense of urgency into is last two words.

'I'm coming, Eddy!' Flora replied, her heart dipping in disappointment as she surveyed the empty deck. Bunny hadn't actually said he would come and say goodbye, but she had hoped he might appear.

Most of the passengers had left the ship, while Flora stayed at the rail, listening to the metallic clang of the winch lines which had sounded a little bereft. Delaying a little longer, she counted to ten in her head, but when no one appeared, she sighed, hefted her portmanteau into her arms and descended the companionway to the saloon deck, aware it was likely the last time she would do so in some time. A governess's salary did not stretch to ocean voyages.

When she had decided it wasn't going to happen, heavy male footsteps pounded down the gangway behind her. Her heart jumped, but when the man came level with her she saw it was only one of the officers. He strode past with a polite nod which she returned, releasing a slow breath.

'What are you waiting for, Flora? Come on!' Eddy bounced on his toes at the end of the gangplank. 'If we don't go now, we'll have to go to the back of this queue.' He indicated the line of carts, carriages and wagons piled high with luggage waiting to leave the dock.

'I'm on my way,' she called and headed his way, then under her breath muttered, 'I'll give him one more minute to catch us up.'

More footsteps sounded behind her, accompanied by a frantic, 'Flora!'

Bunny's shout stiffened her shoulders, but she didn't turn round. He overtook her, then stepped in front of her. 'You're not thinking of leaving without a goodbye, I hope?'

Flora's blood surged in her veins but she kept her expression bland as she took in his high colour, disarrayed hair and his unbuttoned jacket; all evidence he had been running.

'You're late.'

'I know. I'm so sorry. I had to organize Matilda's loading onto the quay and those awkward stevedores didn't have the right canvases. They were about to use hemp rope which would have scraped Matty's paintwork dreadfully.'

'And I thought calling her Matilda was going too far.'

'Jealous, eh?' He shoved both hands in his pockets and grinned down at her. 'This reminds me of our first meeting, when you hit your head on the support and were angry, guilty and defensive all at the same time? You're wearing that same expression now.'

'Thank you for reminding me.' Irritation sent heat into her face. Was she right all along and he saw her as an amusing shipboard dalliance destined to shrivel the moment they stepped onto dry land?

He removed his hands from his pockets, gently gathered her hand in both of his and brought it to his chest. The deck seemed to dip beneath her, but that made no sense as they were standing on the quayside.

'If it's agreeable to you, Miss Maguire. Might I visit you at Cleeve Abbey? I could get down there for Easter.' He held her gaze without speaking, and no matter how much she wanted to look away, she could not.

'You remembered where I live?' She took a step closer, all coyness redundant as she leaned into him, excitement fizzing through her veins. 'Will you bring Matilda?'

'Matilda cannot get much above fifteen miles an hour, whereas a train is far more efficient. Besides,' his gaze softened, drawing her in, one hand lifted and ran a finger down her cheek, 'I suspect my priorities have changed somewhat. After all, she's just a motor car.'

'I never imagined I would hear you say that. However, the sentiment is very much appreciated. And if you can tolerate my penchant for investigating murders, I can probably put up with your other woman.'

He cupped her cheek and when she turned her lips into his hand, he pulled her forward until her mouth was under his.

She relished the taste of him beneath her lips, marvelling at the newness of this intimacy and the strength of her own desire until, at last, but also too soon, he released her, though kept his arm locked around her as if reluctant to let go.

She raised her chin and looked into his eyes where something sat in the blue depths which was hers alone, not caring one bit that a group of sailors were watching from the deck.

'Flora!' Eddy hollered from the quay. 'We have to *go*.'

'That visit? Perhaps we could make it next week instead?' He eased in and claimed her mouth again.

'I had better go,' she whispered against his mouth, as reluctantly she pulled away and strolled slowly to the carriage, a broad smile on her face.

'You kissed him in front of *everyone*,' Eddy whined, hanging out of the open carriage window, shuffling back in his seat as she climbed inside.

'I did, didn't I?' She settled on the seat opposite, her bag beside her. 'Remove your feet from the seat.'

'Huh!' Eddy sniffed. 'At least he didn't pat you on the head like Mr Hersch did to me. Anyone would think I was a sheepdog.'

Laughing, Flora relaxed against the upholstery, her hand lifted in a wave through the window to where Bunny watched from the quayside, his hands jammed in his pockets and a broad smile on his face.

The carriage turned a corner and with a small, satisfied sigh, she settled back against the upholstery, then bolted upright again when she remembered she hadn't warned him about her father.

Ah well, Ptolemy Harrington would discover Riordan Maguire for himself

ACKNOWLEDGMENTS

I would like to thank the brilliant team at Boldwood, specifically Caroline Ridding for her vision in helping me bring Flora to life. To Isobel Akenhead, Sarah Ritherdon, and Sue Lamprell. Also to Boldwood's creative department for the beautiful covers.

ABOUT THE AUTHOR

Anita Davison is the author of the successful Flora Maguire historical mystery series.

Sign up to Anita Davison's mailing list for news, competitions and updates on future books.

Visit Anita's website: www.anitadavison.co.uk

Follow Anita on social media here:

 twitter.com/anitasdavison
 facebook.com/anita.davison
 goodreads.com/anitadavison

ALSO BY ANITA DAVISON

Miss Merrill and Aunt Violet Mysteries

Murder in the Bookshop

The Flora Maguire Mysteries

Death On Board

Death at the Abbey

Boldwood

Boldwood Books is an award-winning fiction publishing company seeking out the best stories from around the world.

Find out more at www.boldwoodbooks.com

Join our reader community for brilliant books, competitions and offers!

Follow us
@BoldwoodBooks
@TheBoldBookClub

Sign up to our weekly deals newsletter

https://bit.ly/BoldwoodBNewsletter

Milton Keynes UK
Ingram Content Group UK Ltd.
UKHW042019021123
431836UK00002B/4